REG

Mischief & Marriage

Anne Herries

MILLS
BOON

Mills & Boon, an imprint of Harlequin (UK) Limited,
Eton House, 18-24 Paradise Road, Richmond, Surrey TW9 1SR

REGENCY: MISCHIEF & MARRIAGE
© Harlequin Enterprises II B.V./S.à.r.l 2011

The publisher acknowledges the copyright holder of the individual works as follows:

Secret Heiress © Linda M. Sole 2010
Bartered Bride © Linda M. Sole 2011

ISBN: 978 0 263 89722 7

052-0312

Harlequin (UK) policy is to use papers that are natural, renewable and recyclable products and made from wood grown in sustainable forests. The logging and manufacturing processes conform to the legal environmental regulations of the country of origin.

Printed and bound
by CPI Group (UK) Ltd, Croydon, CR0 4YY

Secret Heiress

Anne Herries

Prologue

Autumn 1818

'Eliza, my dearest.' Mrs Bancroft held out her hand to her beloved adopted daughter. 'Sit with me, my love. I have something to tell you.'

Eliza smiled and did as she was bid, sitting on the edge of the bed and reaching for her mother's hand. 'What is it, dearest Mama? Are you feeling worse? Is there anything I can do for you?'

'No, I am just as always, but I think we should talk. You know that it is unlikely I shall see the winter out…'

'Mama, please…' Eliza begged. 'Doctor Morris said that you were a little better when he called. When the spring comes you will start to get up again and then…'

Mrs Bancroft squeezed her daughter's hand. 'I know it is hard for you, dearest. We lost Papa two years since and now…' She shook her head as tears sprang to Eliza's eyes. 'No, you must not grieve for me, Eliza. I have loved you dearly, but I fear we have not been quite fair to you. We should have tried harder to discover the name of your true mother.'

'You are my mama,' Eliza said. 'I know that you did not give birth to me, but I love you dearly.'

'You have been everything a daughter should be,' Mrs Bancroft said. 'You have been ours since Papa found you left in the church behind the altar one Sunday morning, but somewhere out there you have a mother and a father. Don't forget that Papa saw a gentleman's carriage driving away and I believe you are the daughter of quality. Your clothes were of the finest materials and the ring I found tucked in with them is beautiful. I have kept it safe for you, Eliza.'

'You showed it to me,' Eliza said. 'It is very beautiful, but I do not see what use it can be. If my mother abandoned me, she must have had her reasons.'

'Perhaps she had no choice. I do not think that any mother would give up their own baby willingly.'

'I dare say you are right.' Eliza smiled and kissed her. 'I only know that I was fortunate to have been found and raised by you and Papa.'

'The ring is at the bottom of my sewing box if you should need it.'

Mrs Bancroft sighed. 'My head aches again. I think I should like a tisane if you would make it for me, dearest.'

'Yes, of course.'

Eliza rose and went downstairs to the kitchen. She had always known she was not the true child of her parents, but their kindness meant that she lacked nothing. However, if she were truthful, she had sometimes thought of her birth mother and wondered who she was and why she had been forced to abandon her newly born baby.

Her mama had mentioned a valuable ring amongst her clothes. Why had her birth mother placed it there—was it in the hope that one day her daughter would look for her?

Eliza had wondered if her mother would one day come to visit and tell her why she had given her up. Since she had not, there was no way of knowing who she was or where she lived. It would be almost impossible to find her—unless she could find someone who recognised the ring, of course.

If her papa had been right about the carriage he had seen driving away belonging to a wealthy man, then her parents might be gentry or even aristocrats. Eliza was not used to moving in those circles, except for the occasional invitation to the local landowner's house at Christmas for the tenants' party. How could she ever hope to find her mother?

She put the bothersome thoughts from her mind as she entered the kitchen. It was small like the rest of the cottage, but there were only the two of them these days; though they had missed the beautiful rectory that had been their home, they had become accustomed to their situation. Eliza did most of the work and the nursing herself, though Betty came in once or twice a week to clean. She had been the Bancrofts's maid for years and insisted on doing what she could for them even though they could pay her very little.

'I would work for nothing,' Betty had told Eliza a few days previously. 'If your mama were not so proud, I would never have left her at all.'

'Mama does not wish to be a burden.'

'It is hardly right that you should do everything, love,' Betty said. 'You know where I am if you need me.'

While the kettle was heating, Eliza gathered the ingredients for a blackcurrant tisane, her mother's favourite. Despite the unfortunate start to her life, she had been loved, cared for and guided in the way she should go. At the moment all her thoughts must be centred on the sick woman upstairs. There would be time enough to think of her future when she was alone.

Chapter One

Summer 1819

Daniel, Lord Seaton, stared out of the window of his London house. It was situated in one of the best areas of the city, in a quiet garden square. It suited him when he visited the capitol. However, he would probably have to sell the property to meet his debts, rather than let it to a tenant, as he had intended when he came up to town.

'Damn you, Marcus,' he muttered. 'Why did you have to land me with your mess?'

He frowned at the letter in his hand. As if he did not have enough problems trying to bring his own estate back from the brink of ruin! His father had died of a putrid fever six months earlier, after foolishly losing more than ten thousand pounds at the tables—and to a man Daniel believed might be both a cheat and a rogue. Cheadle was known for his ruthless play, so what his father had imagined he was about, Daniel did not know. Yet it was not the only mistake the late Lord Seaton had made. Several poor investments meant that Daniel had mortgages on at least half the land. His father had settled the gambling debt, but the mortgages meant that Daniel would struggle for years to put the estate back on its feet again. While his father had every right to spend his fortune as he pleased, Cousin Marcus was another matter.

Daniel scanned the letter again.

Only you can help me, Daniel. His cousin had written the letter two days before the accident that had caused his death just three months previously.

My debts are more than ten thousand and I cannot pay unless I sell my estate. Father might cough up the readies, but he has been ill for months and I think if he knew what I have been about, it would kill him.

To tell the truth, cousin, I have been a damned fool. I got in over my head—-things I am ashamed to own. If you knew all, you would consign me to the devil and think that I deserve whatever is coming. I may be in some danger and if you hear I have died in an accident, I give you leave to doubt it.

There is someone I fear, but I dare not write his name. He would certainly kill me then. Believe me, cousin, I have done things of which I am ashamed—but I did not know the worst of him when he persuaded me to help him. I want to get away, to start again, but I fear he will not let me go. The debt is another matter and the marquis must be paid. Your father was not the only one to fall foul of Cheadle's damnable luck. Forgive me for asking if you can help.

Your wretched cousin,

Marcus

What was he to make of the letter? Marcus had sent it to Daniel's London club and, busy at his estate, he had not received it until he paid a flying visit to town to speak with lawyers about his London property. Now he would have to contact Cheadle and ask for the extent of his cousin's debt to him. At this moment he was not sure if he could find the money without reference to his uncle, but he would certainly speak to the marquis.

However, the remainder of his cousin's letter was a riddle. What had Marcus been trying to tell him? He knew Marcus well enough to be sure that his cousin would not write such a letter without good cause. Who was the man who would not let him go—and, more importantly, had his cousin's death truly been an accident?

At the time of the funeral he had not questioned it. The Earl of Standish told him it was a riding accident, and Daniel had accepted his uncle's explanation without question. Now, his cousin's letter had made him suspect foul play. Marcus had always been an excellent rider. As young men they had been great friends, though in past years they had grown apart. Daniel had chosen to take up a military career and spent eight years fighting with Wellington in various campaigns. It was during his time away that his mother had died and his father had started to drink and gamble. He blamed himself for not being at home when he was needed, and though he had returned when his father became ill, resigning his commission, it had already been too late.

The last thing Daniel needed or wanted at this moment was a mystery to uncover. Yet he knew that he could not simply ignore his cousin's cry for help. Marcus was dead, and perhaps he had done things that would not bear the light of day, but if he had been murdered…

Daniel's mouth thinned. His memories of a young man he had loved as a brother demanded that he seek out Marcus's murderer and bring him to justice.

As for Cheadle, well, he would pay a visit to his club that evening and discover if the marquis was in town.

'You said I could come to you, Betty,' Eliza said when her mother's former maid opened the door of her cottage that evening. 'I am sorry to ask, and I will find work as soon as I can—but may I stay here for a few days?'

'Put you out of the cottage has, he?' Betty shook her head sadly. 'You've no need to ask, my lovely. Come you in and sit by the fire while I make you something to eat. I was afraid Mr Jones would say you couldn't stop there alone once your dearest mother was gone. It only surprises me that he let you stay this long.'

'It isn't his fault,' Eliza said. 'I know the earl would have told him it was his duty to put me out and take another tenant. I can't afford to pay the rent now that Mama's allowance has stopped unless I work—and I shall not find work here. I have asked but no one will take me on. They take one look at my hands and say I'm not suitable.'

'Your hands are not as white as they once were,' Betty replied with a fond glance. 'You worked hard to keep your mama neat and clean and do the cooking. It wasn't easy at the last.'

'Poor Mama. I fear she suffered a great deal,' Eliza said and sighed. She had grieved for the past six months, but knew now she must put her personal feelings aside and look for work. 'What do you think I should do, Betty? If I am not suitable as a maid what can I do— should I try for a governess?'

'I don't think most mothers would take you on, Eliza.

You are too pretty and you might tempt their husbands or their older sons.' Betty looked thoughtful. 'If I were you I should advertise. Offer your services as a companion to an elderly lady.'

'Yes, I suppose that might answer…' Eliza sighed. Her mama's illness had kept her tied to the house for many months, and though she didn't begrudge her mama a minute of her time, she had hoped for something a little more lively in her future. 'I suppose I might find it difficult to find work as a governess, for I have no training—except that I know how to make pillows comfortable and how to mix tisanes that ease discomfort and induce sleep.'

'You are also a good little cook, for I taught you myself,' Betty told her. 'If you take your time and choose the right position, it might be just the thing for you.'

'Yes, I dare say you are right. I have little choice; there is no one to help me.'

'Are there no relatives of your papa who might take you in?' Betty asked. 'You are welcome to stay with me, my love, but it isn't fitting for you. I am sure your mother would like you to mix with people of your own class. She was the daughter of country gentry, as was your father.'

'Yes…'

Eliza did not answer fully. Betty had never been told that she was not the birth child of her parents, and therefore had no claim on their families, though there was a letter from Mama's brother in India. She had found it at the bottom of her mother's sewing box with the ring. Of course she would not dream of approaching him, for they were in no way related.

The ring was valuable. Fashioned of a thick band of gold in which a large deep red ruby had been inset, it had an inscription on the gold band. It was a romantic inscription, which made her think that her parents must have loved each other—but why had they given her up? Leaving her behind the altar on a Sunday had ensured that she was found quickly, but the person who placed her there could not have known that the Bancrofts would adopt her. Had the mystery gentleman been so ruthless that he did not care?

Who had put the ring on the ribbon and hung it about her neck, hiding it beneath her baby clothes? It must have been a woman—her mother? Had she wanted her child to have something of hers—something that Eliza suspected must have been very precious to her?

Why had her mother given her away? Her mama had had no knowledge, of course, but had told Eliza during one of their last discussions that she believed Eliza was a love child.

'Your mother may have been forced to give you up, Eliza. Indeed, I am sure she was, for no woman would give up her baby willingly. I know that I should not, whatever the consequences.'

Eliza had tried to brush the subject under the carpet. Her mama was the only mother she had known and she loved her dearly. While she lived, Eliza had given hardly a second thought to who her birth parents were, even if she could not help wanting to know more about her mother. Now her thoughts turned more and more to her true mother and she wondered if she ever thought of her…wished to see her. Yet how could she hope to discover the truth? Living in the country quietly, as she did, she had no chance of meeting anyone who might recognise the ring.

'I shall send my advertisement to the papers in London and Bath,' she told Betty with sudden decision.

'The kind of position you suggest may be found amongst fashionable ladies who can afford to employ a companion to run around after them.'

'That is the spirit, my love,' Betty said and smiled at her. 'The curate was here earlier. He asked me if I had seen anything of you recently, Eliza.'

'I usually help with the church fête,' Eliza said and looked rueful. 'He has been a little too attentive of late and I have tried to avoid seeing him other than on Sunday morning, when it is impossible not to meet.'

Betty arched her brows at her. 'Your papa was a vicar, Eliza. Young Mr Stanley will have his own living one day. You could do worse than encourage him. Not that you need think of marriage just yet, of course. You are only twenty this summer and there is plenty of time, but being the wife of a clergyman may be better than a companion's life.'

'If I liked Mr Stanley, I should think it an ideal life, Betty—but he is too prissy in his ways. Had he been like Papa, I should have encouraged him long since.'

'Well, I suppose he has some odd mannerisms—and he isn't good enough for a lovely girl like you.'

'I am not pretty, Betty.' Eliza blushed delicately. She was tall and slender, her hair a rich dark brown and her eyes the colour some people called hazel. Her complexion was a little on the pale side, but she had a wonderful smile, and it was when she smiled that she was at her best.

'No, you're not pretty in the accepted sense,' Betty agreed. 'But you have a beautiful nature, Eliza. Any man worth his salt would be fortunate to have you for a wife.'

Eliza laughed, her eyes bright with amusement. 'Betty, you are so good for me. I feel much better being here. I should have given up the cottage sooner instead of trying to keep it on. I have arranged for the few things that I decided to keep to be brought here on the cart. The rest of it will be sold at the market and I shall use it to pay for my keep until I can find work.'

'That you will not unless you want to have a falling out with me and my Ted,' Betty said stoutly. 'He's as fond of you as I am and he won't take a penny of your money, Eliza. You write out your advertisement, my love, and Ted will take it to town this very afternoon when he goes, and send it off for you, but take money for your keep he will not—and that's final.'

Eliza felt tears sting her eyes. She was so lucky to have such good friends. 'I do not know what I should have done without you both while Mama was ill.'

'You would have managed, for you bore the brunt of it,' Betty told her. 'I helped where I could and so did my Ted. He was only saying last night as it was time you had some luck, and so it is.'

'Well, who knows what may happen?' Eliza said. 'I shall advertise for a post and perhaps fortune will smile on me.'

'Go through to the parlour and write your letter in peace and I'll make us some toast and a nice pot of tea for a treat.'

Eliza thanked her and did as she was bid, going into the neat room that was used on Sundays and for company. She sat down at the writing table in front of the window and picked up the pen. There was paper and ink in the drawer; Ted worked as a clerk at the office of the Earl of Standish's estate manager and occasionally brought his work home to finish in the evenings.

She wrote out two adverts, one for *The Times* in London and another for a paper that published in Bath.

The receiving office in Norwich would send them off and accept the fee on behalf of the paper.

Eliza sat for a moment, staring out at the view. Betty's garden was a riot of early summer flowers and their perfume floated in through the open window. While she was here she could at least help with the garden—it was one of her chief pleasures.

Should she also write to Mama's brother and tell him of his sister's death? She was not sure if he already knew or even if he were still alive and living in India. She did not wish to appear as if she were asking for help. However, perhaps it was only polite to inform him.

She hesitated and then picked up her pen once more. She would write a brief note giving the bare facts and leave it at that—surely there could be nothing wrong in informing Mr Henry Jarvis of Mrs Bancroft's death?

Sealing her letter, she picked up her reticule and put on her pelisse. If she hurried to the estate manager's office, she might be in time to catch Mr Wright before he visited the ancient wool town of Norwich this afternoon.

She wondered how long it would be before she received an answer to her request for work. Would anyone be interested in employing a girl like her? She had no experience, except for a little nursing. Perhaps someone would think that sufficient. She could only hope she would receive an answer; despite what Betty had told her, she could not be a burden to her friends for ever.

Betty smiled when she went through to the kitchen. 'Have you written your letters?'

'Yes, I have. I shall walk down to the estate office with them now—unless you need me?'

'There is nothing for you to do,' Betty assured her. 'It is a nice afternoon and the walk will do you good.'

A few minutes later, Eliza set out for the earl's estate office. It was not too far, for the Wrights' cottage was on the Standish estate and the morning was pleasantly warm. Eliza liked to walk whenever she could, though she had had little opportunity the previous summer when her mother was first ill, and had been making the most of this one. In consequence, her complexion was not as pale as it had been.

Perhaps because she was dreaming a little, she did not become aware of the horseman until he was almost on her. Startled, she turned to see the great black stallion racing towards her at speed, so she threw herself to the side of the narrow road, landing on her hands and knees in a bramble bush.

'Damn you, sir! I said whoa,' a voice cried loudly. She heard more cursing and a horse neighing as if in protest as it was reined in, then, moments later, 'Forgive me, miss. My mind was elsewhere and I was not thinking that someone might be around that bend in the lane.'

Eliza rose to her feet as a gentleman in riding dress bent over her. He gave her his hand to steady her and she blushed as she found herself looking up into the bluest eyes she had ever seen. He stood head and shoulders above her and Eliza considered herself tall for a woman. The stranger was broad shouldered and of a powerful build; she thought him one of the handsomest men she had met.

'I…was dreaming myself,' she confessed. 'Had I heard you sooner, I should have moved out of your way, sir. I trust your horse has suffered no harm?'

'That is generously said.' The gentleman smiled at

her, a hint of relief in those devastating eyes. 'Are you hurt, Miss…? Forgive me, I do not know your name.'

'I am Eliza Bancroft,' she replied and her cheeks were pink as he continued to hold her hand for longer than necessary. 'I grazed my hands as I fell, but they will soon mend.'

'May I see your hands?' He turned her hands over and saw the slight graze on the right one and the spot of blood. Bending his head, he licked the wound with his tongue, sending a spasm of shock and incredible feeling curling through her. Eliza jerked and removed her hand from his grasp instantly. He looked surprised, then conscious, as if just realising what he had done. 'Forgive me. I meant nothing wrong. My mother always said that licking the wound took the sting away. I have nothing to help you—unless my neckcloth as a bandage…'

'No! It is not necessary,' she said, feeling embarrassed by her feelings, which were quite inappropriate. 'Thank you, I shall be home soon enough and my friend Betty will tend my hand for me, though I think it is no more than a scratch from the bramble.'

His eyes seemed to burn into her for long moments, then, 'My apologies, Miss Bancroft. My mind was elsewhere. I am on my way to visit my uncle. He is expecting me and I did not wish to be late…' He hesitated, as if unsure of what to do next. 'If there is anything I can do…?'

'No, sir,' she replied instantly. 'I am perfectly able to manage alone, thank you. Pray continue. I should not wish to make you late for your appointment.'

'Standish is a testy old devil at times, but he has been ill and I am anxious about him, so I should go…' He seemed unwilling to leave her, but in quite a hurry.

'Yes, of course, please do,' Eliza replied. 'I would not keep you. I am perfectly able to continue.'

'If only every lady were as forgiving,' he said and, then belatedly, 'My name is Daniel Seaton, Miss Bancroft. I am happy to make your acquaintance. Perhaps another time...'

Eliza was not sure what he meant by that. She inclined her head, dipping a curtsy as he caught the reins and swung up into the saddle, smiling at her once more before giving the horse its head.

Her heart beat faster than normal as she watched the handsome stranger ride off down the lane at a rather more sedate pace. If the earl was his uncle, then he was a man of some rank and would not be interested in the daughter of a parson. His remark could mean nothing. Indeed, it was much better if he had been mouthing a mere politeness, because any attentions from a gentleman of quality would be of the wrong kind.

The earl sometimes held house parties and in the past her mama had warned her not to go walking alone when young gentlemen were staying up at the big house.

'You would not encourage their attentions, my love,' Mrs Bancroft had told her more than once. 'Yet you are attractive enough to arouse the interest of wild young bucks and they are not to be trusted.'

Eliza's instincts told her that Daniel Seaton, as he had named himself, was perhaps the kind of gentleman her mama had warned her of. He had been perfectly polite and behaved respectably enough, apart from the incident when he had licked her hand. No gentleman would do that to a respectable young woman of his own class, but as the daughter of a clergyman she was fair game! She knew that the earl's own son had been both wild and reckless, and he was reputed to have had low morals and had been fond of romping with farm or tavern wenches and drinking a great deal, which was why his violent death while out riding had not been a surprise to the local people. Still, Ted had told them that the earl had been devastated by his son's death and was only half the man he had been before it.

Eliza felt sad for the earl, whom she knew only by slight acquaintance, having seen him at church and the fête that was held once a year in his gardens, as well as a Christmas party he gave for his neighbours. Her papa had been invited to dine occasionally, as the parish priest, but the earl had ceased to entertain in the months following his son's death. It was a terrible thing to lose his only son, though he had a daughter who had given him two young grandsons.

She supposed that one of his grandsons would inherit both the title and the estate, though both were still in leading strings. If the earl were to die before they were grown...but he was only in his late middle years and would surely live until he was sixty at least?

Seeing the estate office ahead of her, she put the thought out of her mind and increased her pace.

'It was good of you to come down again so soon, Daniel,' the earl said and sighed heavily. 'Will you take a glass of madeira with me before nuncheon?'

'If it is that excellent stuff you usually keep, I shall be delighted, sir,' Daniel said and smiled at his mother's brother. He was fond of his uncle, which was one of the reasons he refused to burden him with financial problems. 'How are you, sir?'

'Not too clever, Daniel.' The earl passed him a glass of the rich wine. 'I'm not sure I shall live long enough to see my grandchildren grow to manhood.' He held up his hand as Daniel would have protested. 'No, don't deny it. My heart took a knock when Marcus was killed…'

'He would not want you to grieve too hard, sir. Marcus cared for you deeply.'

'Did he? I am not sure…once, perhaps, but we had grown apart of late. He seemed odd, as though something was on his mind.' The earl sighed heavily. 'I know the lad sowed his wild oats and I cannot approve of things he did, but he was my son. If he had asked for my help, I would have given it.'

'I have spoken to Cheadle, sir. He tells me that you settled my cousin's gambling debt immediately?'

'The damned fellow approached me before my son was cold in his grave. I dislike that man intensely, Daniel.'

'I, too,' Daniel agreed. 'I played a hand with him at my club. He lost heavily that night and was forced to give me this.' Daniel took a ring from his pocket and showed the earl. 'He asked me to keep it and intends to redeem it at his earliest convenience. I shall of course oblige him.'

'I am surprised that you played with him after what happened to your father?'

'I was not drunk, neither was I desperate. I know my limits and when to rise from the table. I had my reasons, sir.'

'I dare say you did.' The earl looked at him through narrowed eyes. 'Did Marcus approach you for help? The young fool! He should have come to me immediately.'

'He did not wish to distress you, sir. He sent me a letter. It was waiting at my club. I did not discover it until I went to visit my lawyer recently.'

'Your father left a damned mess for you, Daniel. You have only to ask if you need help.'

'Thank you, sir. I know it, but I believe I shall manage. I thought I might sell the London house, but for the moment I shall let it to tenants. I shall not be able to afford to visit London much until I have the estate on an even keel again.'

'You won't tell me, but I dare say your father took a mortgage.' The earl nodded as Daniel remained silent. 'Not my business but you might look for an heiress? If she suits you and her father is on the catch for a title you might save yourself years of penny pinching. Besides, you will wish to marry in a year or two, if not now.'

'Yes, perhaps.' Daniel laughed ruefully. 'Marry a fortune to pay my debts—that would be a little hard on the young woman, do you not think so?'

'It is often the case that a young woman of fortune has little else to commend her to a husband. Look for a plain chit, my boy, and she will be grateful to you. She will give you a couple of sons and then you may both live as you please. It is done all the time.'

'I know you are right, sir, but I shall try to sort my problems myself if I can.'

'Well, you don't need advice from me.' The earl frowned, suddenly seeming very toubled. 'It was odd the way Marcus died… His groom told me that he found a sore beneath the saddle when he groomed the wretched beast, which might explain why a man who was an excellent rider fell and broke his neck. I just can't understand how it happened. He should not have taken the horse out in such a state—though Jed swears there was nothing there when he saddled up that morning. If something caused the horse to chafe, it must have got there between Marcus leaving home and returning that evening. He had, of course, been drinking in the village inn, though I have been told he was not drunk when he left.'

'Is the groom still in your employ, sir?'

'No, he left me a week or two back. Lives in the village, name of Jed Bailey—why?'

'Marcus was a damned good rider, but something must have made his horse bolt the way it did…' Daniel frowned, remembering his cousin's confusing letter 'The coroner brought in a verdict of misadventure. Is there any reason to think there might have been foul play? '

'None then and none now,' the earl admitted. 'Marcus was in with a bad crowd, though I do not know who they were—but I sensed he was hiding something from me.'

'I should like your permission to investigate a little, sir.'

The earl looked at him thoughtfully. 'You know something I don't, of course. Don't want to tell me?'

'I know very little, sir—but I intend to find out.'

'Take care, then. If whoever was behind what happened to Marcus learns you are poking your nose in, he won't stop there. I would rather nothing happened to you, Daniel.'

'I shall be on my guard. Besides, there may be nothing in it.'

'You wouldn't be bothering to investigate if you thought that. Is Cheadle behind this, Daniel?'

'What makes you think that, sir?'

'No reason. Just don't trust the man.'

'Well, neither do I—but I don't think him a murderer. He may be ruthless at cards, perhaps even a cheat, though he played fair with me the other night—but I doubt he was involved in my cousin's death.'

'Well, I wish you good luck, but don't get killed, my

boy. I am relying on you to guide my heir if I pop off before he is old enough to manage the estate.'

'I shall be delighted to help young Paul if I can.'

'That was my hope. You will tell me whatever you discover?'

'Of course. When I am certain.'

'You have no immediate plans for marriage, I take it?'

'None at the moment, sir. I am not sure any young woman would put up with me. I have little to offer.'

The earl shook his head. 'Do not put yourself down, my boy. Walk down to the estate office with me, Daniel. I have a building project I should like your advice on.'

'Willingly.' Daniel set his glass down. 'I shall be pleased to see your plans for the new cottages.'

'Well, Miss Eliza, so we shall be losing you soon.' Mr Jones, the estate manager, smiled at her as she explained her reason for bringing in the letter. 'But you will enjoy living in Bath or London, I dare say—more life for you there than here, I imagine.'

'I like being in the country, sir,' Eliza replied. 'I shall miss my friends here, but it is time I started to support myself.'

'Mrs Jones would have taken you at the house if there were a mistress,' the manager said. 'I had a word with her a while ago, but there was only menial work and she didn't think it right that Parson Bancroft's daughter should scrub floors. She will be very pleased to learn you are to apply for a position as a companion to a lady. She was only saying last night that it was what you ought to do.'

'That was kind of her,' Eliza replied. She knew the estate manager had let her have the cottage for longer than he truly ought, because there were estate workers needing a place to live. 'Give your wife my good wishes, sir. I should get back now. I want to give Betty a hand with the garden.'

'I'll send your letters later this afternoon,' Ted Wright promised. 'Take care now, lass.'

'Yes, I shall,' Eliza said and opened the door to leave. She was startled by the arrival of two gentlemen who had been about to enter, flushing as she saw the earl and the man whose horse had almost knocked her down earlier. 'I beg your pardon, my lord.'

'No matter,' the earl said, his eyes narrowing in recognition. 'Ah, yes, Miss Eliza Bancroft. I was sorry to have to ask you to leave the cottage, but Jones told you we had a family waiting for it, I dare say? And I did not feel it was quite safe for you to stay there alone, considering the situation locally. You will have heard of the missing girls, not girls of quality, of course, but still it is worrying. You have settled in with Wright and his wife, I believe?'

'Yes, my lord.' Eliza dipped a curtsy, understanding his reasoning for more than one young village girl had gone missing over the past two years. 'I knew I could not stay for ever, sir. Besides, I hope to find work soon, perhaps in London or Bath.'

'Well, that is excellent news,' the earl said. 'Ah, Jones, I am glad I caught you. I wanted to take another look at the plans for the new cottages.'

As the earl moved off to speak with his manager, Eliza looked at the younger man. His eyes went over her, brows lifted in a question.

'You are recovered from your fright, Miss Bancroft?'

'Yes, thank you, sir. I was not truly hurt at all,' she said, but her heart did a little flip as she caught the pleasant scent of cologne that hung about him. She recalled the feeling that had shot through her when he licked her hand and felt her cheeks burn. 'Excuse me, I must not keep you from your business.'

He inclined his head and moved aside, but she felt his eyes on her as she went out through the open door. After a few steps she looked back and saw he was still watching her. She had never seen eyes quite as arresting as his before. Not knowing why, she gave him a wide smile and a little wave before turning back and walking away. Her heart was beating too fast and she wondered why this second meeting within a short space of time should affect her so much?

Eliza smiled to herself. If Daniel Seaton were going to visit his uncle more often, it might be best that she would soon be leaving Norfolk. It would not do for her to meet him too often, because she could easily begin to like him more than was wise for a young woman of her station.

Chapter Two

'Oh, that is a nuisance,' Betty said as she looked at the milk jug she had taken from the cold pantry the following morning. 'The milk has curdled and I was going to make a rice pudding for Ted's supper.'

'May I go to the farm for you?' Eliza asked. 'I can be there and back in an hour; there will still be plenty of time for you to make that pudding.'

'What a thoughtful girl you are,' Betty said approvingly. 'If you would not mind, it would be a big help to me.'

'It is no trouble at all,' Eliza said, taking sixpence from the shelf and the big jug from the pantry.

She set out for the farm, which was just across the fields from her friend's cottage. Somewhere above her head a lark was singing and the grass in the wild meadow was almost waist high. She was singing to herself, enjoying the warmth of the sun when she suddenly saw the man walking towards her through the long grass. Her heart caught a beat as he smiled and came up to her.

'Good morning, Miss Bancroft. You seem happy this morning?'

'It is such a lovely day,' she replied. She could not help remarking how blue his eyes were, thinking them a match for the cloudless sky. His smile brought an answering one from her. 'How do you go on at your uncle's? Do you mean to stay long?'

'Only a few days, unfortunately,' Daniel Seaton replied and then frowned. 'I think my uncle mends, but he is not as well as I should like.'

'I am sorry to hear that, sir.'

Eliza found that he was walking beside her, clearly intending to accompany her to the farm.

'He took my cousin's death hard,' he continued. 'However, he is better than he was the last time I was down.'

'Did you come at Christmas? I know the earl felt unable to host his usual celebrations.'

'Yes, I was down at Christmas, but I have not seen him since. I have been in London and at my estate...' His eyes darkened, making Eliza think he dwelled on something that pained him.

They had reached the farm gate. He opened it for her and stood back. She felt that he had withdrawn into himself.

'I shall leave you here, Miss Bancroft. I have an errand to run...'

'Goodbye, sir. I hope your uncle will soon be well again.' Eliza watched him walk away, feeling puzzled. For a few moments he had seemed as if he meant to flirt with her, but then something had changed him. It was just as well, for she found him far too attractive.

* * *

Daniel was thoughtful as he left the young woman. He had just come from visiting the home of Jed Bailey. Unfortunately, the groom had disappeared two days previously. His mother said he had been restless and she thought he had taken it into his head to visit his cousin in Bristol.

'There's been something on his mind for weeks, sir,' Mrs Bailey said. 'I asked him what had upset him—and why he left the earl's employ—but he wouldn't tell me. He seemed excited and then…well, to tell you the truth I thought he was scared, sir. Then he came in, in a hurry, like, took his horse and said he was off to Bristol to see his cousin.'

'If he should return, please ask him to come and see me.' Daniel gave her one of his cards.

'Yes, sir, of course.' Mrs Bailey smiled as Daniel slipped a coin into her hand. 'I expect it is just restless feet—you know how young men are, sir.'

Daniel agreed he did and left her. His enquiries in the village so far had been of some help, though he was troubled by what he had discovered. Marcus had certainly been at the inn for two hours on the afternoon of his death. The landlord said he was in a bad mood, and that he sat talking to a gentleman in the corner for an hour or more before the stranger left.

'Did you know the man?' Daniel asked.

'No, sir. He was not local—but a gentleman, I would say. A surly cove. When one of my serving wenches went over to the table and asked if they wanted more wine he told her to stay away, for their talk was private.'

'Is the girl here, landlord?'

'No, sir, more's the pity. Molly was a good worker. She went off the day after your cousin was killed—and

never even told her mother where she was going. She's
not the first, but I didn't think Molly was the flighty
sort. There have been others go off, some would say
gone missing, but I reckon they went to London to make
their fortune—if you understand me. Still, Molly were
a quiet girl and I thought she had a local lad.'

'If you should hear anything you think might interest
me, please send me word.' Daniel gave him his calling
card and two guineas for his trouble.

'Yes, sir. I will let you know if Molly comes back.'
The landlord was thoughtful for a moment. 'Does the
name Cheadle mean anything to you, sir?'

'Yes, it does—why?' Daniel's gaze narrowed intently.

'The name was mentioned between them, sir. Molly
heard them arguing—and your cousin said, "I can't ask
Cheadle to wait for ever." The other man said, "Cheadle
is dangerous. If you cross him, you may regret it, but he
is a poodle compared to you know who…" I don't know
if that is useful, sir?'

'It may be,' Daniel said and frowned as he nodded to
the landlord and gave him another guinea. 'Thank you.
Please contact me if you remember more.'

'You may be certain I shall, sir.' The landlord pocketed the money and smiled to himself.

There Daniel had left his investigations for the
moment. He thought he might have to employ the
services of an investigative agent to search for Molly
and Jed Bailey. It was strange that two young people
had gone off without a word—unless they had run off
together?

His thoughts were busy after his brief meeting with
Miss Eliza Bancroft. The pieces had been all jumbled
up at the start, but they seemed to be coming together

in his mind. He was reaching for something, but was not quite there.

He was determined to discover more about his cousin's death, because he was almost certain now that Marcus had been murdered. The horse had been left outside the inn for some time and it was perfectly possible that someone had tampered with the saddle while it was there.

So the opportunity was obvious, and the likely suspect the man Marcus had been arguing with in the inn—but where was the motive?

It was after meeting Miss Bancroft that Daniel suddenly remembered that both his uncle and the landlord had spoken of other young local women going missing. Could the disappearance of these girls and his cousin's death be linked? It hardly seemed likely and yet Marcus had hinted at something dark and sinister in his letter.

It would bear investigation, even though the truth might be hard to swallow. Drinking, gambling and tumbling the local girls were things that many young gentlemen indulged in—but snatching girls from their homes was quite another. Daniel had no illusions about what happened to the young girls; they would be taken either to whorehouses or, even worse, sent abroad to be sold into the harems of rich potentates.

No, surely Marcus would never become involved in something like that—or had he been drawn into it innocently and then felt trapped? Daniel knew that his cousin had had a wild side, but he did not think him evil. Perhaps he had not known what was going on—and when he had found out he threatened to expose those behind it?

Daniel felt cold. He had no proof whatsoever, but he believed he might have stumbled on a clue.

He was not sure what part the Marquis of Cheadle might have played in this shady business. His name had been mentioned between Marcus and the stranger—but whether he was actually involved with the snatching of local girls was dubious. Daniel would not have thought it—but then, he would not have expected his cousin to become involved in such a disgusting traffic.

The marquis would bear watching. Daniel had been inclined to send back the ring he had won from him to Cheadle's London address, but now thought he would hang on to it. There was an inscription inside it that must be called romantic and therefore it might have some significance to the marquis. Perhaps it might be used as a bargaining tool, for if Cheadle knew something of this murky business he would not disclose it without persuasion.

Having settled the business in his mind, Daniel let his thoughts stray once more to the lovely Miss Eliza Bancroft. He was not sure why she had lingered in his mind. There were other more beautiful girls of his acquaintance who would not be averse to some attention from him, but most of them left him cold. Miss Bancroft interested him.

He would have liked to get to know her better while he was here, but his present situation was not conducive to any kind of relationship with a decent young woman. Had things been otherwise, he might have stayed longer with his uncle and found excuses to indulge in some light dalliance with the young lady—not that she would have permitted more than a kiss or two. He had no doubt that she was chaste, hence the delicious blush he had noticed on earlier occasions.

He would not go out of his way to seek another

meeting with her, Daniel decided, though he could not pretend that he was not intrigued.

No, he must not let his purpose wander! He must seek another meeting with Cheadle at the earliest opportunity and ask him what he knew of Marcus's affairs. If Cheadle lied, Daniel would know—and then he would leave no stone unturned to bring down all those responsible for his cousin's death.

'You asked me to call?' Henry, Marquis of Cheadle, looked at the woman sitting so calmly in her boudoir. In her lilac-lace peignoir and a fetching cap she was as beautiful as she had been years ago when he had fallen madly in love with her. He had not seen her for some years, because she had lived quietly in the country, seldom visiting London or Bath, but it seemed that she intended to make a change now that she was a widow. 'I was sorry to hear about the death of your husband, Sarah. Manners was no friend of mine but I dare say you will miss him?'

'You know my feelings about Lord Manners,' Sarah, Lady Manners, replied, only a tiny pulse in her throat giving a hint of the emotion she was keeping in check. 'I stayed with him because of my son, and for no other reason.'

'You were a fool, Sarah. You should have called his bluff—how often do you see Howard now?'

'Very rarely,' she admitted and sighed deeply. 'My son is exactly like his father. I have seen him once since he inherited the estate. We quarrelled after his father's death and he declines to visit me. Besides, I choose to live in the country and he prefers London.'

'Where he squanders the fortune he inherited. You

should speak to him, Sarah. If he continues as he is, he will come unstuck and lose everything.'

'Howard takes no notice of anything I say.' She raised her eyes to his. 'You know what I want, my lord. You have always known. My health is not good. Soon it will be too late for me to get to know our child…'

'I've told you before, I do not know where the child is now, Sarah. I promised that I would make no attempt to find the babe and I have kept my word. The lawyer saw to everything. I merely paid for the arrangements, as your husband demanded in settlement of his terms. I have never known the name of the people to whom the lawyer gave our child. Had I not agreed to his terms, Manners would have treated you more harshly than he did.'

'But you know the lawyer involved, do you not?'

'Yes, for I made payments for the child's upkeep until last year…' he admitted it reluctantly. 'Are you sure you wish to do this, Sarah? Your reputation has remained spotless. Only a few friends knew of your confinement. Do you truly wish to risk exposure at this stage?'

'I am lonely, Henry. And I wish to atone for my earlier wrongdoings.'

'But how long will it be before the truth comes out?'

'Why should it ever be known? Do not fear that I shall reveal your name, Henry. Even if my part were suspected, you would remain anonymous.'

He looked at her in silence for some moments, then inclined his head. 'Very well. I shall look out the lawyer's address. I believe I have it somewhere.'

'Thank you. I am grateful. I was not sure you would come today.'

The marquis raised his brows. 'I am not the monster

rumour would have me, Sarah. I could not refuse you such a request, though I gave my word to Manners that I would never tell you anything.'

Sarah stood up. She moved towards him, laying her hand on his arm. 'Has life been terrible for you, Henry? I thought of you so often, wished that things had been otherwise. Especially when I heard…'

'That I had gone to the devil?' A wry smile touched his mouth. 'I decided that I would never give my heart again and so I married for money, though later I inherited more than I could ever need. My wife hates me and I have no love for her. I care only for my daughter, Marianne. I ask you not to tell me if you discover the truth about the child. Manners never told me whether we had a daughter or a son—' He put out his hand to silence her as she would have told him. 'It was for the best. I put the whole thing from my mind and to know now might be to open Pandora's box. I cannot afford scandal for Marianne's sake. I have hopes that she will marry into the peerage.'

'I have heard that she is a very beautiful girl,' Sarah said. 'I am glad you have someone, Henry.'

'My daughter is both lovely and innocent. If it were not for her, I should have asked my wife for a divorce long ago.'

'Is there someone else you care for?' Sarah looked at him steadily, without revealing a flicker of emotion.

'You know there was only one woman I loved. If, after Marianne is married, I could arrange a divorce…?'

'No, Henry. It was too long ago, my dear. Once I would have given everything to be with you, but it is too late.'

'We could still be together. We were lovers once. Why not again?'

'Because I was younger then. I am older than you, Henry. It was one of the reasons I refused to leave my husband. I did not wish to ruin your life.'

'How could you have ruined my life? It meant nothing to me without you. Let me take care of you, Sarah— let me make up for the lost years.'

'It is too late. My health is not good, Henry. I have settled for a quiet life in the country. You are still young enough to find a new love. I ask nothing more of you than the address I need.'

'I would ask no more of you than affection.' For a moment his eyes beseeched her, then, as he saw the answer in her face, his expression became cold, withdrawn. 'Very well, madam. I shall send you what you need. I do not expect to hear from you again.'

Sarah sank back into her elegant elbow chair, her hands to her face as the door closed behind him. He was still angry and bitter, blaming her because she had given into her husband's blackmail.

If only she had been stronger. How different her life might have been if she had been brave enough to leave her husband and go with Henry, as he had begged her.

Her marriage to Manners had been a disaster from the start. Her husband had never loved her. He had had a mistress in London and spent all his time with her. Once Sarah had given him his heir, he had not bothered to visit her bed again. Lonely and unhappy, she had turned to a young man who gave her everything she lacked from her husband. Henry had been the most generous of lovers, sweet and giving.

At the time of their affair he had not yet inherited his uncle's title and had had little in the way of fortune. He was also three years her junior and on the verge of making his career in the army. Lord Manners had known at once that her child was not his. He'd forced her to reveal the name of her lover and then threatened to ruin Henry if she went off with him. She had been forced to break off their affair and to give up her lovechild as soon as she was born. Her daughter had been snatched from her arms only hours after she had given birth, taken from her cruelly by her unforgiving husband. Lord Manners had never told her where the child had been taken; even after his death, he had tried to keep the secret from her.

He had inserted a clause in his will to make certain that she could not find her daughter. If she made the attempt, she would give up the right to live in the Dower House at Trowbridge and she would lose her jointure. She would have nothing left but the fortune her grandfather had left in trust for her, which her husband had refused her for as long as he could. Now that he was dead, half the capital and the income was hers entirely, the remainder of the capital to be divided between her children on her death. Her son had not known of the existence of a half-sister until he read the will, and he had accused her of vile things before storming out of the house and taking himself off to London.

Her husband's vindictiveness had not hurt Sarah; she had long ceased to care and nothing he did could surprise or distress her. She would be sorry to leave the house she had moved to after his death, for it was pleasant and enabled her to see her son on the rare visits he paid to his estate. However, she had no intention of letting her husband's unkindness stop her at least trying to discover the whereabouts of her lovechild.

A smile touched her lips. She had loved Henry and in those days he had loved her deeply. The tales she had since heard of him had been distressing; her husband had made certain she heard of the worst of his excesses, but the young man she remembered was still dear to her.

She had reached her decision with the calm deliberation that was her way these days. She would use some of the capital to purchase a house in Bath, a city that suited her much better than London and where she still had a few friends. Then she would try to find her daughter and be damned to the consequences.

'I am sorry, Eliza,' Ted Wright said as she looked at him expectantly. 'There was nothing for you at the reception office again today.'

'Oh...' Eliza sighed. It had been ten days now and she was beginning to think that she would never receive an answer to her advertisement. It seemed as if she might have to go into Norwich and ask at the employment agency for domestic servants. Perhaps she had set her sights too high and would have to settle for something more menial. 'Thank you. I had hoped, but I suppose these things take time.'

'You may need to put in a second notice, but there is no hurry, Eliza. You are very welcome to stay with us for as long as you please.'

Eliza thanked him, but her spirits sank a little for she did not wish to be a burden to her friends for too long. She would wait one more week, then, if she heard nothing, she would look for employment through the agency.

Lady Sarah looked through her post when it was brought up to her by her maid and sighed. Most of it would be invitations to dine or attend the theatre or some other function. She had been in Bath for just three weeks and already she was inundated by invitations. It was very kind and generous of her friends, but she was used to a quieter life and uncertain whether the new social circle she had found here would suit her on a permanent basis.

She could return to the Dower House and give up her search for her daughter, but that would be to admit defeat. She had been waiting for a letter these past several weeks, but so far the lawyer had not replied to her request for details of her daughter's whereabouts. He was being very stubborn and she could not think why.

She opened the newspapers that had been delivered that morning. *The Times* was always a day late, because it was sent through the post from London, and the local paper had lain unnoticed on her dressing chest all the previous day. She had spent the whole day visiting and had decided to keep to her bed a little longer this morning.

She poured a cup of the dark chocolate she enjoyed, sipping from the delicate cup that was part of a Dresden breakfast set. The chocolate was a little bitter, but she preferred it to tea or coffee at this hour. Sipping its richness, she opened *The Times* and turned to the page she was interested in. Although her maid, who had been with her for years, had been perfectly adequate for her needs in the country, Sarah had become aware that she required a companion here in Bath. She had hoped to find her daughter and ask her to stay, but as yet that was beyond her, though if the lawyer did not soon answer her letter she would employ an agent to find the child… girl. Her daughter would be twenty by now.

Running her finger down the list of young women

searching for a position as a companion, Sarah stopped
at one that appealed to her.

The headline read:

Sensible young woman recently bereaved seeks a
position as companion.
I have nursed my mother and am well able to make
beds comfortable, prepare tisanes and read in a
pleasant voice. I can cook, embroider and mend
and I do not mind light cleaning in the house. I
am happy to run errands and look after an invalid.
However, I have no previous experience of employment in this field.

Sarah smiled as she read the few lines. They seemed
to speak from the heart and told her that the writer
had never applied for a position before. The advert was
a little naïve, perhaps, but that made it all the more
appealing.

Sarah was not yet in need of a nurse, merely someone to run her errands and accompany her to the Pump
Room and other functions. The young woman who
called herself Eliza Bancroft seemed eminently able to
fulfil that duty, and, if Sarah's health grew worse, might
be just the person she needed.

She was not going to give up the search for her
daughter. Sarah was quite firm about that, but she saw
no reason why she should not employ a companion in
the meantime. She could afford it; she had the income
from her grandfather's estate. Because her husband had
withheld it from her for so many years it had grown to a
considerable amount. She had been quite shocked when
her lawyer told her how much the accumulated capital
was. Had her husband been able to touch it, she was

sure he would have gambled it away to spite her, but her grandfather had been a canny Scottish gentleman. He had made sure that the capital and income could not be accessed by anyone but Sarah, or her children if she were dead. How that must have irked her husband. He had the power to prevent her from benefiting from the money while he lived, but he could not take it for himself.

Well, she had it now and no one to gainsay her. As yet her son, Howard, had not run through the fortune his father had left him, though she had heard from more than one source that he was likely to do so in time. Well, she would face that when the time came.

Getting up, she slipped on her peignoir, went over to the pretty lady's desk near the window and sat in the elbow chair. She picked up her pen, dipped it in the glass inkwell and began to write. She would invite the young woman to come to her for a trial period of three months. If they suited she would continue the contract. In the meantime she might find her daughter.

Having written the polite invitation to join her in Bath and offered a salary of two guineas a month and her keep, Sarah felt satisfied that she would secure the services of the young woman. A girl of little experience was hardly likely to get a better offer. She hesitated for a moment, then took out a fresh sheet of paper.

My dear Marquis,
I had not intended to ask anything more of you, and I assure you this is the very last thing I shall ask, but I wondered if you could arrange to have a young woman fetched from Norwich? I have given her a day, place and time, which I have copied here for you. I am residing in Bath and it is a long way

to send my carriage, which I need here. I know you have several carriages at your disposal—perhaps you would be kind enough to have Miss Bancroft brought here to me in the Crescent? I am not yet sure she will accept the position, but as the town of Norwich is not far from your Norfolk estate it might not be too much trouble to send the carriage on the off chance. I shall write again if Miss Bancroft accepts, but if you do not hear please send anyway.

Yours truly, Sarah

Satisfied with her letters, Sarah sanded and sealed both with wax and her signet. She was using her grandfather's crest. He had left the ring to her and she liked it, wearing it on the middle finger of her right hand.

Smiling, Sarah returned to bed and resumed her breakfast, breaking the soft roll and spreading butter and honey. Had she been reckless in offering a position to a young woman simply on the basis of an advertisement? Her husband would certainly have disapproved. He had summarily dismissed her last companion as unsuitable despite her protests. After that she had managed with the services of her maid. Now she could please herself.

She was certain the young woman who had placed that advertisement was an honest and caring person, and as such she was more than qualified for the position. Sarah would give the letters to her maid when she came for the tray and then she would stroll to the Pump Room and meet her friends.

'Here you are, my love,' Betty said, coming into the kitchen one morning later that week. 'My Ted picked this up for you this morning at the receiving office.

Rather than wait until this evening to give it to you, he sent it with Farmer Jenkins's boy. I think it must be a reply to your advertisement.'

'At last…' Eliza took it eagerly. More than two weeks had passed and she had almost given up hope of a reply. Breaking the impressive seal, she read the brief message and sighed with relief. 'This is almost too wonderful to be true, Betty. I have been offered a position with a widowed lady in Bath—and on generous terms.'

She read the letter to Betty, who nodded her head with satisfaction. 'Lady Sarah Manners,' she said approvingly. 'She sounds like a proper lady and her letter is everything it should be. It says that if you accept you will be met in Norwich market square on the twenty-fifth of July at twelve-thirty.'

'I must write and accept at once, for that is only two weeks away,' Eliza said. 'I think I shall do it immediately and then perhaps Ted will take it into town for me tomorrow.'

'I think he was going to town this afternoon. If you walked down to the estate office with it, he will take it with him when he goes.'

'Yes, I shall,' Eliza said. 'I had begun to think that I would need to visit the employment office for young ladies in Norwich, but this is just what I need. Do you not think so?'

'Yes, I dare say it may be,' Betty said and smiled at her pleasure. 'It is time something good happened for you, my love.'

'I consider myself fortunate to have such friends as you and Ted,' Eliza said and went through to the parlour to write her letter. When she had finished it, she put on her pelisse and bonnet and set out for the earl's estate office.

* * *

The Marquis of Cheadle frowned over Lady Sarah's letter. He had recognised the handwriting instantly and for a few heart-catching moments he had thought she wanted him to visit her again—that she might have changed her mind and be ready to take the first step towards going away with him. It was a ridiculous notion, but one that had taken root in his mind since he visited her. The idea was impossible, of course, for he had his daughter's future to think of and that must take precedence over his own desires.

Cheadle had lived by his own rules. He was capable of being ruthless, though not actually the rogue some believed. For many years he had suppressed the ache that had never quite gone away, filled his empty life with gambling and high living, but recently the need for something more had overtaken him. He glanced at the letter again before slipping it into the top drawer of his desk as the door opened and his wife entered.

'Yes, madam,' he said coldly. 'Was there something I may do for you?'

'I wanted to make sure you would accompany us to Bath next week,' Lady Cheadle replied, her mouth twisted sourly. 'Accrington hasn't come up to scratch and I think Marianne is moping. As you know, I had hopes that he would follow us from London, but he has not obliged. I have arranged to visit Bath; we may meet with better fortune there—but I wish you to come with us, at least for the first few days.'

'Bath…' The marquis frowned. 'I had thought to return to London. I am not sure you should rush off to Bath in a hurry, Lady Cheadle. We are in no hurry to push Marianne off. If Accrington needs more time to consider, he must have it. I think he was sufficiently struck to make an offer, but his is an old name and family. He will want to discuss things with his family and his lawyers.'

He reached for the ring he habitually wore and felt its absence as he remembered it was lost, at least for now, given as promise of payment to Daniel Seaton. He would not wear another one, for the ring held memories that could not be replaced by another bauble. He frowned as he thought of the man, of whom he had seen nothing since that evening in town. Seaton might well sell the ring for he was entitled to and he could bear no love for a man who had won ten thousand from his father. Lord Seaton had been drunk. Cheadle had warned him to give up, but he had haughtily refused and the result was predictable. Yet Cheadle had a nagging conscience over it, for he had known the older man was too far gone to realise what he was about.

It was with an effort that he brought his mind back to what his wife was saying.

'I am determined to go. If Accrington thinks he may lose her, it should bring him to the point sooner rather than later. Have I your assurance that you will accompany us?'

Cheadle narrowed his gaze. 'Very well, madam. Have it your way. A few days here or there is nothing to me.'

'I shall miss you,' the earl said and sighed heavily. 'Having you here has been a comfort to me, Daniel.'

'I shall be sorry to leave you,' Daniel replied. 'However, there is estate business that takes me home.'

He also had the business of an agent to employ, and had arranged to meet the man in Norwich. He had decided to take up his uncle's cause to find out the truth about Marcus's death, and so had decided to stay with the earl whilst he put things in motion. It had taken a few days for the exchange of letters, because the man he had chosen was a Bow Street Runner and well recommended. Daniel knew that if his chosen investigator got a scent of something he would go for it like a terrier after a rat and he was eager for the man to begin his work.

After leaving his uncle, Daniel rode through the village. He saw the young woman who had been in his thoughts too often of late. She was standing outside the haberdashers, looking into the window, and an older woman was with her. They seemed to be intent on looking at some materials on display.

Daniel tipped his hat to her and slowed his horse to a standstill.

'Good morning, Miss Bancroft. How are you?'

'I am well, sir,' she said. 'I have had good news—I have been offered employment with a lady.'

'Most generous terms they are, too,' her companion said. 'I wouldn't part with my Eliza for the world, but she may get the chance to mix with quality, and that must be good for her.'

'Good day to you both,' Daniel said. 'I must get on, for I have an appointment.'

He rode on by, conscious of the fact that something tugged at him and made him want to turn his head. Yet he conquered the need. He admired the young lady but at the moment he had more weighty matters on his mind than dalliance.

'Are you sure you have all you need? Enough money to come back if the carriage isn't there to meet you?' Betty asked, looking at Eliza anxiously. 'I've packed you some food for the journey, love.'

'Thank you. I have all I need,' Eliza said and hugged her again. She felt very emotional now the time to part had arrived, and her throat was tight. 'You will answer my letters?'

'You know I can't write much,' Betty replied. 'My Ted will read yours to me and he'll write what I want to say—but you are to write as soon as you get there and let us know you are safe and happy. If there is anything you need…anything you don't like…you are to come back to us on the next mail coach. You have a home with us for as long as you like.'

'Thank you, my dearest friend,' Eliza said, tears springing to her eyes. She held them back because if she cried Betty would, too. 'I have been so blessed in my friends. I shall write to you as soon as I can, but I am sure I shall do perfectly well. Lady Sarah sent me a guinea by special post for the journey after she got my letter. Was that not kind of her?'

'I'm glad we made you that new travelling gown and pelisse,' Betty said. 'You look a proper young lady and that is only right for you will be mixing in company, I dare say.'

'I think we may live very quietly. Lady Sarah said that she is a widow and her health is sometimes poor. I do not expect to go anywhere much, except perhaps to the Pump Room.'

'The waters are supposed to be good for anyone sickly,' Betty said. 'Well, always remember you can come home if you're unhappy, my love.'

'Yes, I shall. I had better go, Betty. Ted is ready with the dogcart. I must not keep him waiting; I think he has business in Norwich.'

'Off you go then, Eliza. Have a good time and be as happy as you can.'

Eliza went out to where her friend's husband sat patiently waiting for them to say their goodbyes. The young groom came to help her in, grinned at her and stood back as Ted whipped up his horse.

'She looks a proper treat,' he remarked to Betty as they drove off. 'Anyone would think she were quality.'

'Well, she is and better than most,' Betty said. 'Thanks for your help with the trunk but you had better get off now or they will be looking for you at the stables.'

'Yeah. Ain't got a piece of yer gingerbread, 'ave yer?'

'I might have,' Betty said and smiled. 'Come into the kitchen and I'll see what I can find.'

She cast one last regretful glance at the dogcart and went back into the cottage.

'Well, here we are then, Eliza,' Ted Wright said as he pulled the cart to a halt in the busy market square. He glanced round and nodded as he saw the carriage waiting close by the clock tower. The driver seemed to be looking about, as if expecting someone. 'I'll just go and ask if that's the transport for Miss Eliza Bancroft.'

'Surely it can't be? A carriage like that for me?' Eliza protested, but the groom was getting down and coming towards them.

'Would you be Miss Bancroft?' he asked, tipping his tall crowned hat respectfully.

'Yes, I am. Did Lady Sarah send you to fetch me?'

'I was sent to take you to Lady Sarah Manners in Bath,' he said, an odd look on his face. 'Can't exactly say as she sent me. This carriage belongs to the marquis, miss.'

'The marquis?' Eliza was puzzled. 'I don't understand. You have it right—you are to take me to Lady Sarah, my employer?'

'Those are my instructions, yes. Is that trunk all you have with you?'

'And my portmanteau,' Eliza said. 'I shall carry that—if you would help Mr Wright with the trunk, please?'

'Yes, of course.'

The man turned away. Together, he and Ted strapped the heavy trunk on the back of the carriage and then Ted came back to her. He held out his hand, placing his other hand over hers as she took it.

'Don't forget, you can come home any time you like, Miss Eliza.'

'Thank you,' she whispered, glancing at the groom as he stood with the door open, waiting for her. She climbed in and waved to her friend from behind the window. Her mouth felt dry as she settled back against the comfortable squabs and her throat was tight. She was certainly to travel in luxury and that made her a little apprehensive. Why would the marquis send his carriage—whoever he was? For a moment she wondered if she were being abducted and then the absurdity of such a notion made her smile.

The groom knew the name of her employer. It was quite possible that the marquis was a friend of Lady Sarah and that he had agreed to bring her companion to her.

Feeling relieved to have settled the thing in her mind, Eliza sat back and took out the battered copy of a book she had bought from the second-hand stall at the market. It would serve to pass the time as they traveled, for she knew they would be some days on the road. She would need to take a room at more than one inn and she would have to rely on the coachman to find a decent house that was not too expensive for her purse.

Eliza looked out of the inn window and smiled as she saw it was yet another clear fine day. They had already been three days on the road and she would be glad when they reached Bath, which should not be more than another day at the most, for they had made good time. The Marquis of Cheadle's carriage was well sprung and the journey had been less tiresome than it might have been had she travelled on the mail coach. She had been surprised to find herself staying at the finest inns on the road; when she tentatively asked how much she owed the first morning, she was told that the Marquis of Cheadle's groom had settled the account.

Eliza had immediately tried to settle the debt, but the groom shook his head. 'I was given me instructions clear, miss. You wus to 'ave all the best and he would pay for yer lodgings.'

'Oh…' Somewhat taken aback by this statement, she was at first at a loss for words, then, 'I suppose my employer has settled it with the marquis.'

'Yes, miss. I dare say you are right.'

She moved away from the window and picked up her portmanteau, which contained all she required for her immediate needs. Her trunk had already been loaded on to the carriage and they were ready to leave again.

'How much further have we to travel?' she asked as the groom opened the door for her.

'If we make good time and meet no accidents, we should reach Bath before dark this night, miss.'

'Thank you.' She smiled at him, relieved that only one day of travelling remained. She had finished her book and the last hours of the previous day had seemed tedious. 'You are very kind.'

'You are welcome, miss.' He touched his hat. 'I hopes as it is the lady you're working for, miss.'

'What do you mean by that? I told you at the start, I am to be a companion to Lady Sarah Manners.'

'Right then, miss. Nothing to worry about then. Get in and we'll be orf.'

Sarah climbed into the carriage, feeling puzzled once more. Something in the groom's manner had disturbed her. She wondered why she was riding in such luxury and once again a shiver of apprehension slithered down her spine. Had she been naïve in accepting the first offer she received?

For a moment she felt a *frisson* of fear at the nape of her neck, but then she took a hold of her nerves. She was being very foolish. It was most unlikely that any marquis would go to so much trouble to abduct a girl he had never seen. She was hardly the most beautiful girl in the world. The thought made her laugh. She had been reading too many romances!

Daniel looked across the square and saw the carriage drawn up outside the inn just as the young woman entered it. He frowned, feeling concerned as he recognised her and the crest on the carriage. What on earth was Miss Bancroft doing in the Marquis of Cheadle's carriage? Alarm bells began to ring in his head. He recalled that she had been pleased to receive a generous offer of employment—was she being lured to a false promise? Would she join the legion of the missing?

The thought of Miss Eliza Bancroft being sold into white slavery appalled him. He could not bear to contemplate such a thing. It must not be allowed to happen. He must do something—and quickly.

Eliza must be warned that the marquis was not all he seemed. If he had charmed her into believing that she would be his lover or his mistress…no, he would not permit it.

Somehow he must prevent her from plunging into a life of shame and degradation. Yet how could he prevent her? He must go after her—but how to stop the carriage? What could he say?

An idea so reckless and foolhardy that it made him laugh for sheer mischief came to his mind. He dismissed it instantly, but it returned and he felt that he must risk it for Eliza's sake. He was not sure if she travelled alone, but if the marquis was with her in the carriage it would be necessary to disguise himself. A grim smile touched his mouth.

If Cheadle was involved in the vile gang that he believed was behind his cousin's death, he would find out soon enough that he had an enemy.

Eliza was brought from her reverie by a shout of alarm from the coachman and then a violent jolting as the carriage came to a sudden halt. She was thrown from her seat and for a moment landed on her knees on the floor of the carriage. Picking herself up, she was about to look out of the window when the door was opened.

'You had best get down, miss. I hope you wasn't hurt?'

'No, just shaken.' She took the coachman's hand. 'What happened?' she enquired as he helped her descend. 'Have we…?' She was about to ask if the carriage had suffered an accident, but seeing the masked rider caught her breath. 'What are you doing, sir?' He had a pistol directed at coachman's chest. 'That thing is dangerous…'

For a moment the highwayman seemed disinclined to answer. He sat his horse, staring down at them in silence.

Eliza lifted her head, anger making her impetuous. 'I fear you have mistaken your victim, sir. I have only a few coins in my purse—and this ring.' She felt for the ring she had found in her mother's sewing box. It was still on the ribbon that had been with it, hidden under her baby clothes. She took out her purse and offered both it and the ring to the highwayman. 'Please take these and allow us to go on. I beg you, do not harm these good men—they have done nothing to hurt you.'

'Who are you?' the masked man asked in a gruff voice she suspected was disguised. 'Why are you riding in the Marquis of Cheadle's carriage—what is he to you?'

He had accepted the purse and ring, which she noticed he examined before slipping them into his coat pocket. For a moment he hesitated, then beckoned her closer.

'Come with me for a few minutes. I wish to speak with you.'

'Don't you listen to him, Miss Bancroft. He is a rogue and not to be trusted,' the coachman cried and took a step towards her, stopping as the gun pointed in his direction once more.

'I mean you no harm.' The masked man bent down, offering his hand, then glanced at the coachman. 'Wait for your passenger, man, and do not try to be a hero—or you will regret it. Remember, a wild shot might harm the young lady.' He barked the words at the coachman, his pistol still aimed in his direction. 'If you do anything foolish, your wife will be a widow this night.'

'Please do as he asks. I am not afraid,' Eliza instructed.

She gave the highwayman her hand. He grasped her arm and she clutched his saddle, instinctively jumping as he hauled her up before him.

'Well done,' he murmured in an approving tone that sent tingles down her spine. 'You are quite safe. I do not kill women and children.'

Eliza shivered. At first she had been terrified by the sight of a masked, armed man, but for some unaccountable reason her fear had gone as he rode with her into the trees.

They travelled only far enough to be out of sight of the coachman before he halted. He dismounted and held out his arms. She slid down into them. For a moment he held her and she was aware of the pleasant smell of soap and a breath of cologne. He was very clean for a common highwayman.

'Well, sir,' Eliza said, her heart beating very fast, 'what have you to say to me that could not be said in front of the coachman?'

'Why are you travelling in that devil's carriage?' he demanded. 'Do you have any idea what kind of a man he is? Whatever promises he has made you are likely to prove your downfall.'

'The marquis has made me no promises. I have never met him. I am on my way to Bath, where I am to be employed by Lady Sarah Manners.'

The highwayman stared at her. Eliza felt a start of surprise as she noticed how blue his eyes were.

'Is that the truth?'

'Why should I lie to you?'

'Where did you get this ring?' He took her ring from

his pocket, looking at the inscription inside for a moment before handing it to her. 'What does it say?'

'Love means more. Why do you ask?'

'I have seen a similar ring before.'

Eliza's heart raced. 'I believe it was my birth mother's ring. I never knew her, but my mama found it beneath my clothes when I was given to her as a baby.' Her eyes entreated him. 'Where have you seen a ring like mine?'

'I took it from someone in a card game.' He reached for her purse in his pocket, returning it to her. 'I am not sure whether I should believe you, Miss Bancroft, but I do not rob young ladies who have no more than a few coins in their purse.'

'Thank you.' Her eyes were on his face. The mask covered most of it, but something about the set of his chin seemed familiar, as did the cologne he wore. She was certain she knew him. 'Why were you concerned about my reasons for travelling in the marquis's coach?'

'I would not have an innocent girl fall into that trap.'

Her cheeks were pink. 'You were good to be concerned for me, Mr Seaton, but I assure you I am not about to become any man's mistress. As for the marquis, I have never met him.'

For a moment he was silent, then, 'How did you know me?' He muttered an oath beneath his breath. 'Confound it! This is a coil, Miss Bancroft. I had hoped you would not recognise me. What gave me away?'

'Your eyes and your chin—and your cologne,' she said. 'This is most awkward for us both, sir. Will you accept my word that I shall never reveal your identity on pain of death?'

'Heaven forfend!' Daniel said and laughed as he removed his mask. 'I do not think you need to go so far, Miss Bancroft. Were you to be in danger of your life, you must certainly reveal my name.'

Eliza felt the laughter bubble up inside her. 'How foolish this is! I do not think you are proficient at your profession, sir. May I enquire why you took it up?'

'I must admit that this is my first attempt. I saw you get into the carriage where you made your last stop and feared you might be in trouble. It appears I was mistaken—but I could not allow you to go on in ignorance of the manner of man in whose carriage you rode. However, I did not wish to be seen by Cheadle, so I thought of the disguise to fool him if you were together—a disguise that seems not to have served me that well.'

'I see…' Eliza was thoughtful. 'I must thank you for your concern for me—but, pray tell me, why did you not wish to be seen by the marquis?'

'It is a matter I may not discuss with anyone—but I assure you I had good reason. And I beg you to have a care when dealing with him.'

'I have no need of such advice. I told you, I have no intention of becoming any man's mistress.'

'Sometimes innocent girls are not given a choice in the matter.'

'What do you mean?' Her smooth brow wrinkled in thought. 'Surely you do not think the marquis…? No, sir, that is monstrous. I have been treated with the greatest courtesy by his men. You are reckless and foolhardy and I cannot think you gave this foolish trick much consideration.'

'You have no idea of what you speak,' Daniel said harshly. 'There are men capable of such infamy…things of which you can have no knowledge. Please continue your journey. I am sorry to have interrupted what was such a pleasant experience for you. When Cheadle leaves you pregnant and destitute—'

Eliza reached out and slapped him. Her eyes widened in distress as his mouth thinned with temper. 'Oh, I am so sorry. I did not mean to…'

She turned away in embarrassment, but he caught her arm, swinging her back to face him. She had a moment to notice the angry passion in his eyes and then he caught her to him. His head bent as he took possession of her lips. The kiss was at first demanding, angry, but then it softened, becoming sweet and pleasing. Eliza did not struggle. For some obscure reason she felt relaxed and at ease in his embrace, her lips receptive, slightly parted. When he finally released her, she could only stare at him in bewilderment.

'Forgive me. I was tempted. You provoked me too far.'

'Then I must ask you to forgive me. It was quite unintentional, I assure you. May I leave now? You have my word that I shall not betray you. Nor shall I fall into the arms of a scoundrel. I am truly to work for a lady of quality.'

'You are either a saint or have the patience of one,' Daniel exclaimed ruefully. 'I have no excuse for my behaviour—in holding up your carriage or the kiss.'

'Papa taught me to see good in everyone and every situation.'

Eliza turned away, a smile on her soft mouth. It was as well that he could not read her mind. If he had guessed at her thoughts, which were really extremely shocking, he would know that she had wanted the kisses to continue.

As she walked back to the carriage, where the

coachman was anxiously awaiting her, Eliza's thoughts were churning with unanswered questions. Mr Seaton had not told her from whom he had won the ring that was like hers, but she could not help wondering if it were the Marquis of Cheadle. Was the hold-up all a foolish prank or was there some hidden secret—a secret that might concern her?

'Are you all right, Miss Bancroft?'

'What? Oh, yes, perfectly,' Eliza said. 'It was just a mistake, sir. The highwayman was playing a prank for a bet. He held up the wrong carriage. Shall we go on now?'

The coachman gave her an odd look, but said no more, offering his hand to assist her into the carriage.

Eliza sat back against the squabs. She touched her fingers to her mouth and smiled. Ever since the first time she had seen Mr Daniel Seaton she had wondered what it would be like to be kissed by him. Now she knew and it was even nicer than she had imagined.

Was it wicked of her to have enjoyed his kiss? Eliza knew that she was unlikely to marry unless she settled for someone like the curate. Mr Stanley was a good man, she supposed, but she had never dreamed of being kissed by him, whereas Mr Seaton's face had come unbidden to her mind both when sleeping and when she was awake. It was foolish to think of him—he was the earl's nephew and would have only one purpose for a girl of Eliza's upbringing. For a moment she thought that the sacrifice of name and reputation might be worthwhile for the happiness that an illicit love affair might bring. Then she recalled that she herself was most likely a lovechild. Papa and Mama would be horrified if they knew what was in her mind.

'I am sorry,' she whispered, though she was quite

alone in the carriage. 'I promise I shall do nothing to shame you.'

You could never do that, Eliza.

Tears stung her eyes as she imagined her mother's voice and her gentle smile. She missed her parents and her friends and for a moment she felt terribly alone. It was a huge step to travel such a long way to live with a stranger. Supposing Lady Sarah did not like her? The offer was only provisional and at the end of that period of probation, she might be forced to look for another position.

Chapter Three

The house in the Crescent was imposing and grand. It was very different to the eyes of a country girl who until recently had only visited Norwich once in her life.

Eliza's heart beat wildly as the footman opened the front door to her. His livery was extremely smart and his manner seemed condescending as he beckoned her inside. The black-and-white tiled floor in the hall gleamed and the scent of lavender polish met her as she was shown up the stairs to the first-floor reception rooms.

'Her ladyship is expecting you, Miss Bancroft.'

'Thank you,' she whispered, her throat dry as she followed the footman along the landing to a pair of imposing doors. They were painted white and scrolled with gold swags and bows, the handles of gleaming brass. A maid must have polished them that very morning.

'Miss Bancroft, your ladyship.'

The footman stood back to allow Eliza to enter, closing the door behind her. Eliza saw a woman seated in an elbow chair close to the window. She had obviously been reading, but she placed her book on the wine table close to hand, letting her enquiring gaze rest on Eliza. She had a gentle face and her smile of welcome lit her eyes.

'Please come to me, Miss Bancroft,' she said, standing up and offering her hand. 'I have been looking forward to meeting you.'

'Thank you. I, too, have anticipated this meeting with pleasure, my lady.' Eliza moved forwards. She extended her hand and the lady held it for a moment and then sat down. 'I am grateful for the chance to be of service to you, my lady.'

'Until recently I have been living in the country,' Lady Sarah said. 'Now that I am in Bath I find I need a companion, a young lady who will exchange books at the library, fetch things I need and accompany me to the Pump Room and various functions. I have maids to care for my clothes and the house. I really need a friend to sit and talk with me, perhaps read to me now and then when I have a headache—nothing too strenuous, Eliza. I hope I may call you Eliza?'

'Yes, of course, my lady.'

'Ma'am or Sarah will do. I hope we shall become firm friends in time, Eliza. It will be a pleasure for me to have the company of a young lady.' Lady Sarah smiled. 'Please, bring a chair and sit near me, my dear. I shall ring for refreshments. I should like to hear more about you and your mama—if it is not too painful for you?'

'No, ma'am, I am able to talk of Mama without crying now. I looked after her in the last few months of her illness. My papa died two and a half years ago. It was quite sudden and we had to leave the rectory where he was the incumbent. Mama never quite got over losing him so suddenly. She became delicate and was confined to bed for some months.'

'How sad for her and for you. I am sorry for your loss, my dear. I hope you will not mind going into company so soon? I lead quite a busy social life here.'

'Mama told me I was not to wear black for her,' Eliza said and glanced down at her dove-grey gown. 'I have some other plain gowns in colours, ma'am, but very little suitable for evenings. We did not entertain.'

'Oh, I quite expected to provide some clothes for you,' Lady Sarah said immediately. 'I shall summon my dressmaker in the morning and we shall commission some outfits for you, Eliza. What you have on is perfectly suitable for wearing to the Pump Room, and I may have something you can adapt for evenings until your new clothes are ready.'

'I am good with my needle. If you had some cast-offs, I could alter them for my use rather than purchasing all new…'

'I will find one or two that may do for the moment, but you shall certainly have new gowns. Please do not feel embarrassed, Eliza. It is perfectly in order and quite usual.'

'Oh…in that case I am grateful, my…ma'am,' Eliza said. 'I had not expected so much kindness.'

'You may find me a hard taskmaster,' Lady Sarah replied and laughed softly. 'I am tiresomely forgetful, my dear, and may send you on errands a dozen times a day.'

'I shall be only too pleased to fetch whatever it is you wish.'

A maid entered at that moment, bringing a large silver tray set with an exquisite tea and coffee service of elegant silver with bone handles, and delicate porcelain tea bowls. There was also a plate of tiny biscuits and almond comfits.

'Will you pour for us both please, Eliza? I take my tea with a drop of milk and one lump of sugar.'

Eliza poured the tea into the delicate bowl, added a little milk and used the tongs to select a small lump of sugar, which she added to the bowl. She handed it to Lady Sarah, who thanked her, stirred it once, sipped and nodded her approval before setting it on the wine table at her side.

'Would you like a comfit, ma'am?'

'No thank you, but please try one, Eliza. Cook made them especially in case you arrived.'

Eliza tasted one of the comfits, as she had been bidden, and expressed pleasure as she ate the delicious treat. She poured a cup of tea for herself and resumed her seat.

'What other duties are required, ma'am? So far it seems that I am to be treated as a guest rather than an employee. I should like to be of use to you in whatever way I may.'

'I really require only companionship,' Lady Sarah assured her. 'You will be as…a cousin or a younger sister to me, Eliza. I hope you will accept me as a friend, because that will be more comfortable for us both. There cannot be more than two-and-twenty years between us. My son is but seven and twenty and I married when I was sixteen. My son was born ten months later.'

'You hardly look more than nine and thirty, ma'am.'

Lady Sarah laughed and looked pleased, though she denied it. 'I feel so much older some days. My life has been very quiet until recently. While my husband lived I resided at home in the country, often alone. To have the company of a young lady of your age is a delight for me.'

Eliza hardly knew what to say. She had not considered that she would be so fortunate and found it difficult to realise that she was going to live in such favoured circumstances.

'Now, if you have finished your tea, I shall ring for Millicent Browne. She is my housekeeper here and she will take you up to your room. Please take your time to refresh yourself after the journey and then come down to me. We have a dinner engagement this evening, but this afternoon is free for us to talk and get to know each other. Dinner this evening is just an informal affair with friends, but I shall send you a gown you may like to wear.'

Eliza thanked her again. A woman came in answer to Lady Sarah's summons. She was dressed in a plain black gown with a neat lace collar and a gold brooch fastened at the throat. Her bright eyes looked at Eliza curiously, but her manner was welcoming as she led her along the landing and up a short flight of stairs.

'Her ladyship put you in one of the family rooms, miss. She wanted you close to her apartments so that you could pop in and out when she is resting, as she does some afternoons.'

'Thank you, Mrs Browne,' Eliza said. 'I hope that I shall be of some use and not cause more work for you. I am quite happy to make my bed and keep my room tidy.'

'Well, that is kind of you, miss. Not all guests are so thoughtful, I can tell you, but it will not be necessary. Her ladyship told us you were to be treated as family, and that's how it will be.'

'I must do something to earn my keep.'

'Your nice manners and cheerful smile will cheer her ladyship and that is all that's needed, miss.'

Mrs Browne stopped outside a room and opened the door, ushering her inside. The room was very pretty, furnished with satinwood pieces that struck Eliza as being exquisitely made, and the décor was of pink and cream with a touch of crimson here and there.

'What a beautiful room,' she exclaimed. 'I have never had such pretty things. Thank you for giving me such a lovely bedchamber—and roses on the dressing chest. How very kind.'

'Her ladyship wanted things nice, miss. We are all fond of her and we shall be obliged to you if you can cheer her up—she's not had a good life.'

'Oh…' Eliza wondered what was meant, but was too polite to enquire. It was not for her to gossip about her employer the moment she arrived. 'I am sorry to hear that. I shall certainly do my best to please.'

Left to herself, Eliza took off her bonnet and pelisse, depositing them on a chair. She ran her fingers over the surface of the beautiful dressing chest and the matching writing table and chair, bending to sniff the roses, which gave off a wonderful perfume. She could not quite believe her good fortune.

Sitting down on the edge of the bed, she thought about her extraordinary day yesterday. First the hold-up that was not truly a hold-up at all since the highwayman had turned out to be a man she had previously met and was clearly not very skilled at his work. A little smile touched her mouth as she remembered his kiss and her quite inappropriate feelings.

How foolish she was to feel such a strong attraction to a man who would never mean anything to her. She had been very fortunate in securing such a comfortable position and must do nothing to jeopardise her good fortune. If she saw Mr Seaton again, she would be sure to keep her distance, but it was unlikely that he would come to Bath.

And even more unlikely that he would be interested in a mere companion. A man as well connected as Daniel would surely have no trouble attracting a suitable wife. Yet his smile, his concern for her when he knocked her down, the feeling she had when he kissed her, would linger in her mind.

Daniel frowned at himself in the mirror. It would appear that he had made a fool of himself by holding up Cheadle's carriage. Eliza had travelled alone and was adamant that she was going to be the companion of a lady in Bath. He had felt foolish and angry, and that kiss had been unwise because he had not been able to get her out of his mind since.

An interview with his bank in Bath had revealed that his finances were, if anything, worse than he had imagined. Even if he were prepared to live like a miser and work all the hours of the day and night, he was not sure that he could hang on to the estate. His mind should be focused on his own problems—and his cousin's death. He could not afford to be thinking of a girl with eyes that made him want to kiss her senseless.

He had come to Bath to hear the worst, but also in search of Cheadle, whom he'd learned was due to stay here. It would be his chance to bargain for the ring and see if he could get anything of worth out of him—and he did not mean money, though the ten thousand his father had lost to the marquis was the cause of his immediate problems.

He had not come to Bath to discover if Miss Eliza

Bancroft had been telling him the truth. If they were to meet that would be by the way and of no importance. It would be quite ridiculous if he were to allow himself to be distracted by that impish smile of hers. Quite ridiculous and impossible.

If he were sensible, he would try to find an heiress to marry him, as his uncle had suggested. The notion did not sit well with him, but short of taking up a life on the road he could think of nothing else that would produce enough money to pay those damned mortgages.

Susanne Roberts had been giving him suggestive looks in town when he visited earlier in the Season. He had stayed well clear because he could not imagine himself being tied to such a silly girl. However, beggars could not be choosers. He might bring himself to the point of asking if he could put the memory of Eliza Bancroft's tantalising mouth from his head.

He had an invitation to dine with the Roberts family in Bath that evening—and it would do no harm to keep the appointment.

'That lilac silk becomes you well,' Lady Sarah said as Eliza twirled for her, holding the silk draped across her body. 'Yes, I like it—and the grey is perfect for small evening affairs. However, you will need a ballgown or perhaps two—and I think you should have white. You may trim them with delicate touches of black lace if you wish, but I think white is perfectly acceptable—do you not agree, Madame Millaise?'

The seamstress nodded her approval. 'I do not think anyone would take exception to it, milady,' she said, her accent markedly French despite her excellent grasp of the English language. 'A discreet touch of black is all

that is needed to make it perfectly respectable, *non?*'
She looked at Eliza, as if asking a question.

Eliza hesitated, waiting for her employer to speak.

'Yes, that is my opinion. What do you think, Eliza,
my dear?'

'I will be advised by you and *madame*,' Eliza said,
feeling anxious as she looked at the growing pile of
silks her employer seemed to feel she needed. 'Mama
particularly told me she did not wish me to wear mourning for more than a few days, but I like the grey and
lilac. I should choose those shades at any time. I had
not thought of white, but I am sure it will be perfect.'

'Yes, I believe it will. You are an attractive girl, Eliza,
and will pay for dressing.'

Eliza blushed. She had never thought of herself as
particularly attractive, though Betty always said it, but
wearing good clothes certainly made her feel much more
stylish. She had already adapted two evening gowns that
her employer had given her from her own wardrobe, one
a simple lilac silk, which had had long sleeves. Eliza
had removed the long sleeves and made them shorter,
trimming them with some heavy cream lace. She had
added more lace to the bodice, and, worn with the gold
pin that had been her mother's, the alteration had completely transformed the gown so that even Lady Sarah
had not recognised it. The other was grey silk and had
very elegant lines. Eliza had merely adjusted the waist
and hemline, feeling that she could not improve on its
design.

'Will *mademoiselle* be advised by me as to the style
the gowns should be?' the Frenchwoman asked.

'Yes, thank you,' Eliza replied. 'I am not perfectly
sure of the latest fashion—or what would be appropriate
for a companion to wear.'

'You need not worry about that side of it,' her employ-er said. 'I wish you to feel comfortable in what you choose, Eliza, and I am sure *madame* knows exactly what will become a girl of your age.' She turned to the seamstress. 'That is enough for one day. When can you have the first ballgown ready?'

'By Friday lunchtime, milady.'

'Very well. Eliza can manage with what she has until then. We shall attend the assembly that night, but until then we have only a dinner with friends and a trip to the theatre. You may wear the grey to dinner at the home of Lady Roberts, Eliza, and the lilac to the theatre. Your own walking gown will be sufficient until *madame* has made your new ones.'

Eliza thanked her. Her first visit to the Pump Room and the library had shown her that her clothes were by no means fashionable enough for Bath, at least if she were here on a visit for pleasure, though she thought them adequate for a companion. However, Lady Sarah had made it clear that she wanted her companion dressed suitably when they were in company and, although over-whelmed by what seemed excessive generosity, she accepted the new gowns as necessary—a part of her employment.

That did not stop her being excited by the prospect of wearing such lovely clothes. Lady Sarah's cast-offs were far finer than anything she had ever possessed and she knew that both were almost unworn, though possibly purchased when her employer was younger.

She thanked the seamstress for her help, assisted the young girl who carried out the materials and walked to the door with them both. When she returned to the sitting room, Lady Sarah was sipping a glass of restor-ative wine.

'Come and sit down, Eliza. You must be quite exhausted after that,' she said. 'I always feel drained after fittings for new gowns.'

'It was a new experience for me,' Eliza replied with a smile. 'I always made my own gowns with Mama's help. She was an excellent seamstress.'

'With a little training you could be a fashionable seamstress,' Lady Sarah said. 'Your own gowns are quite acceptable for the country, my dear, but you need a little town bronze.'

Sarah wondered why a companion should need to look fashionable but she did not question her employer. She considered herself fortunate to be treated so well.

'Perhaps you will go to the library for me this afternoon, my dear. I do not like the book I started last evening. It was well recommended, but *The Mysteries of Udolpho* is not to my taste. I should prefer something more sensible, I think.'

'Have you read the story of Tristan and Iseult?' Eliza asked. 'I have just finished reading it and enjoyed it, but I shall see what else I can find that you might like.'

'Lady Roberts recommended the story I asked you to bring yesterday, Eliza, but I think it foolish. I will try the story you recommended, but I think I should like poetry or perhaps something of Miss Austen's—though I believe I have read most of them.'

'I shall see what I can find. In the meantime I will fetch the book I brought with me.'

Eliza went upstairs to put on her bonnet and pelisse. Thus far she was finding her duties light. Indeed, it was like staying with an aunt rather than working for an employer and she felt very spoiled to be leading such an indulgent life. Eliza had always helped her mother in the kitchen and with parish work when her father was the rector, and she found it strange to be so idle.

It took but a moment to find the book and to put on her pelisse. She went back down to the parlour and took her leave of Lady Sarah, setting out for the lending library. The afternoon was pleasantly warm and the walk would be welcome after a morning spent choosing silks and trimmings for her new gowns.

Eliza reached the library without seeing anyone she knew. She had met only a handful of Lady Sarah's friends so far and was not acquainted with any other companions, so did not linger to gossip with anyone. Her search for books that her employer might find rewarding took a little longer, but she came away with three she thought interesting. It was as she came out of the library that a man walking backwards as he said goodbye to a friend almost trod on her toes. She gave a squeak of alarm and dropped her books. He turned instantly, an apology on his lips. The colour came and went in his face as he saw her. Her heart raced, for it was the man she had both longed and yet feared to see again.

'Forgive me,' he said. 'Did I hurt you?'

'No, I stepped back at once.'

He bent to pick up the books, looking at her contritely. 'I must seem a clumsy fool to you, Miss Bancroft. I am so very sorry for causing you to drop these.'

'It was a mere accident, Mr Seaton,' Eliza replied, a slight heat in her own cheeks as she accepted the books and their hands touched. Her stomach fluttered with some disturbing emotion she did not wish to recognise. This was so foolish. To like him so much when she knew it could only lead to distress! 'I assure you I am unhurt.'

'No thanks to me,' he said ruefully. 'May I help to

carry these for you? Perhaps I could buy you tea and cake to make up for nearly knocking you over?'

'I assure you there is no need to do either,' Eliza replied. She longed to say yes, to spend the next hour talking with him over some tea and cake, but her time was not her own. She must remember the vast chasm between them. He was related to an earl and she was a lovechild with a dubious background and no prospects. 'I must take these back to my employer. She is waiting for me.'

'Then I suppose I should let you go,' he said, but turned and walked by her side. 'How are you enjoying your stay in Bath? Is your employer an old dragon?'

'Lady Sarah is neither old nor a dragon. She has been extremely kind to me. I am fortunate to have found such employment. Indeed, there is little for me to do except enjoy myself.'

'That is fortunate.' His eyes were intensely blue and seemed thoughtful as he met her gaze. 'I imagine there are not many companions in that position.'

'Perhaps not,' Eliza replied. 'I did not expect to meet you here, sir. Have you given up your former employment?' Her eyes sparkled as she teased, for she knew that his one and only attempt at highway robbery had been a mistaken desire to save her from a fate worse than death.

'I rather think it gave me up.' Daniel laughed huskily. 'Had my unfortunate encounter been with any other young lady of my acquaintance, I think I should even now find myself behind bars.'

'That would be harsh indeed. You gave the coachman a little fright and that was bad of you, but you caused me no harm. Indeed, I have smiled to myself more than once over the incident.'

'You find me amusing, Miss Bancroft?'

'I found your attempt at highway robbery amusing.' She saw him frown. 'Does that offend you?'

'Yes and no,' he replied honestly. 'I think it was my own fault, but no man enjoys being thought a fool.' She sensed he had withdrawn slightly and regretted her careless remark.

'I did not think you a fool, sir. I see I have offended you. Forgive me. I must get back, for Lady Sarah will wonder what keeps me.'

He tipped his hat to her again, stopped walking and allowed her to go on alone. Eliza did not glance back, though she sensed that he was watching her walk away. She was sorry if she had offended him, but that was better than allowing him to imagine she was ripe for dalliance. He had kissed her once without invitation. It must not happen again. A young woman in her circumstances ought not to be seen encouraging the attentions of a man who was related to an earl.

Daniel watched her walk the length of the street. She had a trim figure and was in many ways unusual, being possessed, he suspected, of a strong sense of humour. It piqued his pride a little to know that she found him amusing. Yet he could hardly blame her. Most women would have thought him a clodhopping fool for nearly knocking her down not once but twice, and then there was the ridiculous hold-up. She was remarkably patient and tolerant, and he discovered that he found her enchanting. There were few enough young women with her wit and sensible manner and he could not suppress a sigh. *If she were only an heiress...* He laughed and shook his head. Such a prize would not be long on the shelf. Had she had money as well as her other attributes she would have been spoken for long ago.

Daniel's thoughts turned to the evening ahead. He had been invited to Lord and Lady Robert's house to dine. As yet he had said nothing to the gentleman about his uncomfortable circumstances. He was reluctant to do so for it was bound to leak out, unless they came to an understanding. Lord Roberts would naturally protect the reputation of his daughter's fiancé if they came to an arrangement, but would he be prepared to come to Daniel's rescue?

It was a situation Daniel wished he could avoid, but he knew that the best solution was to find a wealthy bride. He would have to make up his mind and put all thoughts of Miss Bancroft from his mind.

Eliza dressed with care that evening. Lady Sarah had sent her a simple string of seed pearls to wear with the gown. She understood that they were a loan from a generous employer who wished her companion to look well and accepted them with pleasure.

Lady Sarah nodded her approval when she went to her room, to ask if there was anything she needed.

'You look charming, my dear. That gown suits you far better than it ever did me.'

'You have such good taste,' Eliza replied. 'Your clothes always look elegant without being too fussy.'

'I never did like too many frills and ribbons—though they look well on younger girls. Lady Roberts has a very nice daughter, Eliza. I see no reason why you two should not be friends. It will be good for you to have some acquaintances in Bath.'

'Yes, it will be pleasant when I know more people,' Eliza agreed, though she was not certain that the daughter of a titled lady would necessarily wish to know Lady Sarah's companion.

'Come, my dear. The horses are standing. Coachman never likes his horses kept standing. We must leave.'

Eliza helped her to gather her shawl, fan and reticule, and then they went down to the carriage. Lady Sarah whiled away the journey by looking out of the window and pointing out places of interest or people they passed that she happened to know, but the journey only took a few minutes and could easily have been walked.

The footman came to open the door and let down the steps, helping first Lady Sarah and then Eliza to descend. They went into the hall and then up the stairs, where their hostess was waiting to greet them. Lady Roberts was a tall thin woman with a hooked nose, which her daughter had unfortunately inherited, though she was elegantly dressed. They both greeted Lady Sarah with affection and Eliza politely. Almost immediately, another guest was announced and Eliza noticed that Susanne's face lit with pleasure, making her look almost pretty. Turning her head to look at the newcomer, Eliza felt a shock of recognition. It seemed that she was destined to meet Mr Seaton yet again.

'Lord Seaton,' her hostess gushed. 'How delightful to see you this evening. We were so pleased you could come—were we not, Susanne?'

Eliza felt her cheeks flush. He had not told her that he was *Lord* Seaton and she felt foolish for having misused his name several times.

'Yes, Mama,' Susanne replied and giggled shyly. It was clear that she believed he had come for the purpose of seeing her and enjoyed the prospect of being courted.

'I was happy to be invited, ma'am.' His gaze moved

to Lady Sarah and then Eliza. His expression did not change, though Eliza noticed a little pulse flicking at his temple.

'Have you met my good friend Lady Sarah Manners and her companion Miss Eliza Bancroft?'

'I do not think I have had the honour of meeting Lady Sarah,' Daniel replied. 'However, I had the pleasure of meeting Miss Bancroft at my uncle's estate a few weeks ago. I trust you are well, Miss Bancroft?'

'Yes, thank you, *my lord*.'

'Ah, yes, the dear earl.' Lady Roberts moved smoothly on, obviously not impressed that he should acknowledge acquaintance with a mere companion. 'I believe he was not well a few months back.'

'My uncle still mourns the loss of his son,' Daniel replied with a frown. 'I think his health is well enough otherwise.'

'Yes, such a sad occurrence.' Lady Roberts looked at her daughter pointedly. 'You are released, Susanne. Take our guests into the drawing room. I have only one more guest to greet and then I shall join you.'

Susanne looked expectantly at Lord Seaton. He offered his arm and they moved forwards into the large drawing room, where Lord Roberts was entertaining three other guests and a footman was standing with a tray of champagne. Eliza followed with Lady Sarah. She was offered a glass of champagne by the footman, which she accepted, but made no attempt to drink. Lady Sarah led the way to a rather beautiful blonde lady dressed in grey silk, smiling and greeting her with pleasure.

'Julia Henderson, I had no idea you would be here this evening. I am delighted to meet you again.'

'Sarah dearest. We arrived in Bath only yester-day. How wonderful to find you here.' The two ladies embraced and then Julia turned enquiring eyes on Eliza. 'And this is…?'

'My companion, Miss Eliza Bancroft,' Lady Sarah said.

'Your companion? For a moment I thought… How nice to meet you, Miss Bancroft,' Julia Henderson said and extended her hand. 'How long have you been with my dear friend Sarah?'

'Just a few days, ma'am,' Eliza said, seeing the warmth and affection for Lady Sarah in her eyes. 'But they have been extremely pleasant ones.'

'Well, I shall be calling on you both very soon and I shall look forward to a long chat. I want to hear all about you, Eliza—and you must call me Julia. I absolutely insist.'

'Oh…' Eliza blushed. 'That is very kind of you, ma… Julia.'

'You will soon get used to it,' Julia said and laughed. 'Now, you must meet my daughter Kate—Kate, this is Eliza. You two must absolutely be friends, because you are going to see a lot of one another. I shall want to spend time with Sarah and you two should be prepared to go off on your own somewhere.'

'Mama!' Kate was a younger image of her mother, her blue eyes sparkling with amusement as she came to Eliza. 'You must forgive her, Miss Bancroft. She may command me, but not you, though I hope we shall be friends and you may call me Kate if you wish.'

'Only if you call me Eliza.' Eliza smiled because she liked both the mother and daughter. 'I, too, hope we shall be friends. As yet I have very few acquaintances in Bath.'

'I have loads of them,' Kate said frankly. 'However, only one or two I would actually call friends. I should like to get to know you—and that is not because Mama insists either.' She threw a fond but exasperated look at her mother, who was talking animatedly with Lady Sarah. 'Dear Mama is managing, but she means well.'

'I am certain she does,' Eliza agreed, thinking that she was fortunate to have met a girl she could truly think of as a friend.

Most of the other young ladies she met exchanged pleasantries but did not seem interested enough to become her friend.

Her thoughts were interrupted as the invitation to move into the dining room was given. After some shuffling and searching, everyone sat down and Eliza found herself seated between an elderly gentleman, who proved hard of hearing and Lord Roberts. Her host saw her seated with solicitous care and then proceeded to ignore her as he talked exclusively to the lady on his right.

Obviously, a companion was not deemed worthy of a meaningful conversation. Eliza contented herself by looking about her. She caught snatches of other people's conversation and smiled as she watched Miss Susanne Roberts making up to Lord Seaton. Susanne simpered, giggled and fluttered her lashes so often that Eliza would have asked if she had something in her eye had she been close enough.

Now and then the deaf gentleman muttered something. Eliza nodded or asked if she could pass him a dish or the condiment set. She risked a few glances at Lord Seaton and discovered that he was looking at her and frowning. Once she thought he would address her across the table, but his companion claimed his attention and the moment passed.

It might have been a long and tedious meal, but the

food was actually delicious and Eliza enjoyed watching the company. She saw Kate flirting in an unexceptional way with an older gentleman, and Lady Sarah was clearly enjoying talking with friends.

Eventually, Lady Roberts announced the move to the drawing room, leaving the gentlemen to their port and cigars. Kate immediately gravitated to her side.

'Poor you,' she exclaimed as she linked arms. 'Mr Huddlestone is as deaf as a post and Lord Roberts was awfully rude. I do not think he addressed more than three words to you all evening.'

'I did not remark it,' Eliza assured her. 'I dare say a dowager duchess is more important and entertaining than a companion.'

'How calm you are and kind.' Kate laughed. 'In your position I should have been inclined to talk across the table, but Mama says it is rude to interrupt the conversation of others.' She lowered her voice. 'Besides, Miss Roberts was monopolising the only handsome man in the room—even if Lord Seaton was more interested in looking at you.'

'No, I am certain he was not,' Eliza denied immediately. 'He seemed quite content with his companion.'

'She threw herself at him in town, but he ignored her. Mama warned me that Seaton may be in financial difficulty, for his father was ill for a while before he died and may have neglected the estate. There was a rumour of it, but I do not know the whole. He may be looking to marry a fortune, though I shall think him a fool if he settles for a peagoose like Susanne.'

'That is a little unkind,' Eliza reproved, but could not resist a smile. Kate was certainly outspoken, but she could not help liking her.

Lord Seaton was not a fool, but it was possible that

he needed to marry money. Gentleman often did, for the upkeep of a country estate was expensive. She imagined that Lord Roberts was wealthy and would see his daughter well endowed. However, Eliza had no time to ponder the subject for she was summoned by Lady Roberts to help serve the tea.

When she brought Lady Sarah her cup, her employer frowned. 'This is unfair on you, Eliza, my love. You are here to enjoy yourself.'

'I am enjoying myself very much, ma'am. Serving tea is no hardship for me.'

'It is the manner…' Lady Sarah shook her head. She clearly did not approve of the way Eliza had been commandeered by their hostess, but would not make a fuss in public.

Once tea was served, Kate was called to the pianoforte and she asked Eliza to accompany her.

'Do you know this one?' she asked, playing a few bars of a popular ballad. She smiled when Eliza inclined her head. 'Sing it with me?'

Eliza stood at her shoulder and joined in the second verse. She had a sweet though untrained voice and their voices blended into a pleasant harmony. They had finished the ballad and were singing the words of 'Greensleeves' when the gentleman returned, and were warmly applauded as they brought the old song to an end.

'Well done, ladies. That was a perfect duet,' Daniel Seaton told them, strolling towards the pianoforte. 'May I join you in a verse or two?'

'Of course,' Kate agreed. 'What shall we sing?'

'I have been practising Mr Beethoven's piano sonata,' Susanne said, coming up to them. She looked pointedly at Eliza. 'Perhaps you should return to Lady Sarah, Miss Bancroft. I believe she needs you.'

'Yes, certainly. Everyone has heard quite enough of me for one evening.' Eliza retired gracefully to sit by her employer's side.

She listened appreciatively to the music. Susanne played with more accomplishment than Kate and, when they sang a popular ditty, their voices blended well with Lord Seaton's. She applauded their performance as warmly as anyone.

'I believe we should leave now,' Lady Sarah said when the entertainment finished and the company began to talk amongst themselves. 'I am feeling a little tired.'

'Allow me to escort you to your carriage, ma'am,' Daniel offered, startling Eliza who had not been aware that he was standing so close.

'So kind,' Lady Sarah said and took his arm. 'It was a pleasant evening, but it is late for me. I knew your uncle once, sir. You must call and take a dish of tea with us one afternoon.'

'I should be delighted,' Daniel said, inclining his head.

Eliza gathered up all their bits and pieces. She followed behind, noticing with approval Lord Seaton's consideration for her employer. He walked her to her waiting carriage, helped her inside, seeing her settled comfortably before turning to Eliza. His blue eyes were thoughtful as he offered his hand to help her ascend the steps.

'I hope your evening was not too tedious, Miss Bancroft?'

'Not in the least, sir. I enjoyed your singing immensely.'

'I enjoyed your rendition of "Greensleeves."'

'And Miss Roberts played with remarkable proficiency.'

'She is undoubtedly an accomplished young lady.'

'Yes, I am certain she is.'

What was the message in his eyes? Eliza was not certain; it might be merely imagination, but he seemed to say that he cared nothing for Miss Roberts and very much for her. No, she was letting her feelings run away with her.

It seemed to Eliza that Lord Seaton held her hand for a little longer than necessary. Perhaps only seconds, but enough to make her heart flutter. Her body began to heat and very peculiar sensations made the nape of her neck tingle. She removed her hand from his grasp.

He was too dangerous to allow even the smallest flirtation.

'Thank you, sir. I can manage now. Goodnight.'

'Goodnight, ladies.' He stepped back as the groom closed the carriage door. 'I shall call one afternoon, Lady Sarah.'

Sitting back against the squabs, Eliza refused to feel pleased by his promise. It would be extremely foolish to allow herself to like Lord Seaton too much. Yet she did, she did…already her thoughts dwelled on him far more than was sensible or right.

Chapter Four

Daniel doused his head with cold water and groaned. Whatever had possessed him to drink so much wine after he returned to his lodgings the previous evening? He shook the water from his hair and sank back into the rapidly cooling bath his valet had prepared for him. Last evening's dinner party had been a total failure as far as he was concerned. Not only had he been bored by Miss Roberts, finding her shallow and foolish, he had left without speaking to her father.

'Damned idiot!' he muttered as he rose from the water and towelled himself down, the droplets glistening on skin that was slightly golden in tone.

Why the hell had his father lost so much money to Cheadle? It was the cause of all this bother, the reason he had no choice but to offer for a girl he did not truly admire. He must either marry to advantage or enter the army and sell his estate to salvage what little he could.

Surely there must be another alternative?

The thoughts had been going round and round in his head since waking. He had really believed he could go through with the marriage to Miss Roberts until…he had seen *her* looking at him with those thoughtful eyes.

Miss Eliza Bancroft.

Damn it all, why should the girl affect him like this? She wasn't beautiful by the standards of the day. Perhaps if they had met first in society he would have passed on without a second glance.

Liar!

Daniel groaned as he accepted that Miss Eliza Bancroft had been the reason for his failure to address Miss Roberts. He was intrigued by her manner of plain speaking. She found him amusing, did she? Her careless remark had pricked his vanity. He was accustomed to having young women hang on his every word. Indeed, he might have married long ago if beauty or money had been all he required in a wife.

The woman had bewitched him! What an idiot he was, mooning over a girl's smile like a green youth.

Daniel's mirth vanished as swiftly as it had come. His situation was serious. He had to find some way of paying those damned mortgages.

Eliza looked out of the front window as she heard voices below and was in time to see that Lady Julia and Kate had arrived. They were all to visit the Pump Room together that morning. Picking up the reticule she had been asked to fetch for Lady Sarah, she went downstairs in time to witness their friends being admitted.

'Eliza,' Kate said, 'isn't it a glorious day? I have asked Mama if we may leave her and Lady Sarah for a while once they are settled with their friends. It is far too pleasant to be stuck indoors. Do you not agree?'

'It would be pleasant to walk if Lady Sarah does not need me.'

A walk was exactly what she needed after a night of too much thinking. Despite all her good intentions, Eliza had not been able to dismiss thoughts of Daniel Seaton. She wished she did not know his secret for it seemed to draw her closer to him. Had they met in company for the first time the previous evening, she would not have felt so troubled.

How could he think of marrying such a foolish girl as Miss Roberts? She was far beneath him in every way.

Immediately, Eliza was ashamed of the thought. Miss Roberts was a perfectly pleasant girl, just a little foolish to set her cap at him in public the way she had.

Good gracious! Was she feeling jealous?

Eliza scorned the wayward notion. She had no business thinking of Lord Seaton at all.

Kate's friendly chatter was just what was needed to banish her foolish thoughts. Eliza gave her new friend all her attention as the four ladies were driven to the Pump Room in an open landau.

Lady Sarah seemed happy to be reunited with an old friend, and once the two older ladies were settled in the Pump Room with a glass of the restorative water, Kate persuaded Eliza they should leave.

'Certainly you must go with Kate,' Lady Sarah added her voice to the young lady's. 'I shall be perfectly comfortable here—and we are all to take luncheon together at Lady Julia's house. Do not be late for that, girls.'

'No, of course not,' the girls chorused.

Kate slipped her arm through Eliza's and they left the Pump Room, heading for the fashionable shops that abounded in the town.

'I need a new fan for best,' Kate told her as they

emerged into the warm sunshine. She was dressed in a pretty green walking gown with a bonnet of chip straw trimmed with matching ribbons and white shoes and gloves. 'My favourite snapped in half last time I used it. The struts are so fragile, are they not?'

'I have one that my mother gave me,' Eliza replied. 'I have not...'

She meant to say that she had hardly used it but, seeing the gentleman walking towards them, her heart caught. He was so extremely handsome in his coat of blue with dove grey breeches and boots that shone like gloss.

'Miss Henderson...Miss Bancroft...' Daniel raised his hat to them. 'A beautiful morning, is it not?'

'Lord Seaton,' Kate said and gave him a flirtatious look. 'Are you on your way to the Pump Room? I would not have thought you needed to take the waters.'

'Indeed, no, I should hope not,' he replied and grinned, for her manner was mischievous. 'Indeed, I have heard the taste is so bad that I doubt the health-giving properties they are said to possess. I suppose you are headed for the shops?'

'There is nothing I enjoy more,' Kate replied. 'Unless it is dancing. Do you attend the assembly this evening, sir?

'I am not sure...' His eyes rested on Eliza. 'Do you attend, Miss Bancroft?'

Eliza had deliberately remained silent, but now she was forced to answer.

'I believe it is Lady Sarah's intention,' Eliza said, hoping that she did not sound breathless. Her heart was behaving most oddly. 'It will be my first proper ball, though I was sometimes invited to your uncle's Christmas party, sir. I danced there, of course. Mama taught me—' She broke off with a flush for she had said too much—and she did sound breathless.

'Then I must certainly attend,' he responded gallantly, his words making her feel odd all over. 'You will promise to save at least one dance for me, Miss Bancroft—and I shall also claim one from you, Miss Henderson.'

'I shall be sure to enter your name, sir—and so will Eliza,' Kate sparkled up at him. 'Now you must leave us for shopping is important business, my lord.'

'I am not sure that I ought to dance.' Eliza remembered belatedly that she was a companion. 'I do not know if Lady Sarah will permit it.'

'Of course she will expect you to dance.' Kate retorted. 'Lord Seaton, support me in this please. Eliza must dance, must she not?'

'I am persuaded that Lady Sarah will expect it,' Daniel replied and his eyes were bright with amusement. 'I must not delay you longer. I shall see you both this evening, ladies.'

He tipped his hat once more and walked on by. Kate hugged Eliza's arm.

'Was that not clever of me? He likes you very much. I dare swear he had no intention of attending this evening until you told him it was your first ball.'

'Oh, no…' Eliza was genuinely horrified. 'Please do not suggest such a thing. It would be most inappropriate. Lady Sarah has been kindness itself, but I am her companion. Lord Seaton really should not pay me any attention. Especially if—' she broke off, feeling flustered. 'He should not.'

'You are distressed,' Kate said in concern. 'I was merely teasing you. I would not encourage you to think of him. Lord Seaton is not exactly a rake, but he is known for his flirts. They say the last was a beautiful opera dancer.' Kate gurgled with laughter. 'I heard he fought a duel with someone over her, but I dare say it was all a hum. Oh dear, I should not have mentioned that, should I? Mama says my tongue will be the ruin of me and she is right.'

'I believe many gentlemen have a mistress,' Eliza said, sounding calmer than she felt. 'But…I have no wish to become one of them.'

'No, indeed it is not to be thought of for, then I could not know you and that would be a shame.' Kate's humour was irrepressible. 'Not that I should take a jot of notice but Mama would not approve. You will pay him no mind, Eliza. Unless of course he were to propose marriage. They do say reformed rakes make good husbands in the end.'

'You are a wicked tease,' Eliza told her. 'It is as well I have no intention of having my head turned by a handsome face.'

'So you do like him,' Kate crowed. 'No, no, I shall not tease you, dearest Eliza—but just think how fortunate it would be if he should offer.'

Eliza shook her head. To allow herself even one thought in that direction would be madness. She was not sure she would be permitted to dance that evening or even if it would be wise. Lord Seaton was too far above her and the more she mixed with him the more painful it would be in the end. She might even have to leave Lady Sarah's employ at the end of the month, and then she might never see him again.

The thought brought a sharp swift pain to her heart, but she lifted her head in the air. She refused to be foolish enough to fall for a man she hardly knew and could never know better.

They were approaching the shop they had come to visit and Kate's attention was taken by the array of beautiful fans in the window. Some were of painted paper, others of ivory and lace, some with silver or jewelled handles and very costly.

'Oh, there are so many lovely ones,' Kate exclaimed. 'How do I choose just one?'

Eliza was able to enjoy helping her friend to choose. She was, after all, a sensible girl and she would not fall into a dangerous flirtation simply because a certain man made her heart race whenever he was near.

Daniel walked past the house where Lord Roberts was staying, heading for a popular coffee house in the hope of meeting with friends. His thoughts were once again in turmoil. He had set out with the firm intention of asking Lord Roberts for his daughter's hand and then applying for a loan to settle his gambling debt, which he would repay when he could. However, Miss Henderson had overset his plans by mentioning the assembly. He had been unable to resist the unconscious appeal in Miss Bancroft's eyes when she spoke of her first public ball. The prospect of dancing with her had awoken something inside him that had lain dormant for a while and he anticipated the evening with some eagerness.

Surely it could not matter if he did not speak to Lord Roberts immediately?

Eliza Bancroft.

Daniel wanted to see laughter in those expressive eyes. He wanted to dance with Eliza, hold her body close to his and perhaps take her out into the moonlight to steal a few kisses.

He remembered a previous stolen kiss. He could almost taste her, smell the perfume that was uniquely her own. He wanted so much more! Forbidden thoughts of Eliza lying in silken sheets, her hair spread on the pillow and her lips swollen by his passionate kisses, slightly open as she waited for more...

The sight of a curricle driving past in the opposite direction, interrupted his pleasurable thoughts. A cold shaft of anger shot through him as he saw the cause of all his troubles. The Marquis of Cheadle was in Bath, which meant that they would be bound to meet in company. Therefore, he must arrange a private interview as soon as possible. He would see what advantage was to be gained from bargaining over the ring he held as surety for a few hundred guineas.

Why did the marquis's ring bear the same inscription as that in Eliza's ring? She said it had belonged to her mother—had there been something between Mrs Bancroft and Cheadle? Surely not! The lady was the wife of the Reverend Bancroft and, as far as Daniel knew, of spotless reputation. It was mere coincidence and a trifle that should not enter his head again. He had more important things to consider.

For a moment, Daniel's thoughts dwelled on the possibility that Cheadle might know something of his cousin's death. He must seek him out and ask a few questions before handing over the ring.

Eliza glanced at herself in the mirror as she prepared for the assembly that evening. Her gown was a miracle of white silk tulle, lace and elegant styling. Trimmed lightly here and there with tiny knots of black ribbon, it looked so expensive and fashionable that Eliza was almost frightened to leave her room.

Surely Lady Sarah would not approve of her companion wearing a gown such as this one?

Her heart was sinking as she walked the short distance down the hall to her employer's bedchamber. Lady
Sarah could not have intended her companion to look
so stylish.

'Come in, my dear,' her employer's voice invited her
to enter as she tapped the door.

'I am so sorry,' Eliza began immediately to apologise.
'I thought *madame* would make something more suited
to my situation. Shall I change?'

'What nonsense, Eliza. You look beautiful…' Lady
Sarah beckoned her forwards, her expression intent as
she looked at her closely. 'The gown is elegant and perfect for you, my dear. I knew *madame* would do you
justice, but I had not expected such a change. You look…
very different. Do you not like your gown?'

'I love it,' Eliza assured her. 'I thought…well, does it
not make me look as if I am a young lady of fashion?'

'Exactly. Just as you should look, Eliza. You deserve
something nice and I am happy to be in a position to give
it to you.' Lady Sarah smiled at her. 'I am very pleased
with *madame*'s work. You must thank her when she
comes again.'

'Are you sure it is not too good for a companion?'

Lady Sarah hesitated, then, 'You have become my
friend, Eliza…almost like a daughter to me. We have
not known each other long, but already I am so fond of
you. I want you to be happy while you stay with me.'

'I am happy. I feel so fortunate to have been chosen
by you, ma'am. I would never wish to do anything to
distress you.'

'I am sure you will not.' Lady Sarah nodded, a hint of
tears in her eyes. She knew that she might have gone too
far, but she was enjoying treating Eliza, as she would her
lost daughter when she found her. 'We must go down.

We do not wish to keep the horses standing. This evening is your first assembly. You will not wish to miss a moment—and of course you must dance as much as you please. It will give me great pleasure to watch and to know that you are enjoying yourself.'

'You are so kind to me.'

Eliza made sure that her employer had all she needed, following her down the stairs and out to the waiting carriage. It was strange how close she felt to Lady Sarah, almost as though she had known her all her life.

Eliza was a little overwhelmed by the noise and press of people mingling in the huge assembly rooms. She thought that all Bath society must have gathered for the occasion, their costly jewels glittering in the light from the heavy chandeliers. However, once they had passed into a room where chairs and sofas had been grouped they found friends.

'Come and sit beside me,' Lady Julia invited. 'Kate has been on the fidget since we arrived. Now you may leave us to ourselves and join the other young people.'

'Are you comfortable, ma'am?' Eliza asked, looking at her employer. 'Is there anything I may fetch you before I go with Kate?'

'Lord Melcher is arranging some champagne—' Lady Julia broke off as two gentlemen approached, one tall and dark, the other slightly broader in the shoulder with fair hair and a little moustache. 'Lord Smythe…Mr Thatcher, good evening. You know my daughter Kate, of course—may I introduce you to Miss Eliza Bancroft. She is visiting with my great friend Lady Sarah.'

'Ma'am, Miss Henderson, Miss Bancroft.' Lord Smythe bowed to Kate. 'May I have the honour of this next dance?'

'Only if Mr Thatcher intends to dance with my friend Miss Bancroft,' Kate said with a wicked smile. 'Afterwards, you may both change partners.'

'Kate, you need not…' Eliza blushed, but the fair-haired gentleman bowed to her and smiled.

'Miss Henderson need not have prompted me, Miss Bancroft. I shall be greatly honoured if you will grant me the favour of this dance—and another, if I may have your card for a moment?'

'Oh…' Eliza hesitated and then handed him the little card she wore on a ribbon about her wrist. He wrote his name in a space later that evening and then offered his arm. 'Thank you, Mr Thatcher. It is so kind of you.'

'My pleasure, I assure you.'

She took his arm, feeling an immediate liking for a man who was clearly one of Kate's intimate friends.

'Is this your first visit to Bath, Miss Bancroft?'

'Yes. I have been living quietly in the country. My mother was ill for some months before she died—but Lady Sarah is so good to me.'

'I do not know the lady well, but Lady Julia and Miss Henderson are good friends—and neighbours in the country. Father's estate is in Hampshire.'

'We lived in Norfolk.'

Drawn into what was a lively country dance, Eliza was swept along by the music and enjoyed herself too much to be self-conscious or shy. She had never been given formal dancing lessons, but dances like this had been a part of the celebrations at the earl's home each Christmas. As the vicar's daughter she had been invited and knew how to perform most of the dances creditably.

The next set of dances was slower and more elegant. Eliza watched for a few moments, confident that she knew the steps. When Lord Smythe asked her to dance she felt able to give him her hand.

After the first few dances, Kate and Eliza were reunited, and a steady stream of young and sometimes older gentlemen made their way to the girls to be introduced by one of the ladies or gentlemen present and to request a dance.

In consequence, both girls soon found their cards filled, except for those they had saved in advance. Eliza had kept two free just in case Lord Seaton should arrive later in the evening. He did not appear in the first hour or so and she sat one of them out, taking the chance for some refreshment with Lady Sarah.

It must have been nearly ten o'clock when she saw him coming towards her. Her heart leaped with excitement, because he was so very handsome in his immaculate evening dress and his smile seemed just for her.

'Did you think I had forgotten my promise, Miss Bancroft?' Daniel asked. 'I hope you have kept a dance for me—or have I lost it to another because of my tardy arrival?'

'I did keep the next dance, sir—should you wish it.'

'I most certainly do and I must beg your forgiveness for being so late. I was delayed by some important business.' He laughed as her brows arched. 'No, I assure you. It was a card game with friends and I won—quite fairly.'

'I would never suspect you of anything less,' she replied, a smile in her eyes.

Daniel inclined his head, taking her hand to draw her forwards into the throng of dancers. 'This is a waltz. You have no objection, Miss Bancroft?'

'I have danced a waltz only twice, Lord Seaton. You must forgive me if I am not entirely proficient.'

'Just allow me to lead you. You need not fear, Miss Bancroft. You are in good hands.'

Eliza trembled inwardly as he put his hand at the small of her back, but her calm smile remained intact. As soon as they began to dance she lost all sense of nerves and the sensation was like floating to music. With no one else had Eliza experienced this glorious feeling of lightness and a sense of being far away from the crowd. It was as if she were alone with Lord Seaton and there was no one else in the world. Had she closed her eyes she could have believed she was dancing in the moonlight; there was no one but the man whose arms held her, making her heart beat with slow sure strokes. A little sigh of pleasure left her lips.

'You approve,' Lord Seaton's teasing voice broke the spell. 'I am better at dancing than some other things, perhaps?'

'You must know you are an excellent dancer, sir.'

'It is a pleasure to dance with you, Miss Bancroft. You are like thistledown in my arms. I could wish our dance might last for ever.'

His words so exactly mirrored her own thoughts that she felt a blaze of pure happiness. It was like being in heaven…the most wonderful feeling she had ever known.

When the music ended, Eliza felt a sharp pain of loss as he let her go and stood back. She wanted to be back in his arms, out in the moonlight. She wanted… She made an effort to control her emotions as he escorted her to her friends. This was so foolish! It was just a dance, even though it had seemed so much more.

Lady Sarah was talking to a gentleman Eliza had

never met before. She felt Lord Seaton's fingers tighten on her arm and sensed tension in him. Glancing at his face, she noticed the pulse flicking at his temple.

'Ah, there you are, my dearest,' Lady Sarah said. 'I should like to introduce you to the Marquis of Cheadle, Eliza. As I am sure you recall, it was he who sent his carriage to Norwich to collect you.'

'Yes, of course, and I am extremely grateful, sir,' Eliza said, her keen gaze taking in a man in his late thirties or early forties perhaps, attractive, elegantly dressed with eyes of a greenish-brown that some called hazel. 'It was a most comfortable journey due to your generosity.'

'I am glad to hear it, Miss Bancroft, though my coachman tells me you had an unpleasant incident on the last stage of the journey?'

'Oh…' Eliza resisted the temptation to look at Lord Seaton. 'It was really nothing very much, my lord.'

'Nothing, you say?' The marquis's eyes narrowed. 'Not quite what I expected to hear, Miss Bancroft. But perhaps we should discuss this at another time? If I may call in the morning, I should like to hear your side of the affair.' He inclined his head and then looked at her companion. 'Seaton, good evening.'

'Cheadle. Where are you staying? I must call on you soon.'

'Yes, I have a debt to settle. At your convenience, Seaton. We have a house in Queen's Square.'

'Perhaps the day after tomorrow?'

'If you wish.'

'Eliza, I am ready to leave,' Lady Sarah said. 'Lady Julia will see you home if you wish to stay later?'

'No, thank you, ma'am. I am perfectly ready to leave.'

'Very well. We shall say goodnight to our friends.'

'Allow me to summon your carriage, ma'am,' Lord Seaton said and went off to arrange it.

Lady Sarah smiled as she took her leave of friends, but leaned on Eliza's arm, and she guessed that her employer was feeling tired.

Lord Seaton was there to see them into the carriage. Eliza sensed that he, too, had realised Lady Sarah was a little done up and his care for her employer pleased her.

'Good evening, ladies,' he said and smiled as he stood back to allow the groom to close the door. 'I shall call very soon.'

'We shall always be pleased to see you, sir,' Lady Sarah assured him.

Eliza thanked him but said no more.

When they were settled in the carriage and on their way, she enquired if her employer was unwell.

'Oh, no, my dear. Just a little tired.' Lady Sarah gave her a searching look. 'You did not tell me that you were held up by a wicked highwayman, Eliza?'

'It really was nothing, ma'am. I did not wish to distress you when there was no need.'

'But Cheadle's coachman was concerned for a while that the rogue meant to kidnap you?'

'No…he merely wished to…apologise.' Eliza blushed in the darkness of the carriage. She did not wish to lie to her generous employer, but how could she explain without giving Lord Seaton's secret away? 'I believe he imagined someone else was in the carriage. It was a mere prank, ma'am—a bet, I believe, between friends.'

'How very odd.' Lady Sarah's expression was troubled. 'There is some mystery here. The marquis may have an enemy. I believe he is sometimes suspected of being a ruthless gambler and worse.'

'You say suspected? You do not think it?'

'I think he may not be as black as he is painted. When he was younger...' Lady Sarah sighed. 'That is the past and I must keep an open mind.'

Eliza sensed that her employer could say more, but she made no attempt to press her. Lady Sarah was silent for most of the remainder of their ride home. Eliza had her own thoughts to keep her mind occupied and her employer was entitled to her secrets.

She saw Lady Sarah safely upstairs, made sure she was being looked after by her maid and then went to bed herself. It had been such a strange evening, filled with sharp memories that Eliza knew would tease her for a long time to come.

She had hung her wonderful dress where she could see it, thinking that it must have been the dress that had brought her so many partners at the ball.

It had been exciting for a girl used to the quiet country life, especially her waltz with Daniel Seaton.

No, she must think of him as Lord Seaton! To allow more intimate thoughts of him would be too dangerous. Daniel Seaton had caused her to fall into a bramble bush and then helped her recover. He had held up her coach, ridden off with her and then kissed her. She might have let herself dream of Daniel, but Lord Seaton must marry a rich wife for the sake of his estate.

As such she could never hope to marry a man like Lord Seaton and so must forget the way her heart jolted when he touched her.

Taking her ring from her dressing case, Eliza slipped it on the middle finger of her right hand. As yet she had not worn it—perhaps she was afraid of what she might discover? Supposing she were to find her mother and then learn that she was not wanted—that the lady resented being found? Her life was happy now. It might be better to leave things as they were. Had her mother cared, she would surely not have given her away. Putting the ring away, she turned her mind to other things.

She must be careful when the marquis questioned her the next morning. Lady Sarah had accepted her explanation, but would the marquis press for more details?

Daniel left the assembly after his dance with Miss Henderson. He had attended for the sole purpose of partnering Miss Eliza Bancroft and the sight of her in that white gown had taken his breath away. She looked like one of the Season's top débutantes and already the tongues had started wagging.

'Who do you suppose she is?' one young buck had asked after he returned from escorting Lady Sarah to her carriage. 'Do you suppose she is an heiress?'

A devil must have been sitting on his shoulder at that moment for Daniel smiled enigmatically and said, 'Oh, I doubt there is enough for you, Carstairs. You would run through ten thousand in a year and ruin both her and yourself.'

'Want her for yourself, do you?' Carstairs looked at him suspiciously. 'So she is a secret heiress and you're in the know.'

'Did I say that?' Daniel suddenly felt uneasy as he saw the gleam in the other man's eyes. He realised the young fool was convinced Eliza was an heiress, but shrugged it off. No doubt someone would tell him the truth before long.

As he walked home, Daniel's thoughts were divided between the way Eliza had felt in his arms, her smile and the scent of her—and what he ought to say to the marquis when they met. Cheadle was unlikely to confess if he had conspired in the despicable trade of stealing and selling young women.

He still hadn't spoken to Lord Roberts and was feeling less and less inclined towards a convenient marriage. It would be ridiculous to toss away his one chance of saving his estate because of a young woman's smile. Eliza might have set his body aflame with a need so strong that it had taken all his willpower to stop himself sweeping her up in his arms and running off with her to a spot where he could make love to her.

He frowned, cursing himself for a fool. Love was surely no more than a fleeting thing. The wise course would be to seek Lord Roberts out first thing in the morning, and yet Daniel knew that he would wait. He had won a thousand guineas at play that evening. Perhaps the bank would accept it as a down payment on his most pressing debts.

Chapter Five

Eliza woke with a sigh on her lips. Her dream had been so enjoyable. She had been living at a pleasant house in the country. In the garden children were playing and she had been aware of a feeling of deep content.

The feeling faded as she recalled that the Marquis of Cheadle was calling that morning. He would want to know every detail of what had happened when a masked highwayman held his carriage at pistol point, and there was so much she could never tell him.

Had she been able to avoid what must obviously be an awkward interview, she would have done so. However, she suspected that the marquis did not give up easily. He was determined to have the truth and she must try to oblige him, without giving Daniel's secret away.

Oh dear, she was beginning to think of Lord Seaton as Daniel. She suspected that he had been at the centre of her happy dream the previous night and knew she was being very silly. Kate had told her that he was a consummate flirt, though not precisely a rake. He had a mistress and might consider she was fair game, for a companion was not off bounds as a girl like Kate Henderson would be.

A part of her felt that she had known him for years. She both liked and trusted him despite his brief adventure as a highwayman, yet she must not like him too much.

Dressing in a simple grey gown that was far more suitable for her situation than the gown she had worn the previous evening, she went along the hall to see if her employer needed anything. It would be best for all concerned if she put Lord Seaton out of her mind.

Both Eliza and Lady Sarah were in the parlour when the marquis was announced at a quarter to noon. Eliza felt a sinking sensation in her stomach as he was shown into the elegant room.

However, the marquis seemed a perfectly polite gentleman, enquiring after the ladies' health before sitting down and turning his attention to Eliza.

'Well, Miss Bancroft, perhaps you could explain to me what happened that day? My coachman says that the rogue rode off with you. He was fearful for your safety, but you returned a short while later seeming none the worse for your ordeal.' His gaze narrowed intently. 'Could you explain that little mystery, please?'

Eliza glanced at Lady Sarah and then took a deep breath. 'I am not perfectly certain what was intended, sir. The...gentleman seemed interested in discovering what I was doing in your carriage, sir.' Her cheeks felt hot as she avoided his eyes. 'I hardly like to say what was implied...'

'Indeed?' The marquis was silent for a moment, then,

'May I hazard a guess that the rogue imagined you my mistress?'

'I think something of the kind was in his mind. When I denied it I was allowed to return to the carriage.'

'I see.' The marquis stood up and took a little turn about the parlour before coming back to her. 'It would seem the rogue claims to have knowledge of me. I must have made an enemy. Were you robbed, Miss Bancroft? I shall repay whatever was stolen, for it was clearly I or someone close to me he meant to rob.'

'No. My purse was returned to me and a ring that is precious to me. It is all I have of my mother, you see.'

'And he did not harm or insult you in any way?'

'Not at all, sir.' Eliza faltered. 'I thought it a foolish prank—perhaps for a wager?'

'A prank you think? Had my men used their weapons, he or they might have died or been badly injured. I do not call that a mere prank, Miss Bancroft.' She looked at him. His gaze was so severe that she dropped her head. 'Was there anything you noticed in particular about the rogue? His voice, manner—the colour of his eyes?'

'Oh…' She hesitated, then, 'His voice was rough, but may have been disguised. His eyes may have been grey…or perhaps blue. I could not be certain, sir. I was a little nervous. I am sorry I cannot tell you more.'

'You have told me more than you imagine,' he replied with a nod of satisfaction. 'Plainly, the man is no common thief, but someone with a grudge against me personally.'

'Who do you think it could be?' Lady Sarah asked as Eliza remained silent.

'Someone who knows me well enough to need to disguise himself, though not as well as he imagines. I do not trap decent young ladies into becoming my mistress, though I shall not deny certain accommodations in the past with married ladies who understood the rules.' His expression relaxed a little. 'Please forgive me, Miss Bancroft. I am sorry you were used so ill when under my protection. The rogue will be brought to justice, I assure you. If he is a gentleman, he will meet me for this and think himself fortunate to escape the noose.'

'I am sorry you feel this a personal slight. I am certain it was a harmless prank.'

'I am surprised that you should take this so calmly, Miss Bancroft. Very surprised.'

He looked at Eliza hard and she blushed. What must he be thinking? Perhaps that she was involved with a man of ill repute—and therefore not the proper person to be companion to Lady Sarah?'

She noticed that he rubbed at the little finger of his left hand, as if he were seeking for something he had lost. Lady Sarah noticed it too.

'You do not wear your ring,' Lady Sarah murmured. 'Is it lost?'

'Temporarily. I hope to have it restored soon.'

'Mine was lost years ago, but a ring is just a ring. Memories never leave one.'

During the silence that followed her words, Eliza sensed an undercurrent of feeling—of sharing. It was so intense that she wished she might leave them together without appearing to suggest she understood. In her mind there was no doubt that there had been something special between the marquis and her employer. She could feel the sadness and saw echoes of a lost love in Lady Sarah's eyes. Her senses told her that there was an old mystery here, but in seconds the barriers were in place again. A casual politeness was resumed and the marquis turned to Eliza, his eyes narrowed and thoughtful.

'My wife and daughter are in Bath. They did not attend the assembly last evening for they wished to recover from the journey. I think my daughter must be two years or so younger than you, Miss Bancroft. I shall make certain that both you and Lady Sarah are invited to our ball.'

'How kind of you, sir,' Eliza said.

'We shall be delighted to attend.' Lady Sarah smiled a little wistfully. 'How is Marianne? And your wife?'

'Both are well. In confidence, I must tell you that we are expecting an offer for Marianne quite soon.'

'I am sure she will marry well. She is, I know, a delightful girl.'

The marquis nodded, glanced at his watch, asked to be forgiven and took his leave.

Lady Sarah was silent for a few minutes after he had gone, staring into space as if her mind were elsewhere. Eliza noticed that her hand trembled as she reached for a glass of restorative wine. She gave a little cry as it tipped and spilled a few drops.

'How clumsy of me…'

'So easily done,' Eliza said and swiftly wiped the spill with a napkin the maid had brought earlier with their refreshments. 'There, it was only a little and no harm done…' She turned and saw that Lady Sarah's cheeks were wet with tears. 'Ma'am, are you ill?'

'No, just upset.' Lady Sarah dabbed at her cheeks with a lace kerchief. 'Sit beside me, Eliza. I am going to tell you a secret, because I think you may have guessed at least a part of my story.'

'You need tell me nothing, ma'am.'

'I wish you to know.' Lady Sarah reached for her

hand. 'You will speak of this to no one else. I know I may trust you, my dear. I was once very much in love with the gentleman who has just left us. He was handsome and charming, but at the time not rich. I was married to Lord Manners. He was not kind or loving and spent all his time with his mistresses in town. Because I was lonely, I was drawn into a love affair with a younger man. Henry was charming and he adored me. My husband discovered the affair, but would not release me. When my lover's child was born, he took it away from me and forced me to give up my lover. I was devastated, but my husband was a cold cruel man and Cheadle would have been ruined had I defied him. He was younger than I and I felt it would be unfair to burden him with a woman who could not appear in society and a child—and so I chose seclusion in the country, where I stayed seeing only a few friends until my husband died.'

'Oh, ma'am, how dreadful for you,' Eliza exclaimed in sympathy. 'I am so very sorry. I think you loved the marquis very much?'

'He begged me to go away with him. My husband warned me that he would follow and kill us both. Even had my lover killed him in a duel, which he wanted to do, he would have lost everything. He could not have been an officer in the army with such a scandal hanging over him, and his uncle might easily have disowned him. I could not ruin his life so I agreed to my husband's terms, though it broke my heart. Do you think me weak and foolish?'

'Certainly not. You were trapped. There was nothing else you could do.'

'I felt trapped until my husband died. He never forgave me and took every chance to punish me.'

'I think you must have suffered a great deal.'

'Yes, that is true. I have been lonely despite my friends and my son, who is very like his father. I hope one day to find my lost child, but my husband did not make it easy for me. Should I find her and acknowledge her, I should lose the right to live at the Dower House *and* the portion of his estate he left me. That would not leave me penniless, for I have money of my own, which was denied me while my husband lived—but I should be loathe to lose my home. However, I am determined to find my daughter if I can.' Her hand tightened on Eliza's. 'At least I have you to keep me company. You have brought me a great deal of pleasure, Eliza. Indeed, it is almost like having my daughter with me.'

'I am happy to be of some comfort to you, ma'am.'

For a moment Eliza was tempted to tell her her own story, but she decided that it would sound too particular, as if she were claiming some kind of kinship with Lady Sarah. That would be too much of a coincidence and was a foolish notion, which she instantly dismissed—though the stories were undoubtedly similar.

'You are far more than that. Having you here has given me a reason to live, Eliza. I was quite low before you came.'

Eliza smiled and held her hand until she recovered her spirits. She was surprised and honoured to have been given her employer's confidence. It showed trust and liking on Lady Sarah's part and gave Eliza a warm glow inside. Not since Mama's death had she felt needed or loved in quite this way. Of course no one would ever replace the woman who had given her so much love in her heart, but there was room for a good friend and she had found that friend in Lady Sarah.

'Your invitation to join you was such a wonderful

thing for me, ma'am. I had so little experience and did not know if my advertisement would bring any answers.'

'It was so honest and simple that I knew you would be the right kind of girl. I shall of course keep you with me until you wish to move on, Eliza. I spoke of a trial period, but already I know you so well.' She sighed with relief. 'I feel better for having told you.' She sat up straight in her chair. 'Now we must both get ready. We are going visiting this afternoon. We shall call and take a dish of tea with various of my friends, but first we must have nuncheon here. Just a light meal, for this evening, as you know, we dine with Lady Julia and Kate.'

The afternoon passed swiftly. Eliza found herself looking from the carriage window in the hope of catching sight of Daniel Seaton. Had she known his direction she might have sent a short note to his lodgings warning him that the Marquis of Cheadle intended to discover the identity of the highwayman. She hoped she had not said anything that would give the marquis a clue. She had sensed something between him and Lord Seaton when they spoke the previous evening. Did Cheadle already suspect him? No, no, why should he? Yet there was definitely some hidden antagonism between the two.

The marquis intended to get to the bottom of the affair. Eliza wished that she could warn Daniel, but fate was not kind to her that day. He was nowhere to be seen in the streets they drove through, nor was he invited to Lady Julia's dinner.

It was not until the next morning that fortune smiled on her. Lady Sarah had asked that she visit the library and pick up a small packet from the home of Dr Morgan.

'Doctor Morgan has prepared some new powders for me, Eliza. I could send one of the maids, but I prefer not to disclose private matters to others and the servants will talk. His house is close by the library and it will save the doctor another visit.'

'I shall be happy to fetch the books and your medicine.'

Eliza was pleased with the chance of a walk. She hoped she might have the good fortune to meet with Daniel Seaton and chanced to see him leaving a small hotel opposite the doctor's house.

'Lord Seaton,' she called. 'A moment, if you please.'

He heard her voice and crossed the quiet street to greet her with a warm smile. 'Well met, Miss Bancroft. I was thinking I might call on the chance you were free to drive out with me this afternoon.'

'I fear I have a prior arrangement with Miss Henderson, but I am glad of a chance to speak with you, sir. Had I known the direction of your lodgings, I should have sent a note yesterday.'

'Indeed?' His eyes were suddenly intent and very blue. 'That sounds serious.'

'I believe it may be. The Marquis of Cheadle knows of the hold-up. He questioned me closely. I told him as little as I dare, but he suspects the highwayman may be a gentleman—perhaps someone he knows.'

'I am undone,' Daniel cried and grinned as he saw her start of alarm. 'No, Miss Bancroft, how could he guess? I dare say there are a hundred gentlemen in London who may have a score to settle with Cheadle.'

'I think he suspects there was more to the affair than

I have told him—that I am perhaps in league with a person of ill repute.'

'That might make things awkward for you, for he could try to influence your employer against you.'

'He means to find the man responsible.'

'Well, I think he will find that difficult.' Daniel frowned. 'Still, for your sake, it may be best if we do not appear to be on intimate terms, Miss Bancroft. I would not have you suffer for such a piece of nonsense. However, my advice remains the same—be careful of Cheadle, for I would not trust him. I have good reason for what I say, believe me.'

'I believe he is painted blacker than he truly is, sir,' Eliza said, thinking of what Lady Sarah had told her.

'Indeed? You must know more of him than I, Miss Bancroft.'

'Oh, no…' She blushed under his eagle eye. 'I hardly know him at all. I believe he could be a dangerous man to have as your enemy, my lord. Perhaps you should tread carefully in your dealings with him.'

'You think so?' He looked vastly offended. 'I am not afraid of any man.'

'No! I did not mean that, of course. It is simply that I feel as if I have known you for so long and I care what—' She broke off in confusion—she had said far too much.

The expression of annoyance faded and a twinkle appeared in his eyes. 'Do you, Miss Bancroft? How very odd that is to be sure. I thought it was but a few weeks since I knocked you into the bramble bush and then held a gun pointed at your heart.'

'You like to mock me, sir. You must understand that our—acquaintance—has been a trifle unusual.' She had a tight rein on her feelings now. 'You knew perfectly well what I meant.'

He met her accusing look with one of amusement. 'Perfectly, since I feel much the same. I would go so far as to say you are in my thoughts almost constantly, Miss Bancroft. You have quite overset all my well-laid plans.'

'I do not understand you, sir.'

'Do you not?' He laughed softly. 'Perhaps that is as well, for truly I do not either.'

'You speak in riddles, sir.' Eliza gave him a frowning glance, but her heart raced. There was such a look in his eyes, a look that seemed to challenge and provoke. She knew he was flirting with her, but could not quite squash the tiny seed of hope that had insensibly taken root in her heart. Her senses told her that this growing feeling between them was more than mere liking, but her mind denied it as a foolish girl's dream. The sensible woman in her knew that she could never be more to him than a flirt.

She was a lovechild, a bastard, born of good families and brought up as the daughter of a country parson. Papa had been the third son of an impoverished baron, Mama the daughter of a schoolteacher. Lord Seaton was from another world, another class. She must never forget that, because if she did she would lose her claim to respectability.

'Well, I have told you of the marquis's intent,' she said, recalling her duties. 'Lady Sarah will be waiting for me.'

'When shall I see you again? Do you attend the assembly tomorrow evening?'

He had moved closer, as if he would physically prevent her leaving. She saw his expression, the hot glow in his eyes, and her heart caught. There was something about him that told her he wanted more of her but she instinctively knew that he would think only in terms of a brief affair…a few kisses and more if he could persuade the foolish little companion to forget her modesty.

'I am not certain. I believe we attend the theatre this evening. Lady Sarah wishes to see the production of *The Taming of the Shrew*,'

'One of my favourite of Shakespeare's works,' Daniel declared and smiled. 'It is also my intention to see this production. Who knows, perhaps we shall meet there, Miss Bancroft?'

'Yes, perhaps. Now, if you will excuse me, I really must go.'

'Must you?' His gaze made her tremble. She almost thought he would seize her and kiss her in the street and drew back. He laughed and stood away from her. 'Yes, I suppose you must. Yet perhaps one day I shall have my wish.'

Eliza was not prepared to ask him for an explanation. She walked away, head high, very conscious of his eyes watching her. Lord Seaton had done nothing to make her believe she was special to him, yet she was certain his decision to attend the theatres was an impulse. He had changed his plans so that they might meet for a short time. It was all they could have, just snatched moments of time when she was out walking or they both attended a function. Had she been a young lady of fortune, she would have suspected him of courting her, but as a companion she could not look so high.

Daniel watched her walk away. He knew that he was playing a dangerous game, risking everything by delaying the inevitable. His best interests clearly lay with Susanne Roberts, but he could not bring himself to speak to her or her father.

Amused by his own foolishness, Daniel turned to discover a gentleman he considered one of his best friends advancing towards him.

'Hastings,' he saluted him with a grin. 'What brings you to Bath? I thought you settled in the country for a few months.'

'Necessity,' Jack Hastings grimaced. 'Mama came to visit. She nagged me constantly for a week and so I brought her to Bath. I am told it is time I took myself a bride and set up my nursery. So I must find a suitable girl I can admire—preferably pretty, good-tempered and an heiress, though the money is not as important as the rest.'

Daniel nodded. His friend was dark-hared with grey eyes and a pleasant countenance. Popular with the ladies, he should have no difficulty in finding the right bride.

'Then we are in similar straits, Jack. I need to marry well, though at the moment I have little inclination for it.'

'You seemed vastly entertained by the young lady I saw you talking to just now.'

'Miss Eliza Bancroft?' It was on the tip of Daniel's tongue to tell him that Eliza was a companion and therefore not suitable but an imp of mischief made him withhold the information. 'Ah, yes. She won't do for you, Jack. Besides, I saw her first, so you have no chance.'

'Caught your fancy, has she?' Jack Hastings instantly took up the challenge. 'Miss Eliza Bancroft, eh? I suppose she is an heiress?'

'I couldn't possibly say...'

'Keeping her all to yourself? You sly dog!' Jack

chuckled. 'Well, all is fair in love and war, so they say. We'll see who she prefers. Where is she staying?'

'In the Crescent with Lady Sarah Manners.' Daniel relented. 'I do not think Miss Bancroft is your type, Jack. Cheadle is in town. I rather thought you liked Miss Marianne?'

'Yes, I do.' Jack looked gloomy. 'She had her eye on a duke—at least, her mother did. I may inherit a fortune one day, but I'll never be more than a baronet. Marianne wants more than that.'

'Well, if the duke doesn't come up to scratch she may turn to you. If I wanted her, I would go after her—sweep her off her feet. She will fall in love with you and forget about marrying nobility.'

'Do you really think so?' Jack Hastings looked thoughtful. 'I believed she liked me for a while, then she went cool and wouldn't look at me. Will you walk to the club with me, Daniel? I have a business proposition I want your advice on—if you would oblige me?'

'Yes, of course, though I'm not sure I am the man to ask about money.'

'It concerns setting up a racing stable. With your experience and guidance I think I might just give it a go. I should like you to look some horses over for me and see if you think they would be any good for racing. There are some yearlings and a horse I'm told has huge potential over the hurdles.'

'In that case I should be delighted to give you my advice.'

'It was a stroke of luck meeting you,' Jack said, clearly pleased. 'We could take a look this afternoon, if you like?'

'Why not? I have nothing in particular to do, though I am going to the theatre this evening.'

'We should be back in plenty of time.'

Daniel was pleased that his advice had been sought, because he was considered a good judge of horse flesh. It might be fate that had brought his friend to Bath. He would do well to concentrate on helping Jack to set up his stables and put Miss Eliza Bancroft out of his mind.

The letter from the Bow Street Runner he had employed was waiting for Daniel when he returned to his lodgings. He had been making exhaustive inquiries and thought he was on the trail of something important.

If my instincts are right, and they seldom fail, my lord, I believe we may have uncovered some very nasty goings on. You were on the right track, but this may be much bigger and more widespread than we imagine. I must go down to Bristol, for I think Jed Bailey may provide us with a clue, and it is my information that the girl Molly is with him. They may be in fear of their lives, but I shall write again as soon as I have something more positive.

Daniel frowned over the letter. He had hoped he was wrong, that his agent would say there was no foundation for his suspicions, but it looked as if this affair could turn out to be much worse than he had guessed—and that might result in a terrible scandal. Unless he could keep his cousin's name out of it and somehow bring the culprits to book without giving his uncle more heartbreak.

He would have to give the matter a lot of thought. Something like this could be dangerous, both for him and the man he had employed. He must write and warn him to take no risks. If necessary, Daniel would have to employ more than one Runner to make certain this did not get out of hand.

Eliza knew that she should not let herself hope Lord Seaton would visit their box at the theatre that evening, but the possibility hovered at the back of her mind. She tried to be sensible, for she was enjoying herself and had become fast friends with Kate and her mama, though she suspected they both liked to gossip rather more than was wise.

They spent the afternoon visiting and, rather to her surprise, Eliza found herself warmly received by everyone. Even a chance meeting with Lady Roberts at the home of a mutual friend proved much pleasanter than on previous occasions. The lady gave her some intent looks and her thin lips formed a smile as she nodded to herself, seeming to confirm something in her mind. She mentioned in passing that her nephew would be in town the following week.

Eliza wondered why the lady would think it necessary to give her this information, but there was no doubt that her manner towards Eliza had undergone a distinct change.

Lady Sarah remarked on it as they drove home to rest and then change for the evening.

'Not that I am surprised my friends should take to you, Eliza. You have charming manners, my love. I am certain they must make you acceptable to everyone.'

'You treat me so generously, ma'am. I am sure that is the reason people are being so kind.'

Lady Sarah shook her head, but smiled to herself, seeming satisfied with the explanation.

'My friends have accepted you for my sake,' she said.

Eliza agreed that it must be so.

Lady Sarah was very close to the truth, but she might have been shocked had she realised the story that had begun to circulate. Fortunately, as yet it was only being whispered of by a few ladies and had not reached the ears of the gossipmongers.

However, Eliza could not help being aware that people turned their heads to look at her as she and Lady Sarah took their seats that evening. In the few minutes before the lights were dimmed, she sensed curious looks directed at her. However, she forgot all about them as the curtain went up and the play began.

It was during the first interval that something surprising happened. Not one, but four gentlemen visited their box, two of whom were unknown to Lady Sarah and Eliza. They came with friends and asked to be introduced to Miss Bancroft and Lady Sarah.

In the second interval, Lord Seaton and a friend he introduced as Jack Hastings arrived. Jack was gallant enough to go in search of drinks for them all while Daniel took a seat at Eliza's side.

'Are you enjoying your evening, Miss Bancroft?'

'The play is excellent,' she replied. 'We have had a stream of visitors. I think Lady Sarah must have a great many friends, though she claimed not to know some of the gentlemen who visited.'

'Indeed?' Daniel frowned as a suspicion came to his mind. 'I had noticed some interest in this box myself.

It is a little curious, unless—' He broke off and looked thoughtful. 'I shall discover what is going on and tell you tomorrow afternoon. May I ask if you and Miss Henderson would care for a drive in my curricle? I could ask Mr Hastings to accompany us…'

'I think that would be pleasant.' Eliza leaned forwards to tap Kate on the arm and put the suggestion to her. Kate glanced round at Lord Seaton and gave him an amused glance, agreeing that a drive would be delightful. 'We should enjoy such an outing, sir. At what time will you call?'

'Shall we say two in the afternoon?'

'Yes. Kate must take nuncheon with us. You will, Kate?' Her friend nodded and she looked at Daniel. 'We shall be ready when you call.'

Mr Hastings returned with a waiter and their champagne. The cork was popped and they toasted one another, laughing and smiling.

'I say, that fellow is rather rude,' Jack said, giving a young buck in the audience a frown for his impertinence. 'He had been ogling you for the past ten minutes, Miss Bancroft. Shall I go and tell him to mind his manners?'

'Oh, no, he is probably admiring Kate,' Eliza said. 'She has many admirers.'

'Yes, I am certain she does,' he agreed. 'She is very pretty—but of course you are beautiful, Miss Bancroft— or may I call you Miss Eliza?'

'Oh…' She was flustered by his request. 'If you wish it, I see no reason why not, Mr Hastings.'

'You must call me Jack,' he said and grinned at her. 'I am certain we shall all be great friends. I shall ask Mama to invite you all to her dinner next week.'

As the bell to announce the end of the interval rang

then, Eliza was saved from making a reply as the gentlemen left. She caught the mischief in Kate's eyes, but refrained from asking what she thought so amusing.

The third interval brought another stream of visitors to their box, all of them gentlemen, or, in one case, a lady known to them with her nephew, who had just joined her in Bath. Eliza hoped that Lord Seaton might return, but he did not; though she enjoyed the performance very much, she was disappointed not to have seen more of him.

He was much in her thoughts when she went to bed that evening, but she slept peacefully without dreaming.

Next morning was spent running small errands for Lady Sarah, and greeting Kate when she arrived for nuncheon.

'I am looking forward to our drive this afternoon,' Kate said. 'Mama told me she intends to visit Lady Sarah so you must not worry that she will be alone.'

'Your mama is very kind,' Eliza said. 'Lady Sarah wished to stay home for once, but she will be pleased to see Lady Julia—they are such good friends.'

'Yes, they are,' Kate agreed and put on an innocent air. 'Mama has known her all her life. They remained friends after…the trouble with Lord Manners. Lady Sarah has no secrets from my mother.' Kate's eyes sparkled with mischief. 'Mama generally tells me most things, but she has merely hinted at something concerning you…she thinks she knows your secret, Eliza.'

'My secret?' Eliza's heart pounded. Could Lady Julia have discovered that she was a lovechild? 'I have no secret, Kate. I cannot think what you mean.'

'You need not be afraid. Mama has not told me exactly, and neither of us would wish to harm you—but you may confide in me, you know. You are not quite what you seem—are you?'

'Kate…' Eliza's cheeks burned—it seemed that Lady Julia must know the secret of her birth. 'Please do not mention…I would not wish it generally known.'

'I knew it,' Kate crowed and squeezed her arm 'Not a word shall pass my lips, I promise. Now, tell me, what did you think of Mr Hastings? Does he not seem an agreeable sort of man?'

Eliza was relieved to have the subject changed. She could not imagine how Lady Julia knew that the Bancrofts were not her parents, but it seemed that she did somehow.

'Mr Hastings seems very agreeable. I think he and Lord Seaton are close friends.'

'Yes, that is a fortunate thing,' Kate replied. 'I do hope we shall be invited to dinner. I should like to see more of the agreeable Mr Hastings—would not you?'

'What bee have you got in your bonnet now?' Eliza was determined to put the embarrassing moment behind her. Kate had promised not to reveal her secret, and though the girl loved to gossip, she would surely keep her word?

Kate smiled and shook her head. Eliza laughed, because she suspected her friend thought Mr Hastings might make Lord Seaton jealous.

When the gentlemen arrived they were both driving smart phaetons with beautiful horses, and both had a young tiger standing up at the back. Kate walked confidently towards Mr Hastings's rig and was assisted up the steps to sit beside him on the driving box. Eliza approached Lord Seaton's phaeton with less confidence, feeling a little shy. She had thought they might all go together in an open landau driven by a coachman and was unsure it was a good idea to be seen alone with a gentleman. It was perfectly acceptable for Kate, of course, because the tiger was there for propriety's sake, but Eliza was a companion and she feared it might look as if she were getting above herself. A gentleman of Daniel's rank would hardly be courting a humble companion.

However, Lord Seaton's smile made her forget her fears. His expression was warm, if a little troubled, and he showed great consideration in seeing her settled.

'I do not think it will be too cold for you,' he said as she took her seat beside him. 'However, my tiger has a blanket should you need it.'

'I am sure I shall not be in the least cold. The sun is very warm and the breeze is most welcome.'

'How little fuss you make on any account.' Daniel smiled at her, but she saw a shadow in his eyes. 'Are you always so forgiving, I wonder? I think what I have to tell you this afternoon may prove upsetting, Miss Eliza...I hope I may call you by your name, as Jack does?'

'Yes, certainly, my lord.' Her eyes opened wider as she looked at him curiously. 'You sound very serious?'

'I am. Do you think you could call me Seaton, as my friends do? I think Daniel in private, but that may be a step too far just yet?'

'I think it might be inappropriate, my...sir,' Eliza said and felt her cheeks getting warm. 'There is a distance between us, even though you have been kind enough to make nothing of it. Perhaps you should tell me what is in your mind? I think you are troubled—is it on my account?'

'You are always so perceptive.' Daniel glanced at her as they left the busy main street and turned off into a quiet country lane. 'It might have been better had I waited until we could walk alone—but my tiger may be trusted. Even if he could hear us, he would never breathe a word. Would you, Will?'

'What's that, my lord?'

Eliza smiled. 'Are all your servants so well trained?'

'I rescued Will from the streets of London, where unscrupulous fellows were preying him on. He is grateful for some reason. I really do not know why. I am not an easy master to work for.' A smothered laugh turned hastily into a cough told Eliza that the tiger's hearing was perfectly sound. 'So we may speak freely.' Daniel hesitated, then, 'A rumour has started in Bath concerning you, Miss Eliza. I am sorry to tell you that stories are circulating concerning your fortune.'

'Concerning my fortune? I have none.' She looked at him in surprise. 'No, how foolish! Where do the gossips get these stories?'

Hearing an expelled breath, she turned her head to look at him. 'You do not mean...you could not have thought...'

'If I am the cause of the rumours, it was a careless remark I made to an acquaintance Carstairs on the evening of the assembly,' Daniel said. 'I believe the gown you wore made some people think you were one of the débutantes and he was curious as to who you were. He asked me if I knew your fortune and I told him it would not be enough for him. Unfortunately, he took it into his head that I was trying to put him off, because I intended to make an offer myself. The story has spread, and, as with all such tales, it has grown. You are now believed to be a secret heiress.'

'But that is terrible,' Eliza cried, shocked by his words. 'That must be why all those...how shallow people are...' Her hands trembled in her lap, but she clasped them firmly together. Had that been what Kate meant? She had thought something different. She would take the first opportunity of disabusing her friend of the idea that she was an heiress. 'To make so much of a careless remark...'

'I wish I had bitten off my tongue rather than cause you distress, Eliza. Please forgive me. I did not intend this to happen, believe me—but I should have remembered what a wicked tongue Carstairs has. He is looking for a rich wife, so you may expect him to call.'

'How awkward,' Eliza said. 'I fear he will be much disappointed when he discovers the truth.'

'You will not tell him, surely?' Ahead of them the other carriage had pulled to a halt at a point of advantage to admire the view. Daniel did the same. His tiger jumped down and he assisted Eliza to the ground. 'There is no need for anyone to know.'

Eliza was prevented from replying by Kate, who called to them to come and admire the view a little further along the rise. Eliza gave Daniel a speaking look and walked to join the others, he a step behind her. For some minutes they all admired the view of Bath as it lay below them bathed in sunlight.

Eliza's thoughts were confused, but she quickly had them in order. Had she been looking to marry, the situation might have been awkward, for she must have told any suitor the truth and it would soon have been common knowledge, but since she was not thinking of marrying anyone the rumour could not really harm anyone.

When Kate and Mr Hastings wandered away to explore a little further, Eliza turned to her companion.

'I believe you may be right, sir. In time the truth is bound to come out, but for the moment it is probably best to ignore it. Lady Sarah's friends know I am her penniless companion and will soon set the gabblemongers straight. It would not be proper for me to mention the rumour to anyone, let alone a gentleman who is inclined to speak too freely.'

'I doubt if he would believe you,' Daniel said and frowned. 'Once these idiots get an idea into their heads it is useless to deny it, because they think you are trying to cover it up—though why you should wish to conceal your fortune if you had one is a mystery.'

'I suppose I might be afraid of fortune hunters,' Eliza suggested and gave a gurgle of laughter. 'How silly people are, Seaton. Why can they not judge someone for what they are rather than what they have?'

'I could not agree more,' he said. 'You can see the amusing side to this situation. I admit that I feared you would be angry with me.'

'In part, Lady Sarah and I are to blame. She has bought me such lovely clothes, clothes a débutante might wear. I did ask her if she was sure I ought to wear a gown like that, but she insisted. I hope it will not upset her when she learns what some people are saying. I am sure she will squash the rumours immediately. If some refuse to believe her, they have only themselves to blame. Besides, it cannot matter—I have no intention of accepting an offer from anyone.'

'Indeed?' His brows arched. 'Do you never wish to

be married? Have you a strong dislike of the institution of marriage?'

'No, certainly not. My parents were happy together...' Eliza frowned. Her adopted parents had been the perfect couple, but she knew nothing of her true mother or father. 'I suppose I might marry in the right circumstances, but that is something for the future. While Lady Sarah needs me as a companion I would not think of leaving her.'

'Ah, I see. Your sentiments are commendable, Miss Eliza. She seems extremely fond of you. It is a shame that her generosity towards you has given some the wrong impression.'

'Yes. However, if you and others deny the story, I believe it will soon be forgotten. I may not be so popular next time we attend a ball or the theatre, but I shall not let it overset me.'

'You are such a sensible young lady. I fear a denial may turn some of the old tabbies against you. However, if you smile and say you do not know how the rumour started, I dare say it will go away.'

'Yes, of course,' Eliza agreed. If only he knew she was not sensible at all, for she was very much afraid she had fallen in love with him. 'I am glad you told me, sir, for I am prepared and I shall make a point of telling everyone that I am merely Lady Sarah's companion.'

'Perhaps you need not go so far. I am sure that if I drop a few hints about your fortune having been exaggerated the speculation will die a natural death. After all, Lady Marianne Cheadle is in Bath and she is beautiful and an heiress.'

'I believe she may soon be engaged. I think her parents expect it.'

'So much the better. It will give the gossips something

more interesting to discuss.' He offered his arm. 'Shall we stroll in the direction of our friends, Miss Eliza? I believe we ought, do you not agree?'

'Yes, certainly,' Eliza replied and smiled at him. 'You are forgiven, sir. Please do not trouble yourself further on my account. I am certain you have more important things to tease you.'

'I cannot think of anything more important than the comfort and reputation of a friend,' Daniel replied. 'However, I must tell you that I am going out of town for a day or two. Jack wants my advice in the matter of setting up a racing stable. He has been offered some horses and I am to help him purchase them and engage the services of a trainer.'

'Are you a judge of these things?' Eliza's eyes were bright with interest. 'I have always loved to ride, though I have not been able to for a year or two.'

'That is a shame. When I return to Bath I shall hire a suitable mount and we may go riding—if you would care for it?'

'Yes, perhaps—if my employer does not need me.'

'Your employer seems to wish you to enjoy yourself as much as possible.' Daniel frowned as she turned her head to call out to Kate. Something about her profile made him think of another young girl…but that was impossible. Or was it? He recalled the ring he had taken from Cheadle in that card game and the ring he had seen briefly as Eliza handed it over before he returned it to her. They were very similar in design, though one was obviously meant for a lady's finger. He thought the inscriptions were identical, though he could not be certain the same person had commissioned them. It was perfectly possible that two different individuals had asked for a similar inscription—and yet in a certain position there was a definite likeness.

When Daniel held up the marquis's coach, his first thought had been that she was on her way to become Cheadle's mistress. Eliza had denied it. Her ring came from her mother. The marquis was merely doing her employer a favour by conveying her in his coach. He had accepted her explanation and given the coincidence of the rings no further thought. Now he had begun to wonder.

Was it possible that Eliza was Cheadle's bastard? She was not so like Marianne Cheadle that it struck you immediately, but for a moment in the sunlight he had seen a likeness.

It was possible that he had stumbled on the truth. It was also possible that the marquis had recommended his bastard to a friend as a companion.

So who was her mother? Eliza said the ring was all she had of her mother. Daniel frowned as he puzzled over the mystery. Her parents had been happy together. Obviously her father could not have known his wife had conceived a child by another man…or was he making a mountain out of a molehill?

Daniel smiled at the foolish notion. Of course Eliza was not Cheadle's bastard, though if she were…it crossed his mind that he might use the information as blackmail. He dismissed the idea instantly. He still had Cheadle's ring, but in the morning he would return it and discover what the marquis had to say concerning his cousin Marcus's suspicious death.

However, the notion that Eliza Bancroft might be Cheadle's lovechild remained at the back of his mind. It would explain certain things…the reason why she was being treated so kindly by her employer and the marquis's readiness to be of assistance.

Eliza noticed that her companion was a little quieter than usual as they drove back to the Crescent. She imagined that he was still concerned for her because of the foolish rumours spreading through Bath society. When he handed her down from his phaeton, she smiled at him warmly and thanked him for a pleasant afternoon.

'You are most welcome, Miss Eliza. I am glad you found the outing to your liking.'

'Yes, I did. You were kind to give up your afternoon to us, sir. Perhaps we shall see you this evening at the assembly, before you disappear for the next few days?'

'I am not sure…' Daniel hesitated, fought his natural inclination and lost. 'Please save two dances for me, Miss Eliza. I shall come earlier this time so they will not be lost.'

'I shall look forward to seeing you.'

'Until this evening, then.' Daniel smiled and helped her down from the curricle.

Eliza was smiling as she went into the house and discovered her employer and Lady Julia sitting comfortably together.

'Did you enjoy yourselves, my dears?' Lady Sarah asked.

'Oh, very much,' Eliza replied and saw Kate bend to whisper something to her mother. 'It was very pleasant, was it not, Kate?'

'Yes, indeed, vastly amusing,' Kate said. 'Truly, diverting, Eliza.'

The mischief in her eyes made Eliza wonder what she was up to, but she merely smiled. Kate had a wicked tongue, but she meant no harm.

Chapter Six

The next morning Eliza visited the library and it was on her return that she found Lady Sarah in some distress. She was sitting with a lace kerchief in her hand and had clearly been crying.

'What is it, ma'am?' Eliza asked and ran to her, kneeling by her side to take her hand. 'What has distressed you so?'

'It is mere foolishness,' Lady Sarah said. 'I have had a visitor while you were out—it appears that people have put two and two together and come up with five, as they so often do. Lady Anton had the effrontery to tell me she knew that you were my lovechild and that she applauded me for having the courage to acknowledge you.'

'No! How could she? How could anyone have come to such a conclusion?'

'I think someone told her last night.' Lady Sarah looked at Eliza. 'I am not certain, but Kate may have hinted at something—you did not tell her of what I confided to you, Eliza?'

'You must know I would not.' Eliza gave a cry of distress. 'Oh, no, she couldn't have meant… Kate told me her mother knew my secret and I begged her not to mention it to anyone, but I did not imagine she was labouring under such a misconception.'

'What did you think, Eliza?'

'I was not sure…' Eliza's cheeks were pink. 'It is nothing very terrible, ma'am, I assure you.'

'If you do not wish to tell me, I shall not tease you,' Lady Sarah said and a single tear trickled down her cheek. 'I do not believe this is your fault. If anything, it is mine for wanting to give you pretty clothes. People have jumped to the wrong conclusion; it is foolish but distressing. To have people think…when it is not true— and I wish so much to find my lost child.'

Eliza had been considering whether she ought to confess the truth of her birth to her employer. Lady Sarah surely had a right to know, and yet she might be angry because Eliza had said nothing at the start. When she saw Lady Sarah's acute distress she knew she must say nothing of her own hopes and fears. This was clearly not the time. Lady Sarah might think she had started the rumour herself in order to convince her of its truth.

'Have you tried to discover the child's whereabouts, ma'am?'

'There was a lawyer involved in the affair, but he will not answer my letters. He arranged the whole affair for my husband. The babe was given to a good home and I was forbidden to try to find her. My husband tried to make it impossible for me to do so—but Cheadle was asked to contribute to the child's upkeep and he gave me the man's direction.'

The Reverend Bancroft had found Eliza in the church, therefore the similarity between their stories was at an end. A lawyer paid for his trouble would not simply have abandoned her behind an altar. Her parents had received nothing for Eliza's upkeep. If Eliza had had a faint hope that she might just be Lady Sarah's lovechild, she knew now it was false.

'Could you not employ an agent to find your child?'

Lady Sarah stared at her unhappily. 'I suppose I might, but this gossip has upset me. The same might happen again and it is so painful—not to say awkward for me. If my husband's lawyers hear...' She shook her head. 'No matter. I shall not mind it.'

'Would you like me to leave, ma'am? If you sent me away, the gossip would soon die.'

'Yes, it would—but I shall not allow it to spoil our pleasure. You are a great comfort to me, Eliza. Please do not leave.'

'I shall stay for as long as you need me, ma'am.'

Lady Sarah nodded, but Eliza thought there was a little reserve in her manner. She was no doubt wondering why Eliza would not confide her own secret. Eliza made up her mind that she would do so once the gossip had died down. She would show her employer the ring and then tell her of how she came to be adopted by the Bancrofts. In the meantime, she would take every opportunity to deny the foolish rumours.

Daniel walked from his meeting with Cheadle feeling relieved that the business was over. He had returned the marquis's ring, refused to take the money offered, asking quite bluntly to be told what Cheadle knew of his cousin's affairs.

'Marcus Standish was a fool,' Cheadle said, answering in as blunt a fashion as Daniel asked. 'He was in with a crowd of whom I know little and wish to know less. If you imagine I am mixed up in their shady business, whatever it may be, you mistake the matter. You should address your questions to Kettleton. I believe they were thick together at one time—but I can be of no more help. As far as your cousin's debt was concerned, I regret now that I spoke to Standish of the matter.'

'Had you waited a while, I think he would not have minded as much. A gambling debt must be paid, after all.' Daniel frowned. 'I do not think I know Kettleton—where may I look for him?'

'I think he has a house in the country somewhere. It may be somewhere near your uncle's home, but I can tell you no more. I have played cards with the man—who is a cheat, I may tell you. It was because he tried to fleece me that I was angry over your cousin's debt. I thought it a plot between them to recover Marcus's debt, but I may be mistaken.'

Cheadle frowned. 'I am known to be ruthless in play and I do not suffer fools gladly—but I am not a cheat. Your father drank too much the night he lost heavily to me. I warned him to give it up, but he would not listen. Indeed, he increased the stakes. I dare say you hate me for it, but I could hardly refuse to play with him.'

'My father was suffering from grief after my mother's death. What he did was foolish but, as I said previously, a gambling debt must be paid.'

'Yes, it must. However, had I known of your mother's recent death, I might have forgone the debt. I am sorry for it if it has caused you difficulty?'

'My affairs are my own,' Daniel said stiffly. 'I believe our business is at an end, Cheadle. You have your ring—and I accept that you knew little of my cousin's affairs.'

'Kettleton is a dangerous man,' Cheadle said as Daniel prepared to leave. 'Be careful of him, Seaton.'

'Thank you for your concern. Good day, sir.'

Daniel was thoughtful as he left the marquis. His warning was uppermost in his mind as he walked towards his lodgings.

Eliza wore her white gown again that evening. She glanced at herself in the mirror when she was ready, wondering why people should have become convinced that she was Lady Sarah's daughter. She did not think they looked alike for Lady Sarah's colouring was not the same. Her hair was much darker, her eyes that greenish-brown that some people called hazel.

If Kate had caused this distress, it really was too bad of her!

Putting the troublesome thoughts from her mind, Eliza went along the hall to her employer's room. Lady Sarah looked at her thoughtfully.

'You must hold your head high, Eliza, and do not mind what people say to you—but remember, if you are in distress, we shall go to my home. I am determined not to part with you whatever happens.' She sighed. 'I have decided to employ an agent to find my daughter, as you suggested, but I am not sure how to begin.'

'You must be very careful, for your husband's lawyer might make trouble for you.'

'He might try...' Lady Sarah shook her head. 'I do not care for what he may say, but my son might be upset—and I should not like to be turned out of my home.'

'I am sure one of the Bow Street Runners would be discreet, ma'am.'

'What do you know of such men?'

'Nothing personally, but I have heard that they can sometimes find people.'

'I imagine Lord Seaton might know more,' Lady Sarah said, looking thoughtful. 'I may ask him how one goes about these things when he calls on us.'

'I believe he is going out of town for a day or two,' Eliza said. 'A matter of some horses.'

'Well, I dare say it will keep until he returns.'

The subject was dropped as they went out to the waiting carriage.

The ballroom was even more crowded that evening, if that were possible. Eliza tried to find a seat next to Lady Sarah, for she would have preferred not to dance, but Kate would not allow it.

'You must not allow the gossips to win,' she said and took Eliza's arm firmly, guiding her to the ballroom. 'You will dance with everyone just as before and let people think what they will. And I am sorry, Eliza, if something I said carelessly has led to this gossip. I truly believed you were Lady Sarah's daughter and so did Mama. She is most upset to have distressed her good friend and she's very cross with me—though all I said was that it was fortunate Lady Sarah had found someone she could love as a daughter. I did not mean to start a rumour.'

'Yes, I think I see how it happened. The gossips already imagined I was a secret heiress and it was a short jump from there to thinking that Lady Sarah had decided to introduce her lovechild to society. Were there many that knew at the time, do you think?'

'Her friends must have known. Mama said there was some gossip concerning her seclusion, and people do not forget. Years later they still remember scandal and often make things worse by inventing what they do not know—as we did. I am very sorry, Eliza. I thought it so fortunate for you—but I have hurt you and I would not do so for the world.'

'I should have been plain with you, Kate. I thought you meant something else.' She shook her head as Kate questioned. 'Not here. People already think ill of me. I would not have them overhear something that would convince them all they were right in the first place.'

'Well, it was an easy mistake to make, considering how fond Lady Sarah is of you, Eliza.'

Kate did not know that Eliza had been adopted as a baby or she would have been convinced of the truth of her theory.

They had entered the ballroom and Eliza tried to put her distress from her mind. Almost immediately, gentlemen wishing to dance approached Eliza and Julia. The first were Mr Thatcher and Lord Smythe. Mr Thatcher was as polite as on the first evening. She could detect no change in his manner and acquitted him of being affected by the gossip. Their dance was pleasant, as was the one she enjoyed with Lord Smythe. It had no sooner ended than she saw Daniel coming towards her, a look of determination on his face. Her heart stopped for one moment and then raced on as he inclined his head.

'I believe you have saved two dances for me, Miss Eliza—may I enquire when I am to have the pleasure?'

'The next set of dances, if you please—and a waltz later in the evening, sir.'

'I am delighted to have arrived in time. I was delayed for a few minutes or I would have been here at the start.'

'I did not reserve the first dances for I was not

perfectly sure at what time we should arrive ourselves, sir.'

Without meaning to, Eliza had given something of
her feelings away. Daniel looked at her intently. 'Has
something more happened?'

'No... Yes,' she replied. 'Nothing I can speak of here,
sir. Lady Sarah hopes you will call on her soon.'

'I would do so tomorrow if I could, but I am promised
to Hastings. I shall be away only two days. Will that be
soon enough?'

'I am sure it will.' Eliza smiled. 'I assure you it is not
urgent. Shall we enjoy our dances?'

'Yes, of course.' Daniel took her hand, leading her
into the formal dance. It was the kind where sets of
steps were performed in rotation and partners changed,
returning to one's original partner at the end of the
formation.'

It was impossible to do more than exchange a few
words when they performed their set at the end of each
change. After the music ended, Daniel took her arm and
steered her towards the long windows that led out on to
the terrace.

'Would you not like a breath of fresh air, Miss Eliza?
It is very warm, is it not?'

'Yes, it is a little,' she agreed, glancing at the stern
set of his chin. 'Is something wrong?'

He did not answer until they were on the terrace, and
even then he waited until they reached the shadows at
the far end before turning to her fiercely.

'Why did you not tell me immediately?'

'Oh...you overheard something?'

'One of my partners was agog with the news. She
whispered to me in confidence that you were Lady
Sarah's lovechild.'

'Of course it is utter nonsense,' Eliza said. 'You really should not listen to gossip, sir. People will make these things up. I have no idea why it pleases them to imagine such things.'

'Are you sure it isn't true?' Daniel's gaze narrowed suspiciously as he looked at her. 'Tell me the truth, Eliza.'

'If I thought… It is just rumour,' Eliza said. 'It cannot be true. Even if…no, it is not my story to tell. I shall not add fuel to the flames. You should ignore the stories. They are exaggerated and foolish.'

'I should not be happy if I thought you had made a fool of me, Eliza.' He looked at her hard. 'I will ask you again—is there any chance that these stories could be true?'

'No…' Eliza moved away from him. How could the rumours be true when she had been found in the church and Lady Sarah's daughter had been given to a good family? It was mere coincidence. 'Do not press me. I think I shall return to the ballroom.'

'Eliza…'

She ignored him as he seemed to call her back. It was very wrong of him to demand answers, and at such a time. Anyone might overhear. She could not be sure of anything and she would say nothing to anyone. There was only one person she was prepared to ask for the truth and she would do that as soon as she could.

Eliza returned to the ballroom and sought her employer. Lady Sarah was talking to a rather beautiful young lady, who turned as Eliza approached.

The girl had dark honey-coloured hair and blue eyes. She was very lovely, the line of her cheek perfect, as was her skin. Her dress was white and sewn with sparkling stones that looked like diamonds, and she wore a pendant of diamonds at her white throat.

'Eliza, my love—this is the Marquis of Cheadle's daughter, Marianne. She has just asked us to her dance next week. I have said we shall be delighted to go.'

'Miss Bancroft,' Marianne said and her voice was soft with a lilt of musicality, 'how nice to meet you. My father spoke of you to me. I shall be happy to know you as a friend.'

'Thank you, Lady Marianne. You are very kind...' Eliza hesitated. 'You will think me rude, but you are not like your father?'

'No, I take after Mama in looks.'

'Your mama was a great beauty in her day,' Lady Sarah said. 'And your father is still a handsome man— you would be fortunate to favour either of them.'

'Papa says I am like him in other ways.' Marianne smiled at Eliza. 'Shall we go back to the ballroom together? I know most people here, but I always feel awkward until someone asks me to dance—and we have only just arrived because Mama was not satisfied with my dress and called the seamstress to make some adjustments.'

'Your dress is lovely,' Eliza assured her. Her eyes went to her employer. 'You are quite comfortable, Lady Sarah?'

'Perfectly, my dear,' her employer replied. 'Go and enjoy yourself while you can.'

Eliza nodded. She walked back into the ballroom, standing just inside the doorway at Marianne's side just as Daniel walked back through the French windows. She saw him staring hard, watched his eyes narrow and the thin line of his mouth as he turned and walked into the card rooms.

Eliza's heart beat rapidly. He was angry because she had refused to answer him, leaving him standing on the terrace. There could be no other reason for his hard look.

She was aware that more than one person had turned their head to look in her direction, but accepted that most were staring at Marianne Cheadle, who was undoubtedly one of the most beautiful girls in the room. Within minutes, she was surrounded by young men begging her for a dance, and when Eliza's partner came to claim her Marianne was already dancing.

'Have you known Lady Marianne long?' her partner asked.

'We met just this evening,' she replied. 'I am sure I could introduce you if you wished to ask her for a dance, though she may not have many left.'

'I know Lady Marianne,' he replied. 'I believe she intends to marry a duke…but Accrington's family is very high in the instep. They would cry off at the hint of a scandal.'

Eliza did not reply. Was he hinting that it would not do for Marianne's name to be linked with hers? She felt a hot rush of embarrassment and almost missed her step.

It was so foolish. All this innuendo and gossip over nothing. Yet if it would harm Marianne, an innocent girl of unblemished reputation, to be seen with her, it must be avoided at all costs.

Eliza felt as if she wanted to weep, but would not allow herself to give way. She held her head high and managed to smile and converse with her partners as usual. No one else mentioned Lady Marianne and she told herself she was being too sensitive. No one knew anything for sure. She was not even certain herself.

* * *

Lady Marianne danced for most of the evening, but just before supper she came up to Eliza and took her arm.

'Do say you will eat supper with me, Miss Bancroft.'

'I ought to look after Lady Sarah—' She broke off as she saw the Marquis of Cheadle staring at them. He was frowning as he came up to them.

'Your mama wants you, Marianne.' His eyes moved from her to Eliza as his daughter immediately obeyed his unspoken order. 'Miss Bancroft. I have something I wish to ask you—would it be convenient if I were to call in the morning?'

'Yes, of course, if you wish, sir.'

Eliza was relieved for it meant she would not have to go out of her way to speak to him. He seemed angry, though his anger was controlled, the only sign a flicker at his temple. He bowed his head and walked off, leaving her standing alone.

She turned, intending to look for Lady Sarah when a man moved across her path. Lifting her gaze to his face, she saw that it was Daniel and he still appeared to be angry.

What had she done that was so terrible?

'I came to tell you that Lady Sarah is feeling a little unwell,' he said, his mouth drawn into a thin line. 'Her carriage has been sent for, but she wished you to accompany her home.'

'Yes, of course. I shall come immediately. I was about to seek her out.'

'What were you speaking to the marquis about?' Daniel asked as he took her arm and steered her from the ballroom to the small anteroom where Lady Sarah was sitting. Lady Julia and Kate were both with her, but she looked distressed until she saw Eliza.

'Ah, there you are, dearest,' she said and held her hand out. 'Forgive me for spoiling your evening, but I have such a terrible headache.'

'I am quite ready to leave,' Eliza replied and took her hand, holding it gently for a moment. 'I fear you have been doing too much, ma'am—or perhaps you are upset?'

'Just a little,' Lady Sarah admitted. 'People are so unkind at times. Someone had the effrontery to suggest that you might be a fortune hunter and told me to be careful. I am afraid I was sharp with her. Give me your arm, Eliza. I am rather tired this evening.'

Eliza felt as if someone had poured cold water over her. She pressed trembling fingers to her lips.

'Let me help you, ma'am,' Daniel said and offered his arm. 'I am stronger than Miss Eliza and you do look a little pale.'

He took her hand, placing an arm about her as he helped her from the Assembly Rooms out into the night air, which was considerably cooler.

'That is better. It was rather hot inside,' Lady Sarah said and he helped her into the carriage. 'You are so kind, sir. I thank you for your attention. Please visit me soon. I do need to talk to you quite urgently.'

'I shall call as soon as I return to town.' Daniel looked at her in concern. 'Would you like me to call a doctor for you?'

'No, thank you. It is merely a headache. I shall be quite well once I am at home.'

'I wish you better,' he said and glanced at Eliza sternly. 'Take care of your mistress, Miss Bancroft.'

The coldness in his tone and his manner of address

shocked Eliza. He had never looked at her in quite that way, and she felt his anger once more.

What *had* she done to upset him? Did he think her a fortune hunter, as it seemed others believed?

The question fled her thoughts as she attended to Lady Sarah, finding her smelling salts and then her lozenges in her reticule. Her employer placed a lozenge on her tongue and sat back with a sigh.

Eliza looked at her anxiously. She had not realised how frail Lady Sarah truly was until now. Tears stung her eyes. She would hate to be the cause of so much distress to a woman of whom she was becoming very fond.

Lady Sarah was much recovered in the morning. She declared that it had just been a headache, but Eliza suspected that there was more. However, she did not question her employer—she would surely tell her if she wished her to know.

'I shall stay in bed until noon,' Lady Sarah told her. 'If you wish to go out you must do so, my dear.'

'No, I shall be here if you need me. The Marquis of Cheadle said he would call. He wishes to speak to me, so there is no need for you to get up, ma'am. I dare say it may be something more to do with the hold-up.'

'Yes, quite possibly—or simply the invitation to his daughter's ball. If I am needed, I shall come down.'

Eliza assured her she would let her know if the marquis had some message for her.

Cheadle came at eleven o'clock precisely and was shown into the parlour. Eliza rose to her feet, dropping a respectful curtsy.

'Miss Bancroft. I heard Lady Sarah was unwell last evening. Has she recovered?'

'She is better this morning, but resting. I can take a message to her if you wish.'

'No, my business is with you.' His eyes narrowed. 'Who are you, Miss Bancroft—and how well do you know Lord Seaton?'

Eliza was astonished by his questions and by the tone of his voice. She thought that he was accusing her of something

'Forgive me, sir. I do not see the reason for your enquiry. You know very well who I am.'

'I know your name—but who are your parents? Where did you come from—and what are you after?' His mouth was hard, his tone harsh. 'If you have blackmail in mind, you should address me. Lady Sarah is too vulnerable.'

His harsh tone sent cold shivers down her spine. 'Forgive me, I do not understand you.'

'No? Then why is the whole of Bath whispering that you are Lady Sarah's daughter?'

'Oh…' Eliza drew a deep breath. 'I assure you I did not begin this rumour, sir.' She hesitated, then, 'However, I know Lady Sarah's story…she told me of her child and the way her husband treated her so cruelly.'

'I suggest that you knew it before you inveigled your way into her employment—that you are a schemer and planned this whole thing.' She saw him reach for the little finger of his right hand.

'No, sir, you mistake the matter. I assure you I knew nothing until the day you spoke to me about the hold-up and—' She gave a cry of surprise as she saw the ring he was wearing on his little finger. 'Your ring, sir—may I see it?'

'What significance can my ring hold for you?'

Eliza hesitated, then, 'Please wait one moment, sir. I have something to show you.'

She hurried from the room, rushing up the stairs to her own bedchamber, where she hunted in her drawer and then took out the ring that had lain for years in Mrs Bancroft's sewing box. Running back down to the parlour, she held it out to him.

'When I was a baby, the Reverend Bancroft found me in the church. He took me home and he and his wife brought me up as their own. Before she died, my adoptive mother told me about this ring, which she said she found amongst my clothes when I was given to her. It is, I think similar to your own…' Her heart raced and for a moment she hoped that she might be about to discover the secret of her birth.

The marquis took the ring, looked at it suspiciously, his gaze narrowing. The colour left his face as he read the message inside it. She saw a flash of anger in his eyes and his voice was cold as he spoke. 'Why should I know anything of it? It is just a ring—similar to the one I wear, I grant you, but I dare say many rings are made in this fashion. If you think to blackmail me, I must tell you that I shall not allow it. You may think that the way to reach me is through Marianne, but I make a bad enemy, Miss Bancroft.'

'I am perfectly certain that you would, sir,' Eliza replied, sounding calmer than she felt. 'I would never blackmail anyone and I would certainly do nothing that might blight Lady Marianne's chance of marrying well. It is, I am sure, mere coincidence that I was adopted. I do not claim to be Lady Sarah's lost daughter—or yours— and I have said nothing to her. Clearly I am not her lost child—I understand that her baby was adopted in the proper fashion and that you have paid for its upkeep. My parents received nothing, and as I told you, I was found in the church.'

'I am not sure exactly what Lady Sarah told you...' For a moment he looked uncertain.

'I have already said too much,' Eliza replied proudly, raising her head. Her eyes met his unflinchingly. 'Even if I had some claim on the man who was my natural father, I should not make it. I had hoped to shed some light on an old mystery, but I see you cannot help me.' She held out her hand. 'My ring, if you please.'

'I shall keep it for the moment,' he said. 'Your story will be investigated, Miss Bancroft. If I discover you are in league with someone else to ruin me, or to prey on someone who is dear to me, I shall see that you end your days in prison. You will say nothing of our conversation to Lady Sarah. You would do well to leave her employ and forget your dreams of riches.'

'You are insulting, sir.' Eliza raised her head proudly. 'I ask for nothing but the truth. If you know more than you reveal and are my father, please tell me and I shall not trouble you again.'

'Spread such a rumour and you will find yourself in trouble. I am not Lady Sarah...'

The marquis turned and walked from the room, leaving Eliza to stare after him with tears in her eyes. He had made his feelings very clear. He thought her a scheming adventuress. His reaction to her ring was so violent that she was certain he had recognised it. His anger and allusions to blackmail seemed to indicate that he had a guilty secret to hide. He had advised her to leave Lady Sarah's employ—why? Was it possible after all that she was their lovechild?

No, no, how could that be? The circumstances were similar, but not the same. Lady Sarah's child had been adopted—Eliza had been found in a church. Yet the sight of her ring had undoubtedly affected the marquis. He had refused to return it to her—why? Was he afraid that she would show it to Lady Sarah?

Eliza's thoughts were in turmoil, for she did not know what to believe. The marquis was clearly guilty about something—but what? If he was her father, he was not prepared to admit it.

He had told her that she would be wise to leave her employment. He had threatened her with exposure and imprisonment, but she had done nothing, made no claim on him or Lady Sarah.

Eliza's eyes felt heavy with tears. How could she stay here now?

Refusing to give into her emotions, Eliza went up the stairs to Lady Sarah's room. At the first opportunity she would find an excuse to leave, but not until she was sure the woman she had come to love as a second mother was quite well.

Lady Sarah was sitting up in bed when she entered with a writing board in front of her. 'Has the marquis gone?'

'Yes. It was just more questions, ma'am. Nothing important.'

'I thought it could not be.' Lady Sarah smiled. 'I am feeling much better. I shall get up now and come down. I think I shall rest quietly at home this afternoon, but I should be grateful if you would go to the library for me and pick up one or two packages. You might wish to do some shopping for yourself.'

'I do need some shoes,' Eliza said. 'I may look and see what I can find.'

'It occurs to me that I have not yet given you your wages, Eliza. Please look in the top drawer of the dressing chest and bring me the box you will find there.'

'You have already given me so much,' Eliza protested. 'I consider myself well paid for what little I do.'

'Nonsense. The clothes are my gift to you.'

Eliza fetched the box and Lady Sarah took out three gold guineas, handing them to her.

'I am sure it should only be two guineas, ma'am.'

'That was when I did not know you. I want you to be happy with me, Eliza, and you need money to buy the things necessary for your stay here. Please run along now, my dear. I shall summon my maid in a few moments.'

'Yes, ma'am.'

Eliza's heart ached. She wished now that she had shown the ring to Lady Sarah. She was certain her employer would have been honest with her either way and she would not now be in this turmoil.

After leaving Lady Sarah to rest, Eliza picked up the parcel of books and went out. As she left the house, she noticed a man standing on the other side of the road. He seemed to be staring at the windows, but as he saw her, he turned away. She frowned, but decided that he was merely loitering.

She returned the books to the lending library, picked up some medicine for Lady Sarah, and visited a shop selling good quality shoes, buying a pair of smart boots with shiny buttons that would replace her old ones for walking out. As she left the shop and turned to her right, she saw a group of ladies and gentlemen approaching.

'Miss Bancroft,' she was addressed by Susanne Roberts. 'Have you been shopping?'

'Good afternoon, Miss Roberts. Yes, I have been buying some shoes.'

'You will be able to buy whatever you need now, I suppose,' the girl said with a sneer on her lips. 'How fortunate for you to be taken up by Lady Sarah. She treats you almost as a daughter, does she not?'

The words were accompanied by a snigger that made Eliza's blood run cold. She saw the spiteful look that accompanied the comment and knew that the other girl disliked her very much. Perhaps she blamed her because Lord Seaton had not come up to scratch?

'I am indeed fortunate in my employer,' Eliza replied with dignity. 'Excuse me, I must get home.'

'It would not do to keep your...benefactor waiting. You might lose a fortune...'

Eliza's face was hot, but she refused to be drawn by the girl's spiteful words. 'Miss Roberts, I wish you good day.'

She walked on by, her head held high. Inside, she was seething with anger, but she was glad that she had not let herself reply unwisely. She was unaware that one of Miss Roberts's party had broken away and was following her until the man came up with her.

'That was uncalled for,' he said as he drew level. 'I hope you will not think that everyone in Bath is so unkind, Miss Bancroft.'

'Miss Roberts may be feeling a little out of sorts. I dare say she did not mean to be so...rude.'

'Oh, I think she did. She was expecting Lord Seaton to propose until you arrived. I imagine her pride has received a setback.'

'It is not for us to speculate on Miss Roberts's hopes and dreams, Mr Carstairs. Please excuse me, I must get home.'

He placed a hand on her arm, detaining her. 'No need to get on your high horse, Miss Bancroft. I was just trying to be friendly.'

'Thank you, but I am in a hurry.'

She pulled away from him, and saw his quick frown. 'You may inherit Lady Sarah's money when she dies, but Seaton may not be as wealthy as you think…'

Eliza pretended not to hear as she walked on quickly. If this was what she could expect from Bath society, she would be glad to leave. Her eyes stung, but she would not give way to tears of self-pity. It made her cringe to imagine what people were saying of her. Perhaps not everyone was as spiteful as Miss Roberts, but they must all be thinking the same thing.

Feeling upset, Eliza did not notice the man following her.

Her thoughts were distressing, going round and round in her mind as she walked home, her shadow staying just a short distance behind her. Did everyone imagine that she was a designing hussy after Lady Sarah's fortune? She knew the marquis imagined her to be an adventuress. Even Daniel had seemed angered by the rumours. Surely he could not think her so mercenary?

It was a lowering thought and one that upset her far more than Miss Roberts's spiteful words. She wished he was here in Bath with her, instead of away with his friend Hastings. He was perhaps the one person in Bath she could tell about the ring the marquis had taken from her.

Their business with the horses was soon done. Daniel had advised his friend to buy the best three mares, a fine stallion with devil eyes and a wicked temper, and a thoroughbred he believed had potential on the racecourse.

'The chestnut has potential,' Daniel said. 'It is Irish bred, and though you must take what the seller told you with a pinch of salt, I believe you could have a race winner.'

'The fellow swore it was faster than the wind,' Jack said and laughed. 'I shall probably find it is as sluggish as they come and a complete dud, but the mares and that stallion should be good stock.'

'I will wager that the chestnut wins the first race you enter it in at Newmarket.'

'I'll take you up on that,' Jack seized the challenge instantly. 'A hundred guineas it comes last.'

'I'll wager a thousand that it wins.' Daniel grinned at him. 'Put a thousand guineas on it to win for me and I'll pay you from my winnings.'

'You are on,' Jack said and clapped him on the shoulder. 'I suppose I must turn my mind to other matters now. I danced with Marianne Cheadle the other evening. I swear she is the only girl for me, Daniel. Mother has picked out two other pretty girls she thinks suitable, but I cannot think of anyone but Marianne.'

'I believe her family expect an offer from Accrington,' Daniel said. 'If I felt as you do, Jack, I should ask her as soon as we return to Bath. If you leave it, you may be too late.'

'Supposing she turns me down?'

'At least you will know the truth. There is no sense in mooning after her, man. Ask her and be done with it.'

'Yes, you are right,' Jack said and laughed. 'Nothing ventured, nothing gained. What do I owe you for your advice—about the horses?'

'Nothing at all. I hope it was sound—and that the chestnut is what I suspect.'

'Well, we'll soon know. I'll send the horse down to Newmarket with my trainer and we'll give it a try.'

'Do not forget to put that thousand guineas on for me.'

Daniel knew the bet was reckless, but he could cover the bet by the sale of some heirlooms if necessary, jewels left him by his grandmother and deposited in the bank. The remainder of his debts were more difficult. He was beginning to feel that he would have to sell the estate before everything was lost. He supposed that he might buy himself some colours and make his life in the army. He had found it suited him when he served with Wellington, but an army life might not suit Eliza.

He had been toying with the idea of making her an offer. The rumours flying round Bath must have made her position difficult; he had been angry when he discovered what the malicious tongues were saying, especially when he had seen the distinct likeness between her and Marianne Cheadle.

Had Cheadle seen it—and what would he do about it? Daniel was certain the marquis would never acknowledge the relationship. The mystery of Eliza's birth mother remained.

Was it possible that she was Lady Sarah's daughter? He had thought it just a rumour, but for once the gossips might have it right.

Perhaps he ought to bring this business of his cousin's death to a conclusion before he spoke to Eliza. If Marcus had been murdered, the man responsible would not like Daniel's agent poking about—and his own life could be in danger. It would be best to exercise caution for the moment, because he did not wish to endanger Eliza's life.

The thought chilled him. Until this moment he had

not considered that his investigations could endanger anyone but himself. He would need to keep his wits about him—and he certainly could not risk speaking to Eliza for the moment. He must continue as her friend, but nothing more.

Chapter Seven

'Are you certain you feel able to attend Marianne Cheadle's ball this evening?' Eliza asked some days after the unpleasant interview with the marquis. 'I should be quite happy to stay at home and read a book if you are in the least tired.'

'What foolishness is this?' Lady Sarah smiled at her as they parted to change their gowns. 'You should wear your new yellow gown this evening, Eliza. I am pleased that *madame* managed to get it ready in time. You have worn the white twice to the assembly and it is right that you should have a new one for your first private ball.'

'You are so generous,' Eliza felt her throat tighten with unshed tears, but she smiled through them. She had felt more and more emotional these past few days, because she could not help noticing that Lady Sarah seemed frailer than she had at first.

'I like you to look well,' Lady Sarah said and patted her arm. 'If I found my daughter, I should hope that she was as caring and kind as you, Eliza.'

Eliza had to blink back her tears. She must control her emotions and her tears. She longed to tell her employer that she had grown very fond of her, but the marquis would disapprove if he saw any sign that their relationship had grown closer.

Her situation was difficult, but she was determined to put on a brave face. It was important that nothing should distress Lady Sarah. Eliza would bear anything but being a cause of harm to the woman she now thought of as her true mother.

They were greeted by Lady Cheadle and Marianne when they arrived at the ball. The marquis was talking with other guests and did not immediately notice them, but Marianne was friendly.

'I am so glad to see you, Miss Bancroft,' she said. 'I shall hope to have time for a few words in private later.'

Eliza thanked her and moved on into the first reception room. Catching sight of the marquis at that moment, Eliza saw him frown at her and shivered. She sensed that he was angry because she had not taken his advice to leave Bath.

She had shown him her ring on impulse, but now regretted not keeping it hidden. She had been happy with Lady Sarah and in her heart she knew that the chances of finding her mother had always been slim. It would have been better not to quarrel with the marquis.

Ignoring his angry look, Eliza made her way towards where Lady Julia and Kate were standing, talking to some other friends. They greeted her warmly and Kate took her arm, drawing her towards the ballroom. Almost immediately, both girls were besieged by gentlemen asking for dances. It was clear that the rumours flying around Bath had not harmed Eliza's reputation as far as the gentlemen were concerned. Indeed, one or two of them were if anything more attentive to her. She was determined to enjoy herself, putting the knowledge of the marquis's displeasure to the back of her mind.

It was about halfway through the evening when Daniel appeared in the ballroom. Eliza saw him dance with Marianne Cheadle and Susanne Roberts, and then, at last, when she had almost given up hope of his approaching her, he wandered over just before the dance before supper.

'Miss Bancroft,' he said. 'May I dare to hope that you have a free dance this evening?'

Eliza's heart jerked, as she was obliged to shake her head. 'I am sorry, my lord, my card is full. I did not know if you were attending this evening.'

'I was not sure myself,' he told her with an odd smile. 'If you have no free dances, perhaps I may take you into supper?'

'If you could secure a table by the window for Lady Sarah and myself, we should be grateful. It is warm in here and a little fresh air would be welcome.'

'It shall be as you ask. I regret that I shall not have the privilege of dancing with you this evening. Perhaps another time?'

She nodded her head to him as a young man presented himself for the next dance. Smiling, she gave him her hand, feeling a pang of regret as they walked away. When she looked back there was no sign of Daniel. However, when she accompanied Lady Sarah into the supper room, a waiter came to direct them to a pleasant table by the window.

'What can I fetch for you, Lady Sarah?' Eliza asked. 'Would you care for some chicken?'

'Something small,' Lady Sarah replied, but even as Eliza prepared to fetch something from the tasty nibbles on display, a waiter appeared with a selection of dishes. He was followed to the table by Daniel, who was carrying a silver wine bucket filled with ice and a bottle of champagne.

He nodded to the waiter, who set the dishes down, then deposited his wine bucket. 'May I tempt you to some champagne, ladies?'

'Thank you, Lord Seaton,' Lady Sarah said and gave him a chiding look. 'I have been expecting you for some days. I think you have forgotten me.'

'No, I assure you, ma'am,' Daniel said and smiled. 'I have been delayed by business, but I shall visit without fail tomorrow—at what hour would you wish me to call?'

'Would two in the afternoon be convenient? I do not rise before noon these days.'

'It will be quite convenient,' Daniel replied and glanced at Eliza. 'Perhaps you might care to ride one morning, Miss Bancroft?'

'Thank you, sir. Perhaps the day after tomorrow,' Eliza said.

'I shall arrange for the horses.'

She sipped her drink and then ate one of the delicious morsels the waiter had brought for them. Lady Sarah toyed with a tiny salmon parcel and drank some water. She glanced up as the marquis came to their table.

'Lady Sarah, Seaton…Miss Bancroft,' the marquis said and glared at Eliza. 'I trust you are enjoying your evening?'

'Thank you, sir,' Lady Sarah murmured. 'We

have been royally entertained, have we not, Eliza my dear?'

'Yes, ma'am,' Eliza answered, but without looking at the marquis. She dipped her gaze, but when she glanced up the marquis had moved on. Daniel looked at her curiously, bringing warmth to her cheeks. She turned to Lady Sarah. 'Would you excuse me for a moment, Lady Sarah? I think I must go to the rest room.'

'Of course, please do,' Lady Sarah said. 'I may follow in a moment, but I wish for a few words with Lord Seaton.'

Eliza left the table and made her way through the room. She went up the stairs to the room set aside for ladies. There she tidied her hair, glanced in the mirror, availed herself of various facilities and left, intending to go back to Lady Sarah.

As she walked along the hall, she saw the marquis approaching. Since there was no way she could avoid him, she lifted her head, telling herself to be calm and answer politely whatever was said to her. However, before she realised what he was about, he seized her wrist and dragged her into one of the other bedrooms, shutting the door and standing in front of it to prevent her leaving.

'Why have you brought me here?'

'Why did you ignore my advice to leave Bath?' he countered, glaring at her. 'What can you hope to gain by staying here now? I have the ring and shall not return it to you—though I have no idea how you obtained it. Tell me, did you steal it from someone?'

'I was only made aware of its existence just before my mama's death. She told me that she had discovered the ring tucked into my baby clothes. I know nothing more—and I should be glad if you would return the ring to me, sir. It is precious to me.'

'I have not yet managed to verify your story, but be certain I shall find you out if you are lying.'

'I had no reason to lie to you. I have stayed for Lady Sarah's sake, because she needs me.' Eliza lifted her head, challenging him. 'If you truly believed I was lying, I think you would have spoken to Lady Sarah before this, sir. Why are you so afraid of the truth? Believe me, I have no desire to claim kinship with you, sir.'

'Indeed?' His eyes narrowed. 'Surely you wish for something from me—should I acknowledge that your story is true?'

'No, sir. I wish for nothing from you,' Eliza replied coldly. 'If you please, I should like to leave. Lady Sarah will be looking for me.'

'Go, then,' he muttered. 'Be warned that if any of this comes out it will be the worse for you.'

Eliza inclined her head. He stood aside and she opened the door and went out. She almost bumped into Daniel, who put out a hand to steady her.

'Oh, forgive me. I did not see you.' She blinked because her eyes stung with tears.

'Are you all right, Eliza? You look upset…' He took hold of her wrist, delaying her, and was about to say more when the bedroom door opened again and the marquis came out. He looked shocked to see that Eliza was still standing there with Daniel. 'What is going on?' Daniel's eyes narrowed in suspicion. 'Why were you in that room with Cheadle? Eliza—has he harmed you?'

'No, please. He has not harmed me…I must go.' She pulled free of him and fled down the hall, leaving the marquis and Daniel facing each other.

'Damn you, Cheadle,' Daniel said furiously. 'If you

have done anything to harm Miss Bancroft, you will meet me...'

'Do not be a damned idiot,' the marquis said. 'You are far out in your thinking if you imagine that I have seduced her. It is a very different matter.'

'If I thought that, you would be lying on the floor at this moment,' Daniel replied through gritted teeth. 'Do not fool yourself into thinking I have not noticed a likeness between Miss Marianne and Miss Bancroft, Cheadle. You may think it slight, but I saw it and, believe me, it is only a matter of time before others see it too.'

'It is as I imagined. That masquerade with the hold-up was a part of your feud with me,' Cheadle growled. 'You saw the inscription in my ring and she showed you hers—and the two of you planned this together in the hope of blackmailing me, though how you knew that Sarah...' He broke off as he realised that he had betrayed himself. 'You are a rogue and she is your accomplice.'

'Whatever I may be, Miss Bancroft is innocent,' Daniel replied angrily. He reached out and slapped the marquis across the face with a white glove used for dancing. 'You may name your seconds, sir.'

The marquis glared at him. 'Do you deny that you were the rogue that held my coach up recently? Revenge for your father or cousin, I suppose?'

'Whatever I may have done, you are wrong to suspect Miss Bancroft of duplicity,' Daniel said stiffly. 'Do you accept my challenge?'

'If you wish to make a fool of yourself,' Cheadle said. 'I choose pistols and I warn you that I have a deadly aim.' He inclined his head. 'My seconds will call on you in the morning.'

'I name Jack Hastings and Robert Milton as my seconds. I am certain they will oblige me. Good evening, sir.'

Daniel turned on his heel and walked past the marquis. He went down the stairs and out of the house. He had come only for the purpose of dancing with Eliza and had no wish to stay a moment longer. He had not been wrong in his suspicions. Eliza and Marianne Cheadle were half-sisters. The marquis was Eliza's father—but who was her mother?

The gossipmongers had it that Eliza was Lady Sarah's lovechild and from Cheadle's careless slip it would appear that the rumour was true.

Did Eliza suspect the truth? Did Lady Sarah know her companion was her daughter?

She had asked him to call the next day. He was not sure why, but would discover the reason soon enough.

Unaware that a challenge to a duel had been issued, Eliza made her way back to Lady Sarah. They had decided that they would stay for half an hour after supper, and after making sure that Lady Sarah was comfortable, Eliza danced twice more.

She had asked one of the maids to fetch both her and Lady Sarah's cloak when Marianne Cheadle came up to her.

'Are you leaving already, Eliza? I hope I may call you by your name? I have felt that we could be friends...' Marianne blushed. 'Would you meet me tomorrow afternoon please? I need to talk to someone in confidence— and you are the only person I feel I can confide in.'

'Yes, of course, if you wish,' Eliza replied. She remembered that Daniel was calling on Lady Sarah at two and nodded. 'Shall we meet at two—near the lending library? There is a little shop across the road where we could have tea and cakes.'

'Oh, yes, I know it well,' Marianne said and looked relieved. 'Thank you so much. I do not wish to impose—but I do need to talk to someone urgently.'

'I shall be there at two tomorrow,' Eliza promised and on impulse leaned forwards to kiss her cheek. 'Do not look so anxious. If I can help you at all, I shall.'

'Thank you, Eliza.' Marianne pressed her hand. 'I must go, for my partner will be looking for me. I shall see you tomorrow.'

'Yes…' Eliza parted from her as the cloaks were brought, then helped Lady Sarah to put hers on before they left the house together.

'I saw you with Marianne,' Lady Sarah said, looking at her a little oddly. 'She is a pretty girl, is she not? Do you get on well together?'

'Yes, I think so,' Eliza replied. 'I am to meet her tomorrow afternoon at the same time as Lord Seaton is calling on you, ma'am. I hope that will not inconvenience you?'

'No, of course not.' Lady Sarah looked thoughtful. 'You told me your mama died a few months before you placed that advertisement, Eliza. I did not ask you many questions—were you an only child?'

'Yes, ma'am,' Eliza dug her nails into her hands. 'As far as I know…'

Lady Sarah turned her head to stare at her. 'What can you mean by that, Eliza?'

'I was adopted, ma'am. I do not know who my real parents were. The Reverend Bancroft found me in the church one Sunday morning.'

'Indeed?' Lady Sarah gave a little gasp in the darkness. 'Why did you not tell me this before?'

'It did not seem important, ma'am.'

'No, perhaps not...' Lady Sarah murmured. 'Then again, it might be very important indeed.'

Eliza said nothing. She had been forbidden to speak of her quarrel with the marquis and would do nothing that might endanger the woman she had come to love. Lady Sarah would not replace her mama in her heart, but she had become very fond of her. She saw no point in mentioning the ring, because without it she had no proof of anything.

Lady Sarah seemed sunk in thought. When they reached the house in the Crescent she gave her hand to Eliza and it seemed to tremble a little, but not one word more was said on the subject.

'Goodnight, dearest,' Lady Sarah said and kissed her cheek.

'Goodnight. Sleep well, and do not worry about anything.'

'I think I shall sleep soundly.' Lady Sarah smiled at her. 'Indeed, I feel quite remarkably well this evening. Goodnight, my love.'

Eliza saw her to her room, leaving her to the attentive care of her maid, and then went to her own room. She sighed as she undressed—her life seemed so complicated. By agreeing to meet Marianne Cheadle, she would once again antagonise the marquis, for he would imagine that she was trying to ingratiate herself with his family in order to blackmail him. However, Marianne seemed in actual distress and in need of a friend—and if Eliza's suspicions were correct, the girl was her half-sister.

She would meet her and if the marquis did not like it he could take her to task once more, but she doubted there was much he could do. He was clearly afraid that she would ruin his daughter's prospects and his own reputation. The last thing Eliza wanted was to make trouble for anyone.

Eliza's thoughts turned in another direction. What on earth must Daniel have thought when he saw the marquis follow her from that bedroom? He had suspected her of being Cheadle's mistress at the start. He would probably imagine his suspicions were now confirmed.

Getting into bed, Eliza blew out the candle and closed her eyes. Everything was in such a muddle, but there was little she could do to make things right.

The next afternoon Eliza walked briskly through the town and arrived at the lending library at five minutes to two. Marianne was already waiting. Her face lit up with relief when she saw Eliza and she crossed the road to meet her.

'I was afraid you might not come.'

'I should not have agreed had I not wished to oblige you,' Eliza said. 'I think you are very worried. Shall we sit on that bench before we have our tea?'

'Yes, please. I should not wish anyone to overhear what I have to say…' Marianne looked nervous. 'I think you will be very shocked, Eliza.'

'Shall I?' Eliza smiled. 'It would have to be very bad to shock me, Marianne.'

They sat down together. Marianne played with her white gloves for a moment, then took a deep breath.

'I lied to my mother,' she confided. 'Mama is waiting for the Duke of Accrington to come to Bath and make me an offer, but I know that he won't come. You see, he very obligingly proposed in London and I refused him. She would be so angry if she knew, for she particularly told me to make a push to secure him if I could.'

'I do not know the gentleman. Do you not like him, Marianne?'

'He is too old, though not repulsive or unkind,' Mari-anne replied and bit her lip. 'I thought if I said nothing of this to Mama she would forget in time, but now... there is someone I wish to marry...'

'Ah, I see.' Eliza nodded her understanding. 'You wish to marry another gentleman, but you do not dare to confess the truth to your parents.'

'Mama will be furious with me. She had her heart set on Accrington—and Mr Hastings will never be more than a baronet. He has a fortune and is eligible, but he does not compare with a duke in Mama's eyes.'

'Yes, I see.' Eliza saw how troubled she was. 'You have a problem, Marianne. I think you will have to confess, ask your parents to forgive you and hope they will allow you to marry the man you love. Has he proposed?'

'Yes...' Marianne blushed and her eyes lit up, reveal-ing her happiness. 'I liked him in London, but he never gave any sign of liking me enough...and Mama encour-aged the duke. Jack asked me to let him address my father immediately, but I begged him to wait for a little while.' She pleated the fine linen of her green walking gown. 'Do you think I should ruin myself if I ran away to Gretna with Mr Hastings? I think it is the only way, but I am frightened...'

'You must not do anything so rash,' Eliza told her and reached for her hand. 'It would certainly cause a terrible scandal. Your mother might refuse to speak to you again—and your father might come after you and prevent the marriage.'

'Do you think so?' Marianne dabbed a lace kerchief at her eyes, but a tear escaped and trickled down her cheek. 'I love Jack and shall marry no one else, whatever Mama or Papa say.'

'Yet I think you would not wish to be estranged from them both?'

'No, I suppose not…' Marianne gave a little wail. 'What am I to do? I am sure Mama will say I must wait for a better offer—and she will be furious when she discovers I turned the duke down.'

'Yes, I dare say she may,' Eliza said and squeezed her hand gently. 'I think if you talk to your father first—perhaps he might listen, do you not think so? I imagine he is fond of you, is he not?'

'Yes, he is,' Marianne agreed. She was silent for a moment, then inclined her head. 'I shall speak to him this afternoon.' Her head came up defiantly. 'If he refuses permission for Jack to speak to him, I shall elope whether he disowns me or not.'

'I cannot deny you, but I would advise you to think carefully before doing anything rash. Your parents may be a little annoyed for a while, but I am sure they will come round in the end.'

'Do you truly think so?'

'Yes, if they love you. They will not wish to see you unhappy, Marianne. Just be polite and calm and beg your mother's pardon for not telling her before—but if you speak to your father first, he may support you.'

'Thank you so much for advising me,' Marianne said. 'I was sure you would know what I should do. You do not censure me?'

'Not in the least. I would never marry anyone I did not care for and why should you?'

'I shall not,' Marianne said and her face took on an expression of determination. 'Shall we go and have our tea? They make a wonderful truffle cake here…'

Glancing to her right, Eliza saw a man loitering. She frowned—she thought she had seen him hanging around once or twice before. He looked to be the same man she'd seen outside Lady Sarah's house. Could he possibly be following her? She wondered if the marquis had employed an agent to watch her. It was just the sort of thing he might do—which meant that he would soon learn she had met with his daughter.

Well, let him do his worst. She had no intention of leaving Lady Sarah unless she was dismissed.

When, at a quarter past three, Eliza returned to the house, she discovered that Lady Sarah was not alone. Daniel had visited and gone, but another gentleman was waiting. She greeted him with pleasure, for she knew him as Kate's friend.

'How pleasant to see you, Mr Thatcher. Kate told me that you had gone out of town for a day or two?'

'I returned this very morning and, having seen Kate and heard some rumours, came immediately to visit you and Lady Sarah. I have Kate's permission to tell you that we are engaged to be married, Miss Bancroft. It is a long-standing agreement, which we kept to ourselves until Lady Julia was prepared to allow the engagement. I wanted to tell you that both Kate and I support you, as will all of your friends. None of us believe that you are a fortune hunter or an adventuress. When we are married, we shall want both you and Lady Sarah to stay with us in London or the country.'

'Oh…' Eliza's cheeks were warm. 'How kind of you, sir. I am delighted that you and Kate are to marry. I sensed that there was something between you, but Kate did not say.'

'We promised her mama that we would wait until

just before they returned to the country, because Lady Julia wanted her daughter to be quite certain. She is very lovely and there are others with larger fortunes and grand titles that she might have married if she had chosen.'

'Kate would always marry for love, as most young women will if allowed,' Eliza said. 'I am so very pleased for you. I must buy Kate a present and wish her happy.'

'We are having an engagement party tomorrow evening,' Mr Thatcher said. 'It is not a dance, though we shall hold one in the country before the wedding. I came to deliver an invitation and Lady Sarah has been good enough to say she will come both to the party and the dance—and naturally she will bring you, Miss Bancroft. Kate particularly asked that you be there.'

'We shall be happy to celebrate with our friends,' Eliza said. 'What a lovely surprise. I am so very pleased.'

Mr Thatcher thanked her and left them. Eliza sat down as the door closed behind him. She looked at Lady Sarah, whose expression was thoughtful.

'I felt there was something, but Kate kept her word to her mama. She did not breathe a word.'

'Kate is a good girl for all her flirting and her outspoken ways,' Lady Sarah nodded approvingly. 'I have been thinking that we shall go to my home in the country soon, Eliza. Lady Julia and Kate will leave Bath at the end of the week and I think we might go soon after. You will not mind living quietly in the country?'

Eliza hesitated, then. 'You will not need a companion so much in the country, ma'am. I could travel with you to see you settled and then look for a new position when you felt better.'

'I was thinking you might like to make your home with me, Eliza. I am so fond of you…'

'I am very fond of you too, Lady Sarah,' Eliza said. She hesitated, thinking about what her employer was suggesting. If they left Bath the marquis could not accuse her of trying to blackmail him and the gossip would soon be forgotten. He had warned her she should leave, go back where she had come from—but why should she let him bully her? Lady Sarah needed her and she loved her. 'Yes, I should like to stay with you—and I think it might be best if we left Bath soon.'

'We can return next spring for a little visit or perhaps London if I feel well enough,' Lady Sarah said. 'I do not wish to bury you in the country, Eliza. I have friends at home and we shall dine with them often.'

'I do not mind staying quietly at home with you,' Eliza assured her. 'I shall be quite content.'

'I believe we shall stay another five days in Bath and then go home.' Lady Sarah nodded and looked pleased. 'This gossip has been awkward for you, dearest, but it will pass. Next time we visit no one will think there is anything worth remarking in your being my companion. This nonsense will all be forgotten.'

There was a suppressed excitement about Lady Sarah that made Eliza wonder what was in her mind, but she did not ask. Her employer would tell her when she wished her to know. Her mind returned to Marianne Cheadle and her problems.

It would have been nice to confide her fears for the girl she believed might be her half-sister, but Marianne had spoken to Eliza in confidence and she would not betray her secret to anyone.

'We are going to a soirée this evening,' Lady Sarah

said. 'I believe Lady Julia will be there. If you wish to go out again and buy her a small gift, you may do so.'

'Perhaps in the morning,' Eliza said. 'Kate loves poetry, so I think I shall purchase a book of poems for her as a keepsake.'

'That is an excellent idea,' Lady Sarah said. 'I have some items of jewellery in my room that I had as a young girl. Shall we go and look at them together? You can help me choose something suitable.'

'I should enjoy that.' Eliza stood up and offered her arm. 'Did your visit with Lord Seaton go off satisfactorily?'

Lady Sarah's eyes avoided hers as she replied, 'Yes, indeed, he has promised to instruct an agent for me. He says that he knows the very man…the soul of discretion and very reliable. Apparently, this man has been investigating something for him and has turned up some interesting facts. I am confident that my search will be over quite soon.'

'I am glad he could help you.'

'He asked after you, my dear. I believe he was disappointed not to see you.'

'I was sorry to miss him.'

It was for the best. Daniel clearly believed the worst of her. He probably thought she was the Marquis of Cheadle's mistress and had been lying to him all this time. She would not see him again once they left Bath. The thought made her heart ache, but she was determined not to give into her distress. He had shown some friendship towards her but she would be a fool to hope for more—after all, what prospects could she offer Daniel? He could, and would, surely marry any suitable young lady.

Following Lady Sarah into her bedchamber, Eliza

watched as she took her jewel case from the dressing chest and unlocked it with a key she kept in her reticule. Invited to look at a selection of pretty pendants that were, as Lady Sarah said, suitable for a young girl, Eliza pointed to two of them. One was a single teardrop aquamarine suspended from a diamond and a fine silver chain, the other a sapphire-and-pearl drop on a fancy gold chain.

'I think these are both lovely,' Eliza said. 'Either one would I am certain delight Kate.'

'Then I think I shall give her this one.' Lady Sarah selected the sapphire-and-pearl drop. She locked the jewel case, replaced the key in her reticule and gave Eliza the box to place in the dressing chest. 'These pieces are all of more sentimental value than monetary and were given to me by my father and grandmother. The Manners's family heirlooms are kept at home in a strong room. I still wear the pearls I was given as a wedding gift and some rings, but the rest are at the disposal of my son's wife, as it should be.'

Eliza smiled and left her to rest and change for the evening.

As she went to her room, she wondered where Daniel was and what he was doing. Though she knew it was a hopeless situation, he was never far from her thoughts.

'Are you sure you wish to go through with this?' Jack asked as he sat with Daniel in the gentleman's club they both frequented that afternoon. 'Could it not be resolved in some other way? Duels are frowned on these days and rightly so.'

'The challenge has been issued and accepted. Neither of us can withdraw. Besides, there are things between us…' Daniel frowned. 'My uncle believed that Cheadle had some part in his son's death. I dare say that coloured my opinion of him and I may have allowed it to lead me astray. I am satisfied that Cheadle was not concerned in the affair. It is true that my cousin's death was almost certainly not an accident. My agent, Mr Smith, as he calls himself for professional reasons, is investigating something, which will I believe lead us to the culprits.'

'Cheadle is no angel,' Jack said thoughtfully. 'I would never try to paint him as blameless, but he is the father of the girl I wish to marry. It is dashed awkward, Daniel. I can hardly ask him for his daughter's hand and then be present when you try to blow his brains out.'

'You do not imagine I shall shoot to kill?' Daniel raised his brows. 'If it is awkward for you, Jack, I will ask someone else—perhaps Thatcher or Smythe…'

'Damn it, I never said I wouldn't stand with you,' Jack said, looking affronted. 'Of course I shall oblige you. I must just hope that Cheadle understands there is nothing personal.'

'I dare say I shall fire in the air,' Daniel said. 'I was furious when I threw the challenge, but since then…I have a suspicion that we might be in a similar boat, my friend.'

'What do you mean?' Jack frowned. 'You are not thinking of Lady Marianne?'

'Good lord, no,' Daniel said and grinned. 'She is a lovely girl, but not for me. It is no good looking at me like that, Jack. I'm not absolutely sure of my facts as yet, and even if I were I couldn't tell you.'

Jack frowned, then nodded. 'I thought you rather liked Miss Bancroft. If there is any truth in the rumours about her and Lady Sarah, she must also have a father…?'

'You are surmising, as I am for the moment,' Daniel said. 'But I mean to get to the bottom of the mystery very soon.'

'Then why go through with this stupid duel?'

'Because I cannot withdraw,' Daniel said with a wry laugh. 'Do not worry. I shall fire in the air and I imagine he will do the same.'

'Well, I still think it would be better if the stupid affair was resolved peaceably, but if you are determined…'

'I think there is no alternative,' Daniel said, looking grim. 'I must just hope that it can be resolved between us like gentlemen.'

Chapter Eight

Eliza saw him at once as soon as they entered the room where Lady Austin was holding her soirée. He was standing with a small group of ladies and gentlemen, none of whom was known to Eliza. She met his eyes for a fleeting moment and saw his quick frown. Daniel's appearance at an affair of this sort was a little surprising—she would not have thought he would enjoy such an evening. When he left his friends and approached her a little later, he told her that he was looking forward to hearing the Italian tenor who was to perform for them.

'I cannot stay long, but I hope to hear Signor Rinaldi sing an aria or two,' he said. 'Do you enjoy opera, Eliza?'

'I enjoy all kinds of music, sir,' she replied, her heart fluttering. When he looked at her so intently, she felt all her good intentions slipping away. Was it possible that he didn't think the worst of her? 'I think we should take our seats for the music is beginning.'

'Yes, of course. Pray let me find a seat for you, Eliza—and Lady Sarah.'

'Yes... Oh, I believe she is sitting with friends. Perhaps we should sit here at the back. I think all the front seats are taken.'

'I do not need to see him only to hear his voice.'

'Yes. I have heard that it is remarkable—' Eliza began, but he leaned forwards and put a finger to her lips as the first notes sounded. Her heart pounded as she gazed into his eyes and for a moment she almost thought he was going to kiss her, but of course he would not in public.

She made a supreme effort and withdrew her gaze, staring at the back of a lady's head. She was wearing a huge concoction of lace and flowers, which completely blocked Eliza's view of the guest of honour. However, she soon discovered that Daniel was right. She did not need to see to appreciate the beauty of Signor Rinaldi's powerful voice.

The music was so moving that she felt tears sting her eyes and she gulped. The emotions she had been trying to control for some time welled up in her as the foolish tears slipped down her cheeks. Then she felt his hand cover hers. She glanced at him and his smile was so tender that she gasped.

'Yes, he had that effect on me the first time,' Daniel whispered. 'Magnificent is the word that comes to mind.'

Eliza nodded wordlessly. He offered her a spotless white kerchief, which she dabbed to her eyes and then used to blow her nose.

'I shall return it washed,' she whispered and he nodded, continuing to hold her free hand.

Eliza liked the comfort it gave her, though as the

first aria drew to an end he removed his hand in order to applaud. Afterwards, she almost wished he hadn't, though he had stood to applaud, as some of the other guests had.

'I must leave now,' he said to Eliza as there were calls for more from the tenor. 'I am not sure that I shall be able to keep my appointment to ride in the morning, but I will be there if I can.'

Eliza turned her head to watch as he walked from the room. How very strange! What had he meant by that remark?

She turned her head to watch him leave. He glanced back at her and the look in his eyes made her heart stop and then race on.

What could possibly stop him from keeping his appointment if he wished? Maybe he still had doubts about her, after all. Their conversation had been polite, though when he'd held her hand and then later smiled at her so tenderly she could have sworn that there was something deeper between them. What should she believe?

Eliza dressed the next morning in the riding habit Lady Sarah had given her. She was downstairs in the parlour at nine and sat there waiting patiently until a quarter to noon, when she went upstairs to change into a more suitable gown.

Why had Daniel not kept his appointment to go riding? Had he not been so attentive and kind the previous evening she would have thought he was still angry with her. However, he had all but made love to her at Lady Austin's soirée. It was perhaps foolish of her to have taken such pleasure in the attentions he had paid her, but a part of her did not want to think he had broken his appointment deliberately.

Still, it was Lady Sarah's last At Home day in Bath. Eliza could not leave her alone and even if she had it would not have been proper for her to go to Daniel's lodgings. However, she could not help feeling that something was wrong, and sat down at the writing desk to pen a polite note of enquiry, which she asked one of the footmen to deliver for her at the hotel where she knew Daniel to be staying.

After that, she was kept busy entertaining friends who called. She looked for the footman who had delivered her note, but did not see him. When she asked, she was told that it was Frederick's night off.

Eliza was forced to put her anxiety behind her. She dressed for the evening and wrapped the small book of poems she had managed to purchase for a betrothal present for Kate by walking quickly to the corner bookshop and back after their guests had gone.

Lady Sarah had wrapped the pendant she intended to give Kate, and they left for the evening at just before seven.

Eliza greeted Kate with a kiss. Her happiness shone out of her as she stood by Mr Thatcher's side.

'I would have told *you*,' she said to Eliza as she kissed her. 'But Mama particularly asked me not to tell anyone until the end of our stay in Bath. I think she thought I might change my mind, but of course I did no such thing.'

'I guessed there was something when you bid Mr Thatcher to dance with me, but I did not guess your secret,' Eliza said. 'I like him very much and I believe you have chosen well.'

'I am glad you like him,' Kate said and kissed her on the cheek. 'I want us to be friends always. Henry said that if ever you needed a home you would be welcome to stay with us.'

'How kind of you both,' Eliza said. 'Lady Sarah wants me to make my home with her and I shall. I am so very fond of her.'

'I think she loves you,' Kate said, hesitated as if she would say more, then shook her head. She was forced to let Eliza move on as more guests arrived.

Eliza went into the large reception room. Footmen were circulating with trays of champagne and tiny morsels to tempt the appetite before supper. Accepting a glass, she looked about her hopefully but there was no sign of Daniel Seaton. She was sure that Kate would have invited him and thought it strange he was not there, particularly as she saw Mr Hastings. He was standing with another gentleman and some ladies, but left them to greet a newcomer.

Eliza saw him go up to Marianne Cheadle and talk to her urgently. Marianne seemed distressed, for she shook her head and walked away, leaving the gentleman staring after her. Seeing Marianne make her way out on to the balcony, Eliza went after her.

'Marianne—is something the matter?'

Marianne turned to her with tears in her eyes. 'Eliza—it is all so awful! I spoke to Papa, as you suggested, and he promised to think about it. He even said that Mr Hastings could approach him, but now it has all gone wrong. '

'What happened?' Eliza asked and a chill ran down her spine. 'Please, do tell me.'

'Papa fought a stupid duel with Lord Seaton,' Marianne blurted out. 'Jack was Lord Seaton's second and... now my father will not see him.'

'A duel?' Eliza felt cold all over. 'Was anyone hurt?'

'I do not know. Papa would not say. He was angry and went out again without speaking to me or Mama. She has no idea what happened or she would not have allowed me to come this evening.'

'This is terrible,' Eliza said and pressed her hand. 'I am so sorry. It must be upsetting for you, but I dare say your father will relent in time.'

'He said we are going home the day after tomorrow,' Marianne said, tears in her eyes. 'I shall not go. I have told Jack we must elope tomorrow if he loves me. He said we must not, but I shall insist.'

'Marianne, you really ought not.'

'You do not know Papa. He is very angry.' Marianne blinked back her tears. 'I tried it your way, but now I shall have no choice but to elope. It will just serve Papa right. Why did he want to fight a stupid duel anyway?'

Eliza shook her head. She was feeling a little sick inside, because she was afraid that the duel might be because of what Daniel had seen that night at his daughter's dance.

As Jack came out on to the balcony, Eliza gave him a speaking look and went into the reception room. She was joined by Kate, who asked if something was wrong and why she was frowning.

'Oh, nothing very much,' Eliza said and smiled at her. 'Tell me how long you have known Mr Thatcher and what made you fall in love with him?'

The subject was turned instantly. Kate began to sing the praises of her fiancé and Eliza did her best to say the right things at the right moment. She was terrified that something bad had happened to Daniel Seaton, but could not mention the duel or say anything that would taint her friend's happiness.

Was Daniel alone and in pain? Surely he was not dead? They would have heard by now.

Her heart thumped painfully as she feared the worst and then dismissed it. She would find out in the morning, but for now she must behave as if nothing were wrong for Kate's sake.

Eliza did not notice either Jack or Marianne return to the room as the evening wore on and wondered where they had gone. Surely Jack had not been reckless enough to give into the pleading of the girl he loved?

When Lady Cheadle came up to her later and asked if she had seen Marianne, she denied it.

'I have searched everywhere. No one has seen her for hours.'

'I was speaking to her earlier. I believe she had a headache. Perhaps she went home?' Eliza crossed her fingers, feeling uncomfortable.

'Without consulting me?' Lady Cheadle looked angry. 'My daughter has better manners than you seem to imagine, Miss Bancroft.' The lady frowned at her. 'Unless you have been putting ideas into her head?'

'No, not at all,' Eliza denied. 'I am sorry, but it might be better not to make a fuss. You may find her at home.'

'Indeed? It seems to me that you know more of this than you will say, miss. The marquis will have something to say on the matter. You have not heard the last of this, believe me.'

'Forgive me, but whatever Marianne may have done, she did not do it on my advice.'

'You have not heard the last of this, Miss Bancroft. If Marianne is not at home with a headache, you may expect a visit from my husband.'

'As you wish, ma'am,' Eliza said. 'I truly hope you will find her in bed at home.'

Eliza sighed as the woman left. She had enough problems without being accused of something she had not done.

Lady Sarah came up to her a moment later. She looked puzzled.

'Lady Cheadle seemed angry, Eliza. Is something wrong?'

'She could not find her daughter and thought I might know where she was.'

'Do you?'

'I am not sure,' Eliza replied. 'I may not tell you, Lady Sarah. Marianne spoke to me in confidence yesterday and this evening. I advised patience, but I fear she may have been reckless.'

'I do hope she has not done anything foolish, my dear. Say goodnight to Kate, Eliza. You may not see her again for a while. I dare say she will be busy before they leave.'

Eliza obeyed. Kate hugged her and said she would keep in touch, and then they were out in the carriage and driving home.

Eliza saw Lady Sarah comfortably settled and then went to her own room. She found a note lying on her dressing table and tore it open. It had come from the footman she had asked to deliver her note earlier that day. He had returned from a visit to his family and informed her in a note that the gentleman in question was injured,

The doctor told me the wound was not fatal, but there might be a fever. I thought you would wish to know, he had written.

Eliza scanned the rest of the note. It told her very little, except that Daniel was hurt. She glanced at the clock beside her bed. The hour was late, past eleven, but she knew she could not rest without finding out more.

Slipping out of her evening gown, Eliza dressed in a plain grey gown and a dark pelisse. She could easily walk to the hotel where Daniel was staying and it would take but a moment to enquire about his condition.

She did not wait to leave a note for Lady Sarah, because she would be home again before anyone knew she was gone. Leaving by a side door, she pocketed the key so that she could return without disturbing anyone.

Her heart was racing as she walked swiftly through dark streets. The hotel was partially in darkness, but inside the porter was dozing in his chair. He woke with a start as she approached him and sprang to his feet.

'I've been waiting for you all day, miss,' he said accusingly. 'The physician said he would send a nurse for the gentleman, but you're late.'

Eliza's heart thudded. It was on the tip of her tongue to tell him of his error but if Daniel needed a nurse she could not simply walk away.

'I had another patient,' she said in a low voice. 'Please take me to him.'

'You'll need this, then.' He thrust a chamberstick with a lighted candle at her.

Following the porter, who continued to mutter and grumble all the way, Eliza was feeling so nervous that her nails dug into the palms of her hands. At last he stopped outside a door, unlocked it and gestured for her to go in. Eliza did so. The room was almost in darkness, though some light entered through the open curtains. She went to the dressing chest and lit the candle from the one she was carrying. With two candles there was sufficient light to see the man lying in the bed. She approached with some trepidation, looking down at Daniel in concern. At once she saw that he was sweating, his face flushed. It was obvious that he had a fever.

'Oh, my poor love,' Eliza said as she saw that he was heavily bandaged over his shoulder. 'What did that wicked devil do to you?'

Eliza felt the sting of tears. She glanced about her and saw a jug and bowl on the washstand. She went across to it and poured some water into the bowl, carrying it back to the bed. Setting it down on the table by the bed, she saw a neckcloth lying near by. She dipped it in the cool water and began to bathe Daniel's head. She soothed the cloth down over his arms and hands, hesitating before turning the covers back to his waist. Wringing the cloth out once more, she began to wipe the sweat from Daniel's body.

When she had finished drying his body, Daniel seemed a little easier. Eliza began to take more notice of her surroundings. She discovered a small dark bottle on the dressing chest and a note giving instructions as to its use. Clearly the doctor had left instructions for the nurse who had not arrived.

Eliza measured the medicine into a small cup. She returned to the bed and pondered how best to give him the mixture. Sitting on the edge of the bed, she slipped an arm beneath his head and lifted it.

'Swallow this for me, my love,' Eliza said. 'It will do you good.'

Amazingly, his lips parted and she held the cup to

his mouth, tipping it so that the mixture trickled on to his tongue drop by drop and watched him swallow. He sighed as she eased him back against the pillows.

'Forgive me, Mama…' Daniel murmured. 'Didn't mean to bring shame on the family.'

'You have not,' Eliza soothed and stroked his hair. 'It was not your fault, dearest.'

Daniel's eyes closed. She laid her hand on his brow. Was he a little easier?

She bent over him, pressing her lips to his. 'Please get better, Daniel. I could not bear it if you died…' She stroked his forehead, tears trickling down her cheeks. 'I love you so very much.'

Daniel did not answer. He was sleeping, she thought, peacefully. Eliza glanced at his pocket watch, which lay on the table by the bed. It was almost midnight. She could not leave him yet. She must at least stay until she was certain the fever was waning. He seemed cooler now, but it could return and then he might die.

Eliza knew that she must go before it was morning. If anyone saw her leaving the hotel, her reputation would be finished.

She brought a chair that stood by the writing desk in the window and sat down, feeling sleepy. She would just watch over him for a while.

Daniel cried out in his sleep. 'Do not leave me… please…'

'I am with you,' Eliza said and took his hand. 'I love you, my dearest one. I have loved you almost from the moment we met.'

It was such a foolish confession and one she could never have made had he not been in a fever and unable to understand what she was saying. She sat on the edge of the bed as his fingers curled round hers, holding her firm. Smiling, she shifted a little and found a space to lie beside him, still letting him hold her hand. She smiled as she felt his warmth and snuggled nearer, her love surrounding him, willing him to recover and be well again. It felt so right to be here with him, even though she was aware that if the slightest hint of her reckless behaviour were to be known, she would be ruined. It did not matter. All that mattered at this moment was that Daniel should be well again.

She would rest for a little and then she would leave before anyone was about.

'You should have watched over your daughter, madam.' Cheadle glared at his wife. 'You were her chaperon. How could you have allowed her to go missing for hours without wondering what had happened?'

'Do not blame me, sir. You have spoiled the gel,' Lady Cheadle said. 'From this note I infer that you knew she had turned down Accrington and wished to marry the rogue who has run off with her?'

'She spoke to me yesterday. I had intended to speak to Hastings, but…something happened. I was angry and may have given her to understand that I would not now speak to him.'

'And what does that mean?' his wife demanded. 'You blame me, but it may be your fault she has run away with this man?'

'If she has…' Cheadle frowned. 'What makes you think that Miss Bancroft knows something of this?'

'She and Marianne have been as thick as thieves,' Lady Cheadle said with a scowl of dislike. 'I suppose you know what some of the gossips are saying about her?'

He frowned. 'I heard that she was a secret heiress and might be related to Lady Sarah Manners.'

'And who might be the bastard's father?' Lady Cheadle accused. 'I am not a fool, sir. I have seen the likeness when she and Marianne stand together. I knew soon after we married that there was someone else, but I did not guess until recently who she was—the woman you could never forget.'

'You would be unwise to voice your suspicions outside this room for your daughter's sake.'

'Marianne has ruined herself.' She shook the note that had been delivered to the house minutes earlier that morning in his face. 'She has gone with her lover. No one of any consequences will marry her now.'

'I shall fetch them back if they have gone to Gretna.'

'Of what use will that be once this is known?'

'No one needs to know,' Cheadle said. 'Show some sense for once, madam, and we may yet come out of this with some credit. If Marianne has been dishonoured, the rogue will marry her—but we shall keep this to ourselves. A wedding will be announced and we shall brush through as best we can. Whatever my daughter has done, I do not wish to see her ruined.'

'This is all your fault,' Lady Cheadle said. 'If you had not spoiled her—been a better example to your daughter—she would not have disgraced us.'

'Watch your tongue, madam. I have put up with your sourness for Marianne's sake, but no more. We shall come to some arrangement as soon as I have settled this matter.'

'Where are you going?' she demanded as he walked to the door.

'To ask Miss Bancroft if she knows anything of Marianne's plans,' he said. 'For your own sake, madam, keep this to yourself until we know the truth.'

He gave her a last look of disgust and went out, the door slamming behind him.

Daniel woke to a feeling of soreness in his shoulder, then became aware that he was not alone. Turning his head, he saw the woman lying beside him, her hair rumpled and her face flushed in sleep. He felt a rush of desire, experiencing an overwhelming need to take her into his arms and make love to her. How beautiful Eliza was as she slept, but what was she doing here? He frowned as he wondered how it happened, trying to remember, but recalling nothing after he was shot. He considered waking her, then she stirred, gave a little moan and woke up. For a moment her eyes were wide and startled, and then she smiled. She did not immediately pull away, but lay looking at him, her eyes still hazy with sleep, so delicious that he could barely refrain from making love to her. Her smile wrenched at his insides, making him aware of many things. Not least of how very special she was.

'You are awake. I thought the fever might come back. How are you? Does your shoulder hurt very much?'

Daniel controlled the hunger within. 'No, not too much. What are you doing here?'

'I heard about the duel. I came to the hotel late last night and the porter thought I was the nurse. I gave you some medicine and sat with you, but you would not let go of my hand so I lay down beside you. I must have fallen asleep. I fear I am not a very good nurse.'

'Forgive me. Had I known you were here, I should have sent you home hours ago.'

'The time…' Eliza rolled over and looked at his pocket watch. She gave a little cry and scrambled off the bed, suddenly aware that she had slept for hours.

'It is past nine. I must get back. Lady Sarah might ask for me. If it is discovered that I am missing, she will be worried.'

'Yes, you must go immediately.' He frowned as she hesitated, clearly worried for him. 'It was but a scratch, Eliza. I can manage, believe me. I have suffered worse.'

'Why did you fight Cheadle? Was he wounded, too?'

'I fired in the air and so did he,' Daniel said. 'I have no idea where the shot came from. Jack said he thought he caught sight of a figure in the trees. I do not know why someone would try to kill me, but no doubt I have acquired an enemy.'

'Then it was not the marquis who shot you?'

'No. I remember that he apologised before I passed out. Jack must have settled things afterwards and brought me here. I have no memory of anything…except that I thought of my mother…' His eyes narrowed, as he remembered something from his fever. 'You soothed me, didn't you? Thank you, Eliza. I wish you could stay to continue to nurse me, but you must leave at once. I promise I will call when I am recovered.'

'Yes, I must go.' Eliza smiled. 'Please take care— especially if you have an enemy.'

She resisted the temptation to touch him or kiss him. If she did not hurry, the maids would know she had not slept in her bed all night.

Eliza ran all the way home. She let herself in with her key and hurried upstairs. She changed into a fresh gown and had just finished tidying her hair when someone knocked at her door.

'Yes, what is it?' she asked, pulses racing.

The door opened and one of the maids looked in. 'I
am sorry to disturb you this early, Miss Bancroft, but
the Marquis of Cheadle is downstairs in the parlour. He
is insisting on speaking to you.'

Eliza glanced in the mirror, her heart beat slowing to
a normal pace. It seemed that she had managed to escape
detection. 'Thank you, Mary. I shall come at once.'

Eliza was thoughtful as she went down to the parlour.
She was certain that the marquis had come to blame her
for encouraging his daughter to elope. Facing his anger
was a daunting prospect, but she had weathered previous
bitter encounters with him and was determined to stay
strong.

She paused outside the parlour door for one moment,
then lifted her head and went in. The marquis was standing at the far side of the large room, staring out into the
gardens, his back towards her. He did not seem aware
of her until she spoke.

'You wished to see me, sir?'

'Yes…' He walked towards her and she saw the
uncertainty and doubt in his expression. 'I tell you this
in confidence, Miss Bancroft. Marianne has gone off
with Mr Hastings. She sent a note in which she blamed
me for making her life impossible. She said that I was
not to look for her, because she would not be where I
would expect to find her.'

A little gasp escaped Eliza. She had feared as much
and wished that she had been more persuasive the previous evening for Marianne's sake.

'I am sorry that your daughter has run away, but I
believe she will be quite safe with Mr Hastings. I know
that he did not wish to elope, but she must have found a
way to persuade him. I feel sure that he truly loves her.'

'A man in love will do foolish things to please the

woman he cares for above his life.' The marquis looked oddly humble. 'I fear that it is my own behaviour that pushed my daughter to the edge.'

'Yes, perhaps.' Eliza was surprised. She had expected him to rage at her. 'I have not often met Mr Hastings, sir—but I do not think he would harm Marianne.'

'You have no idea where they went?'

'Marianne talked of going to Gretna Green, but I told her it was unwise…' Eliza was thoughtful. 'Her note seems to dispute that, does it not?' She hesitated, then, 'There is one person who might know where Mr Hastings would take her…'

'You mean Lord Seaton, of course.' The marquis's brow darkened and she thought he would speak to her sharply, but he drew a deep breath. 'It will not set well with my pride to ask anything of Seaton, but for my daughter's sake I shall do what must be done.'

'I do not think you will find Lord Seaton unwilling to assist you in any way he can, sir—when he is able, of course.'

'You know, then, that he has been wounded? I have not heard how he goes on. I shall enquire and ask if he will see me.'

'Marianne told me about the duel, sir.' Eliza's eyes did not meet his squarely, for she knew more than she ought to about Daniel's condition.

Cheadle sighed. 'Yes, she would. It seems my daughter recognised what I refused to acknowledge, Miss Bancroft. She told me that she had sought your advice, because you seemed to be someone she could trust. I think she recognised the kinship between you. She also told me that you had advised her to tell me the truth.'

Eliza's heart jerked painfully. She was not certain

she understood him correctly. 'I am not sure what you are saying, my lord?'

'The ring you showed me was given by me to the woman I loved above all others. I would have taken disgrace and ruin if she would have come away with me, but she would not allow me to sacrifice myself for her. I have never loved anyone else—except for Marianne.'

'I see...' Eliza's throat constricted with emotion, the tears rushing to her eyes. 'Thank you for telling me. I thought it might be so, but I was not completely sure.'

'Seaton told you about the ring he took from me at the card table, of course...' Eliza hesitated, looking at him warily. 'You do not trust me and I cannot blame you. I had worked it out in my mind—I knew you were holding back when you related the circumstances of the strange incident with the highwayman. I was furious because I thought it an elaborate plan to blackmail me.'

'I assure you, nothing was further from my mind, sir.'

'I know the truth now. Seaton wanted to warn you and came up with his ridiculous plan to hold up the coach, not knowing if I would be with you. Do not fear, Eliza. I have no intention of giving Seaton up to the authorities. I see that I have perhaps deserved all that has happened. My behaviour has not been what it ought for years.'

Eliza nodded her understanding. 'Lady Sarah told me that you were not as black as rumour would have it—and my own observations have led me to the same conclusions. A man completely lost to all decency would not care so very deeply for his daughter's reputation and happiness.'

A nerve flicked at his temple. He was silent for a moment before he replied, 'I hardly deserve such consideration from you, Eliza. I have bullied and denied you. You ought to hate me.'

'I do not know you, sir. It would be hasty to judge a man on a few conversations, particularly as I understood why you were angry.'

'You did?'

'You were angry for more than one reason, but I believe the foremost was that you felt I wished to take advantage of Lady Sarah's good nature, did you not?' He inclined his head and she smiled. 'That means you still care for her very much. Since I love her dearly, I could hardly hate you for trying to protect her.'

Cheadle turned away abruptly. He walked to the window and stood for some seconds staring out at the garden. Beneath the exquisite cut of his blue superfine, his shoulders were tense. Without turning, he said, 'You *are* my daughter. I sent someone to question the lawyer who dealt with the business of your adoption. He tried to refuse me, but I offered sufficient inducement to help him change his mind. He is a scoundrel. Instead of giving you to an honest family, he left you in the church and took my money for his own use for years. I have threatened him with arrest and he has taken hasty retirement, though to expose him would cause a scandal I wish to avoid if possible.'

'How wicked he must be!'

'You are not surprised. You had suspected it…ah, you think I bribed and corrupted a man against his will. Let me put your mind at rest, Eliza. No force was used. He is of retiring age and the money I offered was not insignificant.'

'I see…' She smiled a trifle ruefully. 'It is hardly surprising that he refused to answer Lady Sarah's letter.'

'I have found there are few that cannot be bought—but

I believe I met my match in you, Eliza.' A little smile entered his eyes. 'I think you take after me rather than your mother.'

'Yes, perhaps. I believe I have learned to stand up to whatever knocks life sends my way.'

The smile left his eyes. 'Were you harshly treated? I am sorry that I did not set myself to discover your whereabouts before. I was angry and bitter—and then there seemed no point.'

'Until I turned up and you feared I might ruin Marianne's chances.'

'I dare say you will never forgive me for the things I said?'

'On the contrary, sir. I do not see the merit in holding a grudge. My life was happy for the whole of my childhood. It became harder when Papa died and Mama took the move to the cottage so badly. She went into a decline from which nothing would rouse her—but I loved her and I took care of her until she died. I was then fortunate to catch the notice of Lady Sarah, who has been kindness itself to me.'

'You have not told her who you are?'

'I could not, for I had no proof. Besides, I did not wish to distress her.'

'I shall return your ring to you,' Cheadle said. 'It is locked in my safe and I did not think to bring it this morning. Would you like me to break the news to her?'

'I think you have quite enough troubles at the moment,' Eliza replied with a smile. 'I am glad that you have told me the truth, sir, but I am in no hurry to tell the rest of society. I would not harm Marianne or my mother for the world. When we are in the country I shall find the right moment to speak to my mother, and if you would write a letter and confirm the truth if she asks it of you, that will suffice.'

'How did you become so wise and so patient?' The marquis frowned at her. 'I have no right to expect anything of you, but it would be easier if you did not announce it to the world at all—though of course I cannot stop you if you wish.'

'I shall ask Lady Sarah her wishes on the matter. For myself, I do not mind if no one ever knows. To find my mother is such a wonderful thing—something I never expected would happen. To know that she cares for me even without knowing the truth is more than I could ever ask.'

'You humble me, Eliza,' the marquis said and sounded so sincere that her throat caught. 'I do not ask anything of you, but perhaps one day I may do something for you.'

'I expect nothing, sir. Do not feel that you are obliged in any way. I have no claim on you.'

'Do you not?' He laughed softly. 'Perhaps you have more claim than you imagine.' He shook his head as her brows lifted. 'I shall leave you now, but I may call when you are settled in the country.'

Eliza waited until he had gone, then went up the stairs to her mother's room. Oh, how good that felt, to know after all these years: to know she had always been loved and not simply abandoned.

Lady Sarah was sitting up against her pillows, sipping a cup of the bitter dark chocolate she took in the mornings.

'Eliza, I was wondering where you were. Maisie told me you were not in your room when she brought you a tray earlier. Did you go out for a walk, dearest?'

'I have always enjoyed walking early,' Eliza replied,

for she did not wish to lie. 'I have something I ought to tell you in confidence, Lady Sarah. The marquis was here just now. Marianne has eloped with Mr Hastings—except that I do not think he will have taken her to Gretna Green. The marquis asked if I knew where they had gone. I suggested that Lord Seaton might have some idea where Mr Hastings might take her. They are, after all, very close friends.'

'You think they have not gone to Gretna—do you suppose they have gone to France or somewhere else abroad?'

'I was thinking Mr Hastings might have taken her to someone he trusts. I do not know the gentleman well, but he seemed honourable and honest. I believe he would not wish to harm Marianne or her reputation.'

'Cheadle will be most upset. He has doted on that girl, spoiled her, I dare say.'

'Yes, I imagine he has. She was all he had in the world. When she is married he will miss her.'

'We must hope that she will marry.' Lady Sarah looked thoughtful. 'I do hope a scandal will be avoided for Marianne's sake, if not her family's.'

'I suggested that Lord Seaton might know where his friend would be likely to take the woman he loves.'

'An excellent suggestion. We must be careful what we say. If anyone asks where she is, it may be best to say we think she has been unwell.'

'I imagine the marquis will find some reason for his daughter's absence,' Eliza said. 'Now, if there are any errands I may run for you, Lady Sarah, I shall be happy to do so.'

'I think that perhaps you ought to return our books to the lending library. If left to the last moment, they are sometimes overlooked and incur a fine.'

'Yes, perhaps I should,' Eliza agreed. 'I shall start to pack my belongings this evening. If you would like me to assist your maid by packing some of the smaller items—' She was interrupted by a knock at the bedroom door.

'Come in,' Lady Sarah called and her maid entered. 'Yes, Maisie, what is it?'

'Lord Manners has arrived. He told me he would not disturb you before noon, but wished you to know he has come to stay for a few days.'

'Indeed?' Lady Sarah frowned. 'How typical of Howard not to let me know in advance. Well, we shall not alter our plans for him, Eliza. He must just say what he has to say and leave. I imagine he has come to scold me for some reason.'

'Surely not,' Eliza said as the maid went out. 'Lord Manners must visit because he is fond of you.'

'He is usually too busy enjoying himself in London.' Lady Sarah frowned. 'Take the books and go out, Eliza. Speak to no one of what you know, and do not return until just before noon. I wish to speak to my son before you do.'

'He will not upset you? Perhaps I should remain here in case you need me?'

'No, my dearest. I shall hear what he has to say in private. You may come to the parlour when you return— but find some way of amusing yourself for the next few hours. I am sure you would like to try to see Kate before we leave?'

'Yes, I should. If you are certain?'

'Quite certain, my love. Off you go. My son is not my keeper, even if he thinks it.'

Eliza left her. She felt anxious as she went down stairs and out into the street. It was clear that Lady Sarah thought her son had come to scold her, but surely he would not be deliberately unkind? He must know that his mother's health was fragile.

She had an uneasy feeling as she left the house, but then she put it away from her. Eliza had been told to stay away until nearly noon and she must do as she was bid.

Chapter Nine

Daniel had managed to dress in breeches and a shirt when a porter came to his room and announced that a gentleman was downstairs and wishing to speak with him.

'Who is it?' he said. His shoulder was painful, for it had been a struggle to dress alone. It was damned annoying that he had sent his valet to his uncle with a message; he could have done with some assistance. He had no idea how he would have managed if Eliza had not come to his rescue when he was in the fever—and that was a damned coil. If she had been seen leaving...

'He gave his name as the Marquis of Cheadle, sir.'

'Damn him,' Daniel muttered and rubbed at his shoulder. 'Well, he may as well come up.'

If Cheadle had wanted to kill him he could have done it during their duel. Daniel closed his eyes for a moment. He had finished the medicine the doctor had given him and did not wish for more. His shoulder was painful, but it would ease, though the bandages probably needed changing. He might ask for the physician to call once more.

A light tap at the door heralded the marquis's arrival. He entered on Daniel's invitation and stood looking at him in silence for a moment.

'I am glad to see you out of bed, though perhaps you ought not to overdo things just yet.'

'Forgive me if I do not get up.'

'Please do not try. Your wound must be painful.'

'It was merely a scratch. Whoever shot me was not a marksman.'

'Have you any ideas as to why you were shot?'

Daniel considered for a moment in silence, then, 'I have been thinking hard and the only possible explanation I can think of is that, as you know, I have recently been investigating my cousin's death.'

The marquis gave him a steely look. 'I warned you to take care, Seaton. Kettleton and his cronies are a dangerous crew.'

'I knew it, but I did not imagine anything was likely to happen in Bath. I doubt it was Kettleton himself. He has probably had someone watching me in the hope of catching me unawares.'

'I am sure you are right. He is too cautious and would pay to have his dirty work done for him.'

'A duel was the perfect moment, for I was expecting the shot from you, not someone behind me. Tell me, sir, what may I do for you? Do you wish for another chance to shoot me?'

Cheadle frowned. 'I come here this morning to ask a favour of you, sir, not to quarrel with you. In confidence, I must tell you that my daughter Marianne has run away with Mr Hastings. I wondered if you knew where he lives—and where he might take her?'

'The damned idiot!' Daniel exclaimed. 'I told him to make a push for her, but I did not expect him to do something this rash. I apologise for Jack, sir. It is not like him.'

'I rather think it was my daughter's idea, but I am entirely to blame. I had promised to hear him and then I changed my mind…'

'Because of the duel? That was dashed awkward for him. He did not wish to anger you, but he could not refuse me.'

'I should not have let it upset me, but I had other things on my mind,' Cheadle replied. 'I have it on good authority that my daughter had to persuade Mr Hastings. Miss Bancroft seems to think they will not have gone to Gretna.'

'I doubt Jack would want a hole-in-the-corner affair, sir.' Daniel rubbed at his shoulder. 'His mother would never forgive him. She is a bit of a scold… He has always rather liked his godmother, for she understands him.' He nodded and then smiled. 'Lady Runcton lives in Newmarket. I know for a fact that Jack has bought some horses, which he has sent to Newmarket. He plans to race a horse there shortly. I believe Jack would take her there. Jack is all for a peaceful life, sir. He may hope to placate Marianne *and* win you over to his cause. I think he will write to you from Newmarket.'

'You think he took her to his godmother?' Cheadle stared at him, hope dawning in his eyes. 'That would be perfectly appropriate if they were engaged…'

'Just so, sir.' Daniel raised his brows. 'With a little accommodation on your part no one need know anything untoward.'

'I shall go to Newmarket at once, if you will furnish me with the lady's address.'

'Yes, of course.' Daniel said. 'If you would oblige me by bringing my writing slope?'

'Thank you for your help. I appreciate your confidence in the matter of my daughter.'

Daniel frowned as the marquis went out. He hoped he had done right in giving Cheadle Lady Runcton's direction. If Jack and Cheadle could sort things out between them, Marianne's reputation might yet be saved. The reflection made him think of Eliza. He must hope that she had not been seen leaving his hotel at past nine in the morning. He had begun to remember things, though hazily and without certainty. He was sure that Eliza had done things for him that no unmarried woman should do for a man who was not a member of his family, and it hardened his resolve.

Had he been able, he would have paid Eliza a visit and then posted down to Newmarket himself. However, his shoulder was too painful and he must spend at least another day resting in his room. He reached for the bell to summon the porter. Another visit from the doctor who had tended him would not go amiss.

'You will write to me?' Kate asked as she kissed Eliza's cheek. 'And you promise to come to my ball and my wedding?'

'Yes, of course. I would not miss it for the world,' Eliza said and hugged her. 'I hope we shall always be friends, Kate.'

'Yes, well, we shall,' Kate told her. 'We leave first thing tomorrow and the wedding will be in one month. I shall send your invitation to Lady Sarah's home.'

'We go home in three days.' Eliza smiled as she took her leave. 'I am glad to have seen you again, dearest. As your father's estate is not so very far, we shall easily be able to visit you. It is all very fortunate for you, Kate. You look so happy and I know that Mr Thatcher loves you very much.'

'I am so lucky, but one day you will be too, Eliza. I have always thought Lord Seaton liked you very well.'

'I think perhaps we can only ever be friends,' Eliza said and thought of the moment when she had opened her eyes and discovered him looking at her as she lay by his side. 'I shall leave you now, but I will write soon.'

Eliza's thoughts were troubled as she walked home. Who could have shot Daniel if it was not the marquis? He had dismissed it lightly, but she found it concerning. If the rogue's shot had not gone wide, Daniel might have been killed.

She was wondering whether she dared to risk another visit to his room when she walked into the house and heard the sound of raised voices. One of them belonged to a man, the other to Lady Sarah.

'Please do not insult my intelligence, Howard. Eliza is not what you seem to imagine.'

'The gossipmongers have it that she is your bastard and that you intend to leave her your fortune. You must see that I have reason to be concerned?'

'I really do not see why, Howard. Even if Eliza were my daughter, and should I leave my fortune to someone other than you, you have your father's estate.'

'That is beside the point, Mama. You know very well that I am concerned for your reputation. Besides, it is deuced expensive to live in town. If you have money to spare, you should think of my wife and your grandchildren.'

'I shall not be told where to leave my money, Howard. Your father controlled my money while he lived. You may not do the same.'

'Mother...confound it. You know it isn't just about the money...'

Silence ensued and Eliza took the opportunity to enter the parlour. Her eyes went first to Lady Sarah, for she feared that the quarrel might have upset her. However, she seemed to be in control of her emotions and the situation. Looking next at the gentleman, she saw a large thickset man with dark hair and brown eyes. His mouth was drawn into a thin line and he was staring at her with obvious resentment.

'Are you in need of anything, ma'am?' Eliza asked. 'May I do anything for you?'

'You may leave us alone,' the gentleman said rudely. 'We were having a private conversation and you are not welcome, Miss Bancroft—or whatever your name is.'

'You have it correctly, sir.' Eliza faced him calmly. She felt like a tigress protecting her young and would have flown at him with tooth and claw had she not known that would prove more upsetting for her mother. 'I believe I am addressing Lord Manners? I am Lady Sarah's companion and it is my duty to look after her... which I shall certainly do until she dismisses me.'

'Eliza dearest, I am glad you are back. Did you have a pleasant visit with Kate?'

'Yes, thank you, ma'am. She has promised to write and insists that we attend her wedding, which I assured her we should.' She heard a mutter of exasperation from Lord Manners, but ignored it. 'May I do anything for you?'

'Nuncheon will be served in the small dining room. Give me your arm, Eliza. I am hungry. Will you be joining us, Howard?'

'No, Mother. I have some business in town.' He glared at Eliza. 'I should like to speak to you in private when

I return, Miss Bancroft. My mother may be satisfied to take you without a reference, but I shall require at least one.'

'I am sure the Earl of Standish would be happy to supply a reference should it be needed,' Eliza said sweetly. 'Ma'am, shall we have our nuncheon?'

She offered her arm to her mother, feeling the slight tremble of her hand as Lady Sarah leaned on her. Nodding coolly to Lord Manners, she passed him without another look.

In the dining parlour, Lady Sarah sat down in her favourite chair by the open window. She had clearly been more upset by the quarrel with her son than she was prepared to show.

'I believe we have lemon sole with scallops in white wine sauce, minted peas and creamed potatoes today, Eliza. I shall try to eat a little, for it is a favourite dish. Would you serve it for me, please?'

'Yes, of course,' Eliza said. It was their custom to serve themselves from the hot dishes under silver covers on the sideboard and she quite often attended Lady Sarah.

'Thank you, my dear. You know just how I like things.'

Eliza smiled. She had understood from the start that Lady Sarah's appetite was not large and needed to be tempted. Small portions attractively arranged were more enticing to the invalid palate than huge meals.

'I am so fortunate to have you,' Lady Sarah said as the plate was placed in front of her. 'No wine for me, my dear. I should like a little barley water—but please have wine yourself.'

'I would prefer barley water,' Eliza said as she poured the drink and then returned to the sideboard to choose her own food. 'Does Lord Manners intend to stay long?'

'I do hope he will not stay more than the one night,' Lady Sarah replied. 'He was always a noisy boisterous child. I did not have the heart to have him beaten, you see—though his tutor caned him on my husband's orders more than once. Perhaps if I had asserted my authority when he was younger...' A sigh escaped her. 'We shall not speak of him, Eliza. Have you any shopping to do before we leave Bath?'

'I think I have all I need, ma'am. Is there anything you need?'

'Yes, there are one or two things,' Lady Sarah replied. 'I ordered some shoes, which should be ready this afternoon, and there are one or two other small things I have remembered. I have left a list on my dressing table. You will need six guineas to purchase the shoes and you should take another four with you to pay for the other items. You know where my box is...' Lady Sarah took the key from her reticule and placed it on the table.

Eliza pocketed the key and promised she would go after nuncheon. They talked about Kate's wedding for the remainder of the meal, discussing the clothes they would need and what gift they should give the bride.

'I think I shall give her silver,' Lady Sarah said. 'I shall send it as a present from us both, Eliza. However, if you want to buy her a small present of your own, you may take your wage for next month.'

'I shall not need to,' Eliza said. 'Mrs Bancroft left me some beautiful lace. It had been handed down in my father's family. I have several pieces and I think I shall pick two that are rather fine and give Kate those. She can use them to trim a gown or whatever she wishes.'

'That is a lovely idea.' Lady Sarah smiled at her. 'If

you have finished your meal run along upstairs and fetch the list. I shall not bother to come with you, my love.'

Eliza did as she was told. She went into her mother's bedchamber and crossed to the dressing chest. Opening the top drawer, she took out the box containing Lady Sarah's money. She counted out ten guineas and locked the box before returning it to the drawer, sliding it in beside the leather jewellery box that she knew contained the things that her mother considered sentimental rather than valuable. Closing the drawer, she left the room and went downstairs to the parlour, where she returned the key to Lady Sarah.

'I shall not be more than two hours,' Eliza said. 'Is there anything I may fetch you before I leave?'

'I have my netting box,' Lady Sarah replied. 'I shall be perfectly content here until you return.'

Eliza nodded and left her to sit with her work, though she knew that her mother would probably spend most of her time looking out at the garden. Lady Sarah enjoyed watching the birds that came to drink and bathe in the little fountain just outside the parlour window.

It was a pleasant afternoon, and Eliza enjoyed the walk to the shoemaker's. She paid for Lady Sarah's order, then left the little shop, pausing to look in the window of a fashionable milliner before moving on to pick up the various items she was to purchase for her mother.

It was as she was on her way home that she happened to meet Miss Susanne Roberts. The young lady was walking with two friends and Eliza could not avoid them unless she crossed the road, which would have seemed rude.

'Good afternoon, Miss Roberts.' She inclined her head politely.

'Miss Bancroft. I hear you are leaving Bath soon…'
Miss Roberts smirked at her. 'No doubt you have heard
the latest tale. *You* are quite surpassed by the shocking
elopement of Miss Cheadle.'

Eliza held her breath, counting to ten before she
smiled. 'Is that the latest foolish tale to circulate? How
people love to invent things. For your information, Miss
Roberts, Miss Cheadle has gone to stay with friends. I
believe she is engaged, though she told me in confidence
and perhaps I should not say…'

Smiling to herself, Eliza walked on. She laughed
inside as she caught the crestfallen look on the spiteful young woman's face. Crossing her gloved fingers,
she hoped that Marianne was indeed safe and about
to be engaged to Mr Hastings. However, the only way
to nip an unpleasant rumour in the bud was to start
another, which she hoped would have sufficient cre-
dence to at least throw doubt on the story of Marianne's
elopement.

Returning to the house, she discovered that Lady
Sarah had gone up to her room to rest and Lord Manners was standing before the window, staring out at
the garden. He turned as she entered, giving her a hard
look.

'I have been waiting for you, Miss Bancroft.'

'Indeed, sir? Forgive me. I have been out.'

'You seem to have a great deal of freedom for a
companion?'

'I was on errands for Lady Sarah, sir. However, you
are correct in thinking she is very kind to me.'

'You have a way of talking that no doubt inspires
confidence in the unwary and particularly vulnerable
ladies of a certain age—but I know you for what you
are, miss. I am warning you that I shall not tolerate this

situation. My mother has become attached to you and will not let you go—but you should leave while you can.'

'I do not understand, sir.'

'I know you are not as you seem.' Lord Manners moved towards her, glaring down at her. 'I have heard the rumours concerning you, Miss Bancroft. If you imagine that I shall allow you to steal what belongs to me you are much mistaken. I do not know who you are, but I shall be watching you. Make one slip and I shall have you out of here before you can blink. Your kind belong behind bars and that is where you will end if I have any say in the matter.'

Eliza's heart sank. She had endured this once from the marquis. He had apologised to her, but now it seemed she had another enemy.

Lord Manners imagined that she was an adventuress and hoping to cheat him of a fortune that should go to him and his children.

'I am sorry that you should think so ill of me,' Eliza said. She lifted her head proudly, meeting his angry gaze. 'I am very fond of Lady Sarah. I shall do nothing to bring her harm. Believe me, I have her best interests at heart and I am not interested in her fortune.'

'Oh, yes, you would say that,' he grunted. 'Allow me to inform you of something you may not know, Miss Bancroft. My mother is intending to return to her home soon. Well, the Dower House belongs to me. It is a part of the estate. Should there be any truth in the rumour that you are her lovechild, I shall have no hesitation in following my father's instructions. If she acknowledges anyone as her daughter or takes her daughter to live with her—or gives her any part of her fortune—she will lose her widow's jointure and her home.' He laughed harshly as he saw Eliza's face pale. 'Yes, that makes you think, does it not? Oh, I grant you, she still has this house in Bath and money my father could not touch—but she would hate to live here all the time. So think about that and make plans for your future, Miss Bancroft.'

'You could not be so cruel?' Eliza gasped as she saw the malice in his face. 'How could you threaten your own mother with the loss of her home?'

'My father made it a condition in his will,' Lord Manners said, though she saw a flicker of unease in his eyes. 'If you care for her at all you will think very carefully, Miss Bancroft. I intend to make enquiries and if I discover that you are my mother's bastard I shall know how to act.'

Eliza turned away, going out of the room and up the stairs without another word. Her heart was aching. She was caught in a patch of thorns. Lady Sarah loved her. She needed her. How could Eliza leave her—and yet the threat was real.

If Lord Manners discovered the truth, he would force his mother to leave her home and that might have terrible consequences, for living in town was too tiring for her.

Eliza heard from Maisie that Lord Manners had left the next morning for London. She was glad that she did not have to see him again, but she felt that a shadow was hanging over her.

She had said nothing of his threat to Lady Sarah, but she was uneasy in her mind. It was likely that the truth would come out in time and that could mean ruin and heartbreak for Lady Sarah.

Perhaps it might be best if Eliza found some excuse to leave once Lady Sarah was settled in the country. It would break her heart to leave her mother now that she had found her, but she must do what was best for the woman she loved.

She could not leave her yet.

In all the turmoil of packing and the threat from Lord Manners, Eliza had not been able to dwell on Daniel's plight. She had hoped he might call during their last day, but he had not done so and she hesitated to write. If he had wanted to see her he would no doubt have sent word, even if he could not come in person.

She thought wryly that Daniel was the one person in Bath who did not imagine her to be an heiress. The look in his eyes as they had lain side by side for a moment that morning had told her that he was not indifferent. Her heart ached because she knew that she might never see him again, but she told herself that it was for the best. Had he cared sufficiently, he would no doubt have spoken before this—but even though she was the child of gentlefolk, she was also a bastard.

Daniel had a proud name and he would want a girl of good background for his wife.

'Is everything packed, dearest?' Lady Sarah asked as Eliza came into her room just as she fastened her hat with a long pin the next morning. 'I should hate to get home and discover that we had left something behind, though to be sure it is a journey of no more than thirty miles.'

'The maids have been looking everywhere, under cushions and in drawers. I believe everything we shall not need is in the trunks, ma'am, and I have a portmanteau with all the little things we may need on the journey.'

'Do you have the powders my doctor delivered yesterday?'

'Yes, I have one in my reticule just in case and there is water in the basket with our refreshments. The others are packed in your little trunk with your jewels.'

'That will go inside the carriage with us.' Lady Sarah sighed. 'I am always so nervous when I travel, though there is really no need. As I said, it is but thirty miles to my son's estate, but it might as well be a hundred.'

'You have me to look after you this time,' Eliza said and smiled at her. 'There is no need to be nervous, ma'am. I am sure everything will go smoothly.'

'I do hope so. I hate it when something breaks on the carriage—and I should hate to be held up by a highwayman, as you were, dearest.'

'I am sure nothing of the sort will happen.'

'Very well, then, we should go,' Lady Sarah picked up her reticule and looked around her. 'Have I left anything?'

'Your gloves and your fan.' Eliza picked them up. 'I shall bring them for you. You need not fear to lose them.'

'You are such a comfort to me.' Lady Sarah sighed and left the room, going carefully down the stairs. The housekeeper was waiting downstairs to say goodbye and was rewarded with a guinea and thanks for looking after them. 'You will not forget, Mrs Browne, I left a letter for Lord Seaton, should he call. You will see that he receives it?'

'Yes, my lady, certainly. The maids have their instructions. I wish you a good journey. All the staff hope that you will visit again one day soon. We have been pleased to serve you.'

Lady Sarah thanked them and went out, followed by Eliza, who also stopped to thank the housekeeper.

Outside, she looked about her. The weather was cooler and there was a hint of rain in the air. She saw Lady Sarah settled in the carriage and climbed in beside her, taking a last look down the street. It was foolish to hope. Lord Seaton obviously had no intention of calling—unless he was ill again...

Eliza scolded herself for the ridiculous notion that he would attempt to see her before she left town. However, as they were driven away she caught sight of a blue coat from the corner of her eye and, sitting forwards to look back, thought the gentleman standing outside the door of Lady Sarah's house might just be Daniel. He had called too late and would be told that he had just missed them.

Daniel swore beneath his breath when he was told that he had almost caught Lady Sarah and Eliza.

'They have but this minute left the house,' the house-keeper told him. 'Please step in for a moment, sir. Her ladyship left a letter for you. She asked me to be sure and give it to you, should you call.'

'Thank you. I should be glad to have it.'

Daniel waited in the hall while the woman fetched the letter. The house had that empty feeling, which comes when the owner is not at home, and he cursed himself for not coming sooner. His wound had troubled him more than he had anticipated and his doctor had advised rest. Even now he was disobeying orders—he had been told to rest for another three days at least—but his impatience to see Eliza had brought him here—only to discover it was too late.

Why had she not told him she was leaving town?

The answer was plain enough. He had given her no reason to think that it would matter to him one way or the other. He should have told her that morning after discovering that she had nursed him through his fever. Daniel cursed himself for a fool. He could offer her very little, because he would have a thousand or two at best once his father's debts were paid. If, however, she was willing to marry him and become an officer's wife, living in rented accommodation when they were billeted in a garrison town, or abroad, he would strive to make a better life for them.

But for now he had the pressing issue of his father's debts to resolve. He intended to post up to London to arrange for the deeds to his property to be taken from the bank and lodged with his lawyer. Meanwhile, Cheadle was in Newmarket with his daughter. Daniel had had a brief note from the marquis, telling him all was well.

I can hardly thank you enough for your help. I believe we shall brush through this affair with the minimum of scandal. Lady Runcton is a formidable lady and has made it known that it was by long-standing arrangement that her godson brought his fiancée to see her before announcing their intention to wed. It seems you knew your friend well and he is indeed a suitable husband for my daughter. I am glad to see her happy and I hope you will attend her engagement ball. I shall also be asking Miss Bancroft and Lady Sarah. I shall expect to see you there. I have a proposition for you.

Daniel left the house in the Crescent feeling thoughtful. His resentment against Cheadle had gone for some reason. It had been based on his belief that his father was cheated at the tables, but he had begun to realise that perhaps the late Lord Seaton's careless play had been at fault. He must sell his estate, of course. Perhaps Cheadle had guessed he was in trouble and wished to buy it?

First he needed to clear up this business of his cousin's murder. Daniel's agent must have disturbed a wasps' nest when ferreting around for the truth. If someone had risked attempting another murder, he must have a great deal to hide. The would-be assassin had run off at once. No one had caught more than a glimpse of him.

Daniel must go to London and speak with his agent personally. He wanted this cleared up soon, because until then he could not risk publicly announcing his intention to marry Eliza. As far as he knew, no one had any inkling of his feelings for her, which meant that she was safe, but once their engagement was announced— should she have him—Eliza's life might be at risk.

He would not feel certain of her safety until the villain was behind bars or dead, but as he still had outstanding business with Lady Sarah, surely it couldn't do any harm to call upon her and Eliza in the country on his way back from London?

Chapter Ten

Eliza had been to the village to take her letter to Kate and three letters from Lady Sarah to her friends to the receiving office. It had cost sixpence to send her own letter for she had crossed her lines in order to get as much on the page as possible.

Lord Manners's estate was huge and the Dower House was some distance from the main house, which meant that they did not have to meet the family unless they wished. At the moment Lady Sarah's son was in London. Eliza had allowed the feeling of peace and serenity to ease her mind.

Perhaps Lord Manners would not carry out his threat to make her leave his mother's employ. *Her mother, too.* Eliza felt her throat constrict. She must not give way to the temptation to tell Lady Sarah the truth, because if she did so Lord Manners would force her to leave her home.

Eliza had observed how much better her mother was now they were settled in the country. They had been home for ten days and with each passing day she saw Lady Sarah grow stronger. It was evident that she would suffer greatly if she were forced to live in Bath the whole time. The Dower House was comfortable, but not large and they needed few servants to run it. If Lady Sarah was denied her jointure, she might find it hard to maintain her house in Bath, where many more servants were needed.

Eliza knew that she would have no choice but to leave if Lord Manners renewed his threats. It was as she turned off towards the Dower House that she saw a carriage and four heading towards the main house. Her heart sank, because she knew that if it meant that Lord Manners had come to visit she might soon have to leave.

As yet she had not considered where she might go. Betty had told her there would always be a home for her with them, but it would not be right to impose for longer than need be. She would have to look for a new job as soon as she could, which meant she would need a reference. It would be hard to ask her mother, because she would not understand why Eliza needed to leave.

Tears stung the back of her eyes, but she blinked them away. She would have to think of some excuse, perhaps explain that a friend was ill or something of the sort.

How could she leave without telling her mother that she loved her?

If Lady Sarah knew the truth she would not allow her to go—and then she would lose everything.

What was she to do for the best?

'I have heard from Lord Manners,' Lady Sarah told her that evening. 'He has come down with some friends and is to give a large dinner for our neighbours. He requests that we attend, Eliza—and he has sent me the rubies that belonged to his grandmother to wear tomorrow evening.'

'Oh…' Eliza was surprised. 'Are you sure I was invited?'

'Yes, of course. Howard knows that I should not go without you. He may not have liked the gossip in Bath, but we are home now and, as I told him, it will soon be forgotten.'

'Yes, I suppose,' Eliza said and smiled. Perhaps Lord Manners had thought better of his threat. 'I shall be happy to accompany you. It must be an important dinner or he would not have sent you the rubies.'

'I wish he had not bothered. I much prefer my pearls, but I suppose I must wear them as he has requested it.'

'Which gown will you wear, ma'am?'

'I think the grey silk. That is trimmed with dark crimson knots and will set the rubies off well, though they do not become me. I would rather have worn the diamonds or the emeralds.'

'I dare say they are very valuable,' Eliza said. 'You must not leave your jewel case unlocked, ma'am. I know your servants would not touch anything, but it would not do to lose them.'

'You are very right to remind me,' Lady Sarah said. 'It is one of the reasons I seldom ask for anything from my son's strongroom. My pearls are my own; though I should hate to lose them, it would make no difference to anyone.'

'What should I wear?' Eliza asked. 'Would the yellow or the lilac be more suitable for a dinner at Mannington Park?'

'I think perhaps the lilac,' Lady Sarah replied. 'I

shall not sit up late this evening since we are to dine out tomorrow. If you wish to stay up please do, but I shall retire with a book.'

'I shall do the same, ma'am,' Eliza said and kissed her.

She went to bed feeling happier. Perhaps she would not have to leave after all.

Daniel saw her walking through the trees towards him the following morning. He had been to the Dower House, spoken to various people, and stabled his horse, walking back towards the village in the hope of meeting her. Eliza had, he knew, been to the village to see if there were any letters waiting at the receiving office. It was something she did every morning. His heart to heart with Lady Sarah had cleared up many things and left that lady glowing with happiness.

'Miss Bancroft,' he said and saw her startled look turn swiftly to pleasure. 'I hope I did not frighten you?' He smiled, feeling pleasure in the sight of her.

'No, indeed, sir. Have you been to the house? Lady Sarah was, I know, hoping for a letter from you.'

'I came personally to give her some good news,' he said. 'I am sorry not to have come before, but there was a great deal needing my attention.'

'I am sure she was glad to see you, as I am.'

'I have been making arrangements to sell my estate. I have released a small amount of capital from a venture that has nothing to do with the estate and I shall purchase a commission in the Hussars. I believe the army life may suit me, though the pay will not be what I have been used to in the way of income. However, I must cut my coat according to my cloth.'

'I am sorry you are to lose your estate.'

'My father's debts were impossible to meet,' Daniel said. He moved nearer, gazing down at her. 'I have been thinking of the life I might have, Eliza. It will not be one of plenty, but I believe I should have enough to purchase a small cottage when I leave the army—or before if my wife should need a settled home.'

'Your wife?' Eliza swallowed hard. 'Am I to wish you happy, sir?'

'You will make me very happy if you will accept me as your husband, Eliza. I am sorry I can offer you so little, but I find that nothing else will content me but to make you my wife.'

'You…wish to marry me?' Eliza stared at him, her heart racing. 'I…are you perfectly certain, sir? Do you know what you are saying? I may have things in my past, things that would shame you—and your family.'

'I care for no one's opinion but my own,' Daniel said. 'Besides, I know exactly who you are, Eliza. I suspected something when I saw you with Marianne Cheadle in Bath, but I could not be sure. However, I heard from my agent two days ago and I think it is certain. I have spoken to Lady Sarah and told her the good news. You are her daughter—which I am sure you must have suspected after Cheadle's behaviour.'

'You have told my mother?' Eliza stared at him in horror. 'Oh, I wish you had not. You have no idea of what you have done. Why did you not speak to me before telling her?'

Daniel was puzzled. 'I do not understand you, Eliza. Lady Sarah particularly asked me to find her daughter. She told me that she had a feeling you might be her lost child, but she had no way of proving it. Her reaction to the news was very different. She was delighted with the report that proves your connection.'

'I have known it for a while,' Eliza told him and sighed. 'The Marquis of Cheadle was furious, because he thought I might be an adventuress and he believed my mother vulnerable. He threatened me, but then withdrew his threats when he learned that I had tried to help Marianne. He had also discovered the truth and in the end merely asked if I would keep his secret.'

'Then why have you not told her?'

'Lord Manners is not so forbearing. He has threatened my mother if she acknowledges me, which she will do now that she knows the truth.'

'How can Manners threaten Lady Sarah?' Daniel was puzzled. 'He is her son…'

'He will follow the terms of her husband's will and turn her out of the Dower House. She will also lose her jointure.' Eliza threw a despairing look at him. 'We must hurry back, because the news may have overset her.'

'Forgive me. I had no idea about the terms of her husband's will. Surely her son will not carry it out? It would be unnecessarily cruel.'

'You did not hear what he said to me.' Eliza looked at him, tears in her eyes. 'Please, I cannot answer your very obliging offer now. I must return to my mother.'

'I shall come with you.'

'No, I would rather you did not,' Eliza said. 'Would you meet me here tomorrow morning please? I shall have my answer for you then—but I would rather see my mother alone.'

Daniel caught her wrist. He looked at her for a moment, then brought her into his arms. He bent his head to kiss her, his mouth soft and yet hungry on hers. For a moment she allowed him to hold her, swept away by the heady feeling that his kiss inspired.

When he let her go, she gazed up at him in wonder.

'I wanted you to know that I love you,' he murmured huskily. 'Whatever happens, I will look after you—and your mother, if she is in trouble. I am not sure how, but if necessary I shall ask my uncle for assistance. He might make one of his country houses available to her.'

'How good you are to say it,' Eliza said and smiled. 'But she would not hear of it. She has the house in Bath—though I know she loves her home. Forgive me, I must go to her.'

He held her fingers to the last as she trailed them through his hands. He stood, watching her as she ran in the direction of the Dower House, until he could no longer see her. His horse was stabled at the Dower House, but he would not follow her just yet. Instead, he would walk down to the village and take a room for the night at the inn.

As he walked away, Daniel's mind was concentrated on Eliza. He had no idea that they had been watched and their conversation overheard.

Lady Sarah stood up as Eliza rushed into the parlour. Her face was glowing and she was a picture of happiness as she opened her arms wide.

'Eliza, my love. I have wonderful news for you...'

'Lord Seaton should not have told you just like that,' Eliza said and caught a sob. 'I was afraid it might have been too much of a shock...that you might be ill.'

'Come here to me, my love.' Lady Sarah received her with a gentle hug and a kiss. 'How long have you known that you were my lost daughter?'

'I had a ring... I was told it was similar to one the marquis owned and when you told me your story I suspected it. Then I saw the marquis's ring on his finger and showed him my ring, but he thought I was lying.

He accused me of trying to take advantage of your good nature.'

'How could he say such a thing to his own daughter? I shall have something to say to him when we next meet. He knew how much I longed for you, my dearest child.' Lady Sarah's eyes were moist as she drew her daughter to the sofa and they both sat down. 'I felt a bond between us almost from the first, Eliza, but some weeks passed before I began to suspect that by answering an advert, quite by chance I had done something wonderful and discovered the child I had lost.'

'The marquis has realised his mistake. He gave me permission to speak to you…'

'Then why have you said nothing? Foolish girl, were you afraid it might be too much for me? If only you knew how happy this makes me, Eliza. I have never felt better. I want to tell all our friends.'

'I think we must still take care. Everyone must continue to be told that I am merely your companion.'

'Why? I do not mind my friends knowing the truth, my love. I am proud of my beautiful daughter.'

'Have you not thought what could happen?' Eliza hesitated as her mother frowned. 'The terms of your husband's will are so harsh.'

'Oh…' Some of the brightness faded from Lady Sarah's face. 'Yes, I suppose the lawyers could make things awkward if they chose, but perhaps they need not know.'

'Someone may tell them…that person may insist on the terms of the will being observed.'

'You mean my son, of course.' She reached for Eliza's hand. 'I shall say nothing tonight. We must get through this dinner as best we can. However, tomorrow I shall return the rubies in person. If Howard insists, we shall go back to Bath and make our home there. The house there belongs to me. I have sufficient money of my own without the jointure to live comfortably on for the rest of my life. Perhaps when you marry I may stay with you sometimes—in the country if you have the good fortune to marry someone with a house in a pleasant area. I have thought Lord Seaton might make you an offer?'

'I like him very much—but I am not sure…' Eliza felt unable to explain the circumstances in which she would be living if she married Daniel. Besides, how could she leave her mother? Had Lady Sarah been comfortably settled in her home she would have been happy to become his wife and follow the drum, but she could not desert her mother—especially if she had been forced to live in Bath. 'I would not wish to desert you.'

'Foolish child. I will not have you give up your life for mine. If you receive an offer of marriage from the man I think you love, you must take it. I shall be happy for you and we shall spend as much time together as we can.'

'I am so lucky to have found you,' Eliza said, throat tight. 'I do not know quite how it happened, but it is more than I could ever have hoped.'

'We shall spend the rest of the day quietly. I do not look forward to this wretched dinner, Eliza, but we must bear it. In the meantime, we shall sit together and talk. I want to know all about what your life was like as a child—and I shall tell you how and why I fell in love with Cheadle…'

It was an emotional afternoon, nostalgic and coloured by memories. At the end of it, when they went up to dress for the evening, Eliza was filled with a new-found happiness. She had discovered so much about her mother that she could never have suspected. Eliza felt so close to her. She had begun to understand her father a little, realising what he had gone through as a young man and how he had become the harsh man that was the Marquis of Cheadle. Except that a part of the man Lady Sarah had loved was still there—and it showed itself in his love for Marianne.

He had done all he could to protect her. Yes, he was angry, but he had put his anger to one side in his determination to find Marianne and save her from ruin.

Eliza knew that she could not expect him to care for her in the same way. He had never known her, because she had been taken away when she was but a few hours old. Lady Sarah had never given up hope that she would one day find her child again, but the marquis had married and found solace in other ways.

At least he had believed her innocent of malice in the end and that was something.

As she was dressing for the evening, Eliza's thoughts turned to Daniel. If she accepted his offer of marriage, perhaps Lady Sarah could be persuaded to keep their relationship secret. She must see that it would be so much better if Eliza went away and they met as often as possible out of the public eye.

Eliza knew that she loved Daniel. She wanted very much to be his wife. She also wanted to care for her mother. Why could she not have both? In other circumstances they might have taken Lady Sarah to live with them.

Eliza sighed. It was all so very difficult and the choice was too hard to make lightly.

She had just finished dressing her hair when the door opened and her mother walked in.

'I wanted to give you this to wear this evening.' Lady

Sarah handed her the diamond-and-aquamarine pendant that Eliza had once admired. 'I think it will look well on you. I always thought that I would give it to my daughter one day. Please wear it and enjoy it, my dearest. If I had them, I would give you more precious jewels.'

'I should not want them,' Eliza assured her. 'This is perfect for me. I shall treasure it always. Are you sure I ought to wear it this evening?'

'I am at liberty to give what I please to my daughter,' Lady Sarah said and kissed her. 'Do not worry, Eliza. My son is not his father. I do not believe he would turn me out.'

Eliza felt doubtful. Lord Manners had seemed quite determined to her, but perhaps he was less harsh with his mother. Of course, it must be so. His threats were against Eliza and meant to scare her away.

Eliza removed the string of seed pearls and replaced it with the necklace. It looked well with her gown. 'This is beautiful, ma'am. Thank you so much.'

'I shall not ask you to call me Mama this evening, but in future you must do so, Eliza. You are my daughter and I am proud of you.'

'We must talk about it again tomorrow,' Eliza said. 'I think we ought to go or we shall be late…'

The carriage was waiting to convey them the short distance to the main house. Every window of the large, magnificent building was ablaze with light, spilling out on to the gracious forecourt and across the lawns into the shadows at the far end. The wind was a little chilly that evening for the autumn was now truly upon them and the nights had shortened.

Eliza followed Lady Sarah as she led the way. She was greeted with warmth and respect by the servants, which told her daughter a great deal. Her husband might have treated her cruelly, but his servants liked their old mistress very well.

They passed through an echoing hall with an imposing staircase into a grand drawing room. The colours of crimson, dark blue and gold were rich, but a little too formal for Eliza's taste. She much preferred the softer colours at the Dower House, which she imagined her mother had chosen.

Several people were in the room and they turned to look as they entered. One or two came forwards to greet Lady Sarah, the ladies kissing her cheek and the gentlemen taking her hand. They seemed genuinely glad to see her, but not one of them so much as glanced at Eliza. Even at the start in Bath, before the rumours, Eliza had at least been treated politely. Here she might have been invisible, receiving no more than a frosty nod when Lady Sarah introduced her as her companion.

Eliza held her head high, choosing to ignore the incivility of Lord Manners and his guests. She had no doubt that he had warned his friends to cut the upstart who had dared to prey on his mother.

Since no one spoke to her directly, Eliza did not join in the general conversation at dinner, which was all about people in London society, none of whom she had ever met. Whenever she chanced to look at her mother, she smiled at her, but it was not until the ladies followed Lady Manners into the drawing room at the end of the meal that anyone spoke to her.

'You may help me with the tea, Miss Bancroft,' Lady Manners spoke coldly, her pale blue eyes like chips of ice. She was a pretty woman, no more than three and twenty at the most, but her expression was sour, her dress severe. 'That is, after all, what you are, a paid servant—are you not?'

'Serena, please, my dear,' Lady Sarah protested. 'Eliza is a friend to me. I rely on her completely, as I told my son when he visited in Bath.'

Eliza shook her head and smiled at her mother, making her own reply.

'I am Lady Sarah's companion, and, yes, she does pay me.'

Eliza went forwards to take the cups where she was directed. She did her duty with grace and calm civility, and one of the younger ladies gave her a sympathetic smile.

Eliza made no response to anyone. After receiving her own dish of tea, she took it to the far side of the room and looked out of the window, trying to ignore the conversation.

'Eliza my dear, are you ready? I am tired and I think we should leave.'

Hearing her mother's gentle tones, Eliza nodded and stood up. A servant was dispatched to fetch their cloaks and then they were outside, climbing into the waiting carriage despite their hostess's appeal to wait for the gentlemen to join them.

'I have never been so angry in my life,' Lady Sarah said as she reached for her hand. 'Forgive me, Eliza. Had I guessed what Howard meant to do, I would never have attended his wretched dinner. It was a deliberate insult to you. He knows you are my daughter and is determined to make things awkward for you. Promise me that you will not allow him to distress you.'

'I am not distressed, except for your sake,' Eliza assured her. 'Please do not be upset, dearest Mama.

You told me he prefers London. I doubt he will stay long.'

'If he continues in this way, we shall repair to Bath— or find a small house in the country where we can be quiet together.'

'Perhaps it would be better if I left,' Eliza suggested. 'You could employ another companion and we could meet sometimes in private. I do not suggest this for my sake but yours. I should hate to think that you were driven out of your home, because of me.'

'You must promise me not to leave,' Lady Sarah said. 'If you were to marry, I should wish you happy and visit you as much as I could—but I will not have you reduced to working for someone else. You are my daughter, whether Howard likes it or not—and he will just have to accept you.'

'I would never leave without telling you the reason,' Eliza promised.

The carriage was slowing. When the coachman came to let down the steps, Eliza got out first and helped her mother to descend. They went indoors together and Lady Sarah went straight up to her bedchamber. Eliza saw that she was being cared for by her maid and then went to her own room. However, she was not in the least tired and the moonlight called to her.

She put on a dark cloak and went out. She would just take a little turn about the gardens to clear her head, and then go in.

As she moved towards the shrubbery a dark figure came out of the shadows to meet her. Eliza gave a little cry of alarm, her heart racing. Then she saw it was Daniel and her heartbeat slowed to a sensible pace.

'I wondered who it could be,' she said and smiled, holding out her hand to him. 'I am glad to see you, sir. Please forgive me for rushing off so abruptly this morning.'

'You were concerned for your mother. How is Lady Sarah?'

'She seems quite well, if a little tired. We were summoned to dinner at the house this evening, and I fear my reception there has made her angry.'

'I heard that Manners was very like his father,' Daniel said. He took her hands in his carrying them to his lips to kiss the fingers. 'Was it very awful, my dearest one?'

'It was not pleasant,' Eliza admitted. 'Lord Manners is angry that I did not respond to the threat he made in Bath.'

'He threatened you?'

'He said that I would find myself in prison as an impostor and a cheat if I did not leave Lady Sarah's employ. Hardly a word was spoken to me all evening, and then it was merely a reminder that I am only a companion.'

'The wretched snobs!' Daniel said. 'They do not deserve your consideration, Eliza. You are worth ten of any of them—and Lady Sarah knows it.'

'She loves me,' Eliza said and sighed. 'I did not give you an answer, Daniel, for I feel that she needs me. Would it be too much to ask you to wait for a little longer? I do love you...'

'You love me?' Daniel swept her into his arms, gazing down at her in the moonlight. 'I feared you could not love a rogue like me. I do not deserve you, my love—but my heart has been yours almost from the first.'

'I love you very much,' Eliza replied and there was no shyness or hesitation in her. 'I would go with you this very night, except that I promised my mother I would not go without telling her the reason…' She hesitated, then, 'The cottage that you spoke of, Daniel…would it be possible to buy such a house where my mother could visit us in private? It would be a refuge for her if her son is insensitive enough to turn her from her home.'

'Yes, I am certain I can save enough for that,' Daniel replied, downgrading the regiment he could afford in his mind as the house for Eliza and her mother grew larger. 'If you tell me you love me, I am content to wait.'

'Kiss me,' Eliza urged, pressing herself against his body. She trembled with the need to be loved and touched, to know the joys of loving. 'We have this night and I want to spend it with you.'

'Yes, we shall have tonight,' Daniel agreed. 'I think, tomorrow, I should call on your mother and tell her of my plans for the future. Meet me in the woods as we agreed, and we will go to her together.'

'Yes, I believe she would like to talk to you. I know she likes you well, and she wishes me to be happy.'

'It is also my wish. If the estate were still my own, I would offer your mother a home with us, Eliza. Unfortunately, my father's foolishness at the tables has left us with merely enough to live a decent honest life as an officer and his wife, though we shall have the cottage I promised.'

'It is more than enough for me. I have never expected more. To know my mother is comfortable and to be your wife is complete happiness for me.'

'Then I shall speak to her in the morning.' Daniel smiled as he drew her into his arms. 'For now, I think you mentioned kisses?'

'I want to be yours completely,' Eliza said as he took her hand. 'The summerhouse beyond those trees. We can be alone there.'

'I have thought of you so often, wanted you so much,' Daniel said, his arm about her waist. She leaned her head against his shoulder. 'I never dreamed to find such happiness.'

Eliza lay dreaming, snuggled in her bed, which she had not sought until past five that morning. She had spent the night in the summerhouse with Daniel, wrapped in his arms, blissfully happy and content. He had kissed her, touched her, held her, loved her, but he had not taken her maidenhead, though she would have given it willingly.

'I love you too much,' Daniel said. 'I have seen girls ruined, because their lover was too impatient. If anything should come between us—if I should die—I would not have you suffer for it, my love. You have given me so much this night. I shall save the happiness you offer so sweetly for our wedding night.'

Eliza had been too content to argue. It was enough for her to sit with her back against his warmth, held in his strong embrace for hours as they talked and kissed. Daniel had been so gentle, so loving and generous that if she had not been convinced of her own feelings before, she knew them now. Soon she would get up and go to meet him, and then they would visit her mother together.

A knock at her door brought her from her reverie. She called out that the maid might enter and Maisie came in, looking distressed.

'I am sorry to disturb you, miss, but her ladyships is in a state and asks that you come to her immediately.'

'Yes, of course.' Eliza's heart jerked with fear. 'Is she unwell?'

'No, miss. It is terrible. I've never known anything like this to happen before.'

'Why? What has happened?'

'You'd best go to her ladyship yourself, miss.' Maisie was close to tears. 'I'm too upset to speak of it.'

Eliza pulled on her dressing gown. She left Maisie to go about her business and walked down the hall to her mother's room. Lady Sarah was standing by her dressing chest and her jewel case was open on the top. She turned as Eliza entered, giving a cry of distress.

'Eliza, my love. Something terrible has happened. The rubies have gone. I locked them in my jewel case last evening and put the key in my reticule, as always. This morning I was determined to send them back as soon as I was awake. I did not want to wear the wretched things and now they are gone.'

'You are certain you put them there?'

'Yes, quite certain. You reminded me not to leave valuables lying about, even though we both trust the servants—but, as you said, anyone might come in.' She shuddered and looked distressed. 'To think that someone was in my room while I slept. I might have been murdered in my bed. We could all have been murdered.'

'Please, do not disturb yourself, Mama. Had the thief intended you harm it would already have happened. Was anything else taken?'

'No, but as I told you, my trinkets are of little monetary value. My husband always insisted on locking the heirlooms away in his strongroom each night. Oh, why did I not wait and give them back to Howard last night, as I intended?'

'You were angry and tired,' Eliza said. 'I know one of the doors was unlocked for a while last night, and that was my fault. I went out for a walk. Forgive me, this is my fault. I should have taken the key with me, but I did not intend to stay long.'

'Eliza…' Lady Sarah began, but was interrupted by Maisie, who came in looking scared. 'Lord Manners is here, ma'am. He says he has come to fetch the rubies to save you sending them to him.'

'My son…' A look of fright entered Lady Sarah's eyes. 'He will be so angry when he discovers they are lost. You had better ask him to come up, Maisie. I shall receive him in my boudoir.' As the maid left, she reached for Eliza's hand. 'Do not leave me, dearest. And please, do not say anything about leaving the door undone.'

Eliza followed her into the adjoining room, which was a pretty place with a décor of pink and cream and smelled of perfume and powder. Lady Sarah's possessions made it comfortable and she liked to sit there sometimes of a morning and listen as Eliza read to her from their favourite books.

Lady Sarah was clearly nervous. She pleated the delicate lace of her peignoir and jumped as the door was thrust open without so much as a word. Lord Manners strode into the room, his face like thunder.

'I have come for the rubies, Mama. I was disturbed that you did not give them into my safe keeping last evening. Lady Manners was distressed because you left early without waiting to take your leave of me.'

'I am sorry if I distressed your wife,' Lady Sarah said. 'I was feeling a little tired and forgot I was wearing the rubies. I wish I had given them to you last night, Howard. Forgive me, I seem to have misplaced them…'

'Misplaced an heirloom of that value? How could you?' His gaze narrowed and flicked towards Eliza. 'Do you know anything of this, Miss Bancroft?'

'No, sir. Lady Sarah has just this minute told me that she cannot find them.'

'I locked them in my jewel case,' Lady Sarah said and her hands fluttered nervously. 'I am almost certain I did, Howard. The key was placed in my reticule, as always. This morning when I looked for them they were not there.'

'Then you must have placed them somewhere else.' He looked at Eliza. 'Do you recall seeing where the rubies were put last night, Miss Bancroft?'

'No, sir. I was not here when Lady Sarah took them off, but I am certain she placed them in her locked case for safety.'

'Then what has happened to them?'

'Some thief must have come in the night and taken them,' his mother said nervously. 'There is no other explanation, Howard.'

'Indeed?' His eyes narrowed, a speculative gleam in their depths as he stared intently at Eliza. 'When you employ a young woman you do not know without references, what do you expect? I dare say they will be hidden in her room somewhere—unless she has already passed them to an accomplice...'

'Howard! You will take that back at once,' Lady Sarah cried, too angry to be nervous now. 'I did not ask you for the rubies. Eliza has no interest in such things. You are insulting to suggest such a thing about...my daughter.'

'I suppose you believe her lies?' he sneered. 'Who told you she was your lovechild? Was it her lover? Those rubies are worth a small fortune, Mother. A woman like that is capable of any villainy.'

'Eliza loves me and I love her. I shall not allow you to malign her that way.'

'Have you searched her room? No, I thought not. Well, I shall remedy the neglect...'

He strode from the room. Lady Sarah gave a cry of distress and followed him, Eliza one step behind.

'I am so sorry, dearest,' she said and looked close to tears. 'This is abominable.'

'We shall soon discover the truth of this, madam.'

Eliza could only watch as he proceeded to throw her things about as he searched her room, opening drawers and poking amongst her clothes and her reticules. Then he delved under the bed and pulled something out. It was one of Eliza's reticules, but an old one that she seldom used. She stared in horror as he released the strings and tipped something into his hand. The rubies flashed, blood red and accusing in his hand.

'So, Miss Bancroft, perhaps you can explain this?'

'Eliza...' Lady Sarah stared at her in distress. 'Surely...? I cannot believe it. You would not...'

'No, I would not,' Eliza said, lifting her head proudly. 'I did not put the rubies there and I have no idea how they came to be there. I swear on everything I hold dear that I had no knowledge of them until Lord Manners found them.'

'She is a liar and a thief and I shall know how to deal with her,' he said, a gleam of satisfaction in his eyes. 'You have been utterly deceived, Mother. This woman is not your lovechild. She is an impostor and a thief, sent here by her accomplice to rob or cheat you of all she can.'

Eliza's heart sank, because she could see the hint of a doubt in her mother's eyes. Lady Sarah did not wish to believe him, but she had only Daniel's word that Eliza was her daughter.

'I do not believe you,' she said, looking pale. 'Eliza

would not…she could not be what you name her. She loves me…'

'Yes, ma'am, I do love you,' Eliza said. 'I know your son thinks ill of me, but I did not take the rubies—and I have told you only what I believe to be true.'

'I cannot bear…' Lady Sarah said and swooned. Her son caught her and eased her into a chair. 'Please, call my doctor. I feel most unwell.'

Lord Manners went to the door and shouted for help. He had tucked the rubies into his pocket, and when the servants appeared said nothing of the theft. He directed two of the footmen to help Lady Sarah to her room and Maisie followed, looking anxious and scared, while another servant was sent scurrying to fetch the doctor from the village.

Eliza did not attempt to follow. When the others had gone, she looked at Lord Manners.

'We both know I did not take those, sir. I think you know that I was not in my room last night and I believe it was you—or one of your servants—who placed the rubies here beneath my bed.'

A smile of malice touched his lips. 'You will leave this house at once, Miss Bancroft. Do not stay to pack more than a small bag. Anything more may be sent on another time. Go now or you will find yourself locked in a cell by the end of the morning.'

'How can I leave when our mother is so ill?'

'She is not your mother. Any hopes you had of her are gone.' He walked to the door and looked back. 'I am warning you, Miss Bancroft. You will leave now or you will suffer an unfortunate future. I do not imagine you would care for the life in prison. I hear that few survive more than a year or two and a young woman of your fastidious nature would find it hard to bear.'

Eliza closed her eyes as he walked from the room. She walked along the corridor, but at the door of her mother's room, Maisie barred her way.

'I am sorry, miss. His lordship said as you weren't to see her. She is too upset, miss.'

'I have done nothing of which I am ashamed,' Eliza said, her throat tight as she saw suspicion in the maid's eyes. 'You will take care of her? I love her so much.'

'She will be safe with me, miss—but you should be ashamed. The kindness she showed you. How could you do such a thing?'

'I did not steal those jewels. Had I done so, I should not have left them where they could be so easily found.'

Eliza turned and walked back to her room. Lord Manners had not even thought of searching anyone else's room, because he knew they would be in hers. He had made a show of searching for them to convince his mother, and it seemed he had succeeded.

Holding back the tears, Eliza packed the things she could carry with her. She placed the aquamarine pendant on the dressing chest. She had taken nothing she had been given, other than her wages, of which only about half was left.

She must leave at once, even though she was innocent of any crime. Her word would not be believed against that of Lord Manners. Even Maisie thought her guilty. The worst hurt was that her mother would think she was guilty; she would believe that Eliza had left of her own accord, but she would write to her and pray that she received the letter and would be prepared to accept Eliza's innocence.

She must meet Daniel in the woods and tell him what had happened. He would surely believe her? Her disgrace meant that she would not be a fit wife for him, but perhaps they could live together for a while? She would be happy enough to be his mistress, since she could no longer expect him to marry her.

Chapter Eleven

Daniel waited for three-quarters of an hour in the woods. He glanced at his watch several times, frowning over Eliza's lateness. Surely he had not mistaken the place for their meeting? Did she think that he would come to the house so that they could tell her mother together? He decided that he would walk up to the house. There must be a reason why Eliza had not come, as she promised. After the previous night he had no doubts concerning her feelings for him. She could not possibly have changed her mind.

Catching sight of a piece of pale blue material caught on a bramble, Daniel frowned and bent to pluck it from the thorns. There was some damage to the grass and bushes, as if several feet had trampled them. A cold trickle of fear slithered down his spine. Had something happened to Eliza? No, it was not possible. Who would wish her harm? For a moment a picture of Cheadle flashed into his mind, but he dismissed it. The marquis had made his peace with Eliza, accepting that she was his daughter. He would not do something underhand.

Then who might have arranged an accident or an abduction? Was he making a mountain from a molehill?

Daniel hurried on towards the house, his heart thumping. The scrap of material might not have come from Eliza's gown—and yet he was sure she had one something very like it.

The door was opened to him by a subdued-looking maid, who seemed not to know her business, for she stared as if she did not know what to say.

'May I speak to Miss Eliza Bancroft, please?'

'She's gone, sir. Left in disgrace more than an hour ago.'

'Eliza left an hour ago? Are you sure, miss?'

'Yes, sir. I saw her leave. She left an address in Norfolk for her things to be sent on.'

'Why was she in disgrace? I do not understand?'

There was some mystery here for Lady Sarah had been so very fond of her companion, even before she knew the truth.

'I'm not sure as I should say, sir. There has been an uproar and Mrs Bristow would turn me off if I breathed a word—but it might be because of them rubies that went missing...' The girl gasped and looked over her shoulder in fear. 'I didn't tell you that, sir.'

'I think I should see Lady Sarah, if you will please ask her to receive me.'

'I'll ask Maisie, sir. If you will step into the parlour.'

'Thank you.'

Daniel paced about the small but exquisitely furnished parlour. What could have happened since the previous evening? Eliza had been so happy when she left him, content to leave the future in his hands. He was staring out of the window when he heard steps behind him and turned to find himself looking at another maid.

'My mistress asks if you will step up to her boudoir, sir. She is not feeling well enough to come down—but she does wish to speak with you.'

'Thank you, I shall,' Daniel said and followed her up the stairs and along the hall. She knocked at a door, opened it and intimated that he should enter. 'Thank you…' He inclined his head and went inside.

Lady Sarah was lying on a *chaise-longue* with her feet up. She had a lace kerchief in her hand, smelling salts and lavender water to hand.

'Forgive me if I do not get up, sir. I understand you enquired for Eliza?'

'Yes, ma'am. We had arranged to meet this morning at ten o'clock and then we were to come to see you. I waited almost an hour and then I wondered if I was supposed to come here instead.'

'Eliza did not meet you? I had hoped she might. She had spoken of you recently. You are hoping that I know where she is, but unfortunately I have no idea. My son must have sent her away. I know she took only a small bag and left a message that her things are to be sent to Norfolk.' Lady Sarah gave a cry of distress. 'The foolish child. She ought to have waited and spoken to me. Whatever my son said to her could have been sorted. I fear she thinks that I believe she took those wretched rubies.'

'I am not sure—there is a question of some missing rubies?'

'The wretched things were found in her room, hidden under the bed. Of course someone else put them there.

Eliza would not have stolen from me—would she?'
There was a look of unconscious appeal in her eyes, as
though she needed reassurance.

'Eliza loves you dearly. When I asked her to be my
wife, her first thought was of you. She was angry with
me for telling you that she was your daughter. Cheadle
had confirmed it, but still she would not tell you because
she feared that it might upset you. All that concerned
her was that you should not lose your home.'

'I would live anywhere if I could see my dearest child
often,' Lady Sarah told him, tears standing in her eyes.
'Where has she gone to, sir? Will she have returned to
Norfolk? Why did she not meet you if you had arranged
it?'

Daniel reached into his pocket and took out the scrap
of cloth, handing it to her. 'Do you think this might have
come from one of Eliza's gowns, ma'am? I found it on
a bramble bush not far from the house.'

Lady Sarah gave a cry of fear. 'This is from one of
her favourite gowns. We chose it together. Something
must have happened to her! Oh, this is all my fault. I was
overcome and shocked, and I allowed her to think that
I believed she had taken those ridiculous rubies. I am
sure my son planned the whole thing. He knew where I
kept my key and he could quite easily have entered my
room and taken them. Nothing else was missing. Eliza
did not even like jewels of this kind—why would she
take them?'

'She would not,' Daniel said stoutly. 'Do not even
consider it, ma'am. If the rubies were there, someone
put them there.'

'Yes, I think you are right. What can we do, Lord
Seaton? How can we discover where she has gone?'

'I shall go down to—' Daniel broke off as the maid returned, looking distinctly odd.

'Yes, Maisie, what do you want? I am talking privately with Lord Seaton about my dearest Eliza's disappearance.'

'It is the Marquis of Cheadle, ma'am. He said he had come to see Miss Eliza Bancroft, but when I told him she had gone he asked to see you.'

'Let him come up,' Lady Sarah said. 'Please do not leave, Lord Seaton. Three heads are better than one and he may know something of Eliza.'

'Yes, perhaps,' Daniel said. He walked over to the window and was staring out of it when the marquis entered. Waiting a moment until the greetings were over, he turned to see the marquis still holding Lady Sarah's hand and a fond look in his eyes. 'Cheadle. We have a mystery here. Eliza was falsely accused of stealing a valuable heirloom and has since disappeared. Lady Sarah was told that Eliza planned to return to Norfolk where she has friends, but I am not convinced that that is where she is headed. I found a scrap of cloth in the woods near here and I fear that something may have happened to her. You know nothing of this?'

'I had no hand in her disappearance,' the marquis assured him. 'I came to return this to her.' He handed a ring to Lady Sarah. 'Eliza showed it to me when she began to suspect the truth. I took it from her, for at the start I thought her an impostor, but I soon discovered the truth. She is our daughter, Sarah. I intended to give the ring to her and tell her that I have set up an account for her with my bank in Bath. She will have an independence in the future—and there is no need for you to leave her part of your fortune. Your family need never know the truth and you will not lose your home.'

'My son already knows, which is why he set up this false theft and made sure that Eliza took the blame. I did not see it instantly for I was upset, but I know that my daughter would never hurt me. What Howard said to her I do not know, but I intend to find out.'

'You will allow me to speak to him for you,' Cheadle said. He took her hand and kissed it. 'If he is so unkind as to turn you from your home, I shall purchase a house in the country for you and Eliza—you shall not suffer one day more of his unkindness, my love. Lady Cheadle and I have parted on terms agreeable to her now that Marianne's future is assured. She will not divorce me, but agrees to a separation and will live in London. I intend to travel in France and Italy and perhaps settle somewhere of the sort—but we shall speak more of this when Eliza is safe.' He turned to Daniel. 'Will you go down to Norfolk, sir? See if you can discover the whereabouts of my daughter and keep us informed. I want Eliza found—and if I discover that Manners has harmed her he will come to regret the day.'

'You will need to be there before me,' Daniel said, his mouth hard. 'I love Eliza and she has promised to marry me. I have explained that I shall have little to offer, but she is happy to follow the drum as a soldier's wife.'

'Be damned to that,' Cheadle said. 'I have been trying to tell you that I wish to return the money your father lost to me at the tables, for I think I was in the wrong. I should like to make amends for any harm I have caused—especially if you are to marry my daughter.'

'It is a debt of honour,' Daniel said stiffly. 'Perhaps something for Eliza.'

'Stiff-necked young fool,' Cheadle said. ' We shall talk again. Now get off and see if you can find my daughter—and then bring her here to us. I shall be staying here until Sarah's future is decided. If Manners does not care for it, he may do the other thing.'

Daniel could not stop the laugh that escaped him. 'I think I should not like to be in Howard Manners's shoes when you pay him that visit,' he said. 'Lady Sarah, you will excuse me. I shall go immediately to Norfolk and discover if Eliza is there. Cheadle, you will discover if you can if Lord Manners was behind her disappearance?'

'Naturally,' the marquis said. 'I do not think he will deny me. I happen to hold enough of his notes to make him think twice. I have taken the precaution of purchasing them from his creditors in the event that they might come in useful. One word from me, and the lawyers will move in.' He shook his head at Lady Sarah. 'Do not fret, my dear one. Your son needs a fright, but if he is obliging he will come to no harm.'

Daniel inclined his head, feeling almost amused. He might have found the situation funny had he been sure that Eliza was safe. She would not simply have gone off on her own, would she?

Eliza was aware of the jolting of the carriage. Her head was aching and she could not focus when she first opened her eyes. Some moments passed before she realised that her hands had been bound. Gradually, she began to piece the sequence of events together. She had been accused of theft, told that if she did not leave immediately she would find herself imprisoned, and then she had packed a small bag and set out for her meeting with Daniel.

Suddenly, three rogues had pounced on her from behind the trees. She had struggled and cried out but they had placed something over her face and she had fainted. Perhaps they had given her some evil drug, for she had known nothing for hours. It was night now and so far as she knew no one had even come to see if she was still alive.

Eliza's thoughts were clear even though her head still ached and felt fuzzy. She had been abducted. Why? Was it because someone mistakenly thought her an heiress? She was sure she had been followed in Bath, but had thought herself safe in the country. Was Lord Manners her abductor? He had threatened her with dire consequences if she ignored him, but she had been leaving. His ruse had succeeded—Lady Sarah believed that Eliza had stolen the rubies. She might even believe the rest of his accusations.

Tears stung Eliza's eyes. She struggled to control them. Now was not the time to give way to grief. She had to think about what was happening to her. What did her abductors plan to do with her? Was she to be murdered, her body left in some lonely spot until it decayed and she was for ever lost, just a tainted memory in the minds of those who had known her?

It would seem as if she had run away, as if she were guilty. If Lord Manners had planned this, he had been fiendishly clever. The only flaw in his plan was her meeting with Daniel. He would wait and then…surely he would go to the house looking for her.

Daniel would not believe that she was a thief. She felt confident that he would try to find her—but would she still be alive?

Eliza had no idea how long they had been travelling or in which direction she was being taken. However, she was certain of one thing. When her chance came, she must escape. She could rely on no one else to save her from these rogues—she must make a bid for freedom herself as soon as the occasion arose.

'Daniel,' she whispered as she began to move her hands, trying to ease the ropes that bound her. They had cut into her flesh and were painful, but she focused her mind on the night she had spent with her lover and did not notice the cramping in her legs and arms. 'Daniel, I love you so much.'

If she could only get away from her abductors, she would somehow find her way to the man she loved. Even if he no longer felt able to marry her, he would help her.

'Oh, no, sir,' Betty said when she had invited the gentleman to step into her kitchen because of it being such a cold wet day. 'Miss Bancroft is with Lady Sarah Manners. She went to Bath to be her companion some weeks back. My Ted took her himself.'

'Miss Bancroft left Lady Sarah's house over two days ago,' Daniel replied. 'There was a misunderstanding and Lady Sarah is most upset. She wishes Eliza to return.'

'And who would you be, sir?' Betty looked at him a mite suspiciously.

'I am Lord Seaton, the Earl of Standish's nephew,' Daniel said. 'I came to enquire for her—because we think something may have happened to her.'

'Lawks-a-muss!' Betty cried, turning pale. 'You never mean it, sir—something happened to my Eliza? She isn't the sort of girl to get into trouble. She's always been an angel, looking after her mama all that time with never a murmur of complaint. Who would want to hurt my lamb, sir? That is what I should like to know.'

'So should I, Mrs Wright,' Daniel assured her. 'If I

find the man who abducted her, he will regret it. I give you my word.'

'Lord above.' Moved to violent emotion, Betty blew her nose on her spotless apron. 'She wouldn't be the first girl to go missing from these parts, for there was that tavern wench and the miller's daughter, besides others… If anything has happened to my Eliza, I swear I'd beat him with my rolling pin, sir. The wicked fellow what's took her deserves to hang.'

'It is a hanging offence,' Daniel said. 'Yet I fear the rogues that have taken her are but fools who work for money. I pray that she comes to no harm at their hands. You can think of no one who might wish to harm her—or anywhere she would go if in distress?'

'Where else should she go but here, sir?' Betty said. 'She has no one but us. My Ted told her she was to consider this her home for as long as she wished. If she could, I am sure she would come here.'

'Then I fear we must conclude she is being held against her will,' Daniel said and frowned. 'I shall call on my uncle, but then I must go back to Lady Sarah's home and discover if the marquis has had more luck. You will write to this address if you should hear from her?' Daniel wrote down Lady Sarah's home address. 'I shall go here after I leave. Let me know if you remember anything or hear a rumour, however slight.'

'Yes, sir.' Betty clutched his arm as he turned to leave. 'You will find her, sir?'

'Yes. If it takes me the rest of my life I will find her,' he promised.

But would she still be alive? Was Lord Manners behind Eliza's abduction, or was it someone else?

Daniel could only hope that Lady Sarah would have

received a ransom note when he returned. He had hoped Eliza would be here, but now he knew that she might be anywhere.

Eliza had slept some of the time since they had stopped the coach and given her a crust of bread and something to drink. The masked men had untied her hands to allow her to eat and drink, but when they retied them they had not been as thorough as the first time. She had been unable to loosen the knots then, but now she could feel a definite change. The rope was not cutting in as deeply as it had and she thought she would soon be able to work free. At the next change of horses she would try to escape.

She closed her eyes and thought of Daniel. He loved her. He would be searching for her. If she could only evade her captors, she would find him somehow. She prayed that he had not already joined the regiment he had spoken of when he talked about the future. It did not matter, she would find him wherever he was.

The hours passed so slowly and they must have been travelling for some days, at least two, she thought. Where were they heading? If her hands were free she could have pulled back the blinds and looked out, but the knots were so stubborn. Surely soon they would be loose enough to...

Eliza gave a little cry of triumph as one hand came free. The other was soon relieved of the chafing rope. She rubbed at her wrists, feeling the life come back little by little. It was dark in the carriage, but when she risked a peep out of her window she saw that there was a bright moon. The countryside was touched with silver, looking strange and eerie. However, as they passed a gallows, she shivered, but then thought that she recognised the scenery. Surely she had come this way before? She had seen the gallows soon after leaving Norwich on her outward journey.

Eliza let the blind fall and sat up, feeling excited. If she was truly not far from Norwich, it would be easy enough to find her way to Betty and Ted's. Why had she been brought here? Somehow she did not think that Lord Manners would have gone to the trouble of delivering her to her home. No, there was quite another reason. Someone must have a special reason for bringing her here—but what could it be?

Eliza smiled grimly in the darkness. She had no intention of waiting around to find out. As soon as the coach slowed down the next time, she would make her bid for freedom.

'I am glad you came to me,' the earl said when Daniel had finished telling his story. 'I believe I know who killed your cousin—and, if you say someone took a shot at you, he may also be responsible for the attempt on your life.'

'My agent has been making enquiries—but please tell me your ideas, sir. I know there was some talk of a farmer called Jackson, but I do not think it was he.'

'Jackson had reason to hate my boy—the fool dishonoured his daughter—but there is another man, a gentleman of sorts. He lives in a rather run-down manor house a few miles from here, and I have reason to think Marcus may have been involved in some nefarious dealings with the rogue.'

'Uncle?' Daniel was shocked—he had hoped to shield the earl from the unpalatable truth. 'You think my cousin was involved in something not quite legal?'

'I believe this Kettleton fellow may have been

responsible for the disappearance of several girls in the neighbourhood,' the earl said with a heavy sigh. 'Recently, a girl who once worked here as a maid returned to her home in the village. She told a tale of having been tricked and then forced to live and work in a house of ill repute. She had tricked her captors and escaped, being sensible enough to return home and tell her story.'

'Good grief! I have been warned about this man, Kettleton, and concluded that he was involved in some foul business.' Daniel frowned as he saw his uncle's expression. 'I had suspected it, but had no proof. Tell me what you know, please.'

'The girl's father came to me with some tale of Marcus having promised the girl marriage, but when the girl went with him, believing he would keep his word, she was handed over to another man. She says his name is Sir Henry Kettleton, and that he took her to the house where she was forced to do unspeakable things. I asked the father for some proof, but there is only the girl's word, which, of course Kettleton would deny.'

'Naturally, the word of a baronet would be believed above hers,' Daniel said. He took a turn around the room, as some things began to be clearer in his mind. 'I employed an agent, who has been asking questions about my cousin's death. I believe Kettleton was indeed behind the attempt on my life…' Daniel was suddenly struck by a terrifying thought. 'He could well be behind Eliza's abduction. Damnation! If he has her…' He could not put the awful thought into words.

'He may use her as bait to trap you,' the earl apologised. 'I am sorry you were caught up in this miserable affair, Daniel.'

'I chose to become involved,' Daniel said. 'Besides, this man is evil and must be stopped.' His brow darkened.

'He has gone too far. If anything has happened to Eliza I shall certainly see him hang.' The thought of the woman he adored at the mercy of a man like that was unbearable. 'I must find her.'

'I cannot say where he would have taken her. Kitty Robinson says the whorehouse is in London, but Kettleton's own place is not far from here—a matter of ten miles or so to the east of Standish Village.'

'Then I shall go there and have it out with him.' Daniel looked grim. 'I intend to get to the bottom of this somehow.'

'Take care, Daniel. If he killed Marcus he will not hesitate to kill you.'

'I shall be on my guard, but I must allow him to live for long enough to tell me where he has hidden Eliza.'

'We cannot be sure he has her.'

'It is the only explanation. I was puzzled to the reason for her abduction. There were other factors but it all fits: the attempt on my life and then Eliza's disappearance. I am sure it is all in order to prevent my learning the truth about Marcus's death and exposing Kettleton.'

'Yes, I dare say.' The earl looked thoughtful. 'You must take some of my men with you. Ted Wright has an interest in Eliza's welfare—and my gamekeeper Jenkins is a good man with a gun. A couple of the grooms might be handy in a fight.'

'Yes, they may come in useful,' Daniel said. 'I shall go tonight, sir. If I can get into the house under cover of darkness, I might have a chance of taking Kettleton off guard. The most important thing is to discover where he has taken Eliza.'

If anything had happened to her…but it was a thought too far. He could not bear to think of anything happening to the girl he adored. To have her snatched from him after one perfect night together was too cruel. He would never rest until he found her.

Clouds had obscured the moon and it was dark when Eliza felt the carriage slowing to a halt. She tensed, ready to make her escape the moment it stopped. Glancing out of the window, she could just make out the shape of a house at the end of a long, curving drive. The horses were going very slowly now and she decided to take a chance. Wrenching the door open before the carriage actually stopped, she jumped out, falling to the ground in a heap and rolling to the side of the drive. In another moment she was on her feet, running swiftly towards the trees to the right of the drive. She heard the shout from somewhere behind her, realising that her escape had been noticed.

Eliza's heart pounded as she heard the sounds of pursuit, but it was very dark and she believed that, if she could only reach the trees, she might avoid her captors.

Fortune was with her as she entered the dense wood. Eliza's mind was working furiously. If she blundered through the wood in a blind panic she might trip over unseen hazards and injure herself. It would be better to go more slowly, feeling her way and making as little noise as possible. She could hear the men shouting to one another. They were as much hampered by the dark as she was, and from somewhere quite close, she heard one of them say he was going to fetch a lantern.

'If we don't find her, he'll have our hides,' the other man said. 'You must have left the rope too loose when you tied her.'

'It was as much your responsibility as mine. Kettleton is a devil. He'll shoot the pair of us if the girl escapes.'

Eliza held her breath. They had obviously not seen her. She tried to remain absolutely still as one of them returned to the carriage to fetch the lantern and the other one walked past her. He was within feet of where she stood, her back to a tree. She waited until he had gone past, listening to the sounds of rustling.

Then she saw a light moving through the trees. For a moment the bearer paused and then turned away from her, moving deeper into the trees. Eliza hesitated, considering what to do. The men obviously thought that she would have run deeper into the woods in a panic. By holding her nerve, she had gained the initiative. When she could no longer see the light or hear any sound, she walked towards the drive that led to the house. She would follow the road and see where it led her. Perhaps she could find help—a passing carriage—or another house where she could ask for assistance.

Now that she felt less afraid of being recaptured, Eliza had begun to feel the soreness on her hip and thigh where she had landed hard when she jumped from the carriage. Her wrists were sore, too, because the ropes had been tight at the start and she had chafed her skin trying to loosen them. There was a little more light now, because the clouds had rolled away from the moon. She did not know exactly where she was, but had recognised some landmarks before the coach turned off the high road into country lanes, and she believed she was not too far from Norwich and her home. Her captors had thrown her reticule into the carriage with her, though she had no idea what had happened to the remainder of her belongings. Perhaps they were still with the coach. No matter, she had a few coins in her purse and would be able to pay for assistance to reach Betty's home.

* * *

She had been walking for no more than twenty minutes at most when she saw the carriage approaching. Stepping out into the road, she waved at the driver and he brought his horses to a halt.

'Please, you must help me,' she said. 'I have been abducted, but I managed to escape from my captors. I am trying to reach my home…'

The coachman did not reply, but a tall gentleman was getting down from the coach. He came towards her, looking at her oddly.

'Are you in some trouble?'

'My name is Eliza Bancroft and I was abducted from near Lady Sarah Manners's home in Wiltshire. I was held captive for two days, but this evening I managed to escape. I need to get to the village of Standish Hope— could you help me, please?'

'What a terrible experience for you, Miss Bancroft,' the gentleman said. 'I am sorry that you have been treated so ill. Have you any idea who abducted you or why?'

'I do not know why,' Eliza replied, feeling relieved that she had been found by such a respectable gentleman. 'However, I believe it was on the orders of someone called…Mr Kettleton, I think.'

'Wicked,' the gentleman replied. He offered her his hand. 'Please step inside my carriage, Miss Bancroft. My home is not far and my wife will look after you until we can arrange for you to be taken home.'

'How kind you are.' Eliza took his hand, accepting his help into the carriage. She smiled as he took the seat opposite. 'I do not believe you gave your name?'

'Did I not, Miss Bancroft?' The gentleman smiled as the carriage moved on. 'How remiss of me? My name is

Sir Henry Kettleton, and I regret to tell you that I have no wife.'

'You tricked me…' Eliza gasped, feeling stunned. She flung herself at the door, but he grabbed her arm and threw her back against the seat. He took a pistol from his pocket and pointed it at her.

'Are you going to kill me?' A feeling of despair came over her as she realised that she had escaped his hench-men only to be recaptured by the man himself. 'Why— why are you doing this?'

'Because I have a score to settle with a certain gentleman,' Kettleton said. 'Seaton has been poking his nose into my affairs, and I mean to teach him a lesson. Unfortunately for you, you have seen too much—which means I shall have to make certain arrangements for you, though perhaps I may allow you to live.'

Eliza swallowed hard. 'If you meant to kill me, why did you not have your men do it when they captured me?'

'You are quite right,' Kettleton said and replaced the pistol. The carriage had gathered speed. 'I shall not need this. If you jump now you will certainly suffer an unpleasant injury. Your death would be unnecessary. I have something far more interesting for you in mind. A pretty face like yours can be worth a deal of money. I shall probably sell you to the highest bidder, though I may sample your wares before I pass you on to certain of my friends.'

'You are disgusting,' Eliza said. She sat back in her seat again. 'What do you intend to do to Lord Seaton?'

'I shall send him a ransom note; when he comes looking, I shall kill him—or one of the rogues I employ will do it for me.'

Eliza closed her eyes. How could she have been such a fool? Daniel would certainly come looking for her and then he would die. She would not give in so tamely, but it might be better to let her abductor believe she was too frightened to resist further. She took out a kerchief and began to weep noisily into it.

'For goodness' sake...' Kettleton said testily. 'Thank God we're here.'

The carriage was drawing to a close. He had his leg stuck out across the door, giving her no chance to give him the slip. When the door was opened from the outside, he jumped down and then ordered her to get out. Eliza took her time and then pretended to slip, falling into his arms. Her hand went to his pocket and she pulled out the pistol he had threatened her with earlier.

'Put that down, you stupid little fool,' Kettleton growled. 'I'll teach you to threaten me.'

Eliza took a step backwards. 'If you come near me, I shall shoot you,' she warned. 'Do not think I shall fear to do it, sir. I am quite indifferent to any harm you might sustain.'

'Damn you...' Kettle made a lunge at her, trying to grab the pistol. Eliza screamed and the pistol went off without her knowing quite how. She watched in horror as he fell back, a dark tide of crimson seeping from the hole in his chest. 'You little bitch...' He stared at her, then sank to his knees and fell forwards on to his face.

Eliza was aware of his coachman and two others. They were all staring at her. She was terrified that one of them would shoot her, but they seemed stunned, and then she heard the sound of running feet and shouting. Suddenly about six men burst from the trees and came rushing towards her. There was some yelling as

Kettleton's rogues realised they were under attack and all three took flight.

'Eliza…' Daniel's face looked misty as he moved towards her. 'Are you all right? I heard the shot and feared…'

'Daniel. I think I've killed him ' Eliza gave a little sob, took two steps towards him and fainted.

Chapter Twelve

Eliza woke to find herself lying in a soft comfortable bed in a room she had never seen before in her life. She sat up in alarm. Where was she? She had been abducted—twice—but then…a shudder took her as she recalled the terrible scene outside Sir Henry Kettleton's house. He had threatened to kill Daniel and…she shivered as she remembered his plans for her and what had happened afterwards. She had taken his own pistol and shot him. Then Daniel had come.

Eliza could not remember anything more. She thought she had fainted and the rest was hazy. Vague memories of being carried to a carriage and driven somewhere drifted though her mind, but it was all very faint, lost in mist. Her head was aching a little and she realised she had probably fainted because she had eaten hardly anything for days. She was about to try to get up when the bedroom door opened and someone entered carrying a tray. When she saw who it was, she gave a glad cry.

'Betty,' she said, 'how glad I am to see you. Where am I?'

'You are in the earl's house,' Betty said. 'Lord Seaton brought you here early this morning and the doctor gave you something to make you sleep. He said to let you rest until noon and then bring a light nourishing lunch. There is soup and a little chicken with some fresh bread and butter if you should fancy it, my love?'

'I am very hungry,' Eliza said. 'All those men gave me the whole time was one piece of bread and some water.'

'The rogues!' Betty looked angry. 'The earl has them in prison now, my love—and their master will join them if he survives long enough. They are all for the hangman's noose.'

'I did not kill Sir Henry, then? I thought he was dead…all that blood…' Eliza shivered. 'It was horrid, Betty—but what else could I do? He said he was going to kill Lord Seaton and send me to a house of ill repute.'

'He never was?' Betty was shocked. 'If I had heard him say it, I should have killed him myself.' She set the tray on Eliza's lap and smiled encouragingly as she began to eat her soup. 'That's right, my love. Lord Seaton has business with the magistrate for there has been more wicked things going on than we dreamed. He told me to say he would be back this evening and will visit you then.'

'I shall get up when I've eaten,' Eliza said. 'If someone will bring me some hot water and some fresh clothes. I feel as if I have not washed for a month.'

'The doctor advised you rest,' Betty told her. 'But I shall bring the water and some of your clothes that you left behind, and then you may get up if you feel able.'

Eliza thanked her and Betty left her to have her

meal in peace. The soup was delicious and restorative and the chicken was moist and tender. Eliza ate her fill and pushed the tray away just as Betty returned with the water, followed by a maid with some of the clothes she had left behind when she went to work for Lady Sarah.

The thought of her mother brought the sting of tears to her eyes. Did she still think that Eliza was a liar and an impostor?

There was no point in distressing herself. Eliza knew that she might have more to worry her than the accusation of being a thief. She had shot Sir Henry Kettleton as they struggled for the pistol. No one else had heard his threats to her—would she be believed when she told her story to the magistrate?

Daniel would believe her. As yet, she did not understand how he had happened to be at Sir Henry's estate last evening, but somehow he must have discovered what was going on and come in search of her. Perhaps he had some proof that would reveal her abductor for the rogue he was?

Daniel saw his uncle waiting for him as he entered the house. The earl beckoned him into a small parlour, looking anxious.

'What news, Daniel? Is all settled?'

'Yes, sir.' Daniel looked grim. 'It is not certain if Kettleton will live above a few days, but it may be as well if he does not. He will certainly be hung for his crimes. His rogues have confessed it all. You were right to suspect that Marcus was concerned in the affair, but not of his own free will. He owed Kettleton more than ten thousand pounds and was blackmailed into helping him entice a couple of young women to his house. He thought it would just be some sport for friends, but when he realised what was actually happening to the girls he refused to bring any more young women. Kettleton was furious and threatened him. It is fairly certain, though not proved, that he was behind my cousin's murder.'

'I need no further proof,' the earl said and sighed heavily. 'Marcus should have come to me if he could not meet his debts—but we shall not dwell on the past. I wish to thank you for all you have done.'

'Jed Bailey and Molly have been found safe and well. They went off like that because they both knew too much and were afraid of Kettleton. I am sure they will return now that he is safely under lock and key.'

'So all is settled.' The earl was silent for a moment, then, 'I understand you mean to marry Miss Bancroft?'

'Yes, if she will still have me. I love her and I think we shall be happy together.'

'I shall settle the estate at Peterborough on you, Daniel,' the earl said. 'It was your cousin's and came to him through his mother's family, though under a trust and at my direction until he was thirty. It is not entailed and therefore I may do with it as I wish, since it was to pass to me should anything happen to my son as my wife had no remaining family. I think you will not want to live there and you may sell it with my blessing. It is probably worth nearly twenty thousand pounds. Marcus spoke of raising a mortgage on it. I objected to his intention, refusing my permission, but had he told me why he needed the money I should have understood.'

'I dare say he was ashamed, sir. You must not blame yourself for any of this unfortunate business. ' Daniel was thoughtful for a moment, then, 'I do not know how to thank you for your gift. I should indeed wish to sell.

I have some debts, which such a sum will amply cover. How did you know I was in debt?'

'I guessed it when my agent told me you had had your estate valued. You should have told me. I would have lent you the money.'

'I did not wish to ask. I meant to sell and take up a life in the army.'

'I prefer that you keep your estate, Daniel. I shall be needing your help and advice more as the years pass. If it was within my power, I would leave everything to you—but I must think of my daughter's sons. However, the Peterborough estate will become yours on the day of your wedding.'

'You are generous, sir.'

'We shall say no more of it. Go and find Miss Bancroft. I believe she is sitting in the front parlour, which was your aunt's favourite.'

'Eliza has got up?' Daniel frowned. 'I shall go to her at once.'

He walked swiftly in the direction of the small parlour, which, in summer, caught the last of the evening sun. It was quite dull that evening and a fire had been lit. Eliza was standing at the window, gazing out.

'Eliza…' She turned at his voice, her face lighting with pleasure. 'Should you not be resting?'

'Please do not scold me,' Eliza said and came to him with outstretched hands. 'I feel much better. I am not ill, you know. I think I fainted because I was hungry… though the sight of the blood…' A little shiver went through her. 'Is he still alive?'

'Kettleton is not dead, though he might prefer it to imprisonment and a hanging,' Daniel said and looked grim. 'You have nothing with which to reproach yourself, Eliza. Indeed, Mr Justice Rawlings praised you for your courage and helping to bring a wicked villain to book. He was aware that something unpleasant was happening, for at least ten young women had disappeared in the district over the past two years.'

'How awful. Kettleton must be evil indeed.'

'Yes, I believe he is. We are certain that he either killed or had my cousin murdered. Believe me, my dearest, you need have no feelings of guilt.'

'He intended me for his whorehouse,' Eliza said. 'However, the main reason for my abduction was to lure you to your death. I had already escaped once, but he tricked me into his carriage. He threatened me with his pistol and when he tried to pull me from the carriage I fell against him and took the pistol. He tried to grab it from me and…I fired.'

'It went off by accident, which is what I told the magistrate,' Daniel moved in closer, looking down at her with love in his eyes. 'There were three witnesses, all of whom agreed to testify against a man they feared. It would seem that they were all coerced one way or the other into working for him—or that is what they would have us believe. I am not sure it will save them, but that is for the law to decide, not us.'

'I am glad it is over,' Eliza said and sighed with relief. 'But you do not know what happened before I was abducted…at Lady Sarah's house.'

'Certainly I know,' Daniel said. His arms went around her waist and he bent his head to kiss her softly on the lips. 'Lady Sarah told me her son falsely accused you of theft. When I left her, she was being comforted by Cheadle, who, as far as my understanding goes, intends to take care of her. She did not believe you would rob her, dearest. Her main concern was that I should find you. You must know that she cares for you deeply.'

'Yes, I thought so, but for a moment she seemed to doubt me.' Eliza blinked back foolish tears. 'Then you still wish to marry me? You are not afraid of the scandal?'

'What scandal? My uncle insists that the wedding be here, Eliza. You will be able to invite your friends and I shall invite those I particularly like, though I think we shall not want a large wedding.'

'Oh, Daniel…' Eliza looked up at him, her lips soft and inviting as he lowered his head to kiss her. 'I cannot believe that it has all turned out so well. It seems too much like a dream.'

'We are neither of us dreaming, my love, and, because of my uncle's generosity to me, we shall have a home. He has given me a substantial estate, which I shall sell and pay my debts.'

'Oh, Daniel…' Eliza's face glowed as she looked up at him. 'I am so happy…'

'I love you so much, my dearest. When I thought you lost it was unbearable. I am determined never to let you out of my sight again. We shall have the banns called in church this Sunday,' Daniel said. 'I shall make the arrangements for the wedding and you must find someone to sew your bride gown. Would you prefer to stay here or lodge with Betty until the wedding?'

'The earl has been extremely kind, but I think I should go to Betty's until the wedding. It will be quite safe now that your enemy has been placed under lock and key—and I know she will enjoy having me there. I shall buy material in Norwich and Betty will help me make a new gown.'

'You must do exactly as you wish,' Daniel told her, his fingers trailing lovingly down her cheek. 'I shall spend every day with you until the wedding, and for the rest of our lives. We shall have a short honeymoon in Paris and you may buy most of your bride clothes there.'

'I shall not need so very many.'

Daniel kissed the end of her nose. 'You will allow your husband to be the judge of that,' he said, but his eyes were filled with laughter. 'I shall have several thousand guineas left after the sale of my now property, Eliza, and I intend to spend a fair portion on you.'

'We shall see,' she said and smiled. 'Have you written to Lady Sarah? I would not have her worried for my sake.'

'I wrote to Cheadle at her address and he will break the news to her. I am certain he will make sure she is not too distressed.'

'Then it seems we have nothing to do but look forward to our wedding.' Eliza reached up to kiss him. 'I do love you so very much.'

'And I love you, my darling.' Daniel took her hand. 'Shall we go and tell my uncle the good news?'

It was three days later that Eliza returned from Norwich, whence Daniel had driven her in his curricle to buy certain things she needed, to discover a carriage at Betty's door. They both recognised the crest immediately.

'I think your father must be waiting for you,' Daniel said and saw a flicker of doubt in her eyes. 'Do not be anxious, my love. I shall be with you and I assure you he will say nothing to upset you.'

'I do not fear him,' Eliza said. 'I am merely anxious that Lady— Mama…' she cried as the cottage door opened and Lady Sarah came out to her.

'Eliza, my love,' her mother said and rushed to

embrace her. 'I told Cheadle I must come to you and he was so good as to oblige me. I was so anxious that I could not wait another day—and so here we are.'

'I am glad to see you, but where are you staying?'

'I dare say my uncle would be glad to offer Lady Sarah and the marquis a room,' Daniel said. 'Shall we go inside and talk about it?'

They trouped inside and Betty ushered them through to the parlour, where Mr Wright was looking slightly ill at ease as he attempted to make conversation with the Marquis of Cheadle. He rose to his feet as the others entered.

'I'll leave you now, sir. I'm glad to have made your acquaintance.'

'Remember that you may come to me if you ever wish for a change of situation. I am deeply aware of my obligation, Mr Wright.'

Cheadle rose to his feet. His gaze went to Eliza and Daniel and he nodded his head. 'Well, I hear it is all settled. You are to be married. I congratulate you, Seaton. Eliza will make you an excellent wife—and she will not be without a dowry. I have decided to give her the same as I gave Marianne, which is twenty thousand pounds.'

'Cheadle, that is handsome of you,' Lady Sarah said and smiled approvingly. 'I shall give Eliza five thousand, as I always planned to give my daughter when I found her.'

'Are you sure, Mama?' Eliza asked her with an anxious look. 'Will Lord Manners not object?'

'It matters not if he does,' her mother replied, a flicker of defiance in her eyes. 'Cheadle and I have some news of our own. We shall remain in England until both you and Marianne are wed, and until then we shall make no announcements—but after that we are to travel to Italy and perhaps Spain or France. Cheadle has parted from Lady Cheadle, and she has agreed to a settlement. There may be a divorce one day, but we are both old enough to pay that no mind.' She looked at Eliza in an oddly shy way. 'You will not be ashamed of your mother for becoming a kept woman?'

'Mama...' Eliza's eyes danced with laughter. 'I believe it would be several years too late, for I should not be here had you not already become the marquis's lover. This is what you should have done years ago.'

'Exactly what I told her,' Cheadle said and smiled fondly at his love. 'If I can arrange it, Sarah will be my wife one day—but if not we shall live together abroad and be damned to the gossips.'

'Then I must wish you happiness,' Daniel said and looked fondly at Eliza. 'I know this will set Eliza's mind at rest and we may all be comfortable. '

'You will allow me to repay the money I took from your father at the card tables, Seaton. It is much on my conscience and I would like to make recompense.'

'It was a gambling debt, sir. My father lost the money and...' Eliza pressed Daniel's hand, giving him a look of appeal. He bent his head stiffly. 'Very well, sir, have it your way.'

'Now we may all be content and look forward to your wedding, Eliza,' Lady Sarah said. 'I have brought some special lace with me. I understand you are making your gown with Mrs Wright's help and I hope you will find a use for it.'

'I am sure I shall—that was the one thing I could not find today,' Eliza told her.

'Shall we leave the ladies to talk wedding clothes?'

Cheadle asked. 'Give me your company, Seaton. There are a few things I would say to you.'

The two men walked from the cottage together, taking a stroll in the lane. They discussed the outcome of Eliza's kidnap, and Cheadle declared himself well satisfied with the business.

'I am glad it is all settled. I should not liked to have left England while either you or my daughter were in danger of your lives.'

'Kettleton will be no threat to anyone in future,' Daniel assured him. 'He is still living, but if he cheats death now he will not last long—and his underlings have all confessed their guilt and hope to be transported to America rather than hung. I shall say nothing against it for their testimony has brought the truth out.'

'Then we may all rest easy.' Cheadle cleared his throat. 'I must thank you for helping me to be certain there was little scandal concerning Marianne's elopement. I think once it is known that Lady Sarah and I have left the country together it will not take the gossips long to put the pieces together. You will not mind if there is some talk?'

'Not in the least, and nor will Jack. He is head over heels with Marianne, and I fancy she is quite content to be the wife of a country gentleman.'

'Yes, she is. When last I saw her, she was delighted to know that Eliza was her half-sister and I think she wants her to be her maid of honour, if you will bring her down next week. It is close to your own wedding, I know, but Marianne would so much like her sister to be there.'

'Then we shall certainly come,' Daniel said. 'And then we must also attend Kate Henderson's wedding before we return here. I imagine Lady Sarah will not accompany you to Marianne's wedding?'

'Not this time—it was part of my wife's terms.'

'Then she may stay and keep my uncle company until we visit Kate's home, or perhaps go down ahead of us...'

'You look beautiful in that gown,' Lady Sarah said when she went in to give Eliza a kiss and a small piece of diamond jewellery on her wedding morning. 'This diamond pin was given me by my father when I was engaged, Eliza. I should like you to have it.'

'I shall pin it to my lace. The earl gave me a set of diamonds and sapphires,' Eliza replicd and hugged her mother. She touched the diamonds at her throat. 'These were my father's wedding gift to me, and the bracelet and earrings were from Daniel. I think they conferred together because they match very well.'

'Yes, Cheadle and Seaton do seem to get on together these days,' Lady Sarah replied with a smile. 'Everything is so much more pleasant. I even had a note from Howard, telling me that I am at liberty to stay at the Dower House should I wish. I believe he has repented of his wickedness—or Cheadle must have frightened him half to death.'

'My father *can* be quite terrifying when he is angry,' Eliza replied and kissed her mother. 'Wasn't it splendid of Marianne and Jack to put off their trip to Italy until after our wedding?'

'Jack is to be Seaton's best man. They are close friends, I think?'

'Yes, the best, which is perfect for Marianne and I.' Eliza smiled. 'I do not know what I have done to be so very fortunate in my friends and family, Mama.'

'I think you deserve all the happiness that has come your way,' Lady Sarah said. 'I have never had a word of reproach from you, even though you had a right to complain.'

'Nor shall you,' Eliza told her. 'I have no reason in the world to complain for everything is quite perfect.'

'That is not what I meant and you know it, but we shall not mention the subject again.' Lady Sarah straightened a piece of exquisite Brussels lace at her daughter's breast. 'Come, dearest, we should be leaving for the church.'

Eliza turned her head to look at Daniel as the vicar pronounced them man and wife. He lifted her veil and kissed her, to some applause from the congregation. Eliza's heart filled with happiness. Then they were leaving church, her hand on his arm as the bells pealed out joyfully.

'My beloved wife,' Daniel murmured as they sat side by side in the coach taking them back to his uncle's house. 'How good that sounds. I smile when I think that I once found the idea of marriage something to be avoided.'

'Kate told me you were nearly a rake once,' Eliza said and smiled. 'I was sorry she could not be here, but as you know she is on her honeymoon. I had a long letter and a gift from her, and she promises to come and stay as soon as we are all settled in England once more.'

'A rake?' Daniel's eyebrows arched. 'Did she, indeed? I believe your friend has a little too much imagination, Eliza. I was never quite that, I think.'

'Oh? You disappoint me,' Eliza teased, her eyes sparkling with mischief. 'She promised me that reformed rakes made quite the best husbands.'

'You little wretch,' Daniel said, taking her into his arms to kiss her soundly. 'You deserve that I should spank you—but there, you always did find me amusing. I shall have to teach you not to laugh at your husband. Respect is the proper thing, madam.'

Eliza gurgled with laughter for his eyes quizzed her boldly, daring her to defy him. 'Ah, is that so? Then I fear you will have to chastise me a great deal, husband, for I have never been properly respectful. I cannot help but see the amusing side to anything—and you must admit that you made a wretched fist of being a highwayman.'

'How true. I do not imagine I shall have the need to take it up again. Your father insisted on repaying the money he won from my father for his peace of mind, and the mortgages are all paid.' He gave her a mock scowl. 'I confess my pride was piqued when you said I amused you.'

'But I like to be amused,' Eliza replied, reaching up to touch his cheek. 'There is sufficient sadness in the world, Daniel. When you came into my life I was struggling to recover from my grief. My adoptive mother was a kind and generous lady. She gave me all the love a natural mother would bestow on her child—and I sincerely mourned her; indeed, she will always hold her place in my heart. My good fortune was that by chance I was reunited with my true mother.'

'I doubt there was much chance in it,' Daniel replied. 'Oh, yes, the advertisement and your employment were by chance, but Lady Sarah was determined to find you. I am certain she would not have given up however long it took.'

'You are very right—but it has all turned out

extremely well. She was an invalid when I went to her. Now she has a new brightness about her and seems perfectly well.'

'She has rediscovered love,' Daniel told her and drew her close to his body. 'Love means more, dearest. Those are very true words. When I read that inscription in Cheadle's ring, I began to realise that I had misjudged him.'

'I gave my ring back to my mama. She wanted me to keep it, but I told her she could leave it to my daughter if she wished—or my son...'

Daniel's eyes danced with amusement as he looked down at her. 'Have you not yet decided? I should have thought you would have all that mapped out?'

'Even I may not do that,' she replied. 'Yet I think perhaps God may favour us with one or the other—or both.'

'Now that,' Daniel said, 'would be quite perfect...'

Eliza stirred, a sigh of content on her lips as she woke and felt the warmth of her husband's body beside her. They were staying in a small discreet hotel in Paris, which was exactly right for a honeymoon. Daniel had taken her exploring, showing her the sights and taking her on the Seine in one of the boats that plied their trade up and down its waters, beneath the Saint-Michel bridge and past the great Cathedral of Notre-Dame. He had bought her more dresses than she could possibly wear, spoiling her until she protested and begged him to stop.

'And what was that sigh for?' Daniel enquired, reaching out to touch her cheek. He turned on his side to look at her, as they lay in their bed. 'Are you bored in Paris—do you wish to go home?'

'How could I possibly be bored when I am with you?'

she said and leaned forwards to kiss him. 'It was a sigh of content, you dear man. I love you so much, Daniel. I never dreamed I could be this fortunate.'

'I am the fortunate one,' he said huskily, pulling her close so that their bodies touched, silken flesh against silken flesh. She immediately felt the burn of his need and giggled with pleasure as she pressed closer. His hand smoothed down her back as his kiss had her arching into him. Their desire took fire and they were swept away on a tide of passion. 'I am not sure I deserve such happiness, Eliza, my darling.'

Eliza nestled into his body, tasting the salt of his sweat on her lips. Each time he made love to her it seemed only to get better and better. He had taught her the pleasures of loving with gentleness and consideration, but sometimes there was such hunger between them that they did not leave their room for most of the day. She thought that perhaps today might be one of those halcyon times when the hours passed in a haze of love and pleasure.

She ran her hands over his back, feeling the strength of honed muscles and the tiny sprinkling of hair just at the bottom of his spine. She found his sensitive spot and tickled him, laughing as he growled and rolled her beneath him in the linen sheets.

'Now that certainly deserves some punishment, madam,' he threatened. 'Tell me, what shall I do to chastise you today?'

'I think you might keep me in bed until sunset, when you will rise and take me dancing,' she said and laughed as he groaned and gathered her to him.

'Eliza, Eliza,' he murmured. 'What am I to do with you?'

Eliza did not answer—she was too busy kissing him,

beginning with his neck and then his shoulder and then working her way down his body, finding the sensitive spots that made him moan with pleasure. It was, she had decided, time that she showed her husband she could do a little punishing, too

Epilogue

It was just a year and one day later that Daniel walked into the breakfast room to find Eliza drinking coffee. He dropped a kiss on her head and sat opposite, showing her the letter he held.

'This has been delivered by hand, Eliza. It is for you and comes from a solicitor in London. I know the firm, though I have never used them personally.'

'Please open it for me, dearest.' Eliza's thoughts were far from lawyers and business letters. 'I cannot think what it may be.'

Daniel broke the seal and perused the contents for a moment, then, 'Good lord! A man by the name of Mr Henry Jarvis has left you his entire fortune—I have never heard you speak of an Uncle Henry, Eliza?'

'No, for I do not have one.' Eliza was puzzled, then nodded. 'I believe he may be Mrs Bancroft's brother. He lived in India for most of his life. I found a letter in her sewing box and wrote to inform him of her death, making it plain that I was her adopted daughter and no blood relation.'

'Well, it seems your letter touched him. He had no other family and—good grief! He must have been a nabob. He has left you more than a hundred thousand pounds. That is a huge amount of money, Eliza—whatever shall you do with it?

'I have no idea.' Eliza placed a hand on her ever so slightly rounded stomach and smiled. 'Perhaps you could invest it in land and property for our children, Daniel?'

'Certainly, if that is your wish, my love.' His eyes dwelled fondly on her for a moment, because she was carrying their first child so well. Then his eyes lit with mischief. 'You realise what this means, Eliza?'

'I have no idea, but I dare say you will tell me,' she said, seeing the sparkle of humour in his eyes.

'The gossips in Bath were right all along. It seems you were a secret heiress after all, Eliza.'

'So I was,' she murmured in her calm contented manner. 'Would you pass me that delicious peach conserve please, Daniel? I believe I shall have another slice of toast.'

* * * * *

Bartered Bride

Anne Herries

Prologue

Nicolas, Marquis of Rothsay, nine and twenty, tall, strong, handsome, and known to most of society as a cold heartless rake, looked helplessly at the diminutive lady before him. Henrietta, Countess Selby, might reach no higher than his shoulder in her heels but she was the only person he would heed, the only person he truly cared for in the world—and, he sometimes thought, the only person who cared two hoots for him.

'Marry to get an heir, dearest Henri?' he murmured, looking at his godmother with a sceptical expression. 'Who do you suppose would have me? The match-making mamas take one look and stay well clear of me for fear I may corrupt their little darlings.'

'More fool them,' Henrietta replied, a sparkle in her eye. 'Besides, it is no such thing. You know very well that there are many young ladies who would be happy to become your wife.'

'Why, for the sake of my fortune?'

His dark eyes smouldered, a mutinous, brooding expression on lips that could at certain moments be sensual and passionate, but were, these days, more often set in lines of disdain or disappointment. His memory strayed to a woman he had known some years previously, when he was first a green youth on the town.

'The lady will give you an heir—or more than one to be safe. In return, you will keep her in comfort for the rest of her life. Surely an heir is worth a little effort? You owe it to the family, Nicolas. Also, you should remember your father's last request. He did not exactly make it a condition of his will, but it was his dying wish that you should provide the estate with an heir. You are in your thirtieth year, dearest, and while I would not suggest you are past your prime, I should hate you to leave things too late.'

'Should you, dearest Henri?' Only his beloved godmother would dare to say such a thing to him, and only she could make him smile at the idea that he might soon be past his prime. 'I suppose Cousin Raymond might be called my heir?'

'That nincompoop? He has no more brain than a peagoose and thinks only of his appearance and what is the latest scandalous tale upon the town.' Henrietta fixed him with a compelling stare. 'If you will not do it for yourself, then do it for me. Had I to refer to Raymond as the head of the family, I should soon find myself in my grave.'

'Poor Henri.' Nicolas smiled affectionately, becoming in that moment a very different man than was known in the clubs and certain drawing rooms in London. 'Has my cousin been lecturing you on my morals again? He tried to remind me of my duty to the family name recently. I fear I sent him about his business with his tail between his legs.'

'Perfectly understandable. I should have done the same in your place. He has no right to tell *you* how to behave, Rothsay. Yet, do you not see, that makes it all the more important for you to set up your nursery? If Raymond begins to imagine himself your rightful heir, it will make him more conceited than ever—and perhaps resentful if at the last minute you produce an heir. Besides, the children of old men are often weaklings.'

'Henrietta, I adore you.' Nicolas swept his godmother from her feet, planting a kiss on her cheek. She gave him a mocking wrathful look and he set her down carefully. 'Forgive me, but you tempt me so.'

'Remember I am more than twice your age and to be treated with respect,' Henrietta said, but there was a smile in her eyes. 'Will you at least consider marriage, Nicolas?'

Nicolas caught the hint of tears in her eyes and realised that the matter of his heir was important to her. She had no children of her own and, although not precisely lonely, for she had many friends, she must wish for a child to dote on. He suspected that his godmother had not been truly well for a while now. She might be thinking of making her own will, and, while he knew himself her favourite, he believed she would leave her fortune to his son if he had one. She was forever telling him he had more money than was good for him.

In his heart Nicolas knew that her pleas made perfect sense. It was time he produced an heir for the family. His father had begged him to do so on his death bed

and Nicolas had pushed the memory to the back of his
mind, a little resentful that his father should make such
a demand after the neglect of years.

The trouble was that he had become used to his life
as it was and had no wish for a change. Love caused
more trouble than it was worth and he would avoid it at
all cost—but perhaps a marriage of convenience might
suit him? It was, as Henrietta said, his duty. He was not
yet in his dotage, but if his lack of a wife was causing
his godmother distress, he must certainly give it some
consideration.

'For your sake I shall give the matter of an heir some
thought—when I return from Paris.'

'You intend to visit Paris?'

'Yes, for a few weeks. The company grows stale in
London. I need a change of air.'

'What you need is a passionate adventure,' Henrietta
replied. 'I do not mean your opera dancers and actresses,
who oblige you for the sake of the money you lavish on
them. No, Nicolas, you need to fall desperately in love
and to be brought back to life. I fear you have no real
interest in anything.'

'Love is a myth,' he replied, withdrawing from her,
a look of disdain upon his mouth. 'If I marry, it will be
to a woman who understands that I must be free to live
my own way. As you said, there need be no more than a
token marriage on either side. She will give me an heir.
I shall give her a home and jewels and there it ends—if
I find anyone foolish enough to take me, that is.'

Even for Henri's sake, he had no intention of surren-
dering his heart and soul to love. He had witnessed the
way love destroyed a man, making him a shadow of his

former self, and causing him to withdraw into a lonely place inside his head. Nicolas's father had worshipped his mother; when she died, he had shut himself off from everyone, including his only child—leaving Nicolas to cope with the loss of both parents alone.

As a young man he had briefly believed himself in love but learned a sharp lesson when the young lady laughed at his offer of devotion. After Elizabeth, he had decided that he would never let another woman under his skin.

'Believe me, I can do without a romantic attachment, Henri. Love is for fools.'

'Well, I have said my piece. You must go your own way, Nicolas—and now I shall bid you good morning.'

'Leaving already?' The smile had come back to his dark eyes. 'Stay and have nuncheon with me? It is rare enough that you honour me with a visit, Henri.'

'If you visited Rothsay Manor occasionally, I dare say I should see more of you. London is too much of a racket for me these days.'

'You are not truly unwell?' For a moment real anxiety flashed into his eyes.

Henrietta smiled. The boy she had loved was still there beneath the cold aloof manner he had assumed these past years.

'No, dearest, I am not unwell—and, yes, I shall stay and eat with you since you ask…'

Chapter One

'What have you there?' Lady Hoskins asked as Charlotte Stanton entered the parlour carrying a letter. 'Is it from your father?'

'From Clarice,' Lottie answered with a smile. 'She apologises for not having written before, but they have been too busy.'

'Too busy!' Aunt Beth gave a snort as she looked at her favourite niece. 'Too busy to write to her own twin? Well, is that not typical of them both? They leave you here and go gallivanting off to Paris while you have the bother of an invalid.'

'I did not wish to go to Paris with them,' Lottie replied a little untruthfully. She might have wished to go had her aunt been in better health, or if Clarice had agreed to remain at home with her this time. 'Besides, you were quite unwell, dearest Beth. I could not have been happy knowing you were here alone.'

'Nonsense, I have Muffet and the maids,' Lady

Hoskins replied, but the tone of her voice told Beth that she would not have wished to be left alone to cope.

'I would much rather be here in the country with you than racketing around all those hotels and gaming halls with Papa. Besides, someone had to give an eye to the estate, though Mr Jackson is a very good agent and does his best for us.'

'Well, I certainly hope that your sister is not racketing around gambling clubs,' her aunt said looking alarmed. 'It would be quite improper for a young woman of her age. Your father is a confirmed gambler and will never change. It was the death of my poor sister, never knowing where the next penny would come from. That, my dearest Lottie, is what you get for marrying a rake and a gambler.'

'Papa did break Mama's heart,' Lottie admitted, sadness in her eyes. 'She had to follow him all over Europe, never knowing whether they would have enough money to pay for a roof over their heads or the next meal. It was fortunate that Papa was left this house. At least Mama was able to rest here in peace for a few years, though Papa did not stay long with her. He does have a small mortgage on the house, of course, but the bank will not lend him any more. That is just as well, otherwise, I fear we should not have a roof over our heads.'

Lottie looked round the charming room. Although the soft furnishings and curtains were faded and showing signs of wear, it was a comfortable place to sit in the afternoons. At this precise moment the sun was pouring in through the French windows, which they had opened to allow for some air. The furniture was for the most part old, some of it belonging to an age long gone, heavy carved Jacobean pieces that gave Lottie a feeling of permanence, of belonging. However, the previous owner had been an admirer of Mr Chippendale and there was a very handsome bookcase in the best parlour, as well as a set of good chairs in the dining room. Aunt Beth sat in a comfortable wing chair, her sewing table to hand and a book of poetry on the wine table at her side. Lottie, too, had been reading earlier, and her book lay on the small elegant sofa.

'What else does your sister say?' Aunt Beth enquired as Lottie sat down to read her letter.

'She says that Papa lost a large sum of money to an English marquis playing piquet...' Lottie turned the page, scanning some lines of rather indignant writing from her twin. 'Oh dear...that is too bad of Papa. No, no, he really has gone too far this time. No wonder Clarice is angry.'

'Why? Do not keep me in suspense a moment longer!'

Lottie handed the letter to her aunt, who frowned over it for some minutes before returning it to her.

'That is both ridiculous and disgusting,' Aunt Beth said. 'How dare he?'

'What, you mean how dare Papa accept—or how dare the marquis make such an outrageous request?'

'Both,' Aunt Beth said, looking affronted. 'I have never heard of such a thing—to suggest that your father should give him Clarice in payment for a gambling debt—it is the outside of enough!'

'The marquis has said he will marry her,' Lottie said thoughtfully. 'I suppose in a way it might be a good thing for Clarice. Besides, it could be worse—he might have demanded she become his mistress…'

'How can you think so?' Aunt Beth shook her head. 'The marquis must be a rake. He is probably old enough to be her father—a lecherous old devil who will lead Clarice a hell of a life.'

'If he is, she must not marry him.' Lottie got to her feet. 'We shall know soon enough—they are coming home in a few days. Clarice said the marquis provided the money for their return. Otherwise they might have been stuck in France until we could send more money.'

'And where would we get that, pray? I have nothing left but my pearls—which are for you, Lottie, when you marry—and fifty pounds a year. Clarice had the garnets when she was engaged, and she did not return them when she broke off her engagement. What little I have is for you, my dear.'

'Do not speak of such things,' Lottie begged her. 'I pray you will live for many years yet. Besides, I am not sure I shall marry.'

'Why ever not? You are the equal of your sister in looks, and your character is superior. She has had chances enough—why should you not?'

Lottie sighed. 'I should wish to marry for love, but then poor dear Mama married the man of her dreams—and they very soon turned to ashes.'

'My sister was a silly little thing, though I loved her dearly,' Aunt Beth said. 'However, I married a man who had both background and money—and look where that got me.'

Lottie nodded. Her uncle had not gambled away

his money at the tables, but on a series of bad investments—including being caught in a scandal that had been almost as calamitous as the South Seas Bubble, which had ruined so many people in 1720—and had left his widow with very little fortune. Aunt Beth had been forced to sell her home and come to live with her sister and nieces after her husband died in a riding accident. Then Aunt Beth had taken care of her and Clarice after their mother died, and Lottie at least had become very fond of her.

'I suppose if one of us were to marry a rich man we might all be comfortable.' Lottie frowned. 'But Clarice sounds very angry. I do not think she will agree and if she does not...'

'Do you think we might lose the house?' A look of anxiety crossed Aunt Beth's face. 'Where should we go then, Lottie?'

Lottie had no idea. She had lain awake more than one night recently, worrying about what would happen if her father lost what little money he had at the tables. She had begged him not to go on this latest visit to Paris, but he could never rest in the country for more than a few weeks at a time, and Clarice had demanded to go with him. Now her father owed more than he could pay and both he and Clarice were on their way home.

Nicolas threw his gloves and hat on to the sideboard in the spacious hall of his London house. His boots clattered on the marble floor, the resulting sound echoing to the high ceilings. He was not in the best of tempers and it showed in the set of his mouth and the brooding expression in his eyes.

'Did you have a good journey, my lord?' his butler dared to ask.

'No, damn it, I did not,' Nicolas snapped. 'Have Harris lay up some things for me. I shall be going into the country for a few days.'

'Yes, my lord—certainly. Is there anything more, sir?'

'No Yes, you can wish me happy, Barret. I am to be married, and quite soon I think.'

'My lord…'

Nicholas left his butler in shock as he took the stairs two at a time. He smiled grimly. The one consolation in the whole sorry business was that it would set the cat amongst the pigeons once the story got out. A reluctant smile touched his lips. At least he could still laugh at society and himself—but why the hell had he done it?

It was true that he had promised Henrietta he would consider the idea of marriage, but to ask for the hand of a woman—he would not call her a lady, for she was an adventuress—he had only just met was ridiculous.

Nicolas had at first refused when Sir Charles Stanton had offered him his daughter as payment for the gambling debt. However, after a night of reflection, he had decided that one woman was as good as another. His memory of being ridiculed by Elizabeth when he declared his love had made him determined never to offer his heart again. Therefore Sir Charles's offer was a convenient way of solving his problem. Clarice had been brought up as a lady, of that he had no doubt—but he had not known when he'd agreed to the deal that her morals were those of an alley cat.

It was on the night after he had signed the contract Sir

Charles had hastily had drawn up with their joint lawyers that Nicolas discovered his mistake. One of Nicolas's friends had been visiting Paris and they had gone out to a gaming club together, both of them drinking more than usual. Ralph Thurlstone had been three sheets to the wind and Nicolas rather more drunk than was sensible when he discovered his friend in a back room of the club. Ralph was lying senseless on the bed while a very pretty young woman with long spun-gold curls emptied his pockets of what money he had left. From the look of her hair and crumpled gown, he suspected that she had been on the bed with Ralph prior to robbing him.

'What the hell do you imagine you are doing?' Nicolas enquired dangerously.

'Taking what belongs to me,' the woman replied, her green eyes flashing with temper. 'He owes me and this is scarcely recompense for what he took.'

'Are you telling me you were a virgin before this evening?'

'Would you believe me?'

'No.'

'Then I shall tell you nothing,' the woman said and passed him, going out of the room.

Nicolas had let her go. In truth, he was still stunned by what he had seen. Returning to the main rooms a little later, he discovered Sir Charles at the tables, and standing at his back was the young woman he had seen going through Ralph's pockets moments earlier. Nicolas had thought he must have been mistaken, but there was no mistake. Clarice Stanton, his bartered bride-to-be, had robbed his friend while he lay in a drunken stupor.

'Ah, Rothsay,' Sir Charles said, looking up. 'Sit down and join us, won't you? Clarice is bringing me luck tonight. I was down to my last guinea but she brought me ten more and I have won the pot of two hundred.'

Which he would no doubt lose before he rose from the tables, Nicolas thought.

Nicolas looked the young woman in the eyes and saw her flush. Until this evening, he had not met Stanton's daughter, not bothering to propose to her but leaving it to the father to tell her of their arrangement. He supposed that he had intended to speak to her in his own good time. When he recklessly signed the marriage contract, he had been acting on impulse. He had heard on the rumour mill that Stanton's daughter was pretty, but as he was engaged to her already, sight unseen, her looks were not his primary concern. He had thought only that she was available and would give him the heir everyone said he needed.

To his horror, he had contracted himself to marry a thief and a wanton. What a damned fool he had been!

Henrietta had begged him to marry for the sake of the family. He hardly dared to contemplate what she would say if she knew the truth.

He must find a way to withdraw—but how could it be done? Anger smouldered inside him as he saw the young woman continue to encourage her profligate father at the tables. When Stanton rose a winner of some two thousand pounds or more, she flashed him a look of triumph, as if daring him to expose her to the world.

Needless to say, Nicolas had kept his mouth closed. It would have exposed him to ridicule, as well as Ralph, whom he knew to be newly engaged to a respectable English girl. His friend had been feeling a little hedge-bound, because his mother-in-law to be was demanding he dance attention on her daughter the whole time. Ralph had escaped to Paris for a last fling, and would never know that he had not spent all his guineas at the tables. The loss was one he could afford, but Nicolas was affronted by the idea that he had agreed to marry a woman of such low morals.

Nicolas had left Paris the next day, sending his would-be father-in-law a sharp note dictating that he take his daughter back to England to await his further instructions.

As soon as he had set foot in town, Nicolas visited his family lawyer to discover if the contract was watertight, and apparently it was. Nicolas could of course withdraw and compensate the girl for breach of promise. He would no doubt have to pay through the nose to be free of her. His mouth drew into a thin line as he contemplated the scandal.

No, better that he find a way of forcing the woman to withdraw. He would be ridiculed in the clubs whichever way it went, but if Miss Stanton withdrew it could all be settled by a payment for her bruised pride—if she had any—and there would be less scandal.

It was his own fault for giving in to a wild impulse. He could not blame Henrietta, who would certainly not have advised such a reckless affair. Nicolas smiled wryly. The irony of it was that such a marriage would have suited him had the woman not been a thief and a cheat. She was certainly pretty enough, and, if compliant, might have had her own house and done much as she pleased once she had given him a couple of heirs.

So for now, it seemed that he must go through with the formal arrangements. Henrietta must be told of his impending marriage and in due course an announcement must be made in *The Times*. Yet he would hold back on the announcement for a while; there was still a chance he might be able to persuade the young woman to withdraw. He must post down to his country house and put some work in hand. Nicolas seldom bothered to pay more than a flying visit to his family home; it would certainly need some changes if his wife were to live there.

His wife... Nicolas felt as if a knife had struck at his heart. There had once been someone he hoped to make his wife, but Elizabeth had laughed in his face and married an older, richer man. For years he had allowed his hurt pride to eat away at him, but it was time to put it aside. When this fiasco was over, he must look for a suitable wife in earnest.

'I shall not marry him. I told Papa in Paris that I would not. He refused to tell the marquis that the contract must be broken. I know there is a debt, but he won a little before we left Paris, after I wrote to you. I dare say if we sold this house he could pay the debt.'

Lottie looked at her sister's flushed face and wondered how Clarice could be so selfish. Did her twin never give a thought to anyone else's comfort but her own?

'What about Aunt Beth and me?' she asked. 'Where should we go if the house were sold? Aunt Beth has little enough income as it is—and I have nothing at all.'

'I will find a rich husband and rescue you both.' Clarice flashed a beguiling smile at her sister.

'Surely the marquis is rich enough? Papa said he was rolling in the blunt.'

'Well, I dare say he is, but I do not like him. He is arrogant and cold—and I shall not marry him.'

Clarice took up Lottie's hairbrush and began to brush her twin's hair.

'I hate him, Lottie. Papa is mean to say I must marry him. I would rather die—besides, there is someone I really like. I met him in Paris and I think he is in love with me.'

'Oh, Clarice…' Lottie sighed. 'If the marquis is that horrible, I should not want you to marry him. Is he very old, dearest?'

'Oh, middle-aged, I should say…thirty or more.'

'That is not old.' Lottie frowned at her. 'Is he ugly?'

'No, not ugly…stern, I suppose.' Clarice put down the brush. 'You must agree with me or Papa will make me marry him.'

'If he is presentable and rich…' Lottie looked thoughtful. 'It would be the answer to Papa's troubles, Clarice. Could you not marry him for his sake and ours?'

Clarice made a face at her in the mirror. 'If you think he sounds presentable, you marry him. He would never know the difference…' Clarice stared at her in the mirror and her expression became one of excitement. 'Why not? Why do you not wed him in my place? You could be certain that Aunt Beth had a decent home and Papa could come to you whenever he was in trouble.'

'Don't be ridiculous, Clarice.' While it was true that

they were almost identical in looks, apart from a mole on Lottie's right breast that Clarice did not have, they were very different in character. 'Surely he would know the difference? I know that many people cannot tell us apart but he must know you better than most.'

'We have only met once—and he does not know me at all, though he may think he does.'

'What does that mean?'

Clarice shrugged. 'He is so arrogant. I suppose I cannot expect you to marry him, Lottie. Yet I shall not. I would rather run away.'

'You will not change your mind?'

'No, not for the world,' Clarice declared. 'I am sorry if the house must be sold, but I dare say Aunt Beth can find a little cottage to rent.'

'Is that all you care—after she looked after us for so many years?'

'Well, I should not like her to be homeless, but I refuse to marry him. If you are so concerned, Lottie, you may marry him yourself. I do think you could for it would be better than being stuck here in the country the whole time.'

'Do not be so ridiculous. It is you he wants—how could I marry him?'

'You could pretend to be me.'

'No, no, that would be cheating him. It is a foolish idea, Clarice. I cannot consider it.'

'Then Papa will have to tell him the wedding is off,' Clarice said and looked mutinous. 'I shall not marry him and that is an end to it.'

'Have you seen your sister this morning?' Aunt Beth asked when Lottie came back from her walk the next morning. 'Your father wanted to speak to her, because the marquis has written to him, but she was not in her room. I knocked, but she did not answer'

'I expect she is sulking,' Lottie said. 'I'll go up and speak to her at once.'

Taking off her pelisse and bonnet, Lottie went to her own room first. She was thoughtful as she walked along the hall to her sister's room. She had been thinking about Clarice's suggestion that she marry Rothsay in her place ever since their argument the previous day. It was a mad idea that they should change places, yet if Clarice truly dug her heels in, what was the alternative?

Lottie knew her sister well enough to be sure that Clarice would never marry to oblige her family. She must dislike the marquis very much, which meant that he was probably a most unpleasant man. Yet if Clarice refused, their father would lose everything.

Knocking at her sister's door, Lottie waited for a moment, then opened it and went in. The room was empty; by the look of things, Clarice had left it in a hurry. She had clothes strewn everywhere, an odd shoe dropped on the floor—and all her silver combs, brushes and perfume bottles were missing from the dressing chest.

Feeling cold all over, Lottie went to investigate. Looking in the drawers of the tallboy, she saw that some of them were empty of all but Clarice's oldest things.

As she glanced at the bed, she saw a letter lying on a pillow. It was addressed to her. Tearing it open, her worst fears were soon confirmed.

Clarice had run away.

*Tell Papa not to try to find me. I shall never come
back and he may as well sell the house because I
do not wish to marry that awful man.*

'Oh, Clarice,' Lottie sighed. 'What have you done
now?'

As a child Clarice had always been selfish and
thoughtless, and, because most people could not tell them
apart, she had formed a habit of making people think it
was Lottie who had broken their vase or knocked over
her milk or put a stone through a window.

Glancing at the letter again, Lottie saw the post-
script.

*Why not do as we discussed and marry him your-
self, Lottie? He will never know the difference.
He doesn't care two hoots for me, so what harm
can it do?*

Lottie took the letter and went back downstairs. She
met her father as he emerged from his study. He was
looking tired and worried and her heart caught with
pain.

'Father—is something the matter?'

'Your sister has informed me once again that she will
not marry the marquis and I'm damned if I know what
to do. I suppose I shall have no choice but to sell the
house.'

'Perhaps not…'

'What do you mean? Has she changed her mind?'

'You had better read this, Papa.' Lottie handed him
her twin's letter. 'I have no idea where she has gone, but

she has taken most of her things—including the silver that belonged to Mama.'

Sir Charles read it through and cursed. 'She is a thoughtless minx. Well, that settles it. I must sell—and if the marquis sues for breach of promise, I shall probably end up in the Fleet.'

'Papa! He wouldn't sue?'

'He might,' Sir Charles said. 'Rothsay will not take this well.'

'Supposing I did what Clarice suggested?'

He stared at her. 'Take her place, you mean?'

'Yes. She says the marquis doesn't love her.'

'They only met twice to my knowledge.' Lottie's father looked at her with dawning relief in his eyes. 'You wouldn't do it—would you?'

'Yes, I shall,' Lottie blurted unthinkingly, desperate not to see her father suffer any more distress. She almost denied it instantly, but the look of relief in her father's eyes prevented her from turning back. 'Clarice told me that all Rothsay wants from his wife is an heir—and that it was always to be more of a marriage of convenience.'

'Yes, he was clear that was all he wanted.' Sir Charles seemed to have shed ten years in an instant. 'If you could bear it, Lottie—it would be an end to my problems.'

'Yes, of course I can.' Lottie forced a smile. 'Most girls marry for money or position, so why shouldn't I?'

What else could she do in the circumstances? If she did not take her sister's place, Aunt Beth would be left homeless, her father might end in a debtor's prison; though he had given the family nothing but trouble over the years, Lottie remained devoted to her father. No, she couldn't bear for her family to suffer if there was something she could do to prevent it.

Chapter Two

'Are you certain you wish to go through with this, Lottie?' Her father reached for her hand, which was trembling slightly as the carriage horses began to slow to a steady walk. In another few minutes they would arrive at the marquis's country house and it would be too late to run back. 'I can tell him you are unwilling and ask him to give me time to pay.'

'How can you pay, Papa?' Lottie turned her lovely green eyes on him with a hint of reproach. 'I have thought long and hard about my decision. Clarice will not marry him. She's run away and we've none of us any idea where she is; besides, Aunt Beth is terrified of losing her home with you. How could she live on fifty pounds a year? I should have to find work to help support us both.'

'I am ashamed to have brought you to this,' Sir Charles said. 'I know well that your sister is selfish,' he added and looked rueful. 'She takes after me, while you have your mother's giving nature. I would not have minded that devil being married to Clarice, for I know she would have given as good as she got—but you may be hurt, Lottie.'

'I am stronger than you imagine, and, as I've said, there is no choice.' Lottie smiled at him. 'Now, Papa, you must be careful when calling me Lottie.'

'Rothsay knows nothing of you. He will merely think it a pet name, which of course it is, Charlotte.'

'Well, we must be careful all the same.' Lottie took his hand. 'As I told you, Papa—I shall see if his lordship will release us from the debt without marriage, but if he will not I shall become his wife. It is perhaps my only chance of marriage and I know I should like to have children, so it will not be so very hard for me.'

'Will it not, truly?'

Lottie dropped her eyes. She did not wish her father to know that it was the end of her naïve dreams of finding love and happiness. Clarice had told her the marquis was a terrible rake. Clearly, she could not expect to find happiness with her husband, but at least her aunt would have a home—and she might find content in her children.

'No, Father. I believe I shall be quite content—unless the marquis is good enough to relent.'

'I do not think he is likely to change his mind,' her father said and sighed. 'I fear you will just have to make up your mind to marry him.'

Lottie did not reply. The carriage had just now drawn to a halt before a grand and imposing house built at some time in the last century, and her heart was beating so fast that she could not have spoken if her life depended on it.

'The gentleman and young lady have arrived, sir.' Nicolas turned his head as his butler spoke. 'I have shown them into the green drawing room, as you requested. Shall I ask Mrs Mann to take in some refreshment?'

'Yes, you may bring it in ten minutes,' Nicolas said. 'I shall greet my guests.'

He was unsmiling as he walked briskly towards the green drawing room at the back of the house. He had waited for some protest, some inkling that the lady wished to withdraw, but none had been forthcoming. He could only hope that the young woman might give him some reason to request an end to this impossible arrangement.

'Yes, Father, it is very beautiful,' he heard the young woman's clear voice as he stood outside the door. 'I was just thinking how much Aunt Beth would love to live here. I wonder—'

The young woman broke off, turning to look at him with wide eyes as he entered, a faint flush in her cheeks. She was wearing a bonnet of chip straw tied with emerald ribbons, her carriage gown skilfully fashioned of velvet of a similar hue, and he was surprised. In Paris she had worn a gown that was, to say the least, bold, but this morning she looked a modest and very respectable young lady.

How dared she present herself as a demure country miss? Did she imagine he had such a short memory? His lips curled in scorn as his gaze swept over her. He thought the colour in her cheeks deepened. Was she remembering the night in Paris when he had caught her going through Ralph's pockets?

'Miss Stanton,' he said and took two strides towards her, inclining his head. 'Welcome to Rothsay Park. Sir Charles, how do you do, sir?'

'Middling.' Sir Charles looked hesitantly at his daughter. 'I understand you plan to give a ball to announce your engagement to…my daughter?'

'You would have preferred to give it yourself?'

The scorn in Nicolas's voice assaulted his own ears. He was being rude to a guest and, as his father would have told him, that was unforgivable. In his father's day it would have resulted in a beating and no supper. He added hastily to cover up his bluntness, 'I thought it would be easier here for I have a deuced many relatives, and I fear they will descend in droves once the announcement is made.'

'Ah, yes, well…' Sir Charles floundered unhappily.

'I am sure it will be much better held here, sir,' Lottie said and smiled as she removed her bonnet, revealing hair dressed in waves back from her face and drawn into a secure double knot at the nape. In Paris her hair had been loose, tumbling on to her shoulders, as if she had just risen from bed—which she had. 'I know my aunt will be very happy to visit. I do hope you will not mind my inviting her for the ball? There is no one else I truly wish to invite.'

'Indeed? You have no relatives?'

'Mama had one sister, who is now a widow and has no children. Papa has no family at all.'

'Well, there is Cousin Agatha, Lottie,' Sir Charles said. 'You know what a tongue she has on her. If I do not invite her, she will never stop complaining.'

'I think that perhaps I would rather not ask Cousin Agatha,' she replied. 'You should really call me by my name, Papa. The marquis will think my pet name unsuitable for the lady he intends to make his wife.'

'Lottie?' Nicolas raised his brows. 'Is that not more usually given to those with the name of Charlotte?'

'Mama liked the name. It was hers and it is also one of my names—everyone at home calls me Lottie.'

'Do they? I wonder why. I thought Clarice eminently suitable for the young woman I met in Paris. It has rather more sophistication, I think?'

'Yes, I am certain it has,' Lottie agreed. 'I am perfectly happy for you to address me as you please, sir.'

'Are you indeed? Thank you, Miss Stanton. I shall give the matter some thought.' He turned as the housekeeper entered with another maid bearing silver trays. 'Ah, here is Mrs Mann with your tea—and something stronger for you, Sir Charles. If you'll excuse me I have some business to attend to. Mrs Mann will take you up to your rooms when you have refreshed yourselves. I shall see you this evening before dinner.'

'Thank you, sir. We are much obliged,' Sir Charles said and nodded to the housekeeper as she indicated the Madeira wine. 'Yes, ma'am, that will do nicely, I thank you.'

'Miss Stanton, you will excuse me.' Nicolas nodded to her abruptly and left the room.

'Sir.' She bobbed a curtsy, but not before he had seen a flash of anger in her eyes. He felt a flicker of satisfaction; that was better, he was getting to the real Clarice now.

Nicolas frowned as he strode from the house. His business with his agent would have kept, but he was not sure he could have controlled his temper much longer. How dared the lady look as if butter would not melt in her mouth?

Her smile had reminded him sharply of Elizabeth when they first met. She had seemed charming and innocent—but when he offered her his heart, she had laughed and told him she was looking for more than he could offer.

Clarice—or Lottie, as she seemed to prefer—was not Elizabeth, but Nicolas was no longer a green youth. If Lottie imagined he had forgotten that scene in the bedroom in Paris, she would soon learn otherwise.

He would not be rude to her in front of her father, but when they were alone, he would ask her what game she was playing.

Clarice was so right! Lottie's hands curled into tight balls at her sides. What a rude, arrogant, cold, beastly man he was! She would have liked to give him a set down, for he had no reason to be so insufferably condescending. Papa had, it was true, lost more money than he could afford, but Rothsay could have insisted on being paid. He had accepted Papa's offer of his own free will. The least he could do was to treat both Papa and her with respect.

He deserved all he got. During the journey, Lottie's conscience had pricked her for practising this deceit on the unsuspecting marquis. She had feared that he was in love with Clarice and would spot the difference immediately, but he clearly hadn't. Indeed, apart from that scornful glance he had bestowed on her at the start, he had hardly seemed to notice her.

Lottie had hoped that the marquis might relent and release them from the outrageous contract he and her father had made between them. He was everything her sister had claimed and Lottie would not marry him.

Lottie's indignation drained away almost as soon as it flared into being. With no offer of a withdrawal the contract would still stand; if she were to break the terms then it would be her family that suffered. It might not be so bad, she consoled herself, the marquis had a beautiful home and it would be pleasant to live here, especially if, as she suspected, her husband-to-be preferred London life. It was large enough for her aunt to stay on an almost permanent basis, for Lottie had no illusions about her papa's promises of reform. He might be feeling chastened and sorry now, but within weeks he would become bored and once again the gaming tables would draw him like a moth to the flame.

It was a sickness, like Mama's weak chest, which fortunately neither of her daughters had inherited. Lottie loved her family, even her selfish sister, and she knew that if she went through with this marriage she would probably be in a position to help them over the years. Her husband would have provided her with a small income in the marriage contract and she had a frugal nature.

She reasoned that if all the marquis required was an heir he would not wish to spend much time in her company. Perhaps she could bear to accept a certain amount of intimacy with him for the sake of her family—and she would like children of her own.

'Shall I take you upstairs now, Miss Stanton?'

'Oh…yes, thank you, Mrs Mann.'

Lottie recalled her wandering thoughts. She was here and there was no getting out of the bargain her father had made, so she might as well make the most of things and enjoy her surroundings.

'I shall see you later,' Sir Charles said as she prepared to follow the housekeeper. 'Is everything all right, Lottie?'

'Yes…' Lottie raised her head. Her father was relying on her to solve his problems, as was her aunt. She could not let them down. If the marquis had not been such an arrogant brute, she might have felt bad about deceiving him, but he deserved no consideration from her. 'Everything is perfectly all right, Papa. I shall not keep Mrs Mann waiting.'

Following the housekeeper from the small but elegant parlour, Lottie walked up the wide main staircase, marvelling at the spacious beauty of her surroundings, the ornate ceilings and exquisite furnishings. The family that had built and maintained this house must be vastly rich. It had an air of wealth and security, of being the home of important men, like its present owner.

Why would a man like Rothsay choose to take a bride as payment for a gambling debt? There must be any number of eligible young ladies who would be delighted to marry him—unless his rakish reputation had made him an outcast as far as the matchmaking mamas were concerned?

Lottie's thoughts were confused, churning round in her mind and becoming no clearer. Had the marquis been a little warmer at their first meeting, she thought she might have liked the idea of her marriage very well.

Did she have a choice? What would happen if she changed her mind and withdrew at the last moment?

Oh, fiddlesticks! He was an impossible man and she

was being torn two ways. A part of her wanted to run away while she still had the chance—yet in her head a small secret voice wanted to make a fight of it. Rothsay was rude and arrogant. It would give her some satisfaction to prick his pride if she could.

Lottie changed out of her travelling gown, which was fairly new, into one of the more comfortable dresses she wore at home when walking to the village or the vicarage. She had decided to spend the afternoon walking round the gardens and what she reasonably could of the estate.

From her windows she had seen a large park, and in the distance a lake. Being fond of water and wildlife, she was torn between the park, which looked to consist of many beautiful old trees, and the lake, which was, she was sure, newer and man-made. As the sun was shining brightly, she thought the lake might be within distance and set out for it without reference to anyone.

It was a lovely day for walking; the peaceful surroundings soothed nerves that had become ruffled by her dilemma. She still did not know what she ought to do for the best. Being a sensible girl, she had made up her mind to take things as they came. If the chance presented itself, she might raise the question of a postponement or a cancellation of the contract, but if it did not, then she would simply have to marry him.

Enjoying the beauty of her surroundings, Lottie knew that being the wife of a man who took himself off to town for most of the time could not be a hardship for a girl such as herself. There were many young women who married for the sake of a comfortable home and a position in Society. Her marriage would be convenient to her in many ways, though the thought of how the heirs must be produced was a little daunting.

Could she really lie with a man as cold and arrogant as the marquis? A man she didn't even love?

'Oh, bother,' she said aloud and sighed. 'I shall not allow him to upset me.'

It was too nice a day for such anxious thoughts and staying at this wonderful place, even for a short time, was a treat.

Arriving at the lake, she stood admiring the excellence of the landscaping and how well the rock pools and greenery looked. A flock of black swans sailed majestically towards her, clearly expecting to be fed.

'I am so sorry, my lords and ladies,' Lottie said, feeling that royalty deserved the proper address. 'Had I known you were in residence, I should have brought some food for you.'

'They are magnificent, are they not? I've told Rothsay he is lucky to have found such specimens. We have the white variety, but the black species are something special.'

Lottie whirled round, startled by the man's voice. She had had no idea that anyone else was near by.

'Oh…I spoke aloud believing I was alone,' Lottie said, staring at the young man who had come up on her unawares. 'Yet they do command respect, do they not?'

'I was enchanted,' he said and offered his hand. 'Bertie Fisher. I am a neighbour of Rothsay and came to see him on business. He said that his fiancée had arrived earlier. Do I have the pleasure of addressing Miss Clarice Stanton?'

'Yes…though my friends call me Lottie,' she said and then blushed, for it was very forward of her to invite him to use her name. It was perhaps that he was attractive, his smile warm and friendly, and his manner not in the least arrogant. 'I am pleased to meet you, Mr Fisher.'

'It's Sir Bertram or just plain Bertie to my friends,' he replied and grinned as she offered her hand and he took it in a firm cool clasp. 'I hope we shall be friends, Miss Lottie. As neighbours we are bound to see something of each other. I was just telling Rothsay that I shall be leaving for London at the end of the week. I shall naturally return for your engagement dance.'

'Yes, I am certain we shall become friends,' Lottie answered warmly, then wondered if she would be here many days. 'I am looking forward to exploring the estate, and managed the walk to the lake, though I must return now or I may be late for tea.'

'Will you allow me to walk with you, Miss Lottie? I have something I must tell Rothsay, and we may as well walk together.'

'Yes, certainly,' she said and took the arm he offered. Sir Bertie was certainly a pleasant gentleman and if his wife was of the same nature she would have a friend— should she stay long enough to make friends. 'Have you known the marquis long?'

'Oh, all my life. My grandfather bought the estate and my mother still lives here for some of the time, though Mama likes to travel abroad for the sun in the winter. Sometimes I accompany her, though I do enjoy shooting and hunting in the autumn, and she has her friends, you know.'

'And your wife?'

'I am unmarried as yet—though it has been in my mind to marry. I am a few years younger than Rothsay, of course.'

'Yes…'

'I have to say that you are a marvel, Miss Lottie. We had all given up on the idea of Rothsay settling down. I dare say you know his reputation, but they say reformed rakes make the best husbands. No doubt you will soon have him curled about your little finger.'

'Why should Rothsay's marriage be such a surprise?'

'Oh, well, I suppose he has told you about Elizabeth. Everyone thought it was a match made in heaven. She was the toast of the Season, beautiful, clever and an heiress. Rothsay was head over heels; at least, we all thought so. An announcement of their engagement was expected but then he went off abroad and stayed in Paris for months.'

'He gave no explanation for letting her down?'

'It was all brushed under the carpet. She married a man several years older while Rothsay was in Paris, and now has three sons.'

Rothsay had clearly broken the beauty's heart, which resulted in her marriage to an older man. It just showed what kind of a man he was, leading her on and then deserting her without making an offer. Lottie fumed inwardly. No wonder he hadn't bothered to court Clarice. All he wanted was an heir and he had bought himself a wife for the price of a gambling debt. He must be a cold calculating devil and if Lottie's father had not been so desperate she would tell him what he might do with his offer and go home immediately.

Lottie would have asked more questions of her obliging new acquaintance, but for the fact that she had seen the marquis coming to meet them. She stiffened, her hand tightening on her companion's arm. He glanced at her, but made no comment, and Lottie lifted her head. Surely the marquis would not be rude to her in front of a neighbour.

'I thought you had left, Bertie,' he said, lifting his brows. 'Did you forget something?'

'Yes, as a matter of fact I did. I was walking home past the lake and happened to discover Miss Lottie making friends with the swans. It was then that I recalled what I wanted to ask, Rothsay. I decided to walk back with Miss Lottie.'

'And I was going to ask if you would like to stay for tea,' Lottie said, noticing the way the marquis's pupils took on a silver glow when he was intent. He was a very handsome man, she decided. He had a strong face with a square chin and a little cleft, which was rather appealing. His grey eyes could be very cold, but at the moment they seemed enquiring.

'Well, Bertie, since my fiancée has asked, I think we should all take tea together, and afterwards we can repair to the study and you can tell me what was so important that you felt compelled to return.'

'Certainly, my dear fellow,' Bertie replied amiably. 'It is nothing very much, you know—but it is a grand day for walking in the sunshine, especially in the company of a beautiful lady.'

'I dare say,' the marquis replied and glanced at Lottie, as if wondering whether his friend's remark was justified. 'It is, as you say, a glorious afternoon.'

'Do you allow others to feed your swans?' Lottie asked. His comment could be taken for silent consent that she was a beautiful lady, or a snub. She would ignore it for the moment. 'I should have brought food had I known how tame they are.'

'You should not be fooled by their docile appearance. They hoped to be fed, but swans can be vicious at times. One of my keepers had his arm broken by a male swan guarding its mate—and one of the pairs on the lake have young. However, if you insist on feeding them yourself, please give them the special pellets we use rather than bread. My bailiff will show you where the supply is stored—or one of the footmen will fetch it for you.'

'Thank you. I shall be careful to do nothing to alarm them,' Lottie replied. She was still walking with her hand on Sir Bertie's arm, but the marquis was at her right hand. 'Do you have deer in the park, my lord?'

'I believe there may be a few. I rarely visit Rothsay Manor, Lottie. I prefer to live in London for most of the year. Unlike Bertie, I do not enjoy either hunting or shooting, though my keepers encourage the pheasants and we have a regular supply for the table in season.'

'There are certainly deer in my park,' Sir Bertie told her. 'Do you ride, Miss Lottie?'

'I should—had I a suitable mount,' Lottie replied, turning to look at him. 'At home a neighbour sometimes takes pity on me. My father keeps only one hunter and his carriage horses.'

'I should be happy to provide you with a suitable

mount,' Sir Bertie said. 'My mother occasionally rides and I keep a horse for her—but I have another I believe might suit you. You can stable Heavenly here and then, should you wish, ride over to Greenacres with Rothsay or a groom.'

'That is extremely generous of you, sir. It would depend on Lord Rothsay's immediate plans, I imagine.'

'I dare say we have a horse that may suit you,' the marquis said, his tone sharp, causing her to turn her head and look at him once more. 'Your offer was well intended, Bertie, but I assure you I shall see that my bride has all she needs. I dare say she may care to ride over with me in the carriage and meet your mama—perhaps for tea tomorrow?'

'Certainly. Mama would be honoured.'

Lottie wondered if she imagined it, but she felt a slight squeeze of her arm and Sir Bertie's eyelid flickered.

At that moment she let go of his arm, walking into the house in front of the gentlemen. She heard the murmur of their voices behind her, then Mrs Mann came forward to greet her.

'Ah, Miss Stanton,' she said. 'Your father was anxious about you. I think he feared something might have happened to you. You were not in your room and no one knew where you had gone.'

'I went for a walk to the lake,' Lottie replied with a little frown. 'Forgive me if anyone was worried. I am not in the habit of informing anyone when I go out—though I do sometimes tell my aunt.'

'When are we to expect your aunt, Miss Stanton?' The marquis's stern question caught Lottie by surprise.

'I believe she will come for the ball,' Lottie said. 'I

am certain she would have liked to come with us—but I was not sure...'

'You must write to...I am not sure of the lady's name?'

Lottie met the marquis's eyes without a flicker of emotion. Two could play at this game!

'Lady Hoskins. My Aunt Beth. She came to look after...me, when my mother died. I am very fond of her.'

'You should have brought her with you. This is to be your home, Lottie. You must feel free to invite whomever you wish.'

'You are kind, my lord—but there is only my aunt, and perhaps Cousin Agatha. I do not particularly wish to invite her, but she may come if she hears of our engagement...'

'Indeed? A lady of some determination, then?' For a moment a gleam of amusement showed in the marquis's eyes and Lottie found herself smiling along with him, despite herself.

'Yes, most certainly. Both Papa and...Aunt Beth go in fear of her tongue.'

'You do not?' His brows rose.

'No, I have never feared her. She scolds me but I do not mind her. I am, you see, a very independent woman, my lord.'

'Should I take that as a warning?'

'Yes, I believe you should.'

Lottie preceded him into the drawing room that Mrs Mann had indicated. Her father was staring out of the window. He whirled round, relief in his eyes.

'Lottie! I thought you had done a bunk—' Seeing

that the marquis and a stranger followed her, Sir Charles checked himself and his neck turned the colour of brick. 'My daughter has a habit of wandering off alone for hours…'

Lottie was sure that neither of the gentlemen would believe his clumsy excuse. Sir Bertie would be imagining that she was being forced into an unwelcome marriage—and she had no idea what the marquis was thinking.

'Papa, anyone would think I was still your little girl. I assure you I am much too content here to run off without a word to anyone—which would be extremely rude of me. Had I known it would alarm you, I should have told you that I intended to go for a walk.'

'Well, you know how it is, a father will always be anxious for his daughters's safety.'

'Truly, Papa, you have no need to be anxious on my account. I am well accustomed to taking care of myself.'

'Yes, I dare say…' Sir Charles sat down, looking ill at ease as Lottie took a chair by the tea table. 'No tea for me, thank you. I would not say no to some more of that excellent Madeira, Rothsay.'

'I am certain it can be arranged,' he replied and flicked his coat tails as he sat on a chair near the fireplace. The large grate was empty because the room was pleasantly warm, lit by the afternoon sun. 'Bertie takes his tea with lemon, I believe—and I'll have the same.'

'Sir Bertie?' Lottie asked, directing her smile at him. 'Will you also take sugar?'

'No, I thank you, just the lemon. Rothsay knows my tastes well, Miss Lottie. Mama always has cream and sugar, but I prefer the lemon.'

Lottie poured the tea, handing it to a maid who stood waiting to pass it to the gentlemen.

'Would you care for anything more, Sir Bertie? Those almond comfits look tasty—or perhaps a sandwich? What do we have…I am not sure of your name?' She glanced at the young maid, who blushed.

'It is Rose, Miss Stanton. Rose Brown.'

'What kind of sandwiches are they, Rose?'

'Tomato and cucumber from our hothouses, Miss Stanton, also egg and cress…watercress, that is, from our own…'

'That will do, Brown,' Mrs Mann said after offering Sir Charles a glass of Madeira. 'If you would prefer chicken or salmon, I can have Cook make some very quickly, Miss Stanton.'

'I think I should like the cucumber,' Lottie said. 'What a treat. We seldom have it at home, for it is hardly ever to be found locally. You are very lucky to be able to grow your own, my lord.'

'I dare say. I had not considered it.'

'Rothsay takes everything for granted,' Sir Bertie said and grinned at his friend. 'He has been fed with a silver spoon since birth, Miss Lottie, and believes the world owes him the best of everything. It would do him the world of good to be denied something he truly wanted.'

'And I suppose you have had to work the skin from your fingers?' The marquis looked askance at his friend.

'I shall not deny that I too have been lucky to inherit a sizeable amount—but I do not take it all for granted, as you do, Rothsay. I know myself to be a fortunate fellow.'

His gaze dwelled on Lottie. 'Though not at this moment as fortunate as you...'

'It is a long time since we held a ball here,' the marquis said and frowned. 'My people are well able to cope but I feel we need a hostess. I shall ask my godmother to come and stay, but I wondered if your mama would care to help Countess Selby and Lottie compile a list of people who should be invited?'

'I imagine Mama would enjoy that very much—but you can ask her when you ride over for tea tomorrow. When exactly were you thinking of holding the ball?'

'In another two weeks,' the marquis replied, making Lottie catch her breath. 'I see no point in delay—and it will give us time to invite everyone and order whatever is needed from London.'

She had only two weeks to persuade him that she was not a suitable bride or accept her fate and marry him!

Lottie's hand trembled slightly as she sipped her tea. Everything seemed to be going so fast. The marquis had a note of decision in his voice when he gave the date of the ball. It was very strange, but Lottie had thought he might be regretting his decision to take her instead of the money her father owed him, but now she thought she detected a change.

There was, she believed, a gleam in his eyes that had not been there when they arrived.

Chapter Three

Sir Bertie and the marquis went off together after tea, leaving Lottie and her father together in the parlour.

'Well, Lottie, what do you think now you've met him?' Sir Charles asked in a low voice. 'Can you bear it?'

'Yes, I think so—unless the marquis were to relent and release you from the bargain and your debt, Papa.'

'You will certainly have all the luxuries that money can buy, m'dear—but if you should hate the idea I can tell him it won't do.'

'I believe we must be realistic. I am two and twenty and I have no fortune whatsoever. This may be my only chance to marry well. After all, most young women marry to oblige their families, do they not?'

'Your mother chose for herself,' Sir Charles said heavily. 'She made me promise that you and...'

'Papa,' Lottie warned with a glance over her shoulder, 'please say no more. I do not see that we have a choice. Besides, I believe I should be foolish to turn down the chance of living in a house like this—and I have a fancy to be the Marchioness of Rothsay…'

Anyone who knew her would have guessed immediately that she was merely funning, but the marquis, who had returned from seeing his friend off, and stood outside the door heard only the last few words and thought the worst.

His ears were still ringing with the congratulations Bertie had heaped on him, and he had almost begun to think himself more than fortunate to have found such a lovely bride. However, catching the last few words and hearing father and daughter laugh together aroused his ire once more. The scoundrels! Did they imagine they had found a soft nest for the two of them? He would send them both packing and good riddance.

Nicolas was about to go in and have it out with the pair of them when he heard a squealing sound, a murmur of alarm and some very peculiar noises coming from inside the parlour.

'Oh, you poor little thing. What a mess you have got into…'

Intrigued by the new note in her voice, Nicolas walked into the room and saw something that amazed him. The woman he had just decided was a scoundrel was clutching a very sooty and disreputable animal he thought might be a kitten. She was stroking it gently and he could see that the beast did indeed look to be in a sorry state. Glancing at the fireplace, he saw how much soot the kitten had brought down and made a mental note to have the chimneys swept before the winter.

'How in the world did that get here?'

'I imagine it must have gone up on the roof somehow

and fallen down. It feels so thin,' Lottie said and held the creature to her breast, stroking its filthy fur and getting soot all over her gown. 'We have some milk left from tea…' With one hand, she poured a little milk into one of the exquisite porcelain tea bowls. Still holding the kitten gently as she set both the bowl and the creature on the carpet, she allowed it to lap while supporting it with her hands. 'Oh, look how hungry it is. Do you think Cook would spare a little fish of some kind?'

'I imagine she might if you asked,' Nicolas said. 'You are, after all, to be the mistress here, are you not?'

'If it suits you,' Lottie replied without looking up. 'For the moment I am simply a guest. The milk has all gone. I must take Kitty to the kitchens. She needs a little wash, but it must be done carefully so as not to harm her, and she will need to be fed small amounts regularly. I think I shall keep her in my room…'

'She has already covered your gown and the carpet with soot.' Nicolas glared at her for no particular reason.

'Yes, I am sorry about your carpet, my lord. I know soot is difficult to get out. I will fetch a cloth later and see what I can do.'

'One of the servants will see to it. Good grief,' Nicolas said, feeling irritable without understanding what had changed his mood. 'Ring the bell and Mrs Mann will come. One of the footmen can deal with the wretched thing.'

Lottie looked up, her green eyes sparking with anger. 'It may be a wretched thing to you, my lord, but at the moment I believe it is to be pitied. I dare say it has been lost in your maze of chimneys for days, for I think it is near starving. I wish to care for it myself.'

He blinked and then lowered his gaze. 'I did not mean the thing was undeserving of pity. Merely that it would do well enough with the servants. If you wish to care for it, that is your own affair.'

'If you would kindly direct me to the kitchens.'

'I shall ring for Mrs Mann. She will assist you…' he said, but was saved the trouble by the arrival of the house-keeper and a maid to clear the tea things. 'Mrs Mann—a kitten seems to have got stuck up the chimney…'

'Yes, my lord. It is one of the kitchen cat's brood. We did think one was missing. Rose will take it for you, Miss Stanton.'

'Miss Stanton wishes to care for the kitten herself. If you will show her where she can clean it a little and also provide some food for the wretched beast.'

Mrs Mann glanced at him, but made no comment. She turned to Lottie with a smile.

'Rose will show you the kitchen and scullery, miss— if you are sure you wish for the trouble?'

'It won't be a trouble to Lottie,' Sir Charles put in. 'She always had a soft spot for any creature she found in trouble. Clar…uh, that is, *Clara* used to scream when she found wounded birds in the garden, but Lottie did her best to heal them if she could.'

'And who is Clara?' Nicolas asked. 'I thought your aunt was called Beth?'

'Oh, Clara is a just a friend,' Lottie replied, eyes wide and innocent. 'Excuse me, my lord. I must attend to the kitten—I think she has just wet herself.'

'And you, miss,' the housekeeper said. 'You will

have to house train the beast if you mean to make a pet of it.'

'Yes…' Lottie smiled. 'I shall have to teach her better manners, shall I not?'

Nicolas let his gaze follow her as she walked from the room. He had meant to send both her and her father packing. It would be simple enough to cancel the debt and pay a lump sum to ease the lady's pride. Yet the incident with the kitten had made him curious. He could not quite work out in his mind what was going on, but something did not ring true. Lottie had made nothing of the soot on her pretty afternoon gown or the kitten wetting her. How did the girl he had seen robbing his friend while he lay in a drunken stupor equate with the demure and compassionate young lady now staying in his house? She was like two different women!

She must be a consummate actress. Nicolas scowled, for he did not like the way she had played on his sympathies. Miss Stanton was not the only one to care for animals in distress. As a young lad he had rescued enough of them himself… Now what had made him recall his childhood? It was years since he had given it a thought, perhaps because painful memories had superseded the happier times.

He had, he supposed, been fortunate to live in a house like this and to have parents who cared for him, even if they spared him little enough of their time. His tutor and some of the grooms had been his companions, as he roamed the estate, fished with a net for frogs and newts in the streams and ponds, rode his pony and climbed trees. It was a very good place to bring up a family. The pity was that his mother had been a little fragile after his birth, and when she died from a putrid fever, the house had been plunged into mourning, from which it had never quite recovered. Nicolas's father had not remarried, spending most of his time away from the estate, working. Nicolas had been left alone with his grief.

Glancing around the parlour, Nicolas saw that although the furniture was good quality and made to the finest standards, the curtains and décor had become a trifle faded. He had spent only a few days at the house in the last years, and never in this particular parlour. If his wife intended to use it, he must have it refurbished for her.

His wife... Nicolas walked to the French windows and looked out. Was the reason he had been avoiding the subject of marriage down to his disappointment in love years before—or to the fear at the back of his mind that he might love too well, as his father had? Losing his mother at an early age had made Nicolas a little reserved and afraid of giving his affections. When the first woman he had believed himself in love with had also turned him down, he had put up a barrier to protect himself.

For a moment he thought about Elizabeth, the beautiful young lady who had been his first love. He had believed her nature as sweet as her face. The realisation that her gentle manner was false and covered a spiteful character had swept the illusion of love from his mind. He had thought her a woman he could trust, but her dismissal of his declaration had been deliberately cruel and meant to wound, destroying his trust in women and convincing him that love was for fools.

His father had been a fool for love. As a child, Nicolas

had not truly understood why his father could not bear to be in the house after his wife died. Nicolas had imagined the fifth marquis was too busy to be interested in his only son, but as an adult he could guess that his father had simply shut himself off from everyone who mattered because it was too painful; because he was suffering from a broken heart. Perhaps he had grieved as much as Nicolas, but been unable to show it, which meant they might have been more alike than either of them had realised.

No woman was worth the pain love inflicted. Nicolas was determined that he would never again offer his heart to have it crushed beneath a woman's dainty foot.

'Foolish…' he muttered and went out of the French windows. Love was a waste of time. A marriage of convenience was much safer. It was best to keep his mind on practical matters. He would walk down to the stables and speak to the head groom to discover if there was a suitable horse in their stables for a lady to ride.

'Now you must be good, Kitty,' Lottie said and stroked the kitten's fur. It still felt a little spiky and rough but with good food and care she did not doubt it would recover in time. Now that that the soot had gone, she could see that the kitten was a pretty tortoiseshell in colour. 'If you must wet, use the sand tray as I showed you.'

'You talk to her just as if she can understand,' Rose said and laughed. 'She will learn to use the tray in time. My mother puts the cats out to teach them, but they still wet in the house until they get older. Are you sure you wouldn't like me to take her down to the kitchen?'

'I shall keep her here until she is better,' Lottie said. 'If you would pop in and look at her now and then...'

'I'll come before I help with the dishes, miss,' Rose said. 'Cats are loners, you know. I dare say she will wander off when you let her outside. My mother says dogs are the best companions for they give love in return, and cats don't.'

'My aunt has a large and fat tabby that she adores,' Lottie said and laughed. She had taken to the young maid and was pleased that Rose was to look after her. 'I must go down now for the gong sounded five minutes ago. I do not wish to keep the marquis waiting.'

She went out, leaving Rose to tidy up. It would take a little time to get used to the idea of a maid waiting on her. At home they had a cook and one maid of all work, also Muffet, who had come with Aunt Beth and would turn her hand to anything. This meant that Lottie was accustomed to doing dusting and kept her own room tidy. She often cleaned her aunt's room, too. Living here with so many servants to care for just her and the marquis would seem strange—though of course they would probably entertain friends much of the time.

Lottie realised that she was beginning to rather like the idea of living in this wonderful house. She wrinkled her brow, because if she went through with this deception it would mean living a lie for the rest of her life.

Was she cheating the marquis?

She could not help feeling a little guilty. When she had taken Clarice's place, Lottie had tried not to question her motives or admit that she was doing something underhand—and when the marquis first greeted her so arrogantly, he had made her angry and she had felt he deserved all he got. However, her conscience was beginning to nag her. Perhaps she ought to tell him the truth before things went too far?

She was wearing a gown of green silk that evening. It had a dipping neckline, but was not low enough to show the little mole just above her right breast. Lottie was very conscious of the fact that in the more revealing gowns that Clarice wore it would have been easy to see that she did not have such a blemish.

As she approached the bottom stair, she was aware that the marquis had come out of the room to the right of the hall and was gazing up at her.

'I was about to send someone in search of you, Lottie.'

'Oh…' She blushed. 'Forgive me. I did not mean to keep you waiting for your dinner. I was talking with Rose and forgot the time.'

'Talking with Rose…you mean the parlour maid?'

'She is looking after me. We were talking about cats and dogs. Rose's mother prefers dogs, but Aunt Beth loves her cat—' Lottie broke off and laughed. 'You will think the subject obsesses me. I am sure you are used to far more stimulating conversation in London. I fear I do not know any amusing tales of the Regent to tell you. I have never mixed much in society…' She realised that she had made a mistake. 'Apart from the trip to Paris with Papa, of course.'

'You seemed perfectly at home there.' His brows met in the middle. 'Tell me, Lottie—is this an act for my benefit? If so, you are wasting your time. I am not a fool and my memory works perfectly.'

'I would never think you a fool, my lord…' She sensed

there was a deeper meaning behind his words and wondered whether he had seen through her disguise. Clarice had sworn she had met him only once and that he would not know the difference between them, but was there something her sister wasn't telling her about her time with the marquis? She crossed her fingers behind her back. 'I am not sure I understand you?'

'No, then perhaps I should refresh—' He turned his head as the butler came into the hall. 'Yes, yes, Mann. We are coming now.' His eyes narrowed as he looked at Lottie once more. 'We shall speak of this another time. Dinner is ready and Cook will not be best pleased if we keep her waiting.'

'No, that would not do at all,' Lottie said and laid her fingers tentatively on the arm he offered. 'I think it would be best if we talked soon, my lord. I believe there is something I ought to—'

A loud knocking at the door interrupted Lottie. The footman opened it and a lady entered, accompanied by several servants and a small King Charles spaniel, which barked noisily and jumped from her arms to rush towards Nicolas. He bent down and stroked it behind the ears, looking at the new arrival with rueful amusement.

'Henri! You can hardly have had my letter more than a day. I intended to invite you to stay, of course, but this is a surprise.'

'A pleasant one, I hope?' The diminutive lady laughed confidently up at him. 'I decided this morning I would visit you and here I am—and this young lady must be your intended bride?' The lady bustled towards Lottie, exuding lavender and a warmth that seemed to envelop all she touched. 'You are Miss Stanton? I am delighted to meet you. I have waited for this day too long.' She laughed and seized Lottie's hand, kissing her on both cheeks. 'You are wondering who the devil I am, of course. This wretched godson of mine has not thought to introduce us—Henrietta, Countess of Selby. You may call me Henrietta.'

'Ma'am…' Lottie made a slight curtsy. 'I am very pleased to meet you.'

'And I you, though I really know very little about you my dear, not even your name?'

'It's Clarice, but everyone calls me Lottie.'

'Well, it suits you, though I did not think your name was Charlotte?'

'Clarice's second name is Charlotte, which is why she often goes by Lottie. Anyway, enough chatter, Henri. We are late for dinner. Will you join us—or shall I have something sent up to you on a tray in half an hour or so?'

'I shall rest this evening and will take a little soup in my room,' she replied. 'You may come in and see me for a few moments before you retire, Lottie—if it will be no trouble to you?'

'No trouble at all, ma'am.'

'Then I shall not keep you longer. Nicolas has a decent cook. You will not wish to lose her…' She looked behind her, summoning a woman who looked as if she might be her companion. 'Give me your arm, Millicent. That staircase looks daunting after a day spent travelling.'

'You will become used to her,' Nicolas said as his godmother began her colourful ascent of the stairs, her servants fluttering around her, the spaniel bounding ahead up the stairs. 'Henri usually takes over the house when she arrives—though she has not stayed here often since…' He shook his head. 'Dinner awaits and we are now very late. We shall talk later.'

'You must be very fond of her?'

'I have many relations, but she is the only one I care for.'

'I see…' Lottie wondered what he had been going to say before his godmother arrived, but no doubt he would tell her later.

As it happened, Lottie did not learn what had been in the marquis's mind that evening. Dinner had been served in what was more usually the breakfast room because, as he explained, there were so few of them.

'Tomorrow evening I shall invite some of our neighbours,' he said as they all rose at the end of the meal. 'I had intended a period of quiet time for us to get to know one another, Lottie—but now that the countess has seen fit to join us we must entertain.'

'Please do stay and enjoy some port,' Lottie said. 'You need not accompany me to the drawing room. I think I shall visit your godmother and then go to bed. If I want a drink, I am sure Mrs Mann will have a tray sent up.'

'As you wish.' Nicolas frowned. 'I had thought we might talk?'

'Tomorrow morning if you wish,' Lottie said. 'I am a little tired myself and would wish to retire after I have visited the countess.'

'Very well,' he replied, inclining his head.

Lottie sensed that he was not best pleased. She was not sure why she was putting off the evil moment, because she could surely not delay it much longer.

It would be embarrassing, but there was really no alternative. Lottie had been feeling guilty enough about deceiving the marquis himself, even though he did deserve it in a way, but to deceive the lady who had just arrived would be unforgivable.

She would simply go in for a few minutes and explain that she was too tired to talk this evening. It was clear that the countess expected an intimate heart to heart, but that could not happen. Not until Lottie had told the marquis the truth.

If he truly had no preference for her sister, he might be satisfied with her in Clarice's place—but he must be given the choice.

Nicolas frowned over his brandy. He had offered to give Sir Charles a game of billiards but his future father-in-law had declined. They had talked in a desultory fashion of the King's madness, which had resulted in the prince being called on to become the Regent once more, then discussed the price of corn and the weather. Then, after smoking a cigar, Sir Charles had excused himself and gone to his room.

Nicolas sat on alone in his library. He was not sure why his thoughts were so disordered. The day had not gone as he expected at all and he was still undecided what to do about the situation he had created.

He should, of course, have spoken to Sir Charles as soon as he realised what a fool he had been, made some settlement and withdrawn. It was clearly too late now. Bertie would have spread the news all over the neighbourhood—besides, Henrietta had rushed here as soon as she had his letter. The delight on her face when she saw his fiancée had struck him to the heart.

Lottie gave the appearance of being a modest charming woman, exactly the kind of person who would grace his home and make his relatives welcome. He knew that at heart she was a scheming adventuress, but for the moment she seemed determined to play the part of an innocent—why? What could she hope to gain?

His fingers drummed against the arm of his comfortable wing chair. What a dilemma! And he had only himself to blame. He frowned as he recalled the laughing words he had overheard outside the parlour—so she had a fancy to become the next marchioness, had she?

Well, would it be so bad? He had considered she would do before he had witnessed the theft of those guineas. It was that that rankled, he admitted—and the suspicion that she had been making love with—or at least been prepared to be seduced by—Ralph.

The thing was that he found he did not dislike Lottie. He was not sure he could trust her—and he would have to send her father packing after the wedding. Yet he did need a wife and if Henrietta liked her…he supposed she would do.

Nicolas groaned. He was such an idiot to have become embroiled with a pair of adventurers.

Why did he have the feeling that Lottie was playing a part? Had she decided to reform her ways now that she had a chance to move up in society?

Nicolas knew that he would not find it difficult to play his part in this strange marriage. It would be no hardship to make love to her—and her morals could be no worse than some of the ladies he had made his mistresses in the past. His last mistress had been grasping and self-ish, which was why he had felt no remorse in finishing his arrangement with her. He would at least start his marriage without a clandestine attachment. He would certainly not tolerate being played false by *his wife*. If she imagined he would turn a blind eye to any future indiscretions, she would soon discover her mistake!

'Damn it!' he muttered and stood up. He would not find the answer in the bottom of a brandy bottle.

In the morning he would make it clear that, if they went through with this marriage, he would expect Lottie to be faithful—at least until she had given him a son or two.

Feeling unaccountably tired, he realised that for the first time in a while he would sleep as soon as his head touched the pillow.

It must be the country air.

Lottie rose early, as was her custom. She sat up and looked over at the kitten lying on her bed. She had left it in the basket that Rose had provided for her, but it seemed that Kitty had other ideas. Reaching out, she picked the tiny creature up and stroked it, kissed its head and then climbed out of bed and placed it back in the basket.

'That is your place, little one. You must not form bad habits, for I might roll on you in the night and suffocate you.'

Lottie found some water left over from the previous evening and washed her face and hands. She would have a proper wash before breakfast, but she wanted to go for a walk first.

Going downstairs, she surprised a maid already hard at work polishing the furniture.

'I beg your pardon, miss. We did not know you were awake. Do you wish for something?'

'Not until I return. I am going for a walk. I shall be back in time to dress properly for breakfast.'

A sleepy footman opened the door as she approached. She flashed a smile at him and went out into the early morning air. The dew was still on the grass and silky cobwebs hung between the perennials in the mixed border.

Walking across the lawns in the direction of the park, Lottie felt a sense of peace. The marquis's estate was a lovely place to stay and she would have liked to live here, but she had decided that she must tell him the truth this morning.

She entered the park, reflecting that some of the trees here must be very ancient. One particular oak tree had grown so large that she thought it must have stood here for well over a hundred years. Lost in thought, she was startled by the sound of a shot somewhere to her right. Whilst it had come nowhere near her, she was concerned—she was certain that the marquis had said he did not hunt or shoot. Who could be shooting on his lands?

Without consideration, she turned towards the sound and a moment or two later came upon an unpleasant scene. A man had been shot in the leg. He was clutching at his wound, and the blood was trickling through his fingers. He lay on the ground and looked up at the man with the gun standing over him.

'What is going on here?' Lottie asked, walking up to them. 'Why has this man been shot?'

'He was poaching on his lordship's land,' the man who she instantly realised was a gamekeeper said, and touched his hat. 'We do not allow poaching here, miss.'

'My wife is starving. I only wanted a rabbit for the pot...' the poacher whined looking at her hopefully. 'Tell him it ain't right, miss. There's more than enough game in these parts—and his lordship ain't never 'ere to want it.'

'Poaching is illegal and must be stopped,' Lottie said. 'For one thing it is cruel to trap things. You should have come to the house and asked for help. However...' She fixed the gamekeeper with a reproachful look. 'It was not necessary to shoot the poor man in the leg, sir. You will take him to the house, where I shall bind his leg—and then we shall give him some food for his family.'

'I don't know about that, miss. His lordship don't hold with poachers.'

'I dare say he does not, but I do not hold with what you have done, sir. If you will not help him, I shall do so myself.' She looked down at the poacher. 'Can you stand?'

'If he gives me a hand up.'

'I'll carry him over me shoulder,' the gamekeeper said grudgingly. 'You had best take me gun, miss. It ain't loaded now so it can't hurt you.'

'I should not fear it if it were loaded,' Lottie replied. 'My father shoots occasionally. I am used to guns in the house.' She checked that it was indeed harmless and slung the strap over her shoulder, following the men up to the house, round the back to the kitchen. 'Bring him into the scullery. Cook will not want him bleeding over her kitchen floor.'

'Miss Stanton...' Rose came out to them as they reached the scullery door. 'What is going on?'

'This poacher has been shot. He was stealing a rabbit because his wife is starving, or so he says. We shall give him some food to take home—but in future he must work for his wage. I dare say he can be found some kind of work on the estate?'

'That's Sam Blake,' Rose said. 'He has never done a decent day's work in his life.'

'Then it is time he started,' Lottie told her. 'He must obviously rest his leg for a while, but as soon as he can walk, he must be given a job cleaning out the stables.'

'I'll tell Mrs Mann you said to give him food, but you'll have to ask his lordship about giving him a job,' Rose said. 'Sit him down on that stool, Jeb Larkin, and I'll patch him up.'

'I was going to cleanse and bind his wound, Rose.'

'Best you let me, miss,' Rose told her firmly. 'He has a wound in his thigh and it wouldn't do for you to tend him, miss. Besides, I'll be sending your water up with one of the other maids. You'll be wanting your breakfast.'

'Yes, well, perhaps—but don't forget to give him some food.'

'I shan't forget, miss.'

Lottie left the maid to bind up the injured man and went upstairs. She bit her lip as she reflected that perhaps she had been rash to bring the poacher to the house. His story had touched her, but if he was a rogue his wife's plight might be his fault rather than anyone else's.

She hurried upstairs. Her walk had made her hungry, though she would have gone further afield had she not chanced on the poacher.

Lottie was at the breakfast table alone when the ring of booted feet on tiles told her that someone was about to enter. Her hand trembled a little as she sipped her tea. The unpleasant incident had put the thought of her confession from her mind, but it must be made this morning without fail.

'So you are here. What the hell do you mean by interfering in the way I run my estate? You are not mistress here yet.'

Lottie looked up and saw the anger in the marquis's face. He was speaking of the wounded poacher, of course. She rose to her feet, feeling the nerves knot in her stomach.

'Forgive me. The man was hurt. I thought your gamekeeper might have fired in the air as a warning.'

'And so Larkin might had the rogue not been warned a hundred times before. Blake is a thief and a scoundrel. You may feel that taking what belongs to others is acceptable but I think you will discover that others do not. Far from giving him work in my stables, I have called the constable. Blake will see how he likes a few months in prison.'

'That is harsh, is it not? His wife is starving…'

'He has only himself to blame. Besides, his wife never sees any of the game; he sells what he steals to the inn in the village and gets a few drinks in return, I've no doubt. He will be lucky if he does not hang.'

'Oh…I am sorry,' Lottie clasped her hands in front of her. 'And I do not condone stealing. I was just moved to pity for his wife.'

'You do not condone stealing?' He spluttered incredulously. His eyes narrowed dangerously. 'Then pray tell me whether you think taking gold coins from a man's pocket when he is in a drunken stupor is theft? Not to mention going to a bedroom alone with a man in that state.'

'What..?' Lottie felt the blood drain from her face. She was stunned, her mind reeling as she tried to take in what he was saying. 'She… I would never… Where did this happen?'

'You know full well where we were, at that gaming house in Paris. You were going through my friend's pockets as he lay senseless.' Nicolas stared at her intently. She looked so shocked and distressed that it suddenly dawned on him that it could not have been her. What an idiot he was! He should have seen it instantly. 'Who the devil are you? You're not her, are you? I thought from the start that something was different. You've been lying, trying to make a fool of me…'

'No, it wasn't to make a fool of you,' Lottie hastened to reassure him. 'I meant to tell you yesterday…to ask if you would let Papa repay the debt over a period of years. Clarice is my twin. She refused to marry you and—'

'You thought you would take her place. How noble of you—or was it just a clever move to trick me into marriage, because you had a fancy to be the next marchioness yourself?'

'No, of course not.' Lottie's cheeks were burning. 'If you heard me say that to Papa, it was just in fun…to set his mind at rest. I was going to tell you the truth. I realised last night that I could not deceive the countess. She was so kind and—'

'You would have deceived me happily enough, I suppose?'

'At first I thought you deserved it. You have been exceedingly rude to Papa, to Clarice—and to me.' Lottie raised her head, too angry now to care about what he thought.

'Do you think you have deserved my concern?'

'Mere politeness was all that was required. Well, you may set your mind at rest. I do not wish to marry you. Papa will just have to find the money to pay you what he owes. I dare say I shall find somewhere for Aunt Beth and I to live.'

'So you will renege on the bargain you made?'

'I made no bargain. And nor for that matter did Clarice. You made that deal with our father. Foolish Papa thought he could persuade Clarice to go along with your plans with the promise of wealth, but she dislikes you and—' She broke off feeling embarrassed. 'No, that is rude. I shall not be rude to you no matter what you have said to me.'

'Your manners do you credit, Miss Charlotte,' he sneered. 'If only I could believe in that innocent outrage.'

'Believe what you wish. Thank you for your hospitality, sir, but I am leaving.'

'No, you are not.' Nicolas grabbed her wrist as she would have passed him. 'You will not make a fool of me in front of my neighbours and my godmother. Your father signed the contract. He owes me fifteen thousand pounds. If you refuse to marry me, I shall press for payment—and I shall tell the world that your sister is a thief.'

'You would not…' Lottie stared at him in horror. 'How could you threaten to destroy my family? You are as cold and heartless as Clarice said you were. I do not know what happened in Paris, but she must have had good reason for what she did.'

'Perhaps I am heartless,' Nicolas said, his expression set in harsh lines. 'However, when I make a bargain I stick to it—and you will oblige me by keeping your part.'

'You are a devil! To think I felt guilty—almost liked you…'

'Perhaps you may come to find my presence bearable,' Nicolas said. 'I shall endeavour to put my own disgust to one side and we shall muddle through.'

'Why do you wish to continue? Surely you cannot wish to marry the sister of a woman you have named a thief? You clearly have no respect for Papa or me. Release me from the contract and I will make certain Papa pays you every penny from the estate.'

'No. Jilt me and you will be ruined, your father and sister with you.'

'But why?' Lottie was puzzled.

'Because I need an heir. One woman is as good as another in the dark. Your father owes me and you chose to deceive me. You will keep your part of the bargain whether you wish it or not.'

Tears were stinging behind her eyes, but Lottie refused to let them fall.

'Very well, sir. You can compel me to honour my father's bargain—but you will have no joy of your despicable behaviour.' She raised her head, looking him in the eyes. 'I shall be everything your bride ought to be in public. I will give you the heir you desire, but in my heart I shall always hate you.'

'I never expected you to love me. Why should you? Love is a myth and ever was. I dare say you will be content in your role as my marchioness—and I need an heir or two, perhaps, just to be certain. Do your duty and we shall go along well enough.'

'Have it your own way, sir. You hold all the cards, it seems, but you may come to regret this…' She walked past him and this time he let her go.

Chapter Four

'I was sorry not to spend more time with you last evening,' Lottie said when Henrietta came down to nuncheon. 'I felt a little tired, as I told you, but this morning I am much better.'

'Are you, my dear?' Henrietta looked at her speculatively. 'Well, we shall have them put chairs for us beneath the shade of the chestnut trees after nuncheon. We may sit and enjoy the pleasant weather for an hour and talk as much as we like.'

'You mean the stand of trees to the right of the house?' Henrietta nodded. 'I went for a walk in the park early this morning. A poacher had been shot. I fear Lord Rothsay was not best pleased because I had the keeper bring him back to the house to be patched up and gave him food for his family. He says that the man deserves to be in prison.'

'Ah, I thought there was something,' Henrietta nodded wisely. 'Gentlemen do not care for interference in the management of their estates. We ladies are expected to smile and plead for anything we think needs changing rather than dictate.'

'Papa's estate is small, for he has but one farm left, but he leaves what management there is to me—or he did before we came here. He has no interest in the land or the house. I am not sure what he will do once I am married.'

'I dare say the arrangement suited your papa—but it will not do for Rothsay. As I believe you have discovered, he has a temper and these days his manner seems stern. He can be the sweetest man—but I dare say you know that, Lottie?'

'Can he?' Lottie hesitated and then decided to be honest with the woman she had liked from the first. 'You must know this is not a love match, ma'am. The marquis offered for me because he needs an heir. I agreed because my father's circumstances demand that I should make a good marriage.'

'Oh…' Henrietta sighed. 'I suppose I should have known what Rothsay would do. I am sorry. I had hoped to see him deep in love.'

'I fear I am unable to help you, ma'am.'

'I am not so sure. I am certain he feels something for you. As a child, Nicolas adored his parents. He felt it deeply when his mama died and his father neglected him. I dare say he would not care to show his feelings openly. There was also that young woman—Elizabeth. Rothsay allowed me to believe he did not come up to scratch, but I think she broke his heart. He reacted by taking a string of mistresses and has resisted all the matchmaking mamas for years. I know he wishes to oblige me by setting up his nursery, but I think he would not have offered for you if there were not something between you.'

Lottie did not wish to disappoint her further, so she kept the fact of her father's debt and the marquis's brutal demands to herself.

If Rothsay had been as cold and brutal with Elizabeth, Lottie could not blame her for refusing him. Yet if she had truly broken his heart, it would explain his aversion to the idea of being in love.

No, she did not believe that Rothsay had a heart to break. He was the most arrogant, heartless man she had ever met! His behaviour that morning had been abominable. If her situation was not so desperate, she would have liked to give him a piece of her mind. However, she kept her thoughts to herself and let the countess talk happily about the wedding and the benefits Rothsay would gain from having a wife.

At two o'clock she left her companion and went up to change into a pretty peach afternoon gown. Henrietta had refused to accompany them to Lady Fisher's for tea. She preferred to sit on in the shade and have the butler bring her a cool drink.

'I shall see you this evening, Lottie dear. I believe Rothsay has invited Colonel Brand and his wife, the vicar and the Fishers to dine with us. I dare say I shall rest for an hour before I change.'

'I shall look forward to knowing you better, ma'am,' Lottie said.

When she came down at precisely half past the hour,

the marquis was waiting for her. He hesitated, then inclined his head to her.

'I approve of punctuality in a lady, Lottie. I think I owe you an apology. My manner this morning over the issue of the poaching was brusque and I believe I treated you to a show of temper—but you caused quite a stir.'

'There is no need for an apology, sir,' Lottie replied with a cool nod. So he was not going to refer to their argument over her deception? Her anger had cooled, because, being honest, she understood that she had in part deserved his censure, both for tricking him with her identity and rushing headlong into matters on his estate. Still, if the marquis didn't want to address the second issue she would play along, for now.

'I interfered in a matter that did not concern me. I have been used to ordering things for the comfort of my aunt and myself. Papa takes no interest in his estate and I acted as I would have at home. I ought to have remembered that this is not my home.'

'It will be your home, however, and I am sorry that in this instance I was forced to override your instructions. As for the matter of the food, that has been sent to the family in question—but the man has been arrested. If you wished to help the family further, I should not object. I believe the wife to be a decent enough woman. She takes in sewing and there would be nothing wrong in your employing her—should you wish it.'

Lottie turned her gaze on him. His expression gave nothing away, but there was a tiny pulse flicking in his throat and she understood that he was making her a handsome apology by his standards.

'Yes, I think I shall. If she is competent with her

needle, I shall need someone to help me sew my wedding gown. I was not perfectly sure before we came here, sir. I had a new ball gown made by a local seamstress very quickly, but I shall need something for the wedding.'

His eyes narrowed, darkened, as he regarded her seriously. 'Are you always this calm and controlled? I thought you might have demanded that your father take you home after our row today?'

If only he knew how much it was costing her to keep her temper in check! Lottie kept her expression bland, though she was unable to smile.

'My father owes you a debt. I am here to pay that debt, my lord. You made it plain that you would not release us, therefore I have no choice. I believe that such arrangements are common enough.'

'Yes, they are.' Rothsay looked uncertain for the first time. 'Yet I believe there is usually some liking or at least respect on both sides.'

'Indeed?' She raised her sparkling eyes to his. 'Should I like you, sir? Mayhap you will earn my respect in time. Your apology has been accepted. I believe I can behave in a civilised manner—if you can, too.'

'Then you are determined to go through with it?'

'Do I have a choice?'

'Neither of us does, Lottie,' he commented darkly. Then his mood seemed to lift.

'Besides, I know it is my dear Henri's greatest wish to see me married, and I would do anything to oblige her. So, now that we are agreed…' Nicolas took her hand to help her into his curricle '…you will not have cause to complain of my temper again. I can at least be civilised.'

'I am certain you can.' Lottie smiled suddenly, her anger evaporating. His devotion to his godmother must surely reflect some level of compassion in his character. 'We must try to get along for the sake of our families, sir.'

Lady Fisher turned out to be a pleasant woman, if a little fussy in her manner. She welcomed the idea of a new mistress at Rothsay Manor.

'It is years since Rothsay bothered to entertain much. When he comes down for his brief visits he brings friends from London, but seldom gives a dinner for his neighbours. His father used to give the most wonderful Christmas parties. The whole house was decked with greenery and smelled of spices and pines—but that, of course, was when the late Lady Rothsay was alive.'

'Perhaps we shall be able to continue the custom in the future,' Lottie said. 'I believe I shall be living here most of the time. I shall certainly want to entertain often, for I love company, and you will always be welcome to call for tea—or a morning visit. I am an early riser.'

'My son tells me you like to walk and you enjoy the wildlife. We have red deer in our park and in winter they often come close to the house for the food I have put out.'

'That must be pleasant to see.' Lottie looked up as Sir Bertie approached. 'Lady Fisher was just telling me about the deer.'

'We cull them now and then for the venison, but Mama would make them pets if she could. I tell her that the farmers think them a nuisance if they overrun their fields—but if we did not take our share the damned poachers would have the lot.'

'Oh…' Lottie's gaze flew towards Rothsay but he seemed not to notice. 'I dare say poachers can be a trouble to you?'

'Sam Blake has been one of the worst, but Rothsay tells me that his keeper has dealt with the blighter. If they brought him up before me, I should be inclined to hang the fellow, but I dare say Rothsay will be the presiding magistrate as he is in the county. He says Blake will go to prison for a year. Too moderate by half for my liking, I can tell you.'

'Is the theft of a few rabbits really a hanging offence, sir?'

'I know you ladies have tender hearts,' Bertie said with an indulgent smile. 'But you have to make an example of these fellows, m'dear. Let them get away with it and there will soon be no law for anyone.'

'Well, I expect you know best,' Lottie said, deciding on diplomacy.

'That's it.' Bertie nodded and looked pleased. 'Leave all this unpleasant stuff to us. You have enough to think of with the wedding in three weeks. All those bonnets and furbelows. You will need to go shopping in London, I dare say—or shall you be satisfied with what is to be found in Northampton?'

'Three weeks…' Lottie was shocked—it was the first time the actual date of the wedding had been mentioned. Her gaze flew to the marquis but he was frowning and staring at a picture on the wall, apparently far away in his thoughts.

'There are some very good milliners in Northampton,'

Lady Fisher said. 'I dare say they are not up to London standards, but I know of a seamstress I could recommend—and the draper has a good stock of silk just now. I should be pleased to take you in, in my carriage.'

'Thank you. I believe I may need to purchase a few silks and perhaps a new bonnet.'

'You must have far more than that—must she not, Rothsay? Your bride needs a wardrobe to suit her position in society, does she not? I dare say you have plans to take her to Paris, and the local seamstress cannot compare to the elegance of a French gown—but she will need a wardrobe for the journey.'

'What? Yes, I am sure Lottie will need a great many clothes. Countess Selby is sure to advise her, ma'am. I intend to pay a fleeting visit to town myself almost at once. I can order anything necessary while I am there.'

'I think perhaps I would rather see what is to be found in Northampton,' Lottie said. 'Later, I may order what I need from town.'

'Your clothes are important, Lottie.' Nicolas focused on her. 'We have much to talk about. I shall certainly place some orders in town. You should discuss your needs with Henrietta.'

'Oh, yes,' Lady Fisher agreed. 'The countess has wonderful taste and is known everywhere. If she vouches for you, the best seamstresses will fall over themselves to work for you.'

Lottie thanked her, but made no further remark. She did not wish to argue with Rothsay in front of his friends, but she could not see that she would have the least need for a huge wardrobe.

Rothsay gave her a speculative look as they left but said nothing further until they had been driving for some minutes.

'She means well, you know.'

'I have no fault to find with Lady Fisher's advice, sir. Yet I do not think I shall need a huge wardrobe. As I understand it, I am to live here in the country, while you continue your own life in London—is that not what you require from a complaisant wife?'

'Well, yes,' he said and frowned. 'Once we have an heir, you will be free to live where you please—perhaps in Bath? You will have an allowance naturally, to spend as you please.'

'How generous.' Lottie's tone was perfectly pleasant, but she saw a faint flush in his cheeks. 'I think I shall probably be quite content to live at Rothsay with my children—and Aunt Beth, of course.'

'Yes, of course. Your aunt. Have you written to her yet?'

'I thought the invitation should come from you?'

'I shall attend to it immediately.'

'Thank you—that would be kind. I am sure she is anxious to know…to see us wed.'

'Yes, I dare say she may be.'

'What does that mean, pray? My aunt is a woman of good character and…'

What was he implying? Lottie gave him a fulminating glance and was about to launch into more scathing words when the shot rang out. It whistled harmlessly by their heads but the horses bolted and Nicolas was forced to give all his attention to bringing them under control. He was beginning to slow them when the curricle hit a bump in the road and Lottie was thrown to the ground.

For a moment or two she lay winded, her eyes closed. As a man loomed over her, she opened her eyes and stared up at him. For a moment she blinked foolishly and then her senses cleared.

'Are you badly hurt? Damn it, I am so sorry. I thought I had the horses in hand, but the shot took me by surprise.'

Lottie sat up slowly. As her breath came back, she realised that she felt bruised and shaken, but there were no sharp pains.

'I think I could get up if you gave me your hand.'

'Forgive me. I was so shocked. I thought you might be seriously harmed…or dead.'

'No, thank you, I believe I am just a little shocked and bruised.'

'Thank God for it!' He sounded and looked distressed and when she rose to her feet, he put his arms about her and held her until she placed her hands against his chest, giving him a little push. He released her instantly.

'I have never been so shocked in my life. Had you been badly injured I could never have forgiven myself. You are under my protection and this is outrageous.'

'Do you suppose they were shooting at us—or do you think it a random shot intended to scare the horses? Of course, it might have been that someone misfired.'

'In either case the result might have been the same.' He looked at her in a very odd way. 'Do you not realise that you have come very close to death, Lottie?'

She took a deep breath, refusing to give way to hysterics. 'Well, yes, I realise there might have been terrible consequences, but neither of us is much harmed. I think we should concentrate our thoughts on who might have done this, do you not agree? Is it more likely to have been a stray shot from a gamekeeper or a poacher?'

'Do you feel able to continue?' he asked and gave her his hand as she inclined her head. 'My keepers would not fire across the road. It must have been a poacher—or someone who intended me harm.'

'Do you have enemies, sir?' Lottie looked at him in shock, discovering that her chest felt very tight of a sudden. She imagined the consequences if the shot had found its mark and her heart jerked. Rothsay might have died. The thought of that left a hollow feeling in her heart; things were far from easy between them but still she would hate the thought of losing the man who would be her husband. 'I had thought it must have been an accident but…who would hate you enough to do such a thing? You have Sam Blake safely locked up?'

'Yes, though there may be others I have sent to prison before this. I do not often sit in court, but there were some trials last summer that I was asked to give judgement on. A gang of violent poachers was broken up and most went to prison, though I believe one escaped punishment. I do not recall his name.'

'Then the shot might well have been meant for you, though it might have just been a keeper's shot gone astray. We were not travelling at speed and a pistol aimed at you would surely have hit its target?'

'Perhaps.' He frowned. 'My keepers do their duty, Lottie. You must not take them in dislike because of what happened this morning.'

'I assure you I have not, but accidents will happen.'

'I shall make enquiries. If a man was that careless I should not continue to employ him. You might have been riding here alone.'

'I dare say you are right and it was someone with a grudge against you. Forgive me, I should not interfere in your business. I must remember to keep my opinions to myself.'

'That would be a pity.' He smiled at her. 'You were extremely brave, Lottie. I do not think I know another young lady who would have taken this in her stride as you did.'

Lottie felt her cheeks heat. She turned her face aside, as she said, 'I am not hurt. Pray say nothing of this to the countess. I would not have her anxious over your safety or mine.'

'No, indeed, you are very right. We shall keep this incident to ourselves.' He glanced at her before taking up the reins. 'I hope you will forgive me for not taking better care of you?'

'There is nothing to forgive, sir. Pray do not mention it again.'

'Very well.' He gave her a look that she found difficult to interpret. 'You continue to surprise me. I am beginning to think I have not made such a bad bargain after all.'

Lottie did not answer. Her cheeks burned, for his words had been more revealing than he perhaps realised. Had he been regretting his bargain? If so, why had he not simply released her immediately she and her father arrived? No one would have been any the wiser and he could have made whatever excuse he pleased, leaving him free to find a wife more to his liking.

* * *

Had Lottie been privileged to read Nicolas's thoughts, she would have known that they had been very similar at one time. Nicolas had wondered several times why he had not settled with Sir Charles at the start. However, at this moment his feelings had undergone a sudden and startling change.

When he saw her lying with her eyes closed, Nicolas had at first thought she might be dead. The feeling that swept over him at that moment had been one of utter desolation. Relief had followed so quickly that he had had no time to examine his reaction or to understand why he had felt such a sense of loss.

She had retired into dignified silence, which left him time to consider his reactions. How could it matter to him whether this young woman lived or died? Except that he would feel distress at causing harm to any young woman of his acquaintance.

Was that it—just a natural concern for a young life?

Nicolas was nothing if not honest and he faced the truth without flinching. Lottie had somehow managed to get partly beneath the barrier he kept in place. At first he had thought her a beautiful scoundrel, a hardened adventuress—but Lottie was not her twin sister. He believed she was neither a thief nor a light-skirt, though her sister might very well be both.

He frowned, for it might prove inconvenient to have Lottie's twin as a close relation in the future. He would have to try to make some arrangement that protected his wife and his name from Clarice's misbehaviour—but that was for the future.

In the meantime he needed to sort out his feelings for

this beautiful, brave and spirited young woman sitting silently beside him. He had begun to find her company stimulating, though sometimes uncomfortable as she challenged him openly.

The look in her eyes as she spoke of the lines he had drawn for their marriage had struck him more deeply than he liked. Of course he could not expect her to stay always in the country, hidden away as if he were ashamed of her. He would not want to live with her in town, of course—but she might have her own establishment in Bath if she chose.

He could visit her there or here in the country if he felt the need, but she must be able to entertain and live a proper sort of life. Yes, he decided, that would do very well—and yet somehow it was not quite what he wanted.

As she changed for dinner that evening, Lottie examined her arms and legs, discovering some nasty bruises that were just about to come out. She did feel rather battered and shaken, but had not wanted to make a fuss. She would, however, need to wear a stole this evening to cover some of the marks.

She was thoughtful as Rose brushed and styled her hair for her. The look of horror in the marquis's eyes as he'd looked down at her had been rather satisfying. It was good that he had some concern for her, because she was beginning to like him more than she had expected. He was stern and she had evidence of his temper, but he could be pleasant company when he chose. She hoped that they might come to an understanding as they became more comfortable with one another.

He was not in love with her. She would be foolish to look for romance in her marriage, but if they could perhaps become fond of one another it might be an ideal arrangement.

Lottie sighed as she went downstairs. She was to meet more of her neighbours that evening and must manage to give an impression of a happy young woman about to be married.

The marquis had spoken of going up to town for a flying visit. Lottie would have preferred it if he had stayed so that they could get to know one another, but three weeks was a short enough time to prepare her wedding gown. She would hardly have time to miss him.

'Well, I do not see why you must leave us to amuse ourselves here alone,' Henrietta commented, giving her godson a sharp look after the guests had left that evening. 'Surely there is nothing so important that it cannot wait for a few weeks?'

'I have some business I must see to with my lawyers,' Nicolas told her. 'Besides, Lottie will need some new clothes. If she will supply me with her measurements, and you will advise me on what seamstresses I should employ, I shall endeavour to supply the lack.'

'I intend to take care of my own wedding gown,' Lottie said. 'I should like one or two afternoon gowns and perhaps a new bonnet—but you may safely leave that to me.'

'You need not fear to trust him,' Henrietta said. 'Rothsay has excellent taste. I shall give him a note to my own seamstress and she will provide you with what you need for your honeymoon. If you go to Paris you may buy more there, of course.'

Nicolas frowned. 'If you will give me what I require, I shall do my best to please you, Lottie. We shall discuss what else you need on my return.'

Lottie inclined her head, but said nothing. Henrietta looked from one to the other and shook her head. It was clear to her that once again they had had some kind of disagreement.

'Well, I shall do it now for I know you like to start early in the morning. While you are in town, you may ask my doctor for some more of the excellent mixture he makes for my indigestion.'

'Of course,' he said. 'Are you ready for bed, Lottie, or shall you take a turn in the garden with me?'

'I shall take the air with you, if you wish,' Lottie said. 'It is a pleasant evening.'

Nicolas offered his arm and she took it, her hand so light that he hardly knew it was there.

'I wanted to make sure that you had all you need for the moment,' he said as they went out into the garden. 'I had not intended to leave before the wedding but there is something I must attend to—will you be all right here? Your aunt should arrive in a day or so and you have Henrietta for company, as well as your father.'

'Please do not concern yourself, my lord. I have plenty to keep me busy. The invitations are not yet written and I have a gown to make.'

'I could have the gown made in town.'

'It will not be necessary. I have always made my gowns and I like my own style.'

'Your gowns become you, but you might wish to have something a little more…'

'Stylish?' Lottie laughed. 'I shall not be offended if you speak your mind to me. If I intended a Season in town I should certainly seek the help of a seamstress—but I think that is unlikely.'

'It may not be in the future. You may visit town occasionally, I dare say. I am hoping we shall at least be tolerably good friends, Lottie.'

'Yes, I am certain we shall,' she said. 'I am prepared to forgive and forget—if you are?'

'Can you forgive?'

'I think it only sensible to put the past behind us. We shall begin again, my lord.'

'Shall we, Lottie?' He turned, looking down at her in the moonlight.

She was beautiful. Even when he despised her as Clarice, the adventuress, he had known that she stirred his senses. Without knowing why he did it, he reached out and drew her to him, his head bending to reach hers. He kissed her tenderly and then hungrily as he felt her response. Her body was soft and yielding, the scent of her intoxicating, filling him with an urgent need for something he did not understand. For a few moments he held her crushed against him, feeling the burn of desire in his loins. He was tempted to sweep her into his arms and take her somewhere he could make love to her right away, but he controlled his urges.

'A kiss to seal the bargain,' he said, trying for lightness. 'Goodnight, Lottie. I shall be gone only a few days—and then we shall entertain our neighbours in earnest. Henrietta will set you right if you ask her.'

'Goodnight, Rothsay,' Lottie said, sounding so calm that he was irritated by her lack of emotion. 'Do not concern yourself. I am quite able to amuse myself while you are gone.'

Lottie pressed her fingers to her lips. She could still feel the impression of his lips, the burn of his kiss. Had she wondered if it would be difficult to do her duty and provide the heir? One kiss in the moonlight had shown her it would be only too easy. She had wanted him to go on kissing her for ever, but she was foolish to let herself hope for more than she knew he was willing to give.

The marquis would be a skilled and passionate lover. She had been told that he had indulged himself with a string of mistresses after his attachment to Elizabeth was broken. Lottie frowned as she wondered what the woman he had wished to make his wife looked like. Her curiosity was aroused, but it would be most improper to ask Nicolas about his former love.

Lottie put the slight irritation from her mind. Nicolas had made it clear that she could not look for love or romance in their marriage. His kiss was merely to seal their bargain but it had shown her that she felt more for him than she had expected or wanted. She knew that she would enjoy the intimate side of marriage. She would be neither embarrassed or reluctant when he came to her bed—but she was not sure how she would feel when he left it.

If she allowed herself to like him too much, she might find that her heart was broken. The one thing Lottie must never forget was that this was a marriage of convenience.

Nicolas wanted an heir. He had decided to be generous and considerate to her, which was an improvement on his manner at the start.

Was it enough? It had to be, because she did not think she had the strength to break off their engagement now.

Alone in her room, she bent down to stroke Kitty and laughed ruefully.

'Am I a fool? Should I flee now while I can?'

Kitty purred and Lottie nodded.

'You are right. It is already far too late.'

Chapter Five

Lottie awoke to a sense of loss, though it took her a few moments to realise why. Was it only three days since Rothsay had gone to London? It seemed an age. She had begun to miss the sound of his voice and the ring of his boots on tiled floors. Oh, how ridiculous! She did not really know the man at all and she certainly could not spend the rest of her life moping when he was not here.

She threw back the covers with determination. She had done as she'd thought and arranged with Mrs Blake to come to the house and help her to sew her wedding gown, and this morning she was going into Northampton with Lady Fisher to choose some silks. The invitations had gone out for the ball and the wedding. There was more than enough to keep her busy, because the servants awaited their instructions and it could not all be left to Henrietta, who, Lottie was aware, was far from well.

She washed her hands and face in cool water and

dressed. Rose would bring warm water up later and she would change, but first she would go for a walk to the lake. She had got into the habit of feeding the swans. It had become her first task of the morning and gave her something to do before breakfast. After the incident with the poacher she had stayed clear of the park in the early hours, preferring to walk only as far as the lake before breakfast.

It was so beautiful out at this hour. The peace of her surroundings was taking away the small ache she had experienced on waking. She would see Rothsay very soon for he was sure to return before the ball.

Lottie thoroughly enjoyed her trip to Northampton with Lady Fisher and bought some yards of a deep cream silk shot through with gold. Trimmed with some old lace that her mother had given her before she died, it would make a perfect gown for Lottie's wedding and could afterwards be worn for special dinners. Brides often wore their wedding gown in the first year of marriage; Lottie could see herself making good use of hers. She knew exactly what she wanted, the bodice tight with a dipping neckline trimmed with lace, and three-quarter-length sleeves frilled at the elbows with the same lace. She would not wear a bonnet, but an arrangement of fresh flowers from Rothsay's hothouses in her hair.

Her head filled with plans for the wedding, she thanked Lady Fisher when she was set down outside the house later that afternoon.

'Will you come in for some refreshment, ma'am?'

'Thank you, Lottie. Another time, perhaps? I am

expecting visitors this evening and must be there to greet them.'

'Oh, that will be pleasant for you.'

'I am not sure. I find Hunter a difficult guest but he is my late husband's nephew so I must oblige him sometimes. I wish that Bertie was at home, but as you know he left for London this morning.'

'Yes, Sir Bertie said adieu to me yesterday,' Lottie said. 'You must miss him when he is away, ma'am?'

'A little, but I have many friends. Please call whenever you have time, Lottie.'

Lottie thanked her and waved as the carriage was driven away. She was feeling pleased as she went into the house, because now that she had the silk she needed, she would be fully occupied with the making of her gown.

'Did you enjoy your trip, Miss Stanton?' the house-keeper asked.

'Yes, thank you. I have several parcels. Perhaps they could be taken upstairs?'

'Yes, of course, miss. You have a visitor waiting in the front parlour with the countess. I took her some tea. Would you like me to bring fresh?'

'Aunt Beth has arrived?' Lottie's face lit up. 'That is excellent news, thank you. Yes, I should like some tea, please.'

She walked hastily to the small front parlour, hearing the sound of laughter. It sounded as if Aunt Beth and Henrietta had hit it off already, and, as she entered, she saw that they were perfectly at home together.

'Lottie, my dearest one.' Beth stood up, her face wreathed in smiles as Lottie went to embrace her. 'How are you, my love?'

'Perfectly well, thank you,' Lottie said and kissed her on both cheeks. 'I am so pleased to have you here. I see you are already acquainted with Lady Selby.'

'It is the most fortunate thing,' Henrietta said. 'We were acquainted as girls. Beth is some years my junior but we met in Bath when I was first married and she had just come out.'

'So many moons ago,' Beth laughed softly. 'I had no idea that Rothsay was your godson, Henrietta.'

'I was great friends with his mama,' Henrietta said. 'He was such a charming boy, you know. I confess he won my heart when he was no more than five or six, and I have loved him as the son I never had.'

'It is a pity he had to leave on business,' Beth said, her eyes thoughtful as her gaze rested on Lottie. 'You need to get to know one another, Lottie.'

'We have the rest of our lives,' Lottie dismissed her suggestion, as if unconcerned even though it echoed her own feelings. 'There is so much to do in a house like this, dearest Aunt. I refuse to give Henrietta all the trouble of this wedding, though her advice is invaluable for I should not have known how to start.'

'Well, I am here now to help, too,' her aunt said. 'Have you settled the menus? They are most important—your guests will expect only the best in a house like this, Lottie.'

'We made a start last night, did we not, Henrietta? However, no one understands food better than you, Aunt. You must look at my suggestions and tell me if they can be improved.'

'Yes, I shall certainly do so. Your cook has a light

hand with pastry, Lottie. However, there might be some improvements I can make without giving offence.'

Lottie could tell that her aunt was looking forward to ordering the kitchens and hoped that Rothsay would have no objection. She had always left the menus to her aunt, for her own time was taken up with other things. Aunt Beth would be a great help to her when she was mistress here—and if Rothsay had some fault to find he could tell her when he came.

She glanced at the countess. 'I suppose there has been no word from Rothsay?'

'No, he is very provoking, is he not?' Henrietta gave her a gentle smile. 'It is so much more comfortable when the gentlemen aren't here to give their opinion—though I think he will not interfere with your arrangements in the house, Lottie.'

Lottie stifled the faint irritation she felt at her fiancé's absence. 'I dare say his business is important. He will return as soon as he is able no doubt.'

'Excuse me, Miss Stanton…Lady Selby…' The housekeeper had entered the room and looked from one to the other, as if uncertain who to address. 'There is a problem. I am not sure what ought to be done…'

'What is it, Mrs Mann?' Lottie asked. 'May I be of assistance?'

'Perhaps we could speak in private, miss?'

Lottie followed her from the room into the hall. It was obvious the housekeeper was ill at ease, uncertain what to do about something.

'Is there a problem with one of the servants?'

'No, miss. I should not have troubled you with that, for I am able to deal with domestic problems. It is just that Sam Blake was seen in the village. Apparently, he was talking wildly about getting even with his lordship. Mr Barton, that's his lordship's bailiff, was wondering whether to set more men on to patrol the grounds.'

'Has Blake escaped, then? I am certain Rothsay told me he had been sent to prison.'

'He must have escaped, miss. Barton wanted to speak to the countess, but I thought you might be the best person in the circumstances. I did not wish to alarm Lady Selby. To tell you the truth, she don't seem quite like her old self, miss.'

'No, I think she tires easily.' Lottie frowned, because Rothsay had told her not to interfere in estate matters, but she did not see how she could avoid doing so. 'Please tell Mr Barton to set more men on at once. If his lordship should return and be caught unawares he might meet with an accident.' Remembering the shot that had caused her fall, she was anxious. 'A message should be sent to the marquis in London, making him aware of the situation. I shall write the note myself and Mr Mann may send it on.' She smiled at the housekeeper. 'You were very right not to trouble the countess. You may always come to me if you are in doubt on any account.'

'Yes, miss. I thought I might.' Mrs Mann looked relieved. 'I shall speak to Mr Barton immediately—and you will keep this to yourself?'

'Yes, I would not alarm either Lady Selby or Lady Hoskins. They do not need to know about this. I shall tell them it was just a little hitch with the wedding arrangements.'

'Yes, miss. That is very sensible of you.'

The housekeeper departed and Lottie returned to the

parlour. She told her curious friends that it was just a problem with the supply of fresh salmon for the wedding, which had been easily resolved.

'Well, I do not know why Mrs Mann should be concerned with that,' Henrietta said. 'Rothsay will have it sent down from his estate in Scotland, as usual.'

'Yes, I am sure you are right,' Lottie said, but did not enlighten her further. 'Now, I must tell you that I chose the silk for my wedding gown today and it is beautiful. Rose took it up to my room. You must both come and see. I shall begin work on cutting the pattern tomorrow. I asked Mrs Blake if she would come at ten and help me.'

Lottie wondered if the woman would still come after what had been reported. If her husband was on the run from the law, she might be afraid of her reception. It might be best to send Rose with a message first thing in the morning.

Lottie broke the seal of the letter that had just been brought up to her. She frowned as she saw it was from her sister. What could Clarice have to say to her? She scanned the letter, lingering over one particular paragraph.

How clever of you to snare him, Lottie, Clarice had written. *I know you must have agreed for Papa's sake and to give Aunt Beth a home. I am a selfish wretch, but I am in love—and it couldn't matter to you. You will have money and a home, and you can thank me for stepping back and letting you become the marchioness. I may visit you one of these days—and I shan't stop you*

*if you want to show your appreciation for my generosity.
After all, you are supposed to be me—aren't you?*

Clarice went on to describe some of the places she
was visiting in Paris, as if she had not made what might
be a veiled threat of blackmail.

She frowned, because although Clarice had always
been selfish, she seemed to have touched new depths.
Sighing, Lottie put the letter to one side. She was not
sure what Clarice expected, but she would face it when
the time came. In the meantime, she had more pressing
problems.

What ought she to do about Lily Blake after that disturbing news about her husband?

'I wasn't sure you would want me to come after what
everyone was saying.' Lily Blake made a slight curtsy.
'But Rose told me you still needed my help…'

'Yes, I do,' Lottie said. 'Come and sit down, Mrs
Blake. I do not think we need to concern ourselves with
the gossip or your husband's intentions for the moment.
You need to earn some shillings for your work and I
need help.'

Lily looked at her for a moment, then, 'It weren't my
Sam spreading threats about the village,' she blurted
out, her cheeks hot with colour. 'I know he done wrong,
Miss Stanton, and I ain't trying to defend him—but it
were his cousin Dickon what put him up to the poaching.
They look a bit alike but Sam is still where his lordship
put him and cursing the day he got in with a pack of
rogues. It were Dickon as were shouting his mouth off
at the inn.'

'Sam's cousin, you say?'

'Yes. Dickon were alus a bad lot. He lost Sam his first job and after that my husband couldn't get work. No one would give him a chance, miss, and Dickon plagued him to help him with the traps. We've three children all under the age of five and he didn't want to see us starve.'

'Yes, I understand it must have been hard,' Lottie said. 'In future I shall employ you—and when your husband is released from prison I will see what I can do for him, though I promise nothing in his case.'

Lily's eyes brimmed with tears. 'Sam told me you would've helped him, miss. He reckons you be too good fer the likes of his lordship.'

'You must not say such things to me,' Lottie said and smiled. 'Now, I have heard you have some skill with your needle—can you also cut a pattern?'

'Oh yes, miss.' Lily brightened and brushed her tears away. 'Afore I was wed I worked for a high-class seamstress. She had a smart shop in Northampton and I worked in the back room.'

'Then I am sure we can create something special between us, Lily.'

'Yes, miss. With your figure it will be easy. What did you have in mind?'

Lottie explained, bringing a look of admiration to the other woman's eyes. 'It is a style I know suits me and I have made similar gowns for myself and others before.'

'It will suit you, miss—but perhaps we could change a few things here and there. After all, it is your wedding gown.'

'Yes.' Lottie was thoughtful as she watched Lily spread the silk on the floor and explain what she meant about getting the full potential from the hang of the material. Lily was clearly a talented seamstress and she deserved her chance, regardless of her husband's foolish behaviour.

After she was married, she would have a good think about the possibilities for Lily Blake's future.

In the meantime, she was trying not to worry about the orders she had given for Mr Barton to increase the patrols both on the estate and the roads leading to it. Rothsay might not be best pleased when he returned, but he should have been here and then he could have made the decision himself.

Nicolas glanced at the letter that had just been delivered from Rothsay Manor. He did not recognise the handwriting and looked for the signature before reading the contents. Why would Lottie have sent it to him urgently?

He frowned as he read what had happened and the orders she had given to protect the estate and his person should the rogue try to kill him on his return. He had wondered if Blake were behind the shot that had almost resulted in injury for Lottie, but to his best knowledge the man was still locked up in a prison in Northampton. He could, of course, have escaped in the meantime, but it was more likely to have been his cousin. Dickon Blake had served a year for his own misdemeanours and would have been released recently. The pair were similar in looks and could be confused on a dark night, though, unlike Sam, Dickon was violent and dangerous.

Sighing, Nicolas crushed the letter in his hand, tossing it to one side. He supposed he ought to return and sort this mess out. His business had been finished in an hour for it had merely been an addition to his will. Lottie must be provided for in the event of his death. He had visited various merchants, giving them instructions for the wardrobe Lottie would need as the new marchioness. There was no need for him to wait on their delivery, for the clothes and other things would be sent direct to Rothsay—so why had he delayed?

Walking to gaze out of the window, Nicolas faced the dilemma he had created for himself. Lottie was expecting a marriage of convenience. She had agreed for the sake of her family—in truth, he had given her no choice. What he had done was despicable from start to finish. He should have set her free the moment he realised who she was…or, rather, who she wasn't.

He had despised the woman he had seen rifling his friend's pocket in Paris, but he had formed a deep admiration for Lottie. She was different in every way from her sister.

The trouble was he was in danger of liking her too much. Long ago, he had discovered that unrequited love hurt. Even his mother's gentle but detached way of loving her son had been painful, and his father had ignored him after her death—apart from an occasional pat on the head or an instruction to work hard for his tutors.

It was quite ridiculous to hope that Lottie could ever care for him after the way he had treated her. He was in any case not sure that he wanted to love or be loved. He would do much better to continue as he had started, but that was easier from a distance than if he were with her.

That kiss in the moonlight had shocked him. It had

been a mere experiment, just to accustom her to what it felt like to be kissed—but he was very much afraid that he was the one who had been most affected. Lottie had taken it in her stride. Yes, she had seemed to melt into him while he held her, responding so sweetly that he had wanted to make love to her instantly. Yet afterwards, she had behaved in that calm, composed manner that seemed to suggest it meant nothing at all.

Damn it! He wanted more than a complaisant wife. He wanted to know that, when he made love to her, she would want him as much as he wanted her.

He turned with a grim smile on his mouth. He couldn't hide for ever. The ball was in five days and he must be there in time to make sure that everything was in order.

'Lottie, do come and see all the packages that have arrived for you,' Aunt Beth cried as she entered the house that morning after her customary walk to the lake. 'I have never seen so many all at one time. Whatever can be in them?'

'Rothsay said he would order a few things for me in London.' Lottie frowned. 'I told him not to be extravagant—I shall not need a huge wardrobe here. Besides, Lily Blake has made me such a wonderful wedding gown that I think I shall ask her to make all my clothes in future.'

'Yes, she has created something of a miracle,' Beth said. 'Far more stylish than we ever managed alone, dearest. I think she is wasted as the wife of that rogue.'

'Lily loves him, Aunt.'

'Yes…' Beth shook her head. 'We women are such

fools where men are concerned. My poor sister was much let down by your father. I do not know where he has got to these past few days.'

'He went home,' Lottie said. 'He promised to return for the ball.'

'We must hope he does not let us down.' Beth frowned. 'Rothsay has been a long time. I would have thought he would be here by now. If he is not here for—' She broke off, for there was the sound of the knocker and a footman sprang to attention to open the door.

Lottie turned, heart pounding as she saw the tall figure of the marquis enter. She had forgotten how handsome he was, how strong and masculine. Her heart caught as her eyes absorbed every detail of his appearance; it looked as if his dark hair had recently been cut short in a new style and it suited him.

'Rothsay, you are home,' she said and went forwards to greet him, offering her hand. 'I am glad to see you back. My aunt tells me several packages have arrived for me. I have not yet had time to examine the contents, but I think I should scold you for extravagance.'

'My wife must do me credit, Lottie. I cannot have the gossips saying I have a dowdy marchioness.' He took her hand, held it briefly to his lips. His eyes went beyond her to Aunt Beth. 'Lady Hoskins, I presume. Forgive me for not being here to welcome you to my home, ma'am. I am sure Lottie has made you comfortable. You are, of course, welcome to stay here for as long as you choose— though while in London I have instructed my agent on the purchase of a house for Lottie's benefit in Bath, and you may prefer to visit the spa together sometimes.'

'Really, Rothsay—did I not tell you I was perfectly content here?' Lottie's eyes sparked.

'Well, you must do as you choose,' he said easily.

'Thank you, sir,' Beth said. 'I like Bath very much. I am certain Lottie will enjoy visiting the town when she desires a change.'

'Just as you say, ma'am. I see you are a lady of good sense. Lottie, my love—may I speak to you in private for a moment?'

'Yes, of course.'

'In my library, if you please.'

Lottie followed as he strode through various apartments to the large room in the east wing. She had visited it but once in his absence; it was clearly his own preserve and he had left books lying out on the table, as if he wished to return to them without having to hunt. Brandy and glasses were waiting on a side table for his convenience. Mrs Mann had asked if she ought to tidy them away. Lottie had told her to leave all as it was until he returned.

She stood waiting just inside the door as he gazed out of the long windows at the view of the gardens.

'This business of Blake is unpleasant. I am sorry you had to be troubled with it while I was gone.'

'It was not a trouble, my lord. I was merely concerned that I must give orders to increase the patrols. I know that you do not consider I should interfere in your business, but—'

'Good grief, Lottie! What else could you have done in the circumstances? You said you had not told Henrietta or your aunt?'

'Neither of them will be tempted to go beyond the

immediate gardens. They do not need to know of any unpleasantness.' She looked at him as he turned to face her at last. 'You were not attacked as you travelled home?'

'No, not at all. I dare say it is all a lot of fuss for nothing—but you did exactly as you ought. I should have thought of it before I left, but I was not thinking too clearly.'

'You could not have known that Dickon Blake would decide to take revenge for his cousin's imprisonment. Lily told me Sam is still in prison, as no doubt you have learned.'

'It is not only Sam's incarceration that has angered Dickon. He has only recently been released from prison himself. I sentenced him to a year and he must have been freed just over a month back.'

'So it could have been he who fired at you?'

'Most probably. I shall have someone look into it. Extra keepers are all very well, but we must seek the cause and discover what is in his mind. I do not want to leave you alone until this business is resolved, Lottie. I shall hope to have it sorted before the wedding, but in the meantime the patrols will keep you safe.'

'I am certain of it. I have been far too busy to walk further than the lake and I have not yet ridden out—I was not perfectly sure which horse you would wish me to use.'

'I fear I have not treated you well, Lottie. I should have returned sooner. It was wrong to just leave everything to you. If you wish, we could ride out together tomorrow morning.'

'I should like that very much,' she replied. 'I am glad

you are not annoyed because I was forced to take charge. Henrietta could not have dealt with that kind of unpleasantness, you know.'

'Yet you take it in your stride?'

'I am accustomed to managing my father's estate. Very little distresses me,' she replied, a smile on her mouth. 'I believe we have covered everything we could. You were warned not to travel alone and the keepers have increased their patrols.'

'You are an unusual woman, Lottie. My mother would have screamed or fainted had she been asked to deal with such a decision.'

'I doubt it. Most ladies are capable of far more than gentlemen imagine. We are not, as we are so often termed, the weaker sex—though at times we may acquiesce to being thought so.'

'Is that so?' She looked at him in surprise for there was a new teasing note in his voice that she had not heard before. 'I believe I have a lot to learn about the fair sex, Lottie. I am but a man and cannot expect to understand the workings of the female mind. Besides, I think *you* are the exception and not the rule. I stand ready to receive instruction.'

'Now you are being provoking.' A laugh escaped her. 'Henrietta is right. You are the most provoking man.'

'I dare say I am—but perhaps you can teach me better manners?'

'Perhaps…' Lottie's heart raced. In this new mood her fiancé was very attractive. She must keep a tight rein on her feelings or she would end by falling head over heels in love with him. 'We have a great many gifts from your friends and relatives, Rothsay. Aunt Beth and Henrietta have been enjoying themselves going through them. All the cards are displayed with the gifts on a table in the long gallery. You may care to glance at them later.'

'I shall certainly do so. I dare say Great-Uncle Freddie has sent a silver tea-and-coffee service? It is his usual gift. I believe we may have upwards of four already, but I shall thank him with the proper gratitude.'

'You mean Lord Freddie, I suppose,' Lottie said. 'He sent me a very kind letter and a long string of beautiful coral and pearls, and a pair of duelling pistols for you. His letter said he thought you might appreciate them more than silver.'

'Indeed? How perceptive of him. I have always admired his pistols, which I know he once used in a duel with a rival.' Rothsay laughed. 'I am very surprised.'

'Well, I believe he may just have known that you had quite a bit of silver here at Rothsay. However, Lady Botham has sent us a silver service with both tea and coffee jugs so the tradition has been preserved.'

He chuckled. 'You see the amusing side of it, Lottie. I should have been just as happy to receive cards of congratulations, as expensive gifts, but it is a tradition, I suppose, and we must not offend anyone. We should send thank-you cards to everyone.'

'I have already replied to most,' Lottie said. 'I thought it best to attend to the replies once so many gifts began to arrive, otherwise it is easy to forget something and that is offensive, do you not agree?'

His right eyebrow arched in what she could only think a quizzical manner. 'I find myself agreeing with everything you say. You will make an admirable marchioness, Lottie.'

His words were those of praise, but something in his tone made her look at him sharply. He was not smiling and she sensed a change of mood.

'Have I done something to annoy you, Rothsay?'

'What could you have done? You have everything well under control, do you not, Lottie?'

'I have tried to do what I thought would earn your approval.'

'Indeed? Then you have succeeded. I have no fault to find, Lottie. You are everything you ought to be. Excuse me, I dare say you have much to keep you busy—and I must speak to my bailiff.'

Lottie frowned as he turned and walked from the room. He was angry or annoyed about something and for the life of her she could not think why.

Chapter Six

Nicolas had no idea why Lottie's efficiency had made him suddenly angry. It was foolish to resent the fact that she seemed to have the servants hanging on her every whim in just a few days. She was displaying all the right qualities necessary for the next marchioness, managing perfectly well, it seemed, without his help.

Was this how it would be when they were married? He would take himself off to London for a few weeks and return to a calm, smiling wife who could cope perfectly well without him?

Surely he had been fortunate beyond any expectation. He had chosen his bride so carelessly and he might have been hoisted with an adventuress who cared for nothing but spending his money. Lottie seemed more interested in scolding him for extravagance and caring for his estate in way that had been sadly lacking these past years. The perfect wife—except that she showed no sign of having missed him.

Nicolas laughed at himself. He was the one who had shunned love or anything like it for years. He was the one who had set the terms for their relationship—yet now he found himself wanting more.

He had noticed a new atmosphere in the house as soon as he entered; there was life and purpose, where before it had merely been a cold empty place waiting for someone. It appeared to have been Lottie everyone was waiting for. She had certainly made the place her own. She looked confident, composed and had smiled in welcome when he arrived—why, then, did he wish she had run to him, wanting to be caught in his arms and kissed?

She had asked him if she should like him after his abusive words to her, the threat that had made her his prisoner as much as his wife. Nicolas wished he could recall those bitter words. He knew now that she had not deserved them.

He had erected an invisible barrier between them. It was up to him to remove it brick by brick. Perhaps then she might come to like him, if not to love him.

Lottie frowned as she checked her lists, making small changes, adding little things to the tasks she must complete in the following week. The ball was the next evening, and everything was in place for the lavish supper, which would be served at ten o'clock. Henrietta had insisted champagne must flow like water all evening, and there were other wines for those who did not like the sparkling variety. The servants had worked hard to prepare the various delicacies and clean the house from top to bottom. However, there were still things to be settled for the wedding.

Because so many flowers would be used for the ball, the hothouses might not be able to supply all those needed for the wedding itself. Henrietta had mentioned a nursery run by a Northampton firm and she had sent to them to ask what would be available. The fresh salmon was coming from Scotland, more supplies of champagne would be sent from the marquis's extensive cellars in town, and would arrive on the morning before the wedding. Everything else would be supplied from the estate itself since they were almost self-sufficient. Even some of the candles they used were made locally with wax from their own hives.

Over the past weeks, Lottie had discovered the little cottage industries that relied mainly on supplying the big house and its villagers. Carpenters, a blacksmith, masons, farmers, a small brewery, a potter and an elderly lady, who made the most beautiful lace, were just a few of those depending on the marquis and his household to some degree.

It was a big responsibility and she wondered if that was the reason Rothsay disliked spending time at his home. For Lottie it was rapidly becoming the most beautiful place in the world. She enjoyed her work and her leisure, taking rambling walks when she had nothing more pressing to do. It was during her walks that she had met many of the marquis's tenants and was pleasantly surprised by the friendliness shown to her. Everyone was pleased she had come, they told her, for the master needed a wife to look after his interests.

If anyone had asked her what she would like best in

life, Lottie would have told them it was to live with her loving husband in a beautiful place where she could be useful. Here she had all she could possibly desire—except for one thing.

She could see no sign that Rothsay cared about her. He was on his best behaviour now, polite and complimentary of her efforts on his behalf. However, the distance between them was still there. It seemed he had not forgotten that he had been cheated, though he had accepted her in her sister's place.

It would not do to dwell on what was missing from her life. Lottie had faced the world as it was since her mother had died of a broken heart, and her father continued his downward slide. Rothsay would never love her, but, if she continued to show good sense and make no demands, he might in time come to feel affection for her.

She was about to go in search of her aunt and Henrietta, for it was nearly time for tea, when she heard a querulous voice seconds before the door of her private parlour was flung open. Everyone knew that this was the room she chose when she was busy working or wanted a few moments of reflection and it was by unspoken agreement that she was left alone here. Only this particular lady would ignore that and enter so abruptly.

'Cousin Agatha,' she said and rose to her feet with a smile. 'How nice that you could come.'

'No thanks to that father of yours, Lottie. I particularly asked that he should come and escort me, but I've seen nothing of him and I was forced to travel with just my servants.'

'I am sure they took good care of you, Cousin.'

'That is not the point…but there, I should not fuss at

you. Your father is a wastrel and nothing will change that, Lottie. You must make sure that he doesn't try to scrounge from you once you are married. I doubt Rothsay will put up with it. He is a bit of a cold fish I hear? I suppose you took him for the title and the money?'

'If you suppose that you are wrong,' Lottie said. 'As it happens, I have great respect and regard for Rothsay. I was just about to go in search of Aunt Beth and the countess. If you will accompany me, we shall have tea.'

'Henrietta Selby, I suppose.' Cousin Agatha's thin mouth twisted wryly. 'I know her of old. She at least is a decent sort. Don't tell me it's a love match. You've only known him a short time—besides, Clarice told me the whole story.'

'Did she? Perhaps Clarice does not know the whole story.'

'Humph…like that, is it? Well, if you care for him I shan't say another word about it. Clarice is a fool—she will end up in worse trouble if she is not careful. She came to me for money before she went off to Paris. I gave her a hundred guineas and told her not to expect more. She will run through that in five minutes, I dare say. She knows better than to come to me again, so you may expect a visit before too long.'

'Please, Cousin Agatha, may I ask you not to be so outspoken here? I do know how thoughtless Clarice is but I would prefer that others did not know of her foolish ways.'

'Foolish ways, is it? I should put another interpretation on it, but I won't pull caps with you, Lottie. I've always thought you the best of the bunch, my girl. You've a chance to make something of yourself now. See that you make the most of it.'

'Yes, I shall.' Lottie smiled at her. 'I truly will, Cousin—and I am happy you have come to stay.'

'I'd be a fool to turn down a chance like this,' Cousin Agatha said and laughed. 'Whatever you might think of me, Lottie, you know I ain't that.'

Nicolas paused outside the drawing-room door. He could hear the sound of feminine laughter and several voices. It was a long time since he had come into the house and heard something as pleasant. He walked in and his eyes sought Lottie. She looked very at home as she passed tea to the young maid. He noticed it was not Rose, but knew already that Lottie had promoted her to be her own personal maid. For a moment he almost felt a stranger in his own house, and then Lottie noticed he was there and her face lit with a smile of such warmth that he felt as if something had punched him in the stomach.

'Rothsay, please come in. We are all ladies, as you see, but the gentlemen will start to arrive later. Lord Freddie expects to be here for dinner this evening. He waited for your cousin Marcus to come home so that they could travel together—and your cousin Raymond will be here later this evening.'

He was drawn into her charmed circle immediately and walked to the fireplace, standing to get an overview of the room.

'I see we have a new guest, Lottie.'

'This is Cousin Agatha,' Lottie said. 'Lady Fox is my father's cousin, but I have always addressed her as cousin.'

'Indeed? Then perhaps I may also,' Nicolas said and inclined his head to the rather stout lady, who looked to be just a few years younger than Lottie's aunt. 'You are very welcome here, ma'am. I hope you will enjoy your visit.'

'Humph…you ain't quite the cold fish I was led to believe, Rothsay. I wondered if you were good enough for Lottie, but you may just do.'

'Thank you, ma'am.' A little quiver at the corner of his mouth told Lottie he was amused and not angry at the lady's outspokenness. 'Lottie, where is your father? I have something to discuss with him.'

'He went off for a few days. I dare say he will be back for the ball and the wedding.'

'Yes, I see.' Nicolas frowned. He could hardly blame his future father-in-law when he had done much the same thing. 'No doubt my relations will descend in force tomorrow. May we expect any more of your family, Lottie?'

'No, I think not,' she said. 'We are all here apart from Papa.' A faint flush stained her cheeks. 'I believe my sister will not come.'

'Clarice is still in Paris, as far as any of us know,' Cousin Agatha put in. 'She has friends there, I dare say. Besides, it might be awkward if she came, Lottie. You are better off without her.'

'Yes, perhaps.'

Nicolas saw that she was embarrassed. He looked at his godmother and saw the speculation in her eyes. There was no use in denying it, he must put the record straight now.

'I fear I have not been entirely honest with you from

the start, my dear Henri. Though I was engaged to be married to Clarice, Lottie is actually that lady's twin sister. For reasons I'd rather not go into, it was Lottie who turned up to deliver the news that Clarice had reconsidered our betrothal. But it was fortunate indeed for me; by changing her mind Clarice has given me the gift of being free to propose to her sister—and I have been luckier than I deserve in finding such a lovely bride.'

Cousin Agatha gave a derisory snort, but said nothing more. Henrietta looked from one to the other and smiled.

'Yes, I believe I understand, Nicolas. You must tell me more another time. Do sit and have some tea, dearest. It makes my neck ache to look up to you.'

Nicolas sat. Lottie shot him a grateful look and poured his tea just as he liked it. He understood why Lottie had not particularly wanted to invite Cousin Agatha. The woman was a liability, but he would have a word with her in private. He did not wish Lottie to be embarrassed in front of strangers—and Lady Fox must be quite certain of his support for his future wife.

'Lottie—may I speak to you alone please?' Nicolas caught her as she was leaving to change for the evening. 'I should like a few words in private—before the hordes arrive. I fear we shall not have a moment to spare once that happens.'

'Of course. Do you wish to go to the library?'

He led the way and she followed, then turned as he closed the door behind them, an apology on her lips.

'I am sorry, but Cousin Agatha has always spoken her mind. My sister borrowed some money from her, to pay for her trip to Paris, I must presume. Agatha does not approve of Clarice.'

'No, I dare say not. She seems to approve of you, however?'

'Yes, for I stood up to her when Mama died and she wished Clarice and I to leave Papa and go to her.'

'Well, we all have relations who cause us some unquiet moments. You will meet my cousin Raymond this evening.' Nicolas hesitated. 'I wanted to tell you that I have had my lawyer draw up a new contract for our marriage, which I should like you to sign. Your father must also when he returns. To neglect this might have led to complications if anything should happen to me. In order that your jointure is protected and our sons' inheritance secure I have made the changes necessary.'

'I see…' Lottie understood the reasons for his visit to town. 'Yes, it should be done properly. I shall sign—and Papa will do whatever you tell him when he returns.'

'Had it not been so important I should not have left you here to cope alone.' He produced a document from his pocket and placed it on the table with pen and ink. 'Please take a moment or two to read it, Lottie.'

'I am sure you have been impeccable,' Lottie said, looking up at him. 'Does this mean the other contract has been destroyed?'

'I thought it best to start again. Your father has his copy, of course, but no doubt he will accept the new one in its place. I believe the terms are more favourable than before.'

'I hope you have not given Papa anything more than the release of his debts. He will waste the money at the gaming tables.'

'He is to have an allowance, but in return must be discreet. Your own settlement has been increased. I do not wish you to go short of anything, Lottie.'

'I am certain you have been too generous, Rothsay. I have not yet had time to look at all the gifts you sent me from town, but I think you were extravagant, sir.'

'Not sir, please, Lottie. Rothsay or Nicolas, if you prefer.' He watched as she signed. 'You did not wish to read the contract?'

'I do not think it necessary. As I told you before, I shall be content here. Really, the estate is a perfect place to live. We have almost all we need here, you know. Yes, we do have to send to Northampton or London for luxuries, but most of what we require comes from the farms and the hothouses—or the local businesses and craftsmen.'

'Is that so?' He looked at her thoughtfully. 'I have left the management of this estate to others, except for brief visits. You seem to have learned a lot in a brief time, Lottie. I hope you have not found it too onerous a task preparing for the wedding?'

'It was a delight and a pleasure. I shall enjoy entertaining our neighbours, Rothsay—especially when you are at home, though I intend to hold small soirées when you are not.'

'You have it all settled in your mind? I had wondered if you might have suffered a change of heart whilst I was gone?'

'No, not at all. I think I shall do very well in this life you have chosen for us, Rothsay. If there is anything that needs your attention, I shall write as I did concerning the keepers, but otherwise I shall manage well enough.'

'In that case, it is time I gave you this,' he said with a wry twist of his lips. 'Allow me to take your hand, Lottie.' She rose to her feet and he slipped a magnificent ring on to her left hand. 'I had this made for you in town. It took a day or two longer than I hoped, but I am pleased with it.'

Lottie looked at the exquisite square emerald surrounded by white diamonds so pure that they took her breath.

'It is beautiful, Rothsay. I am overwhelmed.'

'It is worthy of you, I think. I have asked for the Rothsay heirlooms to be sent here in time for the wedding. You may take your choice of them and the rest will return to the bank. I think most of them too heavy and old fashioned, but anything you like could be refurbished. I have bought you a wedding gift, naturally. A bride should have her own jewels, though the heirlooms must be preserved for the future.'

'Thank you so much for my ring.' Lottie moved towards him impulsively. She reached up to kiss his cheek, then found herself crushed against his chest.

Rothsay's mouth was soft and yet demanding, drawing a sweet response from her. She could not keep the barrier in place and felt herself melt into him as the heat of desire swirled inside her. A little moan left her lips and she longed for something she had never known—the joining of a man and woman as one, flesh to flesh. Gazing into his eyes, she saw a hungry yearning and knew that he desired her as much as she wanted him.

He *desired* her. He did not love her, though she believed he was coming to respect her and perhaps like her. Happiness pooled inside her, bringing a smile to her lips and her eyes, had she known it.

'You are everything a man has a right to expect in his wife,' he murmured huskily. 'I should not delay you further, Lottie, or you will be late for dinner—but I wanted you to have the ring and to be aware of changes to the contract.'

'Thank you.' He seemed to have withdrawn again, yet Lottie was feeling happier as she went upstairs. Hers was perhaps a strange marriage, but she thought it might do well enough. The anger and resentment she had felt at the beginning had all gone and she was anticipating her wedding with pleasure.

How right Rothsay was to say there would be no time to talk once his relatives began to arrive. Uncle Freddie and his son Marcus were amongst the first. Lottie had appreciated his gift and thanked him for it with a shy smile and a kiss on the cheek. She liked him and his rather handsome son immediately and felt that the feeling was returned. Cousin Raymond was a disappointment. His clothes proclaimed him a macaroni and he strutted like a peacock, showing off his finery, seeming to have no interest in anything but his appearance and the latest *on-dit* in town.

After that, in quick succession, three families arrived that had not been expected until the following day. However, their rooms were prepared and since they had dined on the way and required only a light supper Cook was not much put out.

Lottie might have struggled to remember them all

had not Henrietta grounded her well concerning the family.

'The Cottrells are second cousins but Nicolas rather likes Sir James and his wife. Lady Tilda was the wife of Rothsay's cousin Rupert. She is a widow but her son Robert is the heir to the title for that branch of the family, though not yet of age. Nicolas oversees her affairs, I dare say, as head of the family. Lord William Stowe is a cousin on his mother's side, and his wife, Jane, is a silly little thing, but sweet and docile. They have two small children. There are any number of distant cousins, who will no doubt seize the chance to stay at Rothsay Manor, but most of them will be satisfied with a nod and a smile. In time you will know them all by name—that is, if you choose to ask them to visit, my dear.'

Supper was a lively affair in the drawing room, though Henrietta retired soon after the tea tray was brought in. Some of the gentlemen were in a jovial mood and seemed prepared to stay up all night, and at eleven o'clock the ladies decided to leave them to their wine and cigars.

Lottie smiled at Rothsay as she bid him goodnight. He took her hand and kissed it, bringing a little flush to her cheeks, but earning approval from his male relatives.

'I am sure I wondered if Rothsay would ever marry,' Lady Cottrell said as she walked upstairs with Lottie. 'He seemed so set in his ways, but they say reformed rakes make good husbands. I know he is meticulous in matters of honour. I dare say he will give up his mistress and settle down once you are married. They say she is quite beautiful but then, you are lovely yourself, my dear. Besides, we must forgive the gentlemen their little peccadilloes, must we not?'

Lottie could not look at her as she murmured something appropriate and escaped to her room. She was sure that the lady had not meant to be malicious, but until this moment Lottie had not thought about Rothsay's life in London. Of course he must still have a mistress. Was that lady the real cause of Rothsay's sudden departure for town?

Lottie supposed that he must have been with her in London all this time…yet the kiss he had given her in the library had seemed so full of passion…

Tears stung her eyes and caught at the back of her throat. How lowering it was to think that she had responded so eagerly to his kiss. She must remember that Rothsay wanted a marriage of convenience. He required complaisance in his wife, but nothing more. If she showed her feelings too plainly, he might feel uncomfortable—or even disgusted.

He had not seemed disgusted when he kissed her, but how could he care for her when he had a mistress he continued to visit?

Lottie had hoped that he might come to feel some affection for her, but now she realised that she had allowed herself to hope for too much. Rothsay was generous and meticulous in matters of business and honour. In having the contract changed to her name, he had safeguarded her from any bother in the future—and there might have been had her sister's name remained in the contract. Lottie had not even considered the legal side, but Rothsay had left nothing to chance. However, he had given her no reason to think his feelings had undergone a major change.

He might respect her more than he did her sister, but

that was not love. He was not in love with her—he might even be in love with his beautiful mistress.

Lottie's eyes sparkled with tears as she picked Kitty up and kissed her. The kitten was growing swiftly, its fur much softer now that it was well fed and groomed. Rose had been training the pet for her and there were less puddles than at the start.

Lifting her head, Lottie banished her tears. She would not give way to emotion. She had agreed to this arrangement and she would not renege on her bargain.

It struck her then that had she wished to, she could have refused to sign the new contract. At the time the possibility had not even occurred to her—nor would she have refused if it had.

Lottie wanted to live here and be Rothsay's wife. She just wanted him to be a little bit fond of her.

Oh dear, was she being foolish again? Lottie made a determined effort and succeeded in laughing at herself. She had been through this a hundred times in her mind. She must and would be satisfied with her life in this beautiful place—even if Rothsay's careless manner caused her pain at times.

What she would not do was to let him guess that she was falling in love with him. She had begun to develop feelings for him perhaps from the very first moment she saw him—and if not then, certainly when he held her close after the accident.

She frowned for a moment as she went to bed. Rothsay had said little about the threat to his life. She supposed that he had keepers watching for Dickon Blake. He would have made his own arrangements now that he was back.

* * *

'Poachers, you say?' Uncle Freddie looked at him hard. 'If they come before me I hang 'em or send 'em off to the colonies. Scum, that's what they are and deserve all they get.'

'In the case of Dickon Blake I would agree. I think he misled his cousin. If it would not appear weakness, I should be inclined to let Sam Blake off after a couple of months. His wife is an honest woman and, if he were given some employment, he might reform.'

'Not with his cousin Dickon about,' Uncle Freddie said. 'If the man is the rogue you describe, you will not be free of him until you either hang or transport him. All this liberal talk about giving the deserving poor a chance in life is a load of nonsense in my opinion. The deserving poor know their place and cause no trouble— the others are rogues and need to be kept in line.'

'Yes, that was my father's opinion,' Nicolas agreed. 'I suppose I should give Blake twelve months and have done with it.'

'Don't give it another thought, my boy. Still, it is best not to tell the ladies anything about these matters. They have soft hearts, but they may ease their minds by delivering succour to those who behave themselves.'

'Yes…' Nicolas smiled inwardly. Somehow he did not see Lottie agreeing with such sentiments. She might not say it to his uncle's face, but he believed she would have no scruples in giving him her opinion.

The devil of it was he had begun to wish for Lottie's good opinion. It was unfortunate that the case should come up on the morning of the ball. If he handed down the heavier sentence, he hoped she would not be too upset to enjoy the evening. Yet his uncle was right. It would be foolish to show weakness. Sam Blake had broken the law and ought to serve his proper sentence.

Nicolas would have to try to keep the news from her, until after the wedding if possible. He would visit Mrs Blake, reassure her that she was safe in her cottage, and ask her not to tell Lottie until after the wedding day. The woman was honest enough and he might give her something to tide her over while her husband was in prison—but the man must serve his time.

His decision was made and he would not change his mind, but it did not sit easily with his conscience. He would have been lenient if he could, but weakness would encourage others to think they could trap game in his woods with impunity and that would not do. Especially as he was thinking of bringing in a herd of deer and some exotic game birds.

'Lottie...' Hearing the sibilant whisper behind her, Lottie turned, looking for the source. She was in the shrubbery searching for greenery that she could use to decorate the house and did not at first see the young woman crouching out of sight. 'I'm here, but I didn't want anyone else to see me.'

'Clarice!' Lottie's heart pumped madly as she glanced round. 'What are you doing here?'

'Do not worry, I haven't come to demand that you step aside for me,' Clarice told her. 'Come here so that I can stand properly without being seen. We returned from Paris three days ago and I've been trying to get you alone ever since.'

Lottie's heart sank as she saw her sister's face and

understood why she had come. 'What do you want, Clarice? If you have come to ask for money, I have very little to give you.'

'Don't be so mean, Lottie. You have all this—and it should have been mine.'

'You ran off and left Papa in the lurch,' Lottie said. 'Besides, the estate belongs to Rothsay, not me. As yet I have only a small allowance. I could give you twenty guineas, but that is all I can spare.'

'I never thought you would be so tight-fisted,' Clarice said and looked sulky. 'I suppose it will have to do for the moment—but I shall expect more when you're married. It wouldn't look too good if I told everyone what you had done, would it?'

'Wait here and I will fetch your money, Clarice. I do not mind giving you something when I have money to spare, but do not expect me to give you large sums. Rothsay will give me an allowance, but he will not pay your debts, so do not think I have a never-ending purse.'

'If I had known how mean you would be, I should have married him myself,' Clarice said. 'Make it fifty guineas, Lottie—or I might tell him the truth.'

'He already knows,' Lottie said. 'You cannot blackmail me, Clarice. I will give you twenty guineas now—and, occasionally, I might give you similar sums, but Rothsay is under no illusions and he is satisfied with his bargain.'

Seeing the flicker of annoyance in her sister's face, Lottie returned to the house to fetch the money. She did not grudge her sister a few guineas, but she was afraid that Clarice's demands would not end here.

Chapter Seven

Lottie put the unpleasant incident with her sister to the back of her mind. The wedding was approaching so fast that she did not have time to dwell on Clarice's threats. On the morning of the ball, she was so busy that she hardly noticed Rothsay had disappeared for several hours. She had received so many small tributes from friends and neighbours that she seemed to be opening gifts and admiring bouquets the whole time. Having guests in the house meant that she must be concerned for their comfort and could not go for her usual walk.

'I never expected all this,' she said to Henrietta when that lady gave her a pretty little box that contained a diamond pin. 'You have already given us that lovely painting of Venice and those exquisite lace tablecloths.'

'This is just for you, because I love you,' Henrietta said and kissed her. 'I am so glad Nicolas has you in his life, dear Lottie. I was beginning to think he would turn into a miserable old man and be entirely alone in his later years.'

'No, how could you?' Lottie laughed. 'He has so many friends and relatives. He need never be alone.'

'One can be all alone in the midst of a crowd,' Henrietta said. 'Rothsay was lonely, but he isn't now. Everyone has been telling me what a change they see in him—and I have seen it from the first. I believe he loves you, Lottie. Truly and with his whole heart, as I had hoped.'

'Oh...I do hope you are right,' Lottie said and pressed her hand. Her throat felt tight, but she dismissed the urge to cry. Henrietta meant well, but Lottie knew the truth—her husband would never truly love her. 'Do you happen to know where he is?'

'I believe there may be a court session in Northampton,' Henrietta said. 'He didn't tell me, but someone mentioned it. Rothsay may have been asked to sit. No doubt he will tell you if you ask.'

Lottie nodded. She wasn't sure Rothsay would wish to discuss his business with her or that she ought to ask. They had been getting on so much better and she did not want him to be angry because he thought she was interfering. She hoped he would be lenient with Sam Blake, but she would not ask.

She was still determined not to ask awkward questions when Rothsay joined them after nuncheon. Chairs had been set out under the trees and some of the gentlemen were playing a game of quoits on the grass. Others had walked to the lake, while the ladies took their ease before changing for the evening.

'Is everything all right?' Lottie asked when Rothsay came up to her.

He nodded but she thought his expression strained, his

manner slightly reserved. Lottie decided that she would say nothing that might precipitate a quarrel that evening. Perhaps tomorrow when the ball was over, though it might be better to be discreet and not mention the fact that Henrietta had let slip about the court session.

It was, after all, none of her business what Rothsay chose to do in his position as a magistrate. She might privately wish that he had let Sam Blake go with a reprimand, but she could not expect her opinion to matter. Rothsay was not alone in his opinion that poaching was a crime that needed to be punished severely.

When it was time to go up to change for the ball, Lottie had managed only a few words alone with Rothsay. She held her curiosity in check. Lily Blake was coming that evening to help her dress, just in case any last-minute alterations needed to be done. No doubt she would tell her what sentence her husband had received that morning.

However, Rose brought the news that Lily was feeling unwell and could not come that evening.

'She has apologised and says she will definitely be here for the wedding, Miss Lottie, but she has a terrible headache and cannot come tonight.'

Lottie looked at her reflection in the mirror. 'Well, there is nothing for her to do so it does not matter. I hope she is not truly ill?'

'I think it was just a headache,' Rose said, but Lottie had an uncomfortable feeling that she was hiding something. 'You do look a proper treat, miss. That dress suits you well.'

'It is my usual style, but Lily made a few changes

that made all the difference. I do not think the stylist in Northampton would have done better.'

'No, miss, nor half so well in my opinion.'

Lottie smiled as the girl fastened Aunt Beth's pearls about her throat. She was just about to go downstairs when someone knocked the door. Rose answered it and gave a little squeak of apprehension.

'It is his lordship, miss.'

'Oh, please come in, Rothsay,' Lottie said and turned to face him as Rose escaped into the dressing room and shut the door. 'I was just about to come down.'

'I see you are wearing pearls. I thought you might like these...' He handed her a box, which, when opened, revealed a pair of pearl-and-gold bangles.

'How pretty! Thank you, yes, they will go well with Aunt Beth's pearls.' She slipped them over her long gloves and fastened them, smoothing out the skirts of her pale green gown. 'Shall I do, Rothsay?'

'You look beautiful, as I am certain you know.'

'I am well satisfied with my gown. Lily Blake helped me style it a little. She is very clever with her needle.'

'Yes, so I understand.' He offered his arm. 'Shall we go down? We must be the first so that we can welcome our guests.'

'Of course,' she said. 'Your gift was another lovely surprise. You will overwhelm me with presents, Rothsay. I assure you they are not necessary.'

'I wish my wife to have pretty things.'

Lottie was aware of how very handsome Rothsay was as he stood by her side to receive their guests. Tall, powerful and with clean-cut features that told of his noble lineage, he drew the eyes of all the young women. She saw envy and even jealousy show briefly in their faces, before their mamas drew them away. The more protective mothers might feel he was not good husband material, but as far as breeding, position and wealth was concerned he must be one of the matrimonial prizes of any Season.

Lottie felt both proud and happy to be wearing his ring, which was much admired by everyone. They opened the dancing together with a waltz, and his hand at her waist sent sensual tremors winging down her spine. She gazed up at him, at his mouth, which she knew could arouse such delicious feelings in her, and saw that it was set in a thin line.

'Is something troubling you, Rothsay?'

'Was I frowning?' He glanced down at her and smiled. 'Forgive me, my thoughts had strayed and that is unforgivable on a night like this. Did I tell you that I am very proud of my beautiful fiancée?'

'Proud?' She lifted her delicate eyebrows, her mouth pursued in a teasing smile that was, had she known it, both provocative and sensual. 'That is a great change, Rothsay? I believe it is not a month since you called me a damned adventuress.'

'I must beg your pardon for that, Lottie. I did not know you then. You know I mistook you for your sister.'

Lottie's cheeks felt warm. He already despised Clarice—what would he think if he knew that she had tried to blackmail her?

Realising he was waiting for an answer, she looked up at him. 'And you do know me now? Are you sure?'

'I am beginning to learn more,' he replied and laughed throatily as he saw the expression in her eyes. 'You are a minx, Lottie. If we were not entertaining I should punish you for that, but it would take too long and our guests would miss us.'

Lottie gurgled with laughter. Banter of this kind was amusing. She was very glad she had not brought up the subject of Sam Blake earlier in the day. It would have angered him and thrown a cloud over the evening. As it was, Rothsay seemed to be in a good humour, which meant she could relax and enjoy the ball.

After their dance, she was surrounded by young gentlemen asking her for a dance. Most of them had only been introduced to her that evening and showered her with compliments, asking ridiculous things like why they had not seen her first, and did she really wish to marry a scoundrel such as Rothsay? Since they were clearly his friends and the banter was all in good fun, she merely laughed and assured them that she was very happy with her choice.

It was not until much later in the evening that she danced with Sir Bertie Fisher.

'Are you settling in well, Miss Lottie?' he asked. 'Mama is delighted to have you as her close neighbour. She tells me she hears good things of you—and I believe you have been shopping together in Northampton?'

'Yes, we have, sir. I bought some beautiful silk for my wedding gown.'

'Ah, yes, the wedding is fast approaching. Tell me

where do you go on your honeymoon or has Rothsay kept it to himself?'

'I am not certain we shall go away,' Lottie replied and now her cheeks felt warm. He was not the first to mention the honeymoon and she was perfectly certain that Rothsay had no idea of it. The word had not crossed his lips and she would not dream of asking such a question when she knew very well the reality of her situation. 'I believe Rothsay has business and I have much to do here.'

He said nothing, but she sensed that he thought her answer odd, and perhaps it was. She was not perfectly certain what occurred when two people married for the sake of convenience—did they go through the motions of a honeymoon or simply got on with their independent lives?

At the end of the dance, she smiled at Bertie, then left him and went upstairs to freshen her gown and apply cool water to her cheeks. It had become very hot in the ballroom and she needed a moment to recover.

A lowering thought had occurred to her. The young women who had looked at her with envy this evening would very soon be laughing behind their fans when it was realised that Rothsay had little regard for his wife and meant to carry on exactly as before.

She had known it from the start. She just had not expected it to hurt this much.

Now she was being quite ridiculous. The ball had put a lot of people to a deal of trouble and she would be stupid to spoil it for them or herself. She must go back down and smile and laugh, as if she were the happiest woman in the world—which she would be if Rothsay loved her.

Returning to the ballroom, Lottie stood up with her partners for every dance. Rothsay escorted her into supper and their table was one of the largest in the room, everyone wishing to spend at least a few minutes with them. Lottie forgot her doubts as Rothsay teased her and accepted the teasing of his friends in good spirit.

'You are a dashed lucky dog,' Uncle Freddie said. 'Had I been twenty years younger, I should have cut you out, Rothsay.'

Lottie threw him a laughing glance. 'Had I seen you first, dear Uncle Freddie, it is quite possible that I would have taken you.'

'Sensible gel,' Uncle Freddie said and winked at her. 'Keep 'em guessing, that's the secret of a long and happy marriage. Not that he would be fool enough to stray now that he has found you, m'dear.'

'Thank you,' Lottie replied and glanced at Rothsay. She was shocked by the brooding expression in his eyes. What could he be thinking?

She wondered if he was thinking of his mistress and wished she could ask if he intended to keep a mistress after they were married, but that of course would be quite shocking. Wives and fiancées did not ask such awkward questions.

After supper Rothsay claimed his second dance of the evening. It was once again a waltz and as his hand pressed lightly at her waist, she felt as if she were melting with pleasure. The music was sweet and the air was filled with the perfume of the flowers that had been banked along the bottom of the dais. Overhead, the glittering chandeliers threw showers of light over the dancers and their jewels sparkled at throats and fingers. It was, Lottie thought, a scene of privilege and indulgence. Only the very wealthy could afford to give parties of this kind, and she found it sobering to think that the food left over from this evening could probably feed a village community for a week.

Well, why shouldn't it? Lottie decided that in the morning she would have some baskets of good food made up and taken to the poorer tenants. It was only right that they should share the delights of their lord's celebrations. She would speak to Mrs Mann about it in the morning.

'You are very thoughtful, Lottie?'

'Yes, my mind had drifted,' she said. 'It must have cost you a great deal for this evening—and a great deal more for the wedding.'

'It is no matter.' His gaze narrowed. 'Are you thinking of crying off at the last minute, Lottie?'

'No, of course not,' she replied. 'I have no intention of it. I was just thinking of all the people who would benefit from just a little of the money that we have spent this evening.'

'Well, as mistress of Rothsay I dare say you may dispense charity where you see fit in the future.'

'You will not mind if I send food to the tenants?'

'Why should I? My mother always did so, though the last few years I have seldom been here and these things may have been neglected.'

'Then I shall certainly do so. Forgive me, Rothsay. This is not the moment to speak of such things.'

'No, it is not,' he agreed. 'We must find time to discuss many subjects, Lottie, but I think we could put serious matters out of our minds until after the wedding, don't you?'

'Yes, certainly. This is a very special night, Rothsay. Thank you for giving me something so wonderful. I am not sure I deserve it.'

'Oh, yes,' he said and smiled oddly. 'I think you do, Lottie. Besides, you had all the work of it—so I should be the one thanking you.'

Their dance ended and Rothsay went off to do his duty, dancing with a married woman, who seemed delighted with his attention and flirted with him desperately.

Lottie tried not to mind that he appeared to enjoy her efforts. She had been told that Rothsay had a mistress. For all she knew, the woman might be amongst their guests…might even be the lady he was even now escorting out to the terrace.

She fought an unworthy urge to follow and confront them. Instead, she accepted the hand of her next partner, resisting the temptation to look at the French window through which Rothsay had disappeared with his beautiful partner.

However, he was back in the ballroom within a few minutes and she saw him talking to Aunt Beth and Henrietta, who were watching the proceedings, but not dancing.

'I am past my dancing days,' Aunt Beth protested when Lottie suggested she might care to indulge once or twice.

She saw Rothsay escort Henrietta from the room and

knew that his godmother would have left the ball earlier than most because she could not stand late hours.

However, he had not returned within half an hour, and the lady who had flirted with him so wickedly was also missing.

Lottie felt her throat tighten and her smile became a little forced. Surely Rothsay would not have invited his mistress to his engagement ball? It would be a terrible insult, for everyone would know and pity her.

No, no, she would not deign to think such things. He was no doubt taking the chance of a cigar in the fresh air or perhaps talking with his godmother.

He returned shortly before the guests began to take their leave and joined her as she said goodbye to them. Most would be returning in a few days for the wedding, some were staying and simply went off to their rooms. When everyone had gone, Rothsay poured himself a glass of brandy from one of the decanters set out on a sideboard.

'Well, Lottie, I think we may say it was successful, don't you?'

'Oh, yes, I am sure of it,' she replied. 'I am glad you were satisfied with the arrangements, Rothsay. If you will excuse me, I shall go up now. I am a little tired. Goodnight.'

She left him without another glance. There was a pain in her chest, which she found difficult to bear. The urge to weep was very close, because she could only conclude that Rothsay had been gone so long because he had slipped away to snatch a little time with his mistress.

Once alone, Lottie allowed Rose to unhook her gown at the back and then sent her off to bed, after thanking her for sitting up so late.

'I can manage now, Rose. Thank you so much for looking after me. Goodnight.'

'Goodnight, miss. I hope as everything went well?'

'Yes, it was all delightful. I shall come to the servants' hall tomorrow to thank everyone. At the moment all I want to do is sleep.'

All she really wanted to do was to sleep. Her first rush of emotion resulted in hot bitter tears, but after a while she wiped them away. She was being so foolish. Rothsay did not wish for a clinging bride. He wanted a sensible woman who accepted the fact of his mistress. She could not fault his manner of late. He was polite, considerate, but uninterested in more than a comfortable arrangement.

She was the fool. She was the one who had gone into this with her eyes open. He had kept his part of the bargain in full and she must do the same. Many gentlemen kept mistresses and their wives turned a blind eye. She must do the same—but she had not expected it to hurt as much as it did.

For a moment she was overcome with anger and an urgent desire to weep and rage, but she conquered her feelings.

She must think of all the things that would bring her contentment and make her life worthwhile.

As Lady Rothsay she could do a great deal of good. Rothsay admitted that he had neglected the things that were so necessary for the well being of his tenants. She could repair much of that neglect. Her marriage would be good for her family. Aunt Beth was assured of a home here or in Bath when Lottie chose to visit, since a house there was one of Rothsay's wedding gifts. He had been extraordinarily generous, far more so than she could have expected after the way the business began.

She could not withdraw. She did not wish to withdraw. She had experienced a moment of weakness, but she would conquer it. In the morning, she would become the calm controlled woman the world saw and these needs and longings inside her would be banished to a distant part of her mind.

Nicolas smoked a last cigar in the gardens. He frowned as he wondered what lay behind the withdrawal he had sensed in Lottie. During their first dance, he had felt her happiness and the closeness between them, and had wished that he could whisk her off somewhere to be thoroughly kissed. However, she had seemed changed when they bid their guests goodnight. He wondered what had happened in his absence. Had she heard something that upset her?

After escorting Henrietta to her room, because she was too tired to remain longer, he had been called to attend to some business he would rather not have been troubled with on such a night.

His mouth tightened to a thin line. At the court sessions earlier that day, he had discovered that he was not down to try Sam Blake, but another set of rogues altogether. They were accused of murder and, since they had been caught in the act, the sentencing was easy. He had ordered them to be hung, but their sentences could be exchanged for transportation as a bond servant for seven years should they choose. Men invariably chose the latter and some of his fellow magistrates considered he had been too easy on the rogues.

It was only after the trial, which had taken some hours because he had listened to all the evidence, that he had learned Bertie Fisher had sat on the poaching case. He had sentenced Sam Blake to three years in the local prison, which was, in Nicolas's opinion, far too severe. He had remonstrated with Bertie afterwards, but his neighbour was adamant that poaching needed to be stamped on.

It was, of course, a serious crime, because many violent individuals became involved in the business, which was often linked to other more serious crimes. However, Nicolas had found himself wishing that he had let the man off with a warning in the first place. Especially in the light of what had happened this evening.

He had been given the news that three men had broken free when being taken back to the prison. Two of them were the murderers, who were to be transported—and the third was Sam Blake.

'The damned fool!' Nicolas had been frustrated to learn of Blake's escape. 'Had he accepted his sentence I might have been able to have it cut in a few months. Now he will be a wanted man and may be shot on sight—and he may well hang if he is taken.'

The news had unsettled Nicolas, making him disinclined to return to the dancing. He had, however, rejoined Lottie to say goodnight to his guests.

The point was—was her new mood down to what she had heard or was she merely cross with him for deserting her?

He threw the cigar into the shrubbery and went in, unaware that he had been watched for some minutes from the shadows.

Lottie rose a little after her usual time at nine o'clock. She washed in the water Rose had brought her and went down to the breakfast room. She was feeling rested and perfectly calm, her feelings under control. She did not know for certain that Nicolas had been with his mistress the previous evening. Perhaps she had been too hasty in her conclusions and ought to give Rothsay more credit, for he was a gentleman and such behaviour would not have been expected of a true gentleman. She had allowed her jealousy to mislead her.

A few of the men were already in the breakfast room but there was no sign of the ladies—and she was told Rothsay had been in an hour before her.

'You are an early riser, m'dear,' Uncle Freddie said and smiled at her approvingly.

'It has always been my habit,' she said. 'I do not much care for breakfast in bed, and I like to walk while the dew is still upon the grass.'

'If you go walking this morning, you should take a groom or your maid with you,' Uncle Freddie said with a frown. 'I hear there are some dangerous men in the area. I doubt they will come on to the estate, for Rothsay's keepers are armed and alert, but if you go to the village you should be careful.'

'I do not plan to walk this morning. There is bound to be a great deal of food left from last night, you know. I would not have it wasted. I intend to visit the kitchens after I have eaten and arrange for baskets of food to be taken to our tenants and the poor of the village.'

'That's the ticket. Don't approve of waste meself. We always send the food to the local orphanage, though I'm not sure the children see much of it. I dare say the governors take the best for themselves. Not much we can do about it.'

'Oh, I think one ought to try to improve things where one can,' Lottie said. 'At home I sometimes visited the workhouse. I think I was able to ease the condition of the poor by being elected to the board to see that the improvements I suggested were carried through. As Rothsay's wife I shall be able to do more.'

'Yes, you will if you care to,' he agreed. 'But all work and no play—you know the saying, m'dear. You must have some fun before you settle into the life here. Rothsay will want you to entertain for him in London, I dare say.'

Lottie wondered if that were true. She did not think it but would not tell his uncle. Instead, she chatted to him about the wedding and enquired what he wished to do with himself all day.

'Might take you for a drive this afternoon if you have time for it, m'dear. I was accounted a whip in me young days.'

'Would you drive me about the estate? I have never been much further than the lake or the park. I should like to see the village and some of the farms.'

'Delighted,' Uncle Freddie said, looking pleased with the idea. 'Rothsay should have done it at the start, but he is an odd fellow at times. I dare say he will wake up to his responsibilities once you are married.'

Uncle Freddie was a good trencherman and Lottie left him to the enjoyment of his breakfast, having partaken of a cup of tea and a buttered roll with honey herself.

She visited the kitchens and discussed what Cook felt could be spared from her larder.

'Most of the fancy stuff is finished, Miss Stanton, but there is quite a bit of ham and roast meat left over. It won't keep more than a day or two at most in this weather. We shall need some of it here, but I'll be cooking fresh this evening and a lot will waste if last night's spread isn't sent out. I had it in mind to send a bit to the tenants, but now that you've taken the trouble to consult me I shall send the meat pies and pasties to the village hall. There's a fête today for the children, miss, and they will find it useful.'

'That is excellent, Mrs Bent. In future you have my permission to send what is not needed here for the poor folk. We shall see if the children can be given a few treats during the year—perhaps a tea or supper at the village hall?'

'The marquis's mother used to hold a children's party here once a year, miss. I was wondering whether you might wish to start the tradition again?'

'That is an excellent idea,' Lottie said. 'I am glad you mentioned it to me. I should like to know of anything that I can do to help make our people happy, Mrs Bent. Now I must go, for we have guests and I ought to see if they have all they want.'

Lottie walked from the room. Mrs Bent nodded her approval as the housekeeper entered.

'She will do for us, Mrs Mann. The marquis's fiancée is a real lady if you ask me.'

'Yes, she is,' the housekeeper replied. 'It was a little odd that her father was not here for the ball. We must hope that he turns up for the wedding.'

'Yes, that is a bit strange,' Mrs Bent said, 'but I dare say there is a reason for it.'

Unaware of the speculation in the servants' hall, Lottie carried on being a charming hostess for the rest of the morning. She did venture out into the garden for a stroll amongst the shrubbery when some of the ladies came down to join her, but did not venture further than the immediate gardens.

Catching sight of one of the keepers, Lottie remembered Uncle Freddie's warning and wondered just who the dangerous men were. She could not think that Sam Blake was one of them, for he had not seemed particularly violent to her—just a rather weak man who had let life push him down.

Before nuncheon, she wrote a note to Lily and asked her to call when she was feeling better and sent Rose with a basket of sweetmeats for the children.

In the afternoon, she went driving with Uncle Freddie. She was impressed with the fertile fields and the fat stock grazing in their meadows. Everywhere they went, men took off their hats to her and bowed their heads respectfully. One or two women came to the doors of their cottages and called out good wishes for her wedding—and she smiled to see a group of children playing happily around the maypole that had been set up on the village green with some other amusements.

However, on the way home, they passed a huddle of

very poor cottages that looked in bad repair. Lottie asked Uncle Freddie to stop, which he did reluctantly.

'You don't want to look there, Lottie. That's the Hollow. All the scum of the neighbourhood live there. Rothsay should pull it down. It is a blot on the landscape.'

Leaning over to look, Lottie caught an unpleasant smell, which, she guessed, came from an open ditch that ran through the middle of the cottages. She could see that the people here did not wave or smile, but looked at her with sullen indifference. One man came out to stare at them in a way that made Lottie shiver. He was tall and heavily built, but she saw the resemblance to Sam Blake instantly and realised it must be his cousin Dickon. His look was one of such malevolence that she sat back in her seat.

'I wouldn't come this way again if I were you,' Uncle Freddie said as he whipped up his horses. 'These people are not like the villagers. They resent interference and do nothing to help themselves.'

'It must be very unhealthy to live in such a place,' Lottie replied thoughtfully. 'Perhaps Rothsay would consider putting in a drain for that ditch and at least doing some repairs.'

'He did make some such suggestion once, but it was met with hostility. There are some folk you simply cannot help in this world, Lottie m'dear. Save your efforts for those that appreciate it.'

Lottie murmured something appropriate. She would like to see improvements made to the Hollow but again it was something that might annoy Rothsay and would be best left until after the wedding.

There were only a few days to go now. All she had to do was make the best of things and see her part of the bargain through. No doubt Rothsay would soon take himself off back to London and she would be able to do small things herself. He surely could not object if she spent her own allowance on improving things for the tenants of the Hollow just a little?

Chapter Eight

After that afternoon, Lottie seemed to have little time for thinking of the changes she would make once she was the mistress of Rothsay. More guests arrived for the wedding as the time grew nearer and most of her day was taken in entertaining them and making sure the arrangements for the wedding went well.

She and Aunt Beth, together with Rose and a footman to carry all the paraphernalia, visited the church the day before the wedding and decorated it with masses of beautiful flowers, mostly in white and pink.

'It all looks absolutely lovely,' Aunt Beth said when she had finished. 'Are you happy, dearest Lottie? You seem so busy and there are so many guests...I have hardly had time to speak with you alone for days.'

'Yes, of course I am happy,' Lottie told her. 'Who could not be when everything is so perfect? The house is filled with people who are all very kind, and I have never seen so many lovely things—all those beautiful gifts in the long gallery, valuable silver and jewels to say nothing of wonderful porcelain and all the other things we have been given.'

'I know you have everything in a material sense—but are you happy, Lottie? I thought at first you were, but just recently you have been very quiet.'

'Oh, I have been busy. Forgive me if I have neglected you, dearest. I knew you were quite happy helping with various little tasks, and I think Henrietta has come to rely on you very much.'

'The countess had been kind enough to say I have helped her, but anyone could have done as much. I was not complaining, Lottie. My concern is for your happiness.'

'I am perfectly happy. What more could I want?'

Aunt Beth shook her head. 'Well, if you are as happy as you say, then I am content. I love you dearly, Lottie, and I do not wish you to be miserable in the life you have chosen—not that you did choose it, really.'

'Oh, yes, I did,' Lottie corrected her. 'You must not think I was forced into it.' She frowned. 'I do hope Papa will return by this evening. I am not sure what we shall do if he does not.'

'He has behaved very badly,' her aunt said and frowned. 'I really do not know what has got into him. He knows he must be here for the wedding.'

Lottie nodded, feeling a little uneasy about her father's reasons for not joining the wedding party at Rothsay's before this.

However, when they returned from the church later that morning, she discovered her father sitting with Uncle Freddie and Rothsay, sharing a glass of wine.

'You have arrived, Papa. I was a little anxious.'

'Well, you know me. Not much of a one for all this fuss,' her father said and came to kiss her cheek. 'I had something to do, but I am here now. I couldn't miss my little girl's wedding, could I?'

Lottie smiled and allowed him to charm her, as he always had. He was thoughtless and careless, but he was her father and she loved him.

'Come and see all the wedding gifts,' she said and took his arm. She wanted a little time alone with him and it was a perfect excuse to draw him from the rest of the company. 'People have been so amazingly kind...'

Sir Charles looked at her uneasily as they entered the long gallery. 'Now don't scold me, Lottie. I did not intend to stay away so long, but I got caught up in something.'

'A card game, I suppose?'

'Yes, I cannot deny it—but it worked out very well for me. I won a small fortune, Lottie, and I offered to pay Rothsay my debt, but he has refused me. I signed the new contract, which is very generous for you as well as me.'

'Yes, I believe it has been changed from the original.'

'Did you not read it?'

'No, I had no wish to know what was in it.'

'You will be quite a wealthy young woman should anything happen to Rothsay—and your allowance is extremely generous. I dare say you may not spend the half of it.'

'I shall use some to help others.' She stopped and pointed to the table where so many valuable things had been laid out. 'Look at all these gifts. People have been so generous.'

Her father frowned. 'Do you not think it a risk to leave all this stuff lying around? That sapphire-and-diamond set must be worth a king's ransom.'

'Yes, I expect it is,' Lottie said. 'Rothsay's great-uncle gave us that. I asked Rothsay if it should be put away, but he said it was quite safe. The grounds are patrolled at night, you know—and I am sure neither the guests nor the servants would touch anything. After all, the house is full of treasures, is it not?'

'Yes, I suppose so. Just makes me a bit uneasy, that's all,' her father said. 'I'm in funds at the moment but I know I would find it tempting if I were short.'

'Papa!'

Sir Charles smiled oddly. 'I wouldn't touch anything of yours or Rothsay's. You must know that, Lottie—but I've known the time I might have felt tempted.'

Lottie looked at him. 'Have you heard from Clarice? She is back in England. She hid in the gardens the other day to speak to me.'

'After money, was she?' Sir Charles frowned. 'Do not give in to her blackmail, Lottie. She will spend it all on her lover.'

'Do you know who he is, Papa?'

'I dare say it is that rogue de Valmer. I think she may have married him,' Sir Charles said. 'I would not have allowed it had I been asked—but she is beyond me, Lottie. I have given up on her, to tell you the truth.'

'You must try to discover where she is after the wedding,' Lottie said, looking at him earnestly. 'Clarice is reckless and she behaves in a way she ought not—but

I would not have her fall into desperate trouble. Please see if she is all right, Papa.'

'Yes, well, if you ask it,' he said and sighed. 'Are you settled here, Lottie?'

'Yes, I am. Do not worry for me, Papa. It is Clarice you should be concerned for.'

'She will go her own way.' He fished in his pocket and brought out a small velvet box. 'I refuse to give Rothsay a penny, Lottie. He has more than any one man needs, including you—but I got this for you.'

He offered the box. She opened it to find a beautiful diamond star set in silver on gold and gave a little cry of pleasure.

'This is lovely, Papa. Thank you so very much. I shall treasure it.'

'Well, it is little enough for all you've done for me over the years.'

'It is perfect.' She reached up to kiss his cheek. 'I am so glad you are here. I was afraid you would not come.'

'I've let you down enough times, but I wouldn't let you down on your wedding day.' He smiled at her as they walked the length of the room. 'Tomorrow is your big day, Lottie—after that you will be Rothsay's wife.'

'Yes…' Lottie's stomach clenched with nerves. She had been so busy she had hardly thought about it, but tomorrow night she would be Rothsay's wife in truth. How would she react when he came to her bed? One part of her longed to be his, but a small voice told her that without love her marriage would be a hollow sham. 'It is almost time for nuncheon, Father. We must join the others.'

* * *

Lottie woke suddenly in the middle of the night. She sat up in bed wondering what had woken her, and then she heard the shouts and the sounds of running feet. Throwing back the bedcovers, she went to the window and looked out. Men with lanterns were everywhere and, as she watched, one of the keepers raised his gun and fired into the darkness. The sound shocked her. What on earth was happening?

She hastened to dress in a simple gown and went out on to the landing. Several of the gentlemen were already dressed and moving about the house with a look of purpose that made her call out and ask what was going on.

'Don't come down, Lottie.' Sir James came briskly up the stairs to where she was standing. 'I am sorry you were disturbed, m'dear. There is no real cause for alarm—just an attempt to break into the house. Fortunately, Rothsay had trebled the guards patrolling the ground because of—' he broke off and looked conscious, as if he were in danger of saying too much. 'I suppose some wretch thought to steal your wedding gifts.'

'Papa did say they might tempt rogues to steal from us, but Rothsay did not think it possible.'

'Well, it was not, as it turns out,' Sir James said. 'You should return to bed, Lottie. There is nothing you can do.'

'Very well. I do not wish to cause you more trouble.'

She went back to her room, but did not retire immediately, instead, she sat in the window embrasure and looked out. The activity was dying down now and she thought that the would-be thieves had been scared off. She was about to undress once more when someone knocked at her door. She went to open it and saw Rothsay. He had dressed hurriedly, his shirt open at the neck, his hair looking rumpled. For some reason the sight of him like that made her catch her breath and she felt a spiral of desire spread through her body. She wished that he would reach out and take her in his arms, kiss her until she melted into his body—but she could see that lovemaking was far from his mind.

Lottie moistened her lips. 'Has the rogue been caught?'

'No—may I come in, Lottie?'

'Yes…' Lottie stood back uncertainly, for it was hardly proper, but they were to be wed in the morning. It could not matter now. 'Of course.' She stood watching as he went to the window and fastened it. 'I was about to shut that, Rothsay.'

'I doubt anyone would climb up here, but it is best to be certain. I should not forgive myself if anything happened to you.'

'I think the intruder was after valuables, don't you?'

'Perhaps.' He frowned. 'They chose to try to break in at the back of the house and were spotted instantly. We chased them off and Larkin thinks he may have winged one of them.'

'Then they will surely not come back in a hurry.'

'I do not think it.' He frowned at her. 'I wanted to tell you that Larkin believes Sam Blake might have been one of them. I preferred you to hear that from me.'

'I thought he was in custody?'

'He was sentenced to three years' imprisonment a couple of days ago, but escaped with some others. They are dangerous fugitives, Lottie, because after this they will almost certainly hang.'

'No, surely not?' Lottie looked at him in distress. 'Surely imprisonment… Three years was too long for what he did. I am not surprised he chose to escape.'

'Blake has fallen in with murderous rogues. One of them fired a pistol at the keeper who raised the alarm. If Blake was one of them, I shall not be able to save him from the noose.'

'If…?' Her eyes met his. 'You have some doubts?'

'It may have been his cousin. They look much alike.'

'Yes, except that Dickon Blake is a bigger man—but facially, yes, the resemblance is there.'

'What do you know of Dickon Blake?'

'I think I saw him when Uncle Freddie took me driving the day after the ball.'

'You went to the Hollow?' His face darkened. 'How could he be such a fool as to take you to that hellhole? I have been meaning to have the whole place pulled down. It is a nest of rats and the sooner it has gone the better.'

'Could you not cover the ditch, drain it and make some repairs—for the sake of the women and children?'

Nicolas's brow furrowed. 'Do not interfere in what you do not understand, Lottie. You have a compassionate heart, but this is men's business. Please leave this to me.'

'Very well.' Lottie felt her eyes sting with tears. Nothing had changed between them. He was as harsh and determined to go his own way as he had been at the start. 'Forgive me for interfering. I thought that some gesture of goodwill might win hearts and minds—but you must do as you see fit.'

'Thank you.' There was a note of sarcasm in his voice. 'I am still master in my own house. Goodnight, Lottie. You had best get some sleep or you will be tired tomorrow.'

Lottie stood motionless as he went out. She did not cry or rage, but inside she felt as if she were being torn apart. He had made his feelings quite plain once more. She was nothing to him. Just a means to an end—as he had made plain from the start.

What a fool she was to care.

What had made him snap Lottie's head off that way? Nicolas cursed his hasty tongue as he returned to his room. He had gone to her because he was concerned for her safety and her peace of mind. Then she had told him she had seen the Hollow and touched some secret part of him that was ashamed. In his heart Nicolas knew that the hovels were a disgrace. They had been wretched enough in his father's time. As a young man he had thought he would pull them down and build new when he came into the estate, but then had come disillusion and the constant pursuit of pleasure that had kept him in town. The Hollow had been banished to a distant corner of his mind, though occasionally it pricked at his conscience.

He had avoided the place for years, because he knew that it was a disgrace—and because it had been the cause of his mother's death. For the most part he had been a good landlord; his tenants had no cause to complain of his treatment and his agents had orders to keep the labourers' cottages in good repair. While the village bordered his land, it was not actually part of his estate. He owned some of the houses and they were in perfect order. The church was another beneficiary—but he had ignored the Hollow and he was not quite sure why. It was one of those things that the longer you put off doing something, the harder it became to right the wrong.

The only way to deal with a slum of that order was to pull it down—but where would the occupants of those hovels live then?

Nicolas's brow furrowed because he knew the answer. Most of them would have to camp in the open until they gave in and moved into the workhouse or drifted away from the area. Many of his neighbours would think that a good thing. The petty crimes, which so annoyed the local gentry, could nearly all be traced to the nest of rogues that had settled there over the years. Freddie had told him it was time he tore the whole place down.

Nicolas scowled as he put the unpleasant matter from his mind. In a few hours he would be getting married… and he had sufficient concerns of his own without trying to work out a problem that had defeated his father all of his life.

He had let his damnable temper come between them once more. He could not expect Lottie to care for a man who overrode her every suggestion with what must seem like arrogance. Why hadn't he explained that he had previously considered the repairs she had suggested but found them inadequate? The cottages were so damp and unsanitary that there was only one way to deal with them, like it or not.

'Oh, damn,' he muttered. If he didn't get some sleep he would be like a bear in the morning. 'It would serve me right if she changed her mind...'

Why had she not changed her mind?

The only thing Nicolas could think of was that she was prepared to accept him with all his faults for the sake of a comfortable home and a life of ease—except that Lottie had made it plain she had no intention of sitting around while others worked. Freddie had told him that she was already planning to discover more about local charities and had asked his advice about setting up a school for the children of his tenants.

A rueful smile touched his mouth. Nicolas was beginning to understand that he might have got more than he bargained for when he demanded that Lottie pay her father's debts by marrying him.

'You are so beautiful,' Aunt Beth said, dabbing a lace kerchief to her eyes as Lottie twirled for her in her bed-chamber. 'That dress is gorgeous, Lottie—the nicest you have ever had, I think.'

'That is all due to Lily,' Lottie said and smiled at the seamstress, who had kept her word and arrived that morning to help with dressing her and to make any last-minute adjustments. 'Thank you so much for my dress, Lily. My aunt is right. I've been thinking that you should have your own establishment in Northampton—or even London.'

'I should never dare to set up in London,' Lily said, a flush of pleasure in her cheeks. 'I have thought I should like a little shop in Northampton, but that is not likely.

Especially now...' Her eyes darkened with unspoken sadness.

'Do not despair,' Lottie said and pressed her hand. 'If Sam keeps out of trouble, we may yet find a way to make things better for you both.'

'I know you mean well, Miss Lottie—but you have a soft heart. The magistrates are gentlemen of property and to them Sam is a wicked rogue. If he'd ever had a chance, he could have been a good man, but you know what they say—give a dog a bad name and you may as well hang it.'

'I promise I shall try to help him when the time comes, but if you see him tell him not to get involved in his cousin's misdeeds.'

'It weren't him last night, miss.' Lily said swiftly. 'He knows you've been good to me. Sam might not like his lordship, but he wouldn't lift a finger against you—or he would have me to answer to!'

'And I believe you.' Lottie laughed softly. 'Well, Lily, do your best to keep him out of trouble and I may yet arrange something.'

Lottie turned to her aunt, who was regarding her with anxious eyes. 'Do not look so worried, dearest. When all the guests have gone you and I will be alone here—and I dare say we can think of something. I kept Papa out of prison more than once. I dare say it may be possible to come up with an idea.'

'Rothsay may have something to say.'

'Well, he may not care to stay in the country for more than a few days or so,' Lottie said. She ignored the look of enquiry in her aunt's eyes. 'We had better go down or we shall be late for the church.'

* * *

The sun was very warm as Lottie got down from her father's carriage outside the church. She saw that several villagers were waiting outside to watch and wave as she entered the beautiful Norman church on her father's arm. They smiled and clapped as they saw her, calling out good wishes for her wedding. Lottie's hand trembled slightly on her father's arm, but she controlled the wave of nerves that had swept over her.

She had slept the previous night after Rothsay left her, though her dreams had been troubled. There was a tradition that it was bad luck to see the bridegroom the night before the wedding. Lottie had not given it a thought until she was drifting into sleep. The omens were anything but propitious and the prophets of doom would say that she was bound to feel nothing but disappointment in such an ill-conceived match—if they knew the truth, which they did not, of course. Everyone thought they were the perfect pair, and Rothsay's relations were thrilled with the prospect of an heir for the family.

Lottie's stomach tightened with a spasm of nerves as she saw Rothsay waiting for her in front of the altar. How tall and strong he was, and as he turned to look at her walk down the aisle, she was aware of his masculinity as never before. Tonight he would claim the privilege of a bridegroom. The thought made her lips part on a sigh and desire pooled low in her abdomen. She longed for the moment when she became his wife in truth, yet she was afraid that she would give herself away in a moment of passion. Whatever she did, she must say nothing that made him feel she expected more than he was willing to give.

She turned her head to look at him as she drew to a halt by his side, and her heart missed a beat. He had such a sensual mouth and he was almost too good looking, though at times he could look harsh, that generous mouth tight with anger. She did not understand him, because they hardly knew one another. They had spent so little time alone that it was impossible to form a true picture of his character. He seemed harsh and arrogant at times, but was there another man beneath the mask he showed to the world—or was she deceiving herself?

Lottie forced herself to concentrate on the service. Rothsay was word perfect when giving his vows, but she stumbled over the word obey and his head turned sharply towards her, one brow arching in enquiry. Lottie trembled as the vicar pronounced them man and wife and then Rothsay lifted her pretty veil to kiss her lightly on the lips.

After that it all became somewhat blurred as they left church to the sound of bells ringing joyfully. As they paused on the church steps, Lottie saw several armed men at the edge of the crowd and knew that Rothsay had left nothing to chance. She thought it unlikely that anyone would try to assassinate him in front of the whole village and all his tenants, but, after the previous night, it was best to be prepared.

Nothing untoward happened and they ran for their carriage as a shower of rose petals and rice was thrown over them. Once inside, Rothsay looked at her, an odd smile on her lips.

'So you did not run away despite my show of temper last night?'

Lottie smiled, because when he was the charming

man of fashion she liked so well she felt at ease in his company.

'Did you really imagine I would? I dare say I shall learn not to speak without thinking in time, Rothsay.'

'Shall you? I wonder if I shall learn to control my damnable temper?'

'I am not afraid of your temper, Rothsay.'

'No, I have discovered that for myself.' He looked at her quizzically. 'Do you think you could call me Nicolas now we are married, at least when we are alone together?'

Alone together.

Lottie felt the nerves in her stomach tighten. In a few hours they would be completely alone. His attentions in the marriage bed would not be unwelcome. Her problem was that she might show her pleasure too much and send him hurrying back to London to the arms of his mistress.

Nicolas did not want a clinging wife.

'I imagine I can do that quite easily, Nicolas,' she said and smiled as he leaned towards her, his mouth seeking hers. Her lips parted as his tongue probed and she felt her resolve melting. How could she hold back when she felt this surging desire, the longing to feel his flesh close to hers?

What a wanton she was! Lottie ruefully accepted the truth. Had Nicolas asked her to be his mistress at the start she would probably have accepted—but of course he wasn't interested so much in having her in his bed as the end result. She exercised control and sat back in her seat as he studied her face. Her instincts told her to throw her arms about him and kiss him back, but her mind told her to remember that she was to be no more than complaisant.

'You really are very lovely, Lottie. I am fortunate to have such a bride. My relatives are all enchanted with you—did you know that?'

'Uncle Freddie is a dear and Sir James is a true gentleman.'

'Even Cousin Raymond told me that I was a lucky dog,' Nicolas said and grinned at her. 'I suppose we must entertain them all this evening and slip away quietly in the morning.'

'Slip away?' she asked. 'I am sorry, Nicolas. I am not quite certain what you mean. I thought you would stay here for a few days and then return to London. I have not prepared a trousseau for a wedding trip.'

'I think you have enough for a short stay in the country, Lottie. I have a small hunting lodge in Hampshire. It has been made ready for us and will give us a little breathing space before we return to our own lives. My family would expect us to have a wedding trip and I did not wish to disappoint them. Henrietta thought Paris, but I believe we need to get to know one another in private—do you not agree?'

'Yes, I do,' Lottie said and smiled. 'That is thoughtful of you, R—Nicolas, thank you. It is exactly what I should wish.'

'It does not mean we shall never go to Paris—perhaps another time?'

'Yes, perhaps,' Lottie replied. 'You must do exactly as you please, Nicolas.'

'Must I?' he asked and such a very odd expression came to his eyes. 'Well, we shall see how we go on together, Lady Rothsay. I did not give much thought to the matter when choosing a bride, but I shall certainly pay more attention to my wife.'

Lottie's eyes strayed to her husband again and again during the evening. They had entertained their guests lavishly to a grand reception. There had been music, dancing, cards for those who chose, and then fireworks in the grounds as the night descended and another light supper was served for any that wished for it. Cook and her helpers had worked extremely hard and Lottie sent a message of congratulations and thanks to the kitchens.

The hour was growing late when Nicolas suggested that perhaps she would like to slip away to her rooms. The guests who had travelled only a short distance were leaving and the family members who were staying on for a while were gathering in small groups, preparing to seek their beds.

'I think everyone would excuse you if you went up now, Lottie,' Nicolas said. 'I shall join you in half an hour—if that is convenient?'

'Yes, thank you, of course.'

Lottie's stomach fluttered with nerves. He was so polite, almost a stranger again. Earlier in the day he had laughed and teased her as the toasts were made, but now he seemed to be brooding, keeping a distance between them.

Was he wondering if he could bear to do his duty? Lottie felt the pain slash though her at the thought. Perhaps he was thinking of his mistress and regretting that she would not be waiting for him that night?

She must not allow herself to think such lowering

thoughts. Lottie banished her desire to weep as she undressed and then sent Rose to bed. Alone, she sat at her dressing table and brushed her hair, thoughtful and nervous, but not afraid. She wanted to be Nicolas's wife—was excited by the prospect of being with him that night.

The time drifted by and she realised that he had been longer than he had promised. He must be gathering courage, perhaps having a drink to bolster his sense of purpose. She had noticed that he drank very little at the reception and during the evening.

As the door that led to the dressing room, which connected the master suite, opened slowly and Nicolas came through, Lottie rose to her feet. Her heart began to pound wildly, then she saw that though he had taken off his neckcloth and coat, he was still wearing his shirt, breeches and boots.

'Nicolas?' She was bewildered by his manner as he came to her. 'Is something the matter?'

'Nothing…' His eyes were serious as he met her anxious gaze. 'I came to say goodnight, Lottie. You are expecting to do your duty this evening, I believe, but I find I am reluctant to begin our marriage this way. We are almost strangers. I shall make no demands of you tonight. There will be time enough in the next week or so…when we are better acquainted.' He leaned towards her, gave her a chaste kiss on the cheek, then turned and left.

Lottie stared at the door as it closed behind him. She could feel the tightness in her chest and tears burned behind her eyes. She longed to throw herself down and weep but was afraid he might hear. Not knowing what to expect, she had imagined many things of her wedding night. What she had not even considered was that he would leave her to sleep alone.

Why? Why had he not taken her to bed? If an heir were all he wanted…surely she was not so ill favoured that he could not bring himself to make love to her?

He had called her lovely in the carriage. She was sure that at various times she had seen the hot glow of desire in his eyes when he looked at her. So why had he held back?

Frustration was a part of her suffering—her body cried out for his and she had anticipated his loving with some pleasure. Yet perhaps all was not lost. Perhaps there was reason for hope if he wished them to be on a better footing before he exerted his rights as a husband.

Nicolas's frustration was a hundred times stronger than Lottie's had she but known it. The sight of his new wife in that fetching lace bedgown, the scent of her perfume and the look of invitation in her eyes had all been sorely tempting.

The devil of it was that he knew she was ready to accept him into her bed. She would not lie cold and unresponsive, for he had felt the softness of her lips in the carriage. He could go to her, make her his own and she would accept him, perhaps even welcome him—but for some reason it was not enough.

He could not convince himself that her compliance was more than that, a willingness to make her duties as pleasant as possible for them both. Lottie was a remarkable woman. He would swear there was passion in her—but he had found passion in the arms of a dozen women and somehow it was not what he wanted or needed now.

Ridiculous as it was, he wanted Lottie to love him. He wanted her to be his wife in the true sense of the word, not only the mother of his children but his partner in life—the other half of his self.

What kind of a fool was he? Nicolas laughed at the thoughts chasing round in his head. It was merely lust. He should go back into his wife's room, make love to her and carry on as he had intended in the first place. A brief wedding trip, then bring her here, leave her with her aunt, and return to London to the life he enjoyed. Yet he was not a man to enjoy celibacy and he had vowed since becoming betrothed that he would stay faithful to his wife. It had been several weeks since he had bid his last mistress farewell.

Surely that was it. He had never been short of willing partners to share his bed. This self-imposed restraint was the cause of the burning need he was feeling. It wasn't love for Lottie that was making him ache with the need to hold her in his arms and feel her sweet surrender. No, he wouldn't be such a fool as to fall in love with his wife.

He would be bored with a clinging wife in a week. He enjoyed his freedom and the chase was all; it always had been so, for he seldom found much pleasure once the woman had given into his demands. No doubt it was a fault in him, but it was the main reason that he had not married—or so he told himself. At the moment, he fancied himself in love, but it would soon pass.

He would let Lottie sleep alone tonight and then

perhaps things would happen naturally when they were alone at the lodge, apart from a few servants who would keep well in the background.

Once he had tasted her delights a few times, he would certainly wish to be free once more. It was just so damned inconvenient to feel this wretched frustration...

Chapter Nine

Lottie glanced at the man sitting beside her with his eyes closed. He had ridden his horse for the first part of the journey, leaving her to travel in solitary state, but for the past hour he had been in the coach with her, his long strong legs stretched out in front of him, his eyes closed. She wondered if he were bored with her company.

'You do not need to go through with this if you would rather be in town,' she said and saw his eyes fly open. 'If you are bored, Nicolas, it might be best if we returned to Rothsay and you left me there.'

'Good grief, what makes you imagine I am bored?' His eyes went over her. 'If you must have it, I am a dashed bad traveller, which is why I rode for part of the way. Travelling in a carriage does not suit me—unless I drive the thing myself.'

'Then why don't you?' Her eyes challenged him. 'Are you not capable of driving a team of six horses?'

'Damn it, Lottie,' Nicolas's eyes gleamed suddenly.

'That is very provocative. You realise you have put me on my mettle, I suppose?'

'Well, can you drive six horses? Papa tried once for a bet, but I fear he lost his blunt. He could not manage them and had to be rescued by the coachman.'

'You are a wicked jade,' he said and laughed. Reaching up, he tapped the roof of the carriage with his silver-topped cane and brought it to a halt. Opening the door, he jumped out and called to the coachman.

Lottie listened to the one-sided conversation. She judged the coachman to be uneasy in allowing his master to drive the team of six spirited horses, which was a very different matter to the pair that Nicolas regularly drove about the estate.

'If you are sure, my lord...' he said reluctantly. 'They take some handling, sir—if you don't mind my saying so.'

'I do, damn it. Move over and leave them to me.'

Nicolas poked his head in at the door. 'Hang on, Lottie, for there's a good stretch of road ahead and I intend to let them go.'

'Are you sure?' She was doubtful now, half-wishing she had not challenged him.

'You'll see...' Nicolas grinned at her.

Lottie sat back in her seat and heard him climb up to the driving box. After some argument, the groom went to the back of the carriage and the coachman stayed in place—just in case he was needed.

Nicholas gave the order and the carriage started moving. For a few moments it travelled at a normal pace, then she felt the horses gather momentum and the carriage seemed to lurch forwards. She held on to the strap as it began to jolt and bump, throwing her forwards and then back as the horses raced down the country road. She looked out of the window. Trees, hedges and fields seemed to flash by at an alarming rate, but apart from some discomfort everything was going well.

Lottie did not see the obstruction ahead, but she heard Nicolas's shout of alarm and then felt his efforts to halt the carriage as he tried to stop the horses' headlong flight. She was thrown forwards violently and then just as violently back against her seat. It was uncomfortable but exciting, dispersing the tension that had been growing between her and Nicolas these past few hours. Above her head there was shouting and some argument, she fancied, and then the carriage halted; looking out of the window, she saw they were surrounded by sheep.

The next moment Nicolas jumped down and wrenched open the door. He glared at her and she could not help herself. She laughed at his annoyance.

'Stupid animals. I think we might have rounded that corner ahead if they hadn't blocked the road…'

'You were travelling too fast. I did not want you to kill us all, Nicolas, just to prove you could handle the team.'

'Well, I could until those wretched sheep appeared.' He looked cross. 'You had best get down. There is some bother with one of the wheels—and the sheep farmer is looking irate. I must settle with him for any distress to his beasts. I just hope the repair will not cause us much delay. We do not wish for another night on the road if we can avoid it.'

'Did you not appreciate the inn last night?'

'It was all very well for you, Lottie. I swear I booked

two rooms—you did not have to make do with a couple of chairs in the private parlour last night.'

'You could have shared my room, Nicolas. We are married. My reputation would not suffer.'

His eyes narrowed. 'I do not know what you are up to, Lottie—but be careful. My temper is wearing thin, even if this is supposed to be a wedding trip.'

Lottie smiled. She was not sure why she had provoked him, perhaps she had wanted a little revenge for his neglect of her. Pretending to be asleep when he was wide awake, indeed.

She gave him her hand and was assisted down. Shaking out the skirts of her dark-green travelling gown, she took a stroll up a small incline and looked down over the surrounding countryside. It was very beautiful, a pleasant place to stop. If she had brought a basket of food, they could have had a picnic. Turning as Nicolas came up to her, she said as much.

'I suppose it is pretty enough,' he said and smiled reluctantly. 'All right, I admit I needed help to halt them—but I shall master it, believe me. I am not a member of the four-in-hand club, though I have driven a team of four often enough. Six is rather more tricky. However, next time we travel this way I shall be able to drive them, I promise. If we cannot go on this evening, I shall hire a curricle and pair from the first hostelry we come to and drive us to my lodge. It is not above ten miles from here.'

'Good. I am hungry. I have not eaten much for a day or so.'

'Nor I…' He laughed suddenly. 'We are an odd pair, are we not? I do not know what got into me earlier.'

Nicolas knew very well what had made him pretend to be asleep. The scent of her sitting so close had stirred his senses, his arousal so strong that he had been hard put to keep his distance.

'Shall you forgive me, Lottie? Could we possibly be friends, do you think?'

'Friends?' Her heart leaped as she saw something deep in his eyes. 'Are you sure that is what you want, Nicolas?'

'Damn it, Lottie! I have been trying to be a gentleman and not rush you.' He reached out and drew her into his arms, crushing her against his chest, his mouth seeking hers hungrily. His lips were hard and demanding at first, then softened to a questing kiss that begged for her response. She gave it, unable to hold back as she felt the burn of his arousal when he pressed her closer still. 'I think I have been a fool, have I not?' His hand caressed her cheek, brushed against her sensitised breast, which peaked beneath the soft silk of her gown, bringing a gasp to her lips. A warm sweet sensation moved through her like thick honey and she spoke without thinking.

'You would have been more comfortable in my bed last night, Nicolas.'

'Should I? You hardly spoke to me after we left Rothsay. I thought you were angry.'

'Perhaps a little,' she admitted. 'You ignored me for most of the journey—yesterday and this morning.'

Nicolas laughed. 'So you are like other ladies sometimes? You do have a little vanity?'

'If I have, it has been sadly crushed. I did not think myself so ill favoured that you would leave me to sleep alone every night, Nicolas.'

'I see I have been wasting my time trying to spare you,' he said and laughed down at her. 'I shall make up for lost time this evening, madam.'

Lottie smiled. She did like him so very much sometimes.

'I believe Coachman is trying to attract your attention, my lord. I think we are ready to go on.'

'I believe I shall ride, if you do not mind, Lottie. We cannot be more than an hour or so from my house. I shall ride on ahead to make certain everything is ready.'

'Yes, of course,' she replied. 'You must do just as you please, Nicolas.'

'You keep saying that,' Nicolas said. 'One day you may regret having given me *carte blanche*.'

Lottie stared after him as he walked to the carriage. She allowed him to help her inside, then watched as he changed places with one of the grooms and set off on horseback.

Just what had he meant by that last remark? Did it mean that when he had had enough of her he would go to London and take up with his mistress where he had left off?

When Lottie arrived at the hunting lodge, which was a pretty country house, small by Rothsay's standards, but situated in a quiet park with a pleasant outlook and an approach through perfect countryside, she found the servants lined up waiting for her. There were far fewer than at Rothsay, and, apart from one maid who was to serve her, all the others were men.

Nicolas had suggested that she leave Rose at Rothsay, because, as he put it, he wished to be private with her.

She soon saw that the servants here were discreet and disappeared as soon as the meal had been served. Was it Nicolas's custom to bring ladies here? Lottie wondered. Had his mistress stayed here—or perhaps women of easy virtue that his friends had enjoyed?

Ladies did not have such improper thoughts, but Lottie could not help herself. She hated the little green imp of jealousy that had taken residence in her subconscious, for after all, Nicolas had never claimed to love her. Yet she could not quite squash the foolish thoughts.

However, he did not desert her that evening, but spent an hour reading poetry to her after dinner, before suggesting that she might retire.

Lottie went without a word. Would he simply visit and say goodnight, as he had on the two previous occasions?

She did not have long to wait; the maid had scarcely left her when Nicolas walked through the adjoining door and stood looking at her. He was wearing a long dark-blue silk robe and his feet were bare. Lottie's heart quickened, her pulses racing. She had been sitting at her dressing table. Now she stood up and waited uncertainly.

'I know you would not refuse me,' he said. 'It was a part of the arrangement and you have been meticulous— but may I hope there is some warmth in your heart? Is it just a duty, Lottie?'

'I know well that you do not want a clinging vine,' she replied with a smile, 'but I cannot deny that I shall find pleasure in our marriage, Nicolas.'

'Then it is all I can hope for and must think myself fortunate after the way I forced you to marry me.'

'It was not so very hard to bear once I had met you—and seen your house.' Her eyes sparkled and teased and he gave a shout of laughter as he drew her to him. 'There are compensations in being married to a marquis—even if his reputation as a rake is daunting.'

'You always give as good as you get, do you not?'

'I have found it is best to meet a challenge head on, Nicolas. Life was not easy with Papa, especially after Mama died. Had I not been prepared to fight for what was needed, we might have foundered long before that trip to Paris.'

'I think life has been unkind to you in the past, but I hope you will find it better in future.'

'I am sure I shall...' She tipped her head, her mouth slightly open as she invited his kiss. It was not long in coming. His lips demanded, his tongue explored and teased, while his hand stroked, down over her hip, cupping her buttocks as he pressed her closer.

Lottie could not doubt the strength of his arousal; with little between them she could feel the hard bulge and the heat of him.

'Come, it is time we began to know one another, Lottie,' Nicolas said and took her by the hand. He led her to the bed, reaching for the ties that fastened her nightrail. He untied them, then pulled the filmy garment over her head, revealing her slender hips, slim waist and full breasts. 'You are even more beautiful than I imagined...'

'Am I?' she asked her eyes on his face. She felt oddly shy as he stretched out a hand, stroking the line of her cheek, her throat and then her breast with a light touch that made her shiver.

'Lie down, Lottie,' he said huskily and divested himself of his robe. She saw that he was completely naked and her cheeks heated as she saw that he was fully aroused. 'I think this is your first time?'

'Yes…' she breathed out on a little gasp as he lay down beside her and half-turned to him. 'You are the first, Nicolas.'

'I knew it even when I called you those names, when I believed you to be Clarice.'

His breath was warm on her face as he began to kiss her with little feathery kisses on her brow, her nose and throat; then he took her lips in a much deeper demanding possession that made her sigh and wriggle closer.

Nicolas laughed throatily, his hand stroking the satin arch of her back, down over her buttocks. He pulled her close so that they lay flesh to flesh, silk to satin, looking into each other's eyes as he caressed her.

Lottie's breathing came quicker, her lips parting with sensual pleasure as he bent his head and his tongue caressed her nipple. She moaned and moved towards him urgently, her body seeking something she could not quite understand. Nicolas kissed her, rolled her over on to her back and then raised himself so that his eyes looked down into hers.

'You are so wet and warm. I think you are ready for me, Lottie. I shall try not to hurt you too much.'

His hand had been moving between her thighs, caressing her with a steady, almost languid movement, but now he parted her legs further as he lowered himself down to her. She felt the probe of his manhood, nudging at her, seeking entry into her moistness. She instinctively opened wider, inviting him to take her, though when he thrust deep into her silken sheath she could not prevent a gasp of pain. He stilled for a moment, allowing her to catch her breath.

'The first time it is always so,' he murmured against her throat. 'Forgive me, my darling.'

'It doesn't matter,' she whispered. 'Please do not stop. I want to be yours completely.'

He began to move again and at first it was a little painful for her, but then as she relaxed the pain seemed far away. She let her body follow his so that when his climax came she felt something too, a little cry escaping her as she clung to him and arched into him, her legs wrapping round him.

Nicolas nuzzled his face against her throat. 'It will be better next time,' he murmured. 'You were sweet and lovely, Lottie. Thank you.'

Lottie's hand touched his head. She stroked his hair, tears on her cheeks. So this was what it felt like to be a woman and to love a man. If she had hoped that she would be able to stop herself giving her whole heart, she knew now that it was a vain hope. Somewhere along the line she had given everything. Did he know that—and would he care?

Lottie did not know and she was too afraid to ask, because she did not wish to know the answer. She realised that Nicolas had fallen asleep as he lay by her side, his face buried in her hair. She moved it from his face, leaning up on her elbow to watch as he slept, thinking how peaceful he seemed…so much younger in sleep than he ever was awake.

She touched his cheek lightly so as not to wake him, her heart aching. He had loved her tenderly and she was grateful for his care of her, but was she more to him than a fleeting pleasure? He had wanted her badly but without love how long did physical attraction last?

She must not torture herself this way. Lottie snuggled closer to him, shutting her eyes. She must accept what he gave and not think of tomorrow.

In the days that followed, Lottie clung determinedly to the promise she had made herself. There was always a smile on her face when Nicolas looked at her or touched her. She took pleasure in everything they did: riding, walking, playing cards, reading aloud from their favourite books, and music. Lottie was proficient at playing the pianoforte, but Nicolas had a rare talent. When he played he became wrapped up in the music, an absorbed faraway look in his eyes, as though the music carried him to a world of his own.

'That was wonderful,' she said when he played for her the first time. It was evening and they had sat over their meal and wine until the light faded from the sky. 'I had no idea you were so talented. I have never heard you play before?'

'I seldom do—especially when anyone else is staying. When I am alone I sometimes play for an hour at a time. I do not subject others to a display of my indulgence.'

'I am sure they would take pleasure in your playing, as I do, Nicolas.'

'Would they?' His eyes had that strange haunted look she had seen before. 'I think you are different, Lottie. You are more generous and kinder than some ladies.'

Lottie had not known how to answer him. Had he

really no idea how talented he was? She merely smiled and shook her head.

She was painting a portrait of him. She had begun the sketch when they sat together in a wild meadow, and he lay back with his eyes closed, his face to the warmth of the sun. Since then she had made sketches of Nicolas in almost every pose and now she was painting a head-and-shoulders portrait that she thought she might frame and keep in her room.

'You paint very well,' Nicolas told her. 'You have made me too handsome, but I can find no other fault with your work.'

'Catching a likeness is a skill I do have,' she said, 'but I have much to learn about colour and texture. I do well enough for an amateur, which is all I aspire to be. I think you should have your portrait painted professionally for Rothsay, Nicolas.'

'We shall both have them done,' he said and frowned. 'I should like to stay here longer, Lottie—but I think we should go back. I never intended to stay more than a few days and we have been here nearly three weeks. There are things that need my attention...'

Lottie saw a brooding look in his eyes and her heart sank. Had he begun to be bored here with her? Did he miss his friends and the life he led in London—his mistress?

Their lovemaking had been very satisfactory to her, but her courses had started that morning, which meant the nightly visits must cease for a while.

Was Nicolas disappointed that she had not fallen for a child immediately? He had certainly loved her thoroughly these past days, sometimes three or four times a night, but she had failed to give him a swift result.

'I am sorry that I have not conceived, Nicolas.'

'In heaven's name, why should you be sorry? You are not a brood mare, Lottie. It will happen in time.'

'I thought you might be disappointed?'

'As it happens, I would prefer to have you to myself for a while longer.' He smiled at her. 'I am in no hurry, Lottie.'

She felt warmed by his smile. Their time here had been pleasant and she felt that she had begun to know him so much better. She had no right to ask for more. He had given all he had promised and more.

'So what are you thinking?'

'I was just thinking it had been very pleasant here, Nicolas.'

'Yes, it has, but it is not real. We should return to Rothsay and reality before it is too late.'

'I am not certain I understand you?'

'Why should you? I am not certain I understand myself.' He frowned. 'Do you love me at all, Lottie?'

'Yes, of course.' Her heart thumped because she was afraid of betraying herself and would not look at him. 'I am very fond of you, Nicolas. You are my husband.'

'Yes, I thought so,' he replied. 'I think I shall go for a long ride, Lottie. Do not expect me back to supper. There are some friends I wish to visit. Tell the servants to pack. We shall leave first thing in the morning.'

Lottie felt as if he had slapped her. What had caused him to suddenly withdraw from her? Had she showed her feelings too plainly? Tears stung her eyes. She had tried so hard not to impose conditions or strings—but to no avail. He had grown tired of her as she had expected, though she had hoped he might find contentment in their arrangement, as she had.

'Yes, of course,' she said. 'You are quite right, Nicolas. There is a great deal to do at home. This has been a pleasant interlude, but it is time to move on.'

He inclined his head and walked purposefully from the room, leaving Lottie to fight her tears.

Nicolas did not come in until the early hours of the morning. Lottie heard him moving around in his room. There was the sound of something falling, as if he had knocked over a stool or small table, and then he swore. She waited for a few minutes, then, as everything went quiet, took a candle and went into his bedchamber. Nicolas was lying on his bed, wearing his breeches, shirt and boots. His eyes were closed and he was snoring.

'Nicolas…is something the matter?'

He did not answer, but a little snore told her that he was fast asleep. She went closer and caught the smell of strong drink. He was drunk!

Lottie was shocked. She had never known Nicolas to drink too much and it made her feel very guilty. She had failed him and he had been driven to drink to get away from her. Or perhaps he had felt trapped because she had shown him too clearly that she was in love with him.

'I am sorry, dearest,' she said and went to remove his boots. They came off with a series of sharp tugs. He stirred once and muttered something but she continued to pull them off and then went to cover him with a light blanket. 'Forgive me…'

'Damn it, Elizabeth,' he muttered. 'You knew I adored you—why didn't you tell me? I suppose it doesn't matter if you break hearts…'

Lottie drew back, feeling as if he had thrust a dagger into her heart. Here at last was the key to that bleak look she saw sometimes in his eyes. He was still in love with Elizabeth—and she had obviously hurt him very badly when they parted. Lottie had been told right at the start by both Bertie and Henrietta that Nicolas had once been madly in love, but she had put it out of her mind. Now she felt as if she had been doused in cold water.

It was little wonder that he felt trapped by his marriage. He had wanted to marry Elizabeth, but she had broken his heart and he had sought comfort in the arms of various mistresses. He had married for the sake of an heir, but Elizabeth was the woman he dreamed of and regretted even now. Lottie would be a fool if she hoped that one day he would love her.

She went back into her own room and sat down on the edge of her bed. Her heart felt as if it were breaking, but she refused to cry. Nicolas had never promised to love her. She had mistaken his kindness for something more and that was her fault, not his.

She got into bed and shut her eyes. Tears were trickling down her cheeks. She could no longer control them. It was useless. Her honeymoon had been so very pleasant that she had been lulled into a false security, believing that Nicolas was ready to settle to marriage. Now she understood why he never could.

No wonder he had not cared who he married. He was still suffering from his blighted hopes and did not care who he took to wife.

All he wanted was an heir and Lottie had failed to provide him with that small thing. No wonder he wished to return to Rothsay. He would probably be off to London soon after they arrived.

Lottie was feeling tired when the carriage pulled up outside the house. Nicolas had ridden his horse for most of the time. She had hardly seen him other than the night they had spent at the inn or when they had stopped for refreshment. He was polite and concerned for her well being, but had made no attempt to kiss or touch her. Of course, there was no chance of making an heir while she had her courses. If she had needed confirmation of what she meant to him, this was it.

Lottie had cried herself to sleep for two nights, but now she felt numb. She had decided that the best defence was to keep her distance, be polite, as he was, but reserved. Inside, she was hurting, but she had no intention of letting Nicolas see that he had broken her heart.

She got down from the carriage with a sigh of relief. Now they were home they need not be forever in each other's company. Indeed, she thought it might be less painful if he took himself off to London. Every time she looked at him she was reminded of the way his lips felt on hers, or the touch of his hand, the feel of him inside her, giving her such pleasure.

'You will forgive me if I do not come in with you, Lottie,' Nicolas said. 'I must speak to the bailiff and I dare say you will enjoy an hour or so to chat with your aunt.'

'Yes, certainly I shall,' she said. 'Please, Nicolas, you

must do just as you wish. I am perfectly capable of finding something to do—especially now that we are home. I have it in mind to do something for the children of our tenants.'

'Freddie said something about a school,' Nicolas said and smiled for the first time in days. 'I approve of the idea, but hope you do not intend to teach them yourself?'

'Certainly not, though I might have enjoyed it had I not had other duties. I shall employ a young man to teach them. I am certain there must be suitable young men of good education in need of such work.'

'I am certain there must.' Nicolas laughed suddenly. 'I think I have been abominably rude to you these past two days, Lottie. Please forgive me, if you can?'

'There is nothing to forgive. I understand, Nicolas.'

'Do you?'

'I dare say you found a diet of my company tedious. You will wish to be off with your friends again soon. Do not imagine I expect you to dance attendance on me all the time.'

'Do you not?' He frowned. 'I see I have no need to apologise. I shall be late this evening, Lottie. Do not wait up for me.'

Now what had she said to upset him? Lottie was thoughtful as she went into the house. It seemed that there was no pleasing Nicolas in this mood.

Lottie spent a pleasant hour having tea with her aunt. She was told that the countess had gone home soon after they left for Rothsay's hunting lodge, but she had written

to Aunt Beth telling her that she intended to visit London
in the very near future and inviting her to stay.

'We got on very well,' Aunt Beth said. 'I am quite
content here, Lottie—but should you wish to be private
with Rothsay for a while I have a standing invitation
from Lady Selby.'

'You must visit her if you wish,' Lottie said. 'I have no
intention of being private with Rothsay and you will be
of help to me here, but I shall not deny you the pleasure
of a visit to town.'

'Well, I might go for a while later. The Season will be
over by then, but I like to visit the theatre and too much
racketing about is not for me—though of course there
are always some hostesses who never entirely desert the
capitol.'

'Yes, I suppose there must be.'

Aunt Beth hesitated, then, 'I had a visit from Clarice
while you were away, Lottie.'

'She came here to the house?'

'She wore a hat with veiling. No one but I would have
seen her face, Lottie. She asked me for money. I gave
her ten pounds, but I think she hoped for far more.'

'Yes, I dare say she did. She asked me for money
before the wedding. I gave her twenty guineas.'

'You must not make a habit of it, Lottie.'

'No, but she is my sister. I cannot forget that we were
close once—and, if it were not for her, I should never
have met Rothsay.'

'Well, I suppose there is that, but do not let her take
advantage, dearest.'

'No, I promise I shall not.'

After her aunt went up to rest before dinner, Lottie

discovered that she was too restless to do the same and decided to go for a walk.

Clarice might be a problem in the future. She would never be satisfied with small handouts, but what else could Lottie do? The jewels she had been given were not truly hers to sell or give away—at least she would feel badly if she disposed of a wedding gift in order to pacify her sister. How could she look Uncle Freddie in the eye if she sold his necklace? Besides, even if she gave Clarice a thousand pounds, it was unlikely to be her last request.

Oh, bother, she would not let Clarice upset her!

She set out for the lake, enjoying the feel of the breeze in her hair. It was good to be home. She had come to think of Rothsay as her home and was content to spend her life here, though she might take Aunt Beth to visit Bath in the autumn for a few weeks.

Lottie stood staring at the opposite shore of the lake. There was an old summerhouse there, which Nicolas had told her had been shut up for years. Lottie wondered if it might be suitable for the school she was planning. The building looked sturdy enough. It was too far to explore further this evening, because she would be late changing for dinner, but in the morning she would see whether or not it would do. About to turn away, she thought she saw something at the window—a face or a flash of white.

She was certain Nicolas had told her the building was locked, because he had mentioned the key being in the bailiff's office, and she had planned to fetch it the next day. Perhaps it was just a trick of the light, and yet she could have sworn she had seen something.

She was thoughtful as she turned and walked back

to the house. It was as she reached the rose arbour that someone came up behind her. She turned and saw Lily, her instincts telling her immediately that the seamstress was in some distress.

'Lily—did you wish to speak to me?'

Lily hesitated, then, 'Yes, my lady. Forgive me—I was wondering if you would help me? I need some money...' She glanced over her shoulder, as if frightened of being overheard. 'It is for Sam...he needs to get away, Miss Lottie. They have put a price on his head. I've seen the posters up everywhere. His price is fifty guineas. People will give him away. It is a fortune to most folk.'

'Yes, of course, it must be,' Lottie said. 'He is hiding at the moment?'

'Yes...' Lily glanced back towards the lake and Lottie understood what she had seen earlier. Sam must be hiding out at the old summerhouse. He was in a very dangerous situation, because he could be discovered at any moment. 'There's someone who would help him get away to the coast. If he could find a ship and go to France he might be safe there.'

'What about you?'

'I shall stay here until he finds work and can send for me. I'll work for you for nothing until I have paid back anything you give me.'

'That would not be necessary...' Lottie thought quickly. If she gave Lily money knowing that it was intended for a fugitive, she would be breaking the law— but Sam Blake had been unfortunate. She did not think he deserved a price on his head for what he had done. 'Come to the house with me now, Lily. How much do you need?'

'Would twenty guineas be too much?' Lily looked doubtful. 'I know it is a lot to ask…'

'No, I can give you that quite easily,' Lottie said. 'You need not worry about paying me back, Lily. I had intended to make you a present for making my wedding gown so beautifully—and that will do very well. You may continue to work for me if you wish, but I had thought of helping you to set up a small establishment in Northampton, if you should like it?'

'You are so generous. If things had been otherwise it is just what I should have liked—but Sam will send for me soon. I shall take the children and follow him to France just as soon as he is settled there.'

'Then I can only wish you good luck. I am glad we returned in time to help you.'

Lily looked over her shoulder once more. 'I know I shouldn't have asked, but Sam is desperate. He says if they catch him he will hang for sure this time.'

'Yes, I know. I am so sorry, Lily. It isn't fair that he should be treated so harshly. I do not think his crime so very terrible.'

'You are a good woman, my lady. There's not many as care about folk like us. His lordship…' She shook her head. 'No, I shouldn't say, but Sam says he's a fool to trust that Larkin…'

'What makes you say that, Lily?'

'He's the one been selling game to the inn, my lady. My Sam only did it the once when he were desperate. He needed medicine for me when I had the last babe—but mostly it was just a rabbit for the pot.'

'Larkin is cheating my husband? Are you sure, Lily? And Sam can prove this?'

'It's only his word, miss. No one would listen to a convicted fugitive, would they?'

'No, they wouldn't. I am so sorry, Lily.' Lottie felt pity for the woman and her husband, but there was little she could do other than to give her some money. 'Come up to my room now and I shall give you the twenty guineas…'

Chapter Ten

Aunt Beth had gone to bed and Lottie was sitting in her favourite parlour reading when she heard the ring of hurried feet and then the door was flung open and Nicolas strode into the room. Raising her head to look at him, she saw that he was angry. She rose to her feet apprehensively.

'Is something wrong?'

'Do you know anything about this?' He threw down a purse of something that clinked. It landed on the floor at her feet with a little thud. 'Blake claims that you gave him the money—is it true?'

Lottie swallowed hard. 'Has he been caught? Why couldn't you have just let him go, Nicolas? He doesn't deserve to be hung for stealing a few rabbits.'

'It wasn't just my rabbits. Bertie has lost deer and the game birds have been disappearing too fast to be the work of just one man. There is a gang of the rascals at work in the area.'

'Sam Blake wasn't one of them. He sold game only once when Lily was ill.'

'I suppose she told you that?' Nicolas glared at her. 'And you believed her—and you gave her twenty guineas for Sam?'

'Yes, I did.' Lottie raised her head defiantly, meeting his furious gaze. 'She told me something else, too—but I dare say you would not listen if I told you who was behind this outbreak of poaching?'

'I would not believe anything Blake said—and you are a fool to believe his wife.'

'I gave Lily the money as a present, but I knew she intended it for her husband. He was going to France and she was to join him once he had found work there.'

'Very likely. The man was a lazy good-for-nothing and would never have done an honest day's work.'

'Was…' Lottie shivered. She felt sick as she looked at her husband's face. 'Are you saying…what happened to him? You didn't…?'

'Larkin shot him. He was searched, questioned and told he was being taken to prison—he knocked a man down and ran off,' Nicolas grated. A pulse flicked in his throat. 'I am sorry, Lottie. I know you like his wife and you had sympathy for the man—but he would have hanged had we caught him. He was seen leaving the area of the lake and some of the keepers went after him. He was warned several times, but he continued to run and he was shot. I am afraid he was killed outright.'

'No! How could you allow that?' Lottie stared at him in horror. 'I thought you had some compassion in you— how could you let your keeper murder a man just like that?'

'I was not present or I would have stopped it. However, Larkin acted within the law. Blake had a price on his head, which meant he could be shot on sight. Larkin says he intended to wing him, but…the shot killed him instantly. He couldn't have suffered.'

'Lily and their children will suffer terribly,' Lottie said. Her eyes stung with tears. 'Larkin is the man who is taking your game, Nicolas. Sam Blake knew the truth. Larkin killed him to cover his crimes.'

'That is ridiculous,' Nicolas said, his mouth set in a harsh line. 'You do not expect me to believe my own keeper is stealing from my neighbours and me?'

'No, Rothsay, I do not expect you to believe it,' Lottie said and raised her head proudly. 'Yet I believe it—and in time you may, too. I just hope that nothing happens that makes you wish you had listened.' She glanced down at the purse on the floor. 'That money belongs to Lily Blake. She will need it if her children are not to starve.'

Leaving it lying on the floor, she walked past him and from the room, going upstairs to her room. Once alone, she sat on the bed, trying not to give way to her emotions.

How could Nicolas have allowed his keeper to kill a man just for the crime of stealing a few rabbits? If he thought that justice, then he was not the man she had thought she loved.

'Damn you, Lottie.' Nicolas caught her as she reached her bedroom door, following her inside. 'I will not leave this there—nor shall I be made to feel in the wrong over this business with Blake. The man was a fool to fall in with hardened rogues—and Larkin was within the law to shoot him.'

'Be damned to the law,' Lottie said, rounding on him furiously. All caution was gone as her feelings reached boiling point. 'Have you no compassion at all? I believed you a man of honour, but now I begin to think I was mistaken. You are not the man I thought I was marrying.'

'Indeed?' Nicolas looked at her, his expression frosty. 'I hardly think you are in a position to preach to me of morals, Lottie. You were ready to deceive me—to allow me to think you your sister. You are as much a schemer as she—perhaps worse, for at least she refused to be part of the deal.'

'You forced me to keep the bargain.' Lottie's cheeks flamed with heat. She felt as if he had slapped her. 'I confessed and begged you to let me go.'

'You had chances enough to break it off. You need not have signed the contract. You knew I would have let you go then. Do not pretend otherwise.'

'I thought I liked you,' Lottie said. 'I knew it would never be a love match—but at least I thought you would deal fairly with me. Now I am not sure that I like you at all.'

'So, now we have the truth at last.' His expression was dangerous, his eyes glittering with anger. 'You married me because you had a fancy to be the marchioness, I suppose. I thought you very different from your sister, but it seems the difference is slight after all.'

'Damn you!' Lottie lashed out, striking him across the face with the palm of her hand. 'Why don't you go back to your mistress—or your precious Elizabeth? It is she you love, is it not?'

'Who told you about Elizabeth?' Nicolas's face was white apart from the red mark where she had struck him. He reached for her, catching her wrist as she would have turned away, his fingers clasping her like a ring of iron. 'Answer me, Lottie! Who has been feeding you these tales?'

She lifted her head proudly, refusing to let the tears fall. 'I know that you could never love me,' she said. 'Let me go, Nicolas. You can seek a separation or a divorce if you prefer—but let's stop this pretence now. You despise me and I—wish I had never met you.'

'You are my wife whether you wish it or not—and I have no intention of seeking a divorce. You made a bargain and you will stick to it.'

'You may force me to be your wife—but I shall never love you.'

Nicolas stared at her in silence for a moment, then turned and walked from the room, slamming the door behind him.

Lottie sank to her knees, covering her face with her hands as she wept.

Nicolas woke and groaned as he felt the pain in his head. He looked round and saw that he was the library, where he had gone to get drunk after the bitter quarrel with Lottie. He had said such things to her—but it was Lottie who had delivered the most telling blow.

She wished she had never met him.

Why had he gone after her and forced the quarrel on her?

He had been so angry when he discovered what she had done. Larkin had given him the money and reported what the man said, though pretending not to believe a word. Nicolas had been furious, though he could do nothing about the man's impertinence. Lottie was in the wrong. Had Blake told his tale to someone else, Lottie might have been in some trouble for helping a fugitive.

Nicolas regretted that Blake had been shot while trying to run away. He had remonstrated with Larkin, but the other keepers backed up the man's story. Blake had been warned and he had struck one of them before making his escape. Larkin's action was within the law. The posters offered the fifty guineas' reward dead or alive—and Larkin would no doubt share the blood money with the others.

Leaving the library, Nicolas felt the bad taste in his mouth. It was partly down to the drink he had taken after Lottie walked out on him earlier, but also the unpleasant feeling he had that someone was pulling the wool over his eyes.

Could Lottie be right about the keeper? He walked up the stairs into her sitting room and saw her curled up on the daybed, fast asleep. Why was she not in bed? Had she been frightened that he would enter her room and force her to do her duty?

His wicked, wicked temper! She must have thought that he was threatening her, telling her that she must do her duty as his wife and give him an heir. He had behaved in a disgusting manner—and the worst of it was he could not be certain that he would not give in to temptation if he continued to sleep in the next room. He knew that seeing her every day would drive him mad if he could not have her. The memory of her warm body close to his and her sweetness pricked at his heart.

She hated him now.

He must go away, remove his unwanted presence.

Lottie would not miss him. She had shown herself perfectly at home here, and after the way he had spoken to her the previous night, she would be glad to see him go.

'I am so sorry,' he said softly. 'I would beg you to forgive me, but I don't think I could bear to see the disgust in your eyes. You will be better off without me.'

By forcing her into a marriage she clearly regretted, he had ruined Lottie's life.

He walked into the dressing room and found some water, dipping his face in its coolness. He would leave as soon as it was light, taking only a few things with him. His town clothes were in London and the sooner he was gone the better. He would write to Lottie from London, tell her she could do pretty much as she pleased here, and he would instruct his agent before he left that Lottie was to have complete control. It was small recompense for what he had done to her, but he must hope she would forgive him in time. He could do little about Sam Blake—but he would make some enquiries about Larkin.

Nicolas's mouth drew into a thin line. He would send a couple of Bow Street Runners down here to keep an eye on the man—and someone to watch over Lottie. If the man *was* a rogue, he might try to harm her.

Nicolas hesitated. Should he stay here and try to make it up with her?

No. He shook his head. There was no point. She must hate him. To see scorn in her lovely eyes would destroy him. It would be best to end this now before he was in too deep. He would have Larkin investigated and make sure she was protected—but she need know nothing about it.

Lottie woke feeling stiff and with a neck ache. She sat up and looked about her, wondering why she had been sleeping on the uncomfortable sofa when she had a soft bed. As the memories flooded back, she frowned. She had sat here and cried herself to sleep, too miserable to seek the comfort of her bed.

She had had such a terrible quarrel with Nicolas. They had both said cruel things—and she regretted it bitterly. To argue with the man she loved over something that was not truly his fault was foolish.

Lottie hated the system that allowed men like Larkin to shoot another man with impunity just because he was a wanted fugitive. Sam Blake might have been a poacher, but he was a husband and the father of three children. What must his poor wife be thinking now?

She decided that the first thing she would do this morning was to visit Lily and apologise for what had happened. Lily might resent her because she was the wife of the man whose keeper had shot her husband, but in time perhaps she would forgive and accept Lottie's help.

She would ride over with one of the young grooms, and on the way back she would take another look at the Hollow. Lottie intended to ask Nicolas again if he would consider cleaning the place up—or at least give the occupants alternative accommodation before he tore down their homes.

She considered speaking to her husband first, but

thought that he might still be angry with her. Dressing in an old riding habit that she had owned long ago, she glanced at herself in the mirror and was satisfied with her appearance. It would be ridiculous to go to a place like the Hollow dressed in something that cost as much as a family might need to live on in a year.

Nicolas had been generous with her allowance. Lottie doubted that she would spend the half of it, which meant she could redirect it in other ways.

She left the house and walked down to the stables, making a brief inspection of the horses until she found one she thought looked a suitable mount.

'Would you saddle this one for me?' she asked a young groom who had tipped his cap to her and was watching curiously. 'And please saddle one for yourself. I want to visit Lily Blake's cottage—and the Hollow on the way back.'

The lad's mouth opened in surprise. She thought he was about to protest, but then he merely touched his greasy cap and set about saddling the mare she had selected. Lottie waited until he had his own mount ready, then led hers to a mounting block and mounted without assistance. Once her hands were on the reins she felt the mare's restiveness and knew she had chosen a spirited beast, which was what she had hoped for.

She glanced at the lad. 'What is your name, sir?'

'I be Willis, ma'am, and the mare be Red Ruth,' he said. 'That 'un ain't bin out fer a couple of days. She'll be a mite fresh.'

'Thank you, Willis. I can feel she wants her head, but she will have to behave. I have serious business this morning.' Lottie smiled at him. 'Now, can you show me the way to Mrs Blake's cottage?'

'Yes, ma'am,' Willis said and grinned. 'I reckon I can. I like Lily. She's a good 'un—too good fer the likes of that Sam Blake. Me pa alus did say it.'

Lottie nodded. The groom moved off and she followed him. They walked the horses until they were clear of the yard and then broke into a trot. She felt her horse pull, as if it wanted to gallop, but she held her reins steady and would not give into the mare's desire. On another day she might have done so, but she did not wish to take any risks this morning.

Lily was red eyed and had little to say when she saw Lottie at her door that morning. Her manner was angry and resentful and the look in her eyes cut Lottie to the heart.

'I don't blame you, miss,' she said. 'You've been good to me and I know you would have helped Sam if you could—but the rest of them don't give a damn.'

'I am sure that isn't true, Lily. Some people are harsh and poaching is a crime, whether we like it or not, but I am sure a lot of people will think what happened was very wrong. I know you are grieving and angry—but when you are ready, come to me. Let me help you set up your own business in Northampton.'

'Thank you, my lady—but I can't ask for more than you've done already, though I am still willing to sew for you to pay my debt.'

'I asked my husband to return the money that was taken from Sam. It is yours, Lily. Please do not be too proud to take it for the sake of your children.'

'I'll think about it—if it happens.'

Lottie left her cottage feeling saddened. She could not expect Lily to welcome her with open arms or to accept her apology. Lily's grief was sharp and it would take time for her to think of a future without the man she had loved.

The visit was something Lottie had had to do, and now there was something more she must see to—even though she expected an even more hostile reception at the Hollow.

'Are you sure you want to stop here, ma'am?' Willis asked as they approached the little cluster of hovels. 'They be a rough lot at the Hollow.'

'They do not have much chance to be otherwise,' Lottie said. 'That open ditch is unhealthy and it smells vile. Who would not resent living near to something like that?'

'Just be careful, ma'am. Not that they'll touch you while I'm around. They know my father and uncles would come back and thrash 'em.'

'Thank you, that makes me feel much better.' Lottie smiled at him. She did not know it, but her manner and her smile had won her a staunch friend that morning.

They dismounted at one end of the hamlet, because Lottie wished to see the true condition of the houses for herself. She lifted her long skirt, hanging it over her arm so that it did not drag in the filth. The smell was vile, but she bore it without flinching, though she was amused to see that Willis covered his nose and mouth.

As she walked the length of the street, people started to come out of the houses. Every now and then she stopped to look at a house. It seemed to Lottie that some of them could be restored, though some would need to be replaced. There was no doubt that it was not an easy project, but she thought it could be done with a little thought and management. The most obvious need was to have the ditch drained and covered.

Intent on her inspection, Lottie was not aware that the crowd had grown until Willis touched her arm and gave a little nod of his head. She turned and saw that they had all gathered at the end of the street, and one man stood at the front, as if intending to block her return to her horse.

Their mood was clearly hostile and she could hardly blame them after what had happened to Sam Blake. However, Lottie was in no mood to be intimidated.

'I have seen enough,' she told Willis. 'We shall leave now.' She saw the discomfort in his face and smiled. 'Do not worry, Willis. I know they are angry, but I do not think they will harm me.'

As they reached the small group at the end of the street, Lottie saw that Sam Blake's cousin Dickon was at their head.

'Good morning,' she said pleasantly in a voice that would carry. 'I dare say you are all wondering what I am doing here this morning?'

'You shouldn't 'ave come 'ere,' Dickon growled. 'Pokin' yer nose in where yer ain't wanted.'

'Unless someone comes, these houses will become nothing but ruins within a few years,' Lottie said. 'It is my intention to repair those that can be repaired. Some will have to be torn down, but they will be rebuilt—and we shall begin by putting in drains and covering over that awful ditch.'

'We don't want yer interference, missus. Clear orf and don't come back or I'll make yer sorry.'

'Speak for yerself, Dickon,' one of the other men said. 'My wife and baby suffer every winter with the damp; our first lad died of a fever on his lungs. If her ladyship means what she says, I'll give a hand with the ditch.'

'I intend to start the repairs at once,' Lottie announced. 'I shall use local labour if possible—so if any of you have building skills, please let me know.'

'I've been a builder,' one of the men said. 'And Sid Carne is a roofer. Most of us can use a spade or a hammer. We would have repaired the houses ourselves if we had the money.'

'Anyone who is willing to work should be here tomorrow morning. I shall be bringing my husband's agent at eight sharp and he will draw up a list of the houses to be repaired and what must be done—and he will pay those who work each day.'

'What about them houses you said 'ad ter come down?' Dickon asked. 'Where will the families go then?'

'I shall begin building a little further through the Hollow. As one house is finished, so one of the houses that cannot be saved will come down; we shall start with the worst and continue until the end, though that may take some time. I hope that you will be as patient as you can, for I cannot do it all at once.'

'Give 'er ladyship a chance, Dickon,' one of the other men said. 'No one but 'er 'as bothered about us fer years. Let 'er see what she can do.'

'I shall be here tomorrow,' Lottie said. 'Be prepared to work. I should prefer that you earned the money yourselves, but of course that is entirely up to you. I can bring in outside craftsmen if I have to.'

The crowd parted to let her through. Willis helped her to mount and they rode away.

'If you are serious about the building, my lady, my elder brother could do with some extra work. Tom can turn his hand to anything—and I reckon as there will be a few more glad of some extra money.'

'Tell him to be there, Willis,' Lottie said.

She could not help feeling a little nervous as she dismounted in the stables and walked into the house. Nicolas might well say that she was interfering in his affairs, and she was—but something had to be done. Lottie was prepared to pay for the repairs with her own money. She just hoped Nicolas would not be too angry with her.

'My husband has gone to London?' Lottie did not know how she managed to hide her surprise and disappointment when Mrs Mann told her why Nicolas had not come down to nuncheon. 'Ah, yes, I believe he did mention some business. I was not perfectly sure when he meant to leave.'

Her heart felt as if someone had taken a knife and stabbed her. So it was all over. He had soon tired of her company and after their quarrel he had decided to return to London—and his mistress, perhaps.

For a moment she recalled the look in his eyes when she had spoken of Elizabeth. He had looked stunned and then angry, as if enraged because she had dared to speak his beloved's name.

Grief and disappointment threatened to overwhelm

her. What was she to do with her life now? For a moment it seemed as if there was nothing left to live for—then she lifted her head as pride came to her aid.

She conquered her disappointment and decided to speak to her husband's agent after nuncheon. Lottie was a little apprehensive, for she imagined he might resist her ideas for the Hollow, but he listened in silence and then nodded his agreement.

'I told his lordship that some of the houses might be saved, but he was insistent it should all come down—perhaps because of things that happened in the past, my lady.'

'I am not sure I understand you, Mr Masters?'

'The late Lady Rothsay was like you, ma'am. She was forever trying to help people—she took a fever after a visit to the Hollow and died within two days. His lordship was but a lad at the time and I dare say he took it hard.'

'That is sad,' Lottie said. 'Surely the best way to prevent something of the sort happening again is to drain that awful ditch and cover it over.'

'I dare say it would help,' Simon Masters agreed. 'There will need to be a cesspool to dispose of the... I beg your pardon, my lady. I should not speak of these things to you.'

Lottie laughed. 'Who else should you tell, sir? I need to know everything that goes on, because I want the work to start immediately.'

'Then perhaps I should draw up a schedule of works for your approval?'

'Yes, of course. I am not sure how fast I can do

all the work, but I want to do as much as I can afford immediately, and then we'll see.'

'Naturally, the repairs will come from the estate revenue, my lady. His lordship left orders that you were to have a free hand—I am certain he would expect to pay himself for any repairs.'

'Nicolas said that I might have a free hand?'

Lottie was surprised and pleased. This was the last thing she had expected.

'Yes, my lady.'

'Very well, we shall begin first thing tomorrow and use as much local talent as we can for the labouring work. Some of the residents may be craftsmen and we must give them the chance, but I shall be guided by your experience in the matter.'

'You may safely leave it in my hands, my lady.'

'Oh, I intend to be there myself at the start,' Lottie said. 'I shall be keeping an eye on what happens—and do not let them cheat you, Mr Masters. I want to help them, but they must do a fair day's work for a fair day's pay.'

The agent smiled. 'Just so, my lady. May I say that I believe things will prosper now that you are here—and perhaps his lordship will take more interest?'

'We must hope so, sir.'

Lottie returned to the house. It was time to take tea with Aunt Beth. Perhaps by working hard every day and concentrating all her thoughts on the unfortunate people of the Hollow, she could forget that Nicolas had deserted her and that her heart felt as if it had split in two.

Chapter Eleven

'Lottie, look at the state of you,' Aunt Beth scolded some three weeks later. 'I approve of what you are doing for those people, naturally, but I did not expect you would actually work yourself.'

'I helped one of the younger women to move from her house into a cottage Mr Masters found for her on the estate. Once her new house is built she will move back to the Hollow,' Lottie said and laughed. 'She has three children and her house is the first to come down. I fear the baby has deposited the contents of his napkin all over my gown. It is just as well I was wearing an old one.'

'You should change before the countess sees you. She would be horrified. I fear you smell, Lottie.'

'Yes, it was my intention to go straight up before seeing anyone,' Lottie said and frowned. 'I thought the countess was in London?'

'She says she needs to speak to you, dearest—but please change before you see her.'

Lottie hurried to change. She knew that she must look terrible, but she had hardly sat still a moment these past weeks since Nicolas left. It would not be true to say that her heartache had eased, but she had little time to think of him, at least during the day. At night her loneliness was hard to bear, but bear it she must, for there was nothing else to be done. Nicolas did not want or need her and she must fill her life with good works.

Having changed into a clean gown and scraped her hair back into a knot at her nape, Lottie went down to the parlour. Henrietta was there alone, and her eyes went over Lottie with disapproval.

'It seems there is not much to choose between the two of you,' she exclaimed. 'I came down to tell you that my godson is on a course set straight for hell and will not long be for this world if something is not done. Now I find you in hardly better shape. You have lost weight, Lottie. What in the world has got into the pair of you?'

Lottie flushed—she knew she had not bothered with her appearance of late. 'Forgive me for not making more effort, Henrietta, but I have been working at the Hollow. I spent the day helping a young woman to move house and—'

'Surely you have servants enough without working yourself to the bone?' Henrietta frowned at her. 'I thought you might see sense, but it seems you are no less stubborn than my godson—did you hear what I said about Nicolas?'

Lottie frowned. 'I heard, but I did not understand you. Is Nicolas ill?'

'Not yet, but he mostly certainly will be if he continues this way. He has been drinking and gambling, and I've never known him to be so careless of his appearance. I called on him the other morning and he looked terrible.'

Lottie's heart contracted with pain. 'I am sorry to hear that, Henrietta, but I really do not see what I can do about it. Nicolas would take little notice of me.'

'You are his wife, Lottie. Do you not care what becomes of him? I have never seen him like this. I do not understand what has changed him—he is like a man possessed, driven to destruction. Indeed, he reminds me of his father just after the marchioness died.' Henrietta's eyes narrowed. 'Have you quarrelled with him, Lottie?'

'No…at least nothing that should upset him in the way you describe. I believe he may regret that he married me. He was not in love with me, Henrietta. There was someone else he cared for deeply.'

'Are you certain of that?' Henrietta looked puzzled. 'He was always moody, of course. Not when he was younger, but these past few years—but then he seemed much happier. I really thought you were the perfect wife for him.' She looked at Lottie intently. 'Do you care for him at all?'

'I love him with all my heart—but please do not tell him so. I fear I drove him away. He does not wish for a clinging wife.'

'Ridiculous! What Nicolas needs is to love and be

loved. If you cared for him, you would do something before it is too late.'

'Would you have me send for him? I doubt he would come—and if he did I could not keep him against his will.'

Henrietta was about to answer, but Aunt Beth entered the room and she thought better of it.

Lottie was thoughtful as she handed out tea and cake. Was Nicolas really behaving that badly? Could he be upset over their quarrel? She had not thought it would affect him—or perhaps he was simply being reckless because he felt trapped?

It was a problem, for she could not simply ignore Henrietta's appeal for help. Her mind was busy with all the alternatives as she went upstairs to change for the evening. If Nicolas wished to be free she would oblige him, but first he must be honest with her and tell her what he wanted from her.

Lottie did not think there was much point in sending for her husband. He would either ignore her or pay a flying visit that would do no one any good. For a while she could not think what she ought to do, but as she was dressing the idea came to her. She had not bothered to purchase many clothes, for she had thought she would have no need of them, but she had been invited to dine several times by her neighbours, and if she were to visit Bath with her aunt she would certainly need more fashionable clothes.

Her plan was bold and risky—Nicolas would be within his rights to be angry. She had agreed to his terms, which were that he would be free to go to London while she stayed here or visited the house in Bath. If she turned up at his London house on the pretext of needing to buy clothes, he would quite possibly be furious.

Well, if they had a row, it might clear the air. Lottie faced the prospect head on. If Nicolas wanted a separation he must tell her—otherwise he would simply have to put up with having her around.

'Go to London to buy clothes?' At dinner that evening, Henrietta looked at her in silence for a moment, then she smiled. 'I think that is an excellent idea, my love. We shall all stay at Nicolas's house while you refurbish your scanty wardrobe. If you will be guided by me, I think we can soon have you looking more the thing, Lottie.'

'I think I shall need your advice if I am to acquire a little town bronze, Henrietta. I do not expect to become the toast of the town, but I should like to be well received.'

'I see no reason why you should not be—and I know my friends will be happy to take you under their wings, my dear. People have been asking why you had not come up with Nicolas. I could not explain, for I had no idea.'

'That is simple—my aunt was poorly, but she is recovered now, are you not, Aunt Beth?'

'What are you up to, Lottie?' Aunt Beth said. 'If you do not mind, I shall stay here, dearest. I may pay your father a little visit, just for a week or two while you are away. He wrote to me and seems worried about your sister.'

'Yes, of course. Go to him if you feel he needs you,' Lottie said. 'But please come back to me soon, aunt.'

'I shall not desert you, Lottie,' Aunt Beth said. 'But

I think you will do better with the countess in town. I have no wish to be racketing around.'

'I dare say we shall not be out so very much,' Lottie said innocently. 'I may be gone only a short time—it depends on what I find…'

Lottie was thoughtful as she went to bed that evening. Perhaps she was a fool but there was no point in staying here pining for something that might never happen. Nicolas was obviously not going to return of his own accord. He might be furious with her, but that would be better than this silent indifference. If they were to part it would be better done now—though in her heart Lottie knew that she would never love anyone else.

She could not stand by and see Nicolas go to the devil without at least trying to discover the cause.

Nicolas stared at himself in his shaving mirror and cursed what he saw. He looked as if he had been dragged through the gutters the previous night; for all he knew, he might have been. He had visited various clubs, discovered that endless gambling bored him and returned home to lose himself in a brandy bottle.

The trouble was, he suspected, that he was missing Lottie. Her perfume seemed to haunt him and he was conscious of a hollow place inside that had been filled for a little time by her presence. He could not get her out of his mind. The drinking and gambling had done nothing to ease the ache inside him or the sense of shame he felt for having abused his wife.

She would hate him now, of course. From the very beginning he had done nothing but insult her—and that last quarrel was unforgivable. How could he go home, which was increasingly where he wished to be? Lottie's clear eyes would show her disgust too plainly and it would kill him to know he deserved her hatred.

Of course he was not in love with her. Romantic love was a myth, but he had enjoyed her company and he wanted her affection—her respect. And though he felt sure that he could never return it, he'd selfishly wanted her love.

Well, he had forfeited it and there was no going back to before that night, but it was time to bring an end to the mad behaviour of the past weeks. He would ruin himself or end up dead in the gutter.

Perhaps he would write an apology to his wife. If she accepted it, he could at least visit her sometimes.

Feeling better, he decided to visit the fencing master he sometimes patronised. It would sharpen his wits and get rid of the sluggish feeling, which was the result of too much wine of late.

'His lordship said nothing of your coming, my lady,' the startled housekeeper said when Lottie and the Countess of Selby arrived on the doorstep of the London house that morning. 'It won't take above half an hour to prepare your rooms—if you would step into the parlour and partake of some refreshments?'

'I dare say my husband did not get my letter,' Lottie said blithely, though she had sent none. Had she informed him, she was certain that Nicolas would have told her not to come. 'We shall be quite content to sit and drink a dish of tea while our rooms are prepared, Mrs Barret.'

Lottie glanced around her as they were taken into a

very elegant salon. It was furnished with delicate satin-wood furniture inlaid with porcelain plaques and looked as if it might be French in style. Perfect for entertaining one's friends, but not as comfortable as her parlour at home.

Lottie frowned, because she had been used to thinking of Rothsay as her home and that might change quite soon. She lifted her chin, putting on a brave face. Henrietta had spoken of Nicolas as being in a parlous state, but she would judge for herself when he came in later. It seemed that he was expected for dinner that evening.

What would he say when he discovered his wife had come to stay? Would he be furious and ask her to leave first thing in the morning?

Why should she leave until she was ready? Nicolas had bullied her into marrying him when she would have released him from the contract. Now he must just put up with the inconvenience until she was ready to leave.

'So what do you think of the house?' Henrietta asked. 'Nicolas had it refurbished when he was first on the town. Personally, I feel it is stylish, but not truly a home.'

'I think it is perfect for entertaining, though if I were often here I should like something more comfortable for the afternoons when I was alone.'

Henrietta laughed. 'Lottie, my dear, I can see this is your first visit to town. The whole point of being in town is that one is never alone—one is always coming or going or entertaining. I dare say your boudoir may be more comfortable.'

'My boudoir? Do you imagine I have one here?'

'Yes, certainly. Nicolas must have prepared the master suite for the comfort of the lady he intended to be his wife. You may care to sit there sometimes—if you are at home—but I am sure that once I tell my friends you are here you will not have time.'

Lottie looked at her uncertainly. The countess seemed very certain that she would be welcomed into society by everyone. As yet, Lottie was not quite so sure.

'Lottie…' The door that divided her suite of very attractive rooms from those that Nicolas used when in town was suddenly flung open and her husband strode in. Her heart caught as she saw him, because she had temporarily forgotten how very handsome he was. 'I could hardly believe it when Barret told me you were here.'

'Nicolas.' Lottie's pulses raced as she looked at him. 'I am sorry you did not get my letter. I hope you will not mind my coming up to town, but I find I cannot manage with the clothes I have. Though you were undoubtedly generous with the gowns you organised for me before the wedding, I have been entertained by most of our neighbours and if I am to take Aunt Beth to Bath, I need some town bronze. Henrietta was kind enough to say she would help me choose the right seamstresses.'

For a moment Nicolas was silent, his manner uncertain, as if waiting for something, then, 'Of course I do not mind, Lottie. I told you that you would need more clothes, did I not?'

'Certainly you did, Nicolas.' Lottie kept her expression bland, wanting to give nothing away as she searched his face for signs of the depravity the countess had spoken of. He looked tired and there were shadows beneath his eyes, but at the moment he was sober and she could see no sign of desperation. 'I dare say it will only take me a few days to be suited and then you may be peaceful again.'

'Please stay as long as you wish, Lottie.' She noticed a little pulse flicking at his temple. 'Are you quite well? I think you have lost some weight? You look thinner than I remember.'

'Perfectly well, thank you,' she replied and allowed a cool smile. 'You will not pull caps with me, Nicolas. Mr Masters said that you had given me a free hand—and I fear I have taken advantage. We have started work on the Hollow, using mostly local labour. I must tell you that one of the new houses is almost built and that terrible ditch has been covered in and drained into a cesspool.'

'Masters wrote and informed me,' Nicolas said, his eyes narrowed and intent. 'I should, of course, have seen to it years ago—but for reasons I prefer to remain private, I favoured pulling the whole place down.'

'It would be a pity to drive people from their homes when a few repairs and some rebuilding will make it a perfectly decent place to live. Now that the open ditch is gone I am sure everyone will be healthier.'

'Yes, I am certain you are right.' He hesitated, then, 'Dare I hope—have you forgiven me, Lottie?'

Lottie wrinkled her smooth brow. 'I am sorry that Sam Blake was killed, but you were not present and the law was on your keeper's side. I have offered to set Lily Blake up in her own establishment in Northampton. There is no way I can make up for what she has lost, but I hope that in time she will be able to move on and begin a new life.'

'I did not mean…' Nicolas shook his head. 'Then you

do not hate me?' he asked, an odd expression in his eyes. 'You said it the last time we spoke.'

'I must apologise for the things I said to you, Nicolas. I was angry but—I could never truly hate you,' Lottie said. 'I know that I have broken the terms of our agreement by coming here—but perhaps you will not mind too much just for a little while?'

'I find that I do not mind at all,' Nicolas said. 'Do you have enough money? If not, you must send the bills to me. I would wish my wife to appear in society in a manner befitting the Countess Rothsay.'

'Thank you, I shall try not to let you down, Nicolas.'

'How could you do that?' he said. 'I have an appointment to play cards with a party of friends this evening and ought not to cancel it—perhaps tomorrow evening we could go somewhere together?'

'Henrietta says we are invited to a soirée tomorrow evening, Nicolas. If you care to accompany us that will be perfectly acceptable—if not, then perhaps another time. You must not think that you are obliged to dance attendance on me. I am perfectly able to entertain myself—at least with Henrietta's help I shall be.'

'Very well, I shall not interfere with your plans.'

'Or I with yours,' Lottie said. 'It is not unknown for a husband and wife to attend separate affairs, I believe.'

There, she was being the perfect convenient wife.

'It is often the case. We should hold a dinner ourselves—if that is agreeable to you?'

'Perfectly. We may attend some of the same affairs, of course,' Lottie said. 'It must be just as you wish, Nicolas.'

'So we are back to that…' Nicolas nodded thoughtfully. 'Very well, my love. I see we shall go on just as before.'

'I hope that we may be friends again,' Lottie said. 'Have you forgiven me, Nicolas?'

'There was nothing to forgive,' he replied smoothly. 'I thought—but perhaps I was mistaken… I find I cannot read you as well as I imagined, Lottie.'

'Perhaps as time goes on you will know me better,' she said. 'Pray do not let me keep you from your appointment, Nicolas.'

He stared at her uncertainly, inclined his head and went back through to his own room, shutting the door with a little snap.

Lottie stared at the door and wondered. Had she noticed signs of frustration in Nicolas? Could it be that he had missed her just a little?

Nicolas's thoughts were in turmoil as he left Lottie to change for a quiet evening at home. He found himself wishing that he might stay with her and talk about the future for them—but his pride refused to let him speak too openly of his feelings. She seemed to have forgiven him for that night or at least to have put their quarrel to one side. In Lottie's estimation, it seemed, the only thing needful of forgiveness was what had happened to Sam Blake—and it appeared that she had accepted he could not have prevented it.

Nicolas was still having Larkin watched. As yet nothing out of the ordinary seemed to be happening. The man went about his work in an exemplary way—but did he know he was being watched?

Damn it! He could not worry about such things when Lottie was suddenly here and in the next room. Her manner was no different than it had ever been—it was almost as if they had never quarrelled. He could not be certain whether she was indifferent or merely making things easy for him.

Now all he had to deal with was his hunger for the woman who would be sleeping in the room next to him for the next week or two.

Would Lottie be prepared to go back to the way it had been on their honeymoon?

Nicolas's pulses raced at the thought. He badly wanted to go back now and kiss her senseless, to take her to bed and make love to her until they fell asleep in each other's arms.

Now he was being a damned fool! Lottie might permit his lovemaking, but she did not love him. She had told him she would never love him, even if he obliged her to do her duty. Why did that matter so much? Nicolas dismissed the notion that he might be in love with her. He wanted her, liked her, and appreciated her good qualities—but love? If he felt the kind of love for her that his father had felt for Nicolas's mother, it would lead to nothing but heartbreak.

He remembered the golden days when his mother had been the heart of their home and it had seemed that his father was always there, always good mannered, smiling and loving towards his son. How suddenly those days had vanished!

His mother's death and the sudden withdrawal of his father's affection had devastated Nicolas. He had not understood as a child that the silent stern man who went away for long periods and hardly noticed his son when he returned was sunk in a terrible grief that had hastened his death. Only later, after an unhappy love affair with a woman who had thought him an object of amusement, had Nicolas begun to understand his father's loss. He thought that he had not truly understood it until recently.

Surely he was not caught in the trap he had meant to avoid by arranging a marriage of convenience? Love was too painful when it ended. He had not wanted to feel that pain again. Yet he could not regret that Lottie had come into his life.

She was beautiful, but there was so much more to her—so much more to discover.

He would be a fool to allow himself to care, Nicolas reflected as he changed for the evening. If there were a chance that Lottie cared, perhaps—but her manner was so unemotional. He could not think that she cared for him in any meaningful way. She was prepared to be the mother of his children, because she had given her promise—and he knew now that she would keep it.

Why could he not just accept that and be content to live his own life, as he had intended?

Nicolas groaned as he suspected that he was caught in a trap of his own making. Yet he would not admit to it, because if he did…

Shaking his head, he took the evening cloak his valet offered and went out of his room and down the stairs. This evening he would take care not to drink more than a single glass of wine. Otherwise, he might find it too tempting to go through that connecting door.

* * *

Lottie heard Nicolas come in. She was surprised he was so early. It was scarcely much past eleven, which for a man who had reportedly been burning the candles at both ends was unprecedented.

She lay for a while, wondering if he might come to her, but the door between their rooms remained firmly closed. She wished she had the courage to open that door and go through to him, but was afraid of his rejection. If he wanted to lie with her he would surely come to her?

Nicolas had accepted her, even telling her to stay as long as she wished, and to send her bills to him if she had not enough money. Why was he so generous and yet so removed from her in every other way?

The frustration grew as she thought of him lying so close. A little moan of need issued from her. She wanted so much to lie in his arms and feel his lips on her—but she must hide her need and wait until Nicolas came to her. He would surely do so in time, because he needed an heir.

Lottie faced the fact that she was in love with her husband. She had sworn she would not love him, but she did. He was indifferent to her, though at times he had a need for marital relations. Was he still seeing his mistress? She supposed he must be—might even have visited her that evening.

The thought was so painful that she dismissed it instantly—yet it would not go away completely.

What did this woman have that Lottie did not? How could she make him want her rather than this unknown woman who haunted his dreams?

If only there was a way to make him jealous! Lottie

could not think of one, however hard she tried. She knew she was not unattractive, but it needed more than that to arouse a man's passions. Perhaps if he thought that other men were interested… Lottie's thoughts went round and round in her head. How could she convince her husband that other men thought her interesting or desirable?

She sighed as sleep claimed her at the last. It just was not going to happen.

Chapter Twelve

'Countess Rothsay.' The young buck smiled at Lottie winningly. 'I know I am late—but dare I hope there is one dance left on your card?'

'I think…' Lottie consulted and then inclined her head. 'Just the dance before supper—if you would care to write your name?'

'May I also take you into supper?' Mr Bellingham asked hopefully.

'I have already been asked several times,' Lottie replied. 'If you would care to join us all, I should be happy to see you, sir.'

'Then I shall certainly do so, Countess. May I say that we all perfectly understand why Rothsay tried to keep you hidden in the country. Were you my wife, I should not wish to share you either.'

'Oh, it was nothing of the kind,' Lottie said with a laugh. 'My aunt was unwell and I stayed until she felt much recovered. I assure you there was no such intention on Rothsay's part.'

'Then he is a fool,' Mr Bellingham replied. 'I shall return for my dance later.'

Lottie nodded and turned to her next partner. This was her first dance since coming to town, for she had needed several gowns made before she could think of attending a society ball of this size. The large rooms were overflowing and very warm, but as yet Lottie had not been tempted outside, though more than one gentleman had asked if she would like to take the air.

She had been hoping that Nicolas would approach and ask her for at least one dance, but thus far he had kept his distance. It was for his sake that she had kept the supper dance until the last, but since he was clearly not interested, she had given it away to Mr Bellingham.

Her popularity at every event she attended had made no impression on Nicolas. He had escorted her and Henrietta to a couple of card evenings and spent most of them in the room set up for cards, leaving Lottie alone to make her own friends and enjoy herself as she would.

So much for her hopes that he would be just a little jealous. He seemed not to have noticed that she was being lionised by most and that the gentlemen flocked to her side every time she stood and watched the dancing for a moment.

She smiled as her next partner presented himself, bowing to her reverently. 'My dance, I think, Countess?'

'Yes, sir.' Lottie's heart thudded. Mr Gerard Hunter was Lady Fisher's nephew. Sir Bertie had introduced them and therefore Lottie had felt obliged to accept his name on her card, but she was a little nervous of him. Of all the gentlemen she had so far met in London, Mr

Hunter was the most particular. His eyes seemed to convey a message and when he held her, there was a certain possessiveness about him—as though he was trying to draw her into a more intimate relationship. Lottie was not sure whether or not she trusted this particular gentleman. 'I believe it is…'

The dance was a waltz. As the young man put his hand at her waist, she realised that she had been unwise to allow him a waltz. His manner was altogether too intimate, his eyes seeming to burn into her as he looked down at her.

She was relieved when the dance came to an end and she could thank him and move away.

Running upstairs to the chamber set aside for the ladies to refresh themselves, she bathed her face in cool water and tucked a stray lock of hair into place behind her ear, before leaving to go downstairs. At the head of the stairs she saw Nicolas and realised that he must have been waiting for her.

'Was Hunter annoying you, Lottie?'

'Just a little,' she said. 'He seems almost too attentive at times—but he is not the only gentleman to pay me foolish compliments.'

Nicolas's gaze went over her slowly, his eyes dark and thoughtful. 'You certainly look very beautiful this evening, Lottie. That gown becomes you, though perhaps the neckline is a little revealing.' His eyes dwelled on her birthmark. 'It is unlike you to let that show?'

'I asked *madame* to make certain the neckline would cover it, but she assured me it was attractive and said the fashion was lower this year. Henrietta said I should be guided by *madame*—but perhaps a little lace at the neck would make it more modest?'

'Why should you hide your charms when every other lady in the room is revealing theirs? A gentleman must learn when his attentions are not wanted. Shall I have a word with Mr Hunter, Lottie?'

'I think it would make a statement if you were to dance with me,' she replied. 'Perhaps your indifference gives other men the wrong impression?'

'Yes, perhaps it does. Do you have a free dance on your card?'

'No. I gave the last to Mr Bellingham.'

'Harry will not mind if I cut in,' Nicolas said. 'I shall have to make it plain that you are my property.'

'Shall you, Nicolas?' Lottie replied and hid her smile. 'How very boring for you.'

'I do not think I shall find it boring to dance with you,' he replied, but his eyes were stormy and she sensed his anger.

Something told her that Nicolas did not care to see other men flirting with his wife too openly.

Nicolas cut in after Lottie had taken half-a-dozen turns around the room with Mr Bellingham, who held her in a perfectly polite manner and did not give her smouldering glances.

'Damn you, Rothsay,' the young man said, but gave way with good grace. 'You should have reserved your own dance—but I suppose I must allow you to claim her. You are a damned lucky devil and always have been.'

Lottie went into her husband's arms. Immediately, she was aware of a feeling of pleasure as Nicolas swept her about the room. How wonderful it felt to waltz with Nicolas. She wished that their dance would go on and on for ever, but all too soon it came to an end.

'Now I shall take you into supper and that should be enough,' Nicolas said. 'Forgive me for neglecting my duties, Lottie. It never occurred to me that Hunter would decide that you were available.'

'No, I am sure it did not,' Lottie replied. 'He was mistaken. I am not available, Nicolas. I am your wife and even though you may not particularly want me—I shall not conduct a clandestine affair behind your back.'

'Shall you not? I am relieved to hear that, my dear.' He offered her his arm, but frowned as if deep in thought. 'What may I fetch you for supper?'

'Oh, just a syllabub, I think, Nicolas. I am not very hungry.'

'You must not neglect yourself, Lottie. I do not wish you to become too thin—you were perfect as you were when I married you.'

'Indeed?' Her eyes sparkled. 'Now that is a compliment, sir. I have received several this evening—but what can top perfection?'

'Nothing.' His brow furrowed. 'You must know that you are one of—if not the—most beautiful women in this room?'

'How kind of you to say so, Nicolas, but you really have no need to flatter me.'

'I was not aware that I was flattering you. I imagined you knew me well enough to know that I speak as I find.'

'The shame is, Nicolas, that I hardly know you at all.'

Lottie went to sit down at an empty table while Nicolas departed to fetch some champagne and a syllabub. When he returned, he discovered that at least four young gentlemen were vying with each other to fetch Lottie some supper. She seemed to have recovered her appetite, because she was nibbling delicately at a tiny almond pastry someone had brought for her.

Nicolas joined the group about her, noticing the way her eyes lit when she responded to their teasing, and the softness of her lips as she licked a crumb from them. He was conscious of a strong desire to lean forwards and lick the crumb from her lips himself, but would not do something so revealing in company.

It was hardly surprising that half the men in the supper room were observing Lottie with barely disguised lust. Even those who were not dancing attendance on her were staring at her with admiration and at him with envy. He was torn between irritation and pleasure that his wife should arouse so much attention.

Yet the frustration he had felt the first night she came up to town was building. He hardly knew how to control himself, because if he simply walked through that adjoining door he could have what every other man in the room wanted.

He wondered when Lottie had become so very desirable—or had she always been and he just had not seen it? Was he a fool to hold back when he might have spent several nights in her arms?

Just what did he want from her?

'Nicolas, how lovely to see you.'

Nicolas turned his head as he felt the touch on his

shoulder. He saw Elizabeth's beautiful face and bowed over her hand, lifting it to his lips.

'Lady Madison, how are you?'

'Oh, well enough, I suppose,' Elizabeth said and sighed. 'My marriage is not all I imagined it would be, Nicolas. I think I made a mistake when I refused you. The years have given you a presence you did not have when we were younger.'

'It is merely age. The years have been kind to you, Elizabeth. I think you are more beautiful than ever.'

'I have been invited to visit Lord Hartwell's country house next month. My husband does not accompany me. It would be pleasant if you were there.'

Nicolas hesitated. Her meaning was clear enough. She was not the first lady bored with her marriage to hint that she would be happy to indulge in an affair.

'Forgive me, Lady Madison,' Nicolas said. 'I believe I shall be in the country with my wife.'

Glancing across the room, Lottie saw Nicolas kiss a lady's hand. She was an exceptionally lovely woman with hair the colour of jet. Turning to Mr Bellingham, she smiled and enquired the name of the beauty.

'Oh…you mean Lady Elizabeth Madison,' Bellingham said and looked slightly uncomfortable. 'She is beautiful, though before her marriage she was an Incomparable. We all wanted her, though she seemed to prefer—' He broke off, embarrassed. 'All in the past and long forgotten.'

Lottie knew at once that she must be *the* Elizabeth— the woman Nicolas cried for in his sleep.

'She is very beautiful,' she said. 'I find I am a little

warm, sir. I should like to take the air on the veranda—if you would oblige me?'

'Of course,' he said and offered his arm. 'Rothsay is a fool if he neglects you for her—she has the tongue of a fishwife.'

'Oh, no.' Lottie trilled with laughter and tapped him with her fan. 'How wicked you are, sir.'

Her laughter had made Nicolas glance her way, but she was genuinely amused and did not see his frown.

Lottie was tired when they returned home that evening. The countess had gone earlier, complaining of a headache, but insisting that Lottie remain and ask for Nicolas's escort to see her home.

'It is time he did his duty by you, Lottie. Nicolas was always a provoking man—but this time he has gone too far. He is your husband. He should act in the proper manner towards you. I wash my hands of the foolish man.'

Lottie smiled and shook her head. Henrietta did not understand the bargain she had made. No matter how much it irked Lottie that her husband remained indifferent, she would not make demands on him. She was perfectly well able to enjoy herself in town without Nicolas running after her.

However, she had been glad of his interference that evening. Mr Hunter was too insistent and it would not do for Lottie to be thought to be fast. She was Nicolas's wife and as such must remain above criticism—at least until his son was born. Yet how was she to give him a son if he did not come to her bed?

It was a problem; the longer things remained the

way they were, the more difficult it would be to resolve them.

How could she break down her husband's reserve? What must she do to bring him back to her bed? She was not as beautiful as Lady Elizabeth Madison—but she was his wife. Surely he had cared for her a little when they spent such happy times together on their honeymoon. Could she make him forget his first love?

She hesitated when she said goodnight, hoping that he might speak, but he merely inclined his head. Lottie turned away and went up to her room, feeling the frustration mount. She undressed and sent her maid away, sitting to brush her long hair in front of the mirror. It was as she was about to go to bed that she noticed she was still wearing her pearls. She reached to unfasten them at the back and discovered that they had snagged on the lace of her night chemise and would not come free. She was reluctant to send for her maid and instead went to the adjoining door. She knocked and Nicolas's voice invited her to enter. He had removed his breeches and long boots and was standing in just his shirt, which came down to his thighs. His face registered surprise as he saw her.

'Yes, Lottie—what may I do for you? You are not unwell, I trust?'

'Oh, no, I am quite well,' she replied and suddenly her earlier tiredness had fled. 'It is these bothersome pearls, Nicolas. The clasp has caught in the lace and I did not want to send for my maid at this hour.'

'Let me see what I can do,' he offered.

Lottie swept her hair up with one hand, turning so that her back was towards him and he could see the clasp.

'I did not realise they were caught until I tried…' She caught her breath as she felt his hand at her nape. The touch of his fingers sent delicious shivers down her spine and she could not speak. He had freed the lace and his hand caressed her throat as he removed the pearls. She turned slowly and looked at him, her lips parting as she saw something in his eyes. 'Nicolas.,,' she breathed and instinctively swayed towards him.

'Lottie—damn it…' he muttered hoarsely and caught her to him, his mouth seeking hers. She melted into his body; her lips parted to invite his seeking tongue, feeling the heat of desire begin to build low in her abdomen. 'Will you…do you want me to continue? I have not dared to ask after that night…you said you hated me.'

'Oh, Nicolas,' she murmured against his mouth. 'I told you I did not mean it, my dearest. It was a foolish quarrel that I have regretted.'

'Was that all? I thought…I might have given you a dislike of my character.'

'No, nothing like that. I was angry, but I—admire you and like you, truly.' She reached up to stroke his cheek with her fingertips, suddenly daring. 'I have missed you, Nicolas. Would you sleep in my bed tonight?'

'Yes, Lottie, I shall,' he said and grinned. Bending down, he caught her behind the knees and swept her up in his arms, striding back into her room. Placing her carefully on the sheets, he stripped off his shirt and she saw that he was naked and fully aroused. 'I have been wanting to do this for a while now. I think we will have this pretty thing off, don't you?'

He pulled her nightgown up over her head and let it

fall to join his shirt on the floor. His gaze feasted on her naked flesh and then he bent his head to kiss her lips. In another moment he was beside her on the bed, lying with his heated skin touching hers, his hand stroking the satiny arch of her back as he pulled her closer still.

Lottie sighed with content, allowing him to stroke and touch her for a few minutes, then, because she could no longer hold back, she began to stroke his shoulders and to kiss his neck. Her nails lightly raked his flesh as she arched and moaned, not trying to hold in the feelings he was arousing in her. Nicolas did not want a clinging wife and she had done her best to keep something back, but her need was too great. She had lain alone too many nights, knowing that he was close and that she loved him, wanted him. Even if he guessed that she loved him, she could not hide her pleasure in his loving. Her screams and the desperate need she felt to have him inside her again and again had driven all else from her mind. He was her husband and she wanted his loving. She wanted him to possess her, to own her, to be a part of his flesh.

She wanted to make him forget the beautiful Elizabeth if she could.

Nicolas seemed to respond to her wanton need, driving into her again and again relentlessly, their cries mingling until at last she shuddered, gripped in a climax that was almost like dying, and he suddenly collapsed against her, his seed deep inside her.

For quite a long time they lay still, silent, holding each other, the desperate need satiated.

'Nicolas,' she whispered at last. 'You won't leave me again, will you?'

'Go to sleep, Lottie,' he said and kissed her brow. 'I have to think. Tomorrow we shall have time enough to talk.'

Lottie woke and stretched. At first she could not remember why she felt so good, then she ran her tongue over lips that still tasted of Nicolas and everything came back. They had made love in such a tumultuous fashion, and then they slept. In the night she had woken once to find Nicolas still at her side. He had wanted her again, making love this time with a slow, sensual tenderness that left her weeping. He had hushed her, stroking her hair as her tears wetted his shoulder, and she mumbled something about love and then hoped he had not heard.

Nicolas would hate it if she tried to put chains on him. She had begged him not to leave her again and then told him she loved him. She would have only herself to blame if he asked her to go home or ran away himself.

Getting up, she wrapped a lace peignoir about her and went to his room. There was no sign of him and she guessed that he had gone out to ride, as he often did early in the morning. He had told her he needed time to think. Was he trying to find a way to tell her that he did not love her?

He had wanted her. Lottie was in no doubt of his need the previous night—but perhaps seeing that other men were attracted to her had aroused his interest. Or perhaps there was some other reason. He had been speaking with Elizabeth and been desperate because he could not have her. Lottie had gone to him, offered herself to him and he had taken advantage. That did not mean he loved her.

She must not expect it…even though he had said things as they lay together.

Lottie used the water her maid had brought her and dressed in a pretty yellow silk gown. She would go down to nuncheon in a moment, for she had slept late. A jewel case was lying on the dressing table, but it was not one Lottie recognised. She opened it and discovered a beautiful diamond necklace. The stones were so large and so white that she gasped with amazement. Then she saw the little square of paper.

> *Family heirlooms. I had them reset for you, Lottie. You deserve the best. Nicolas.*

Lottie stared at the note. She held the necklace to her throat. The diamonds were certainly fabulous, far more valuable than anything else Nicolas had given her. Why had he left them here? She felt a little nervous for they should certainly be locked away in Nicolas's strong room except for special occasions.

She closed the box and stood up, remembering that she had left her pearls in Nicolas's room. She went through and saw them on the dressing table. Picking them up, she returned to her own room and then halted as she saw the woman standing there. She had her back to Lottie but she knew her at once.

'Clarice—what are you doing here?'

Her sister turned. She was wearing a racy hat with heavy veiling. As she lifted it, she revealed an oddly guilty look on her face. 'I wondered where you were. Is that Rothsay's room through there?'

'Yes. I was retrieving something I left there last night,'

Lottie said and felt defensive as her sister's eyes went over her with a flash of jealousy. She was aware that Clarice's gown looked a little outdated, as if she had not had a new one for a while. 'Why have you come, Clarice?'

'Do I have to have a reason?' Clarice asked. 'That isn't very nice, Lottie—considering you have me to thank for all this…' Her eyes travelled round the room and there was jealousy in them.

'Yes, I know. I am grateful that you pushed me into it, Clarice. I did not expect to be happy, but I am.'

'Aunt Beth told me he spoils you.' Clarice fingered the pearls Lottie had placed on the dressing table. 'These are nice. I suppose you have plenty of pin money—you couldn't lend me a couple of thousand, could you?'

'I don't have anywhere near that much, and, as I told you at Rothsay, even if I did I couldn't give it to you.' Lottie said. 'Are you in trouble, Clarice?'

'Philippe is—he owes thousands. If he doesn't pay some of it, he will be arrested and imprisoned. What shall I do then, Lottie? You have all this and I have nothing.'

'This…' Lottie indicated the room about her. 'This belongs to Nicolas. He shares it with me but I do not own it. I cannot give you a thousand pounds, Clarice—at the moment I have no more than two hundred pounds.'

'Give me that, it will help for now.' Clarice said. 'Don't be mean, Lottie. You would have none of this if it were not for me.'

Lottie felt guilty. In much the same way that she always forgave her father his faults, she loved her twin just as dearly. To see her suffer broke her heart. After all, she was so lucky to be Nicolas's wife and she owed her happiness to Clarice. If she had not spent so much on clothes she could have given her sister more. She opened the top drawer of her dressing chest and took out a wooden casket, opening it to remove the small bag of gold coins.

'There you are, Clarice. I am sorry it isn't more, but I have spent my allowance for this quarter.'

'I'll come back for the rest another time,' Clarice said, flew at her and kissed her cheek. 'Goodbye, Lottie. Remember that you owe me.'

She pulled the veiling over her face again and turned to the door. She opened it, looked out and then disappeared through the aperture, leaving Lottie staring after her. She felt slightly sick. How on earth had Clarice managed to reach her room without being seen or announced? Her reminder that she could have been Lady Rothsay had she chosen had left Lottie feeling uneasy. She wished her sister had not come.

Something made her look at the jewellery case that Nicolas had left lying on the dressing table that morning. Her stomach clenched and she reached for it somehow knowing what she would find. She opened it and saw that the necklace was missing. Clarice had taken it. Her own sister was a jewel thief. She had taken a priceless heirloom and then had the effrontery to ask for money.

Rising to her feet, Lottie went out and ran along the landing to the top of the stairs to look down at the hall. Clarice had gone. She must have fled the instant she left the room, knowing that Lottie would look for the necklace sooner or later.

How had she managed to get into the room while

Lottie's back was turned? She had been wearing veiling over her face. They were identical in build and height. If the servants had seen her walk up the stairs they would have assumed she was Lottie; Clarice had probably even been admitted to the house and mistaken for her. It was likely that no one would know she had been to the house.

What was she to do? Lottie sat staring at the empty jewel box, then opened a drawer and slid it inside. Could she contact her sister and demand that she return the necklace? Clarice would simply deny having taken it and Lottie could prove nothing. If no one had seen her, there was no proof that she had ever been in the house. Besides, how could Lottie admit to Nicolas that her sister was a thief?

She remembered that he had accused Clarice of stealing some guineas from his friend's pocket in that gaming house in Paris. He had been disgusted by her behaviour then—what would he think if he knew that Clarice had come here on purpose to rob them? Lottie wondered uneasily if her sister had taken anything else. She glanced around the bedchamber, but everything else seemed to be in place.

'Oh, Clarice,' she whispered. 'Why did it have to be the diamonds?' If it had been her pearls or something less important, it wouldn't have mattered so much—but Nicolas was bound to ask about the necklace.

Nicolas would expect her to thank him. He would naturally expect to see her wearing them—and what could she say?

Lottie was close to tears. She had hoped that they would be closer after last night—but if she told Nicolas that Clarice had stolen the diamonds he would be so angry. He might accuse her of having given them to her sister—or of being the thief herself.

She did not know what to do for the best. Feeling restless, Lottie decided that she would go out for a walk. She could not go shopping because she had no money left, but she was too upset to sit in the house and wait for Nicolas to return.

When she met Mr Hunter as she was entering the park, Lottie was glad that she had brought her maid with her. It had been tempting to go alone, but it would not be thought proper for the Marchioness of Rothsay to walk alone.

'Lady Rothsay,' he said, sweeping his hat off and making her an elegant bow.

'Mr Hunter.' Lottie inclined her head coolly, hoping to be allowed to walk on, but it was not to be. He stood deliberately in her path, making it clear he meant to make the most of this chance meeting.

'I shall join you on your walk. It is a pleasant day, is it not—though I believe a mite cooler than of late?'

'The summer has deserted us,' Lottie replied. Since he would not take a hint and leave her to walk in peace, the weather was a safe topic. 'I dare say you will soon leave for the country, sir?'

'Oh, no, I have every intention of staying in town for a while.'

'I plan to return to the country quite soon. Excuse me, I see Lady March and I must speak with her. Good morning, Mr Hunter.'

She beckoned to her maid, who had dropped behind,

and headed for a young woman she had met recently whom she rather liked. Mr Hunter had accepted his dismissal this time, but she was conscious that his eyes still watched her as she walked away.

What she did not know was that the brief interlude had been seen by a man on horseback.

Nicolas was frowning as he left his horse in the mews and walked back to his house. Why had Lottie been walking in the park with Mr Hunter at this hour of the day? He had left her sleeping and had imagined she would not go out before the afternoon, when he had intended to take her shopping.

The diamond necklace he had left on her dressing table was only the first of several gifts he intended to give his lovely wife. He was thinking that they might take a short trip to Paris, which was where he should really have taken her after their wedding. There were so many plans in his head concerning the future that he had gone out for an early ride to blow the cobwebs away.

Why had she slipped out in the early morning to meet Hunter in the park? He had only caught a brief glance of them, talking earnestly, it seemed to him, and had no idea of how long they might have been together.

He fought his unworthy suspicions, forcing them to a small corner of his mind. Lottie might have met with Hunter by chance. He must not jump to conclusions, but it had made him realise that he did not care for other men paying his wife too much attention. Yet there was surely no harm in what he had witnessed. Just because Elizabeth had led him on, allowing him to believe that she loved him, only to laugh in his face when he proposed to her, it did not mean that other women were the same. Lottie was warm and loving and the previous night he had believed that she truly cared for him.

He still hesitated to use the word *love*. Lottie had enjoyed their lovemaking and clearly felt something for him. Since Nicholas did not believe in love he would name it affection and admit that he felt the same for her.

Yes, he was fond of Lottie. She had somehow managed to get beneath his skin and he would hate to lose her now.

Chapter Thirteen

Nicolas returned in time for nuncheon. He smiled as he joined Lottie at the table in the smaller of the two dining parlours. Since there was just the three of them the formal dining room would seem awkward and too large. He took his place at table and smiled on the two ladies already seated.

'Forgive me if I have kept you, ladies,' he said. 'Tell me, what are your plans this afternoon?'

'We must call on some of my friends,' Henrietta told him and nodded to the footman serving soup. 'Thank you, Henderson, just a little.' Her gaze transferred to Nicolas. 'Had you a particular reason for asking?'

'I thought Lottie might like to go shopping with me?'

'Thank you,' Lottie said, her cheeks a little pink. 'I should like to go another day, Nicolas, but Henrietta thinks I should meet some ladies who do not often go into society. Also I must thank you for the beautiful gift you gave me, Nicolas.'

'I am glad you liked the necklace, Lottie. You should wear the diamonds tomorrow evening when we attend the Duchess of Argyle's annual ball. It is one of the largest of the summer and generally means that she will be leaving town. After next week only the hostesses who seldom leave London will be entertaining. Their dinners are usually for politicians and academics and rather dull affairs—unless you have an interest in such things?'

'I must say that I do prefer a gathering of artistes and musical evenings, but I dare say some such company may still be found?'

'Then you do not intend to return to Rothsay just yet?'

'Perhaps I may stay another week or two,' Lottie said and helped herself to a dish of turbot. 'If that does not inconvenience you, Nicolas?'

'Why should it? I was thinking of inviting a shooting party to Rothsay for the autumn, but that is a few weeks away yet.'

'In that case I shall return a week ahead to make sure everything is in order.' Lottie glanced at Henrietta. 'Will you remain in London, dearest?'

'Not after you have gone,' Henrietta said and smiled at her. 'I visit occasionally, but stayed longer this time for the pleasure of introducing you to society, dearest Lottie. I think we may say that your début has been successful—would you not agree, Nicolas?'

'Yes, Lottie has caused a stir, especially amongst some of the gentlemen.' Nicolas looked at his wife. 'Did you enjoy your walk this morning, Lottie?'

'Yes, I walked in the park for a while, Nicolas. Did you happen to see me?'

'Just for a moment or two, Lottie. I like a ride first thing, you know—but I was surprised to see you. I thought you might have wanted to sleep in a little?'

'Oh, well, when I woke I felt the need of some exercise.'

'I see...' Nicolas inclined his head. 'I shall not see you this evening. I have a card party and may be late. Do not wait up for me, Lottie.'

'We have a soirée,' Lottie said. 'If you are late, I shall see you in the morning, Nicolas.'

Lottie glanced down at her plate. The succulent turbot tasted like dust in her mouth. It seemed that nothing had changed. She had imagined that after last night Nicolas would suddenly become the charming lover of her dreams, but he seemed to have withdrawn once more and she had no idea why.

If she had not been feeling so guilty over the loss of the diamonds, Lottie thought she would have excused herself to Henrietta and spent the afternoon with her husband. It was becoming increasingly obvious to her that they must talk seriously. Nicolas could not blow hot and cold for ever and expect her to accept his moods. They must come to a proper arrangement so that she understood what he expected of her—did he want a wife who was always willing to welcome him to her bed or not? Last night he had taken her with such passion she could swear he cared for her, but this morning the mask was in place once more.

She saw him looking at her, his eyes dark and

brooding, and she sensed that he was angry, but fighting his anger. What on earth could she have done to make him angry? Surely he couldn't know about the diamonds already?

What on earth was she to do about them? If Nicolas had not suddenly gone cold on her again she might have told him the truth, but she was afraid that he would not believe her. Something was definitely troubling him.

True to his word, Nicolas was out late that evening. Lottie heard him come in well into the early hours of the morning. She lay listening for a few moments, hoping that he might change his mind and come to her, but he did not.

She could not bear this a moment longer! Getting out of bed, Lottie went through into her husband's room and saw him lying fully clothed on the bed. He had not even bothered to take his boots off. Had he been drinking again?

Lottie frowned as she bent over him, but could not smell excessive wine on his breath. She pulled off his long boots and peeled back his hose. His feet looked white and soft; tempted beyond bearing, she bent her head and kissed one. Then she pulled a cover over him and sat on the edge of the bed, gazing down at him. Her hand reached out to brush hair that was a little too long back from his forehead.

'My dearest love,' she whispered, then bent and kissed his forehead. 'Please try to love me, Nicolas. I do love you so.'

She got up and walked to the door between them,

shutting it softly. Behind her Nicolas stirred, but did not wake from his pleasant dream.

Lottie had spent the day visiting and taking tea with ladies she had met and liked. They were, like her, interested in improving the lot of the poor and under-privileged and she had been asked if she would join a debating society. She had explained that she would be leaving for the country soon, but would be pleased to join them in Bath later in the year.

Returning home with Henrietta, she went upstairs to change for the ball that evening. She was standing in her petticoat when the door to Nicolas's room was flung open and he came striding in.

'You may attend your mistress when she sends for you,' he flung at the maid, who shot a terrified glance at Lottie and scurried off. 'Well, Lottie,' Nicolas fixed his angry gaze on her. 'I see you are not yet wearing your diamonds. May I fasten them for you?'

Lottie swallowed hard, hesitating. 'I...the clasp was not quite right for me, Nicolas. I have sent them to the jeweller's to be mended.'

'Indeed?' His mouth thinned to a hard line. 'Then it is as well that he sent for me and I was able to collect them for you, was it not?' He took something from his pocket and she saw the glitter of diamonds hanging from his fingers.

'Oh...' Lottie gasped, her heart sinking. She had been hoping she might somehow recover them—that Clarice might repent and return them to her. 'Where—I mean, how did you find them?'

'The jeweller recognised them. It was not clever of

you to take them to a prestigious London dealer, Lottie. Unfortunately for you, his was the firm I used to have them cleaned and reset. He knew them instantly and you, my dear. I suppose you have run through your allowance. You should have asked me for more money if you needed it—they are worth far more than he paid you, perhaps because he knew he would need to return them to me—for a small consideration, naturally.'

'He couldn't have…' Lottie said but knew that her sister was enough like her for a stranger to be certain he was dealing with the Marchioness of Rothsay. 'Nicolas… it wasn't the way it seems…'

'Was it not, my dear?' His voice cut her like broken glass. 'In my opinion, theft is always as it seems, a most sordid business. I told you the necklace was an heirloom. You must have known that meant you had no right to sell the diamonds.'

Lottie turned away from the accusation in his eyes. 'You should not have left them where you did, Nicolas. I did not ask you for such a valuable gift—they were a temptation for anyone.'

'Are you saying you did not sell them? The man told me he served you himself.'

'Well, I am sure he was right,' Lottie said. 'You called me a thief when we first met, Rothsay. It is your own fault for marrying me. You knew that I was as bad as the rest of my family, did you not? I am sorry it has cost you money to get the diamonds back. Perhaps in future you will not leave them lying around. I certainly have no wish to wear them.'

'Lottie?' Nicolas looked at her uncertainly. She turned on him then, her eyes blazing. 'What? You are angry—but if you did not…your sister? Did she ask you for money?' Lottie was silent. 'No…has she been here? Did she take them? Or did you give them to her? Has that been the plan all the time—to get what you could from me for your wretched family?'

She recoiled as if he had slapped her. How could he think that of her—how could he?

Lottie refused to answer him. 'Please leave me now, Nicolas—and take your diamonds with you. I have a headache and shall not be attending the Duchess's ball this evening. If you intend to go, please make my excuses if you will.'

'Not go?' Nicolas glared at her. 'Why will you not answer me? If I have accused you falsely, tell me.'

'I feel most unwell. Please allow me to rest.'

'Very well.' He inclined his head stiffly. 'If I was misinformed, I apologise.'

'You are forgiven. Goodnight, Rothsay.'

Nicolas stared at her in silence for a moment, then turned and walked from the room. Lottie stood where she was for a moment, staring at the door. She was hurting too much to weep. There was no relief for her in tears after what Nicolas had said to her. She had thought that he had begun to care a little, but even after she had given him all the love inside her he could still believe that she was a thief. Yes, she ought to have told him the truth at once. Lottie acknowledged her fault, but he ought to have known that she would never steal from him. Why should she when he had been so generous? It was obvious that she had still to gain the trust of her husband.

She looked about her, wondering what to do. She could not stay here a moment longer. Nor could she return to

Rothsay Manor. Her pride had been hurt as well as her heart. She wanted to be alone for a while. The only place open to her was her father's house—she wanted nothing that Nicolas had given her. At this moment she did not know what she would do in the future, but for now she wanted to be as far away from Nicolas and those cold, cold eyes as possible.

She would send for her maid, pack a small trunk with the most inexpensive clothes she could find and leave tonight while Nicolas was out. She would take none of the jewels he had given her, but she must borrow a horse and carriage, for she had given all her money to Clarice. The future looked bleak, but at this moment she could only feel; her mind was too numb to imagine what she would do with the rest of her life.

Much later that night Nicolas knocked at the door of his wife's room. There was no answer. Frowning, he opened the door and walked into her bedchamber. It was empty, as was her boudoir, as he discovered a moment or two later. A cold shiver went down his spine. Lottie had claimed to have a headache, so where had she gone?

He rang the bell and a few moments later a maid appeared. He did not think she was the one who usually waited on Lottie.

'Where is my wife?'

'She left earlier this evening, my lord. She sent for the carriage and went out with Rose, her ladyship's maid. They took a small trunk and a portmanteau with them, sir.'

'Did my wife receive bad news? Did she say where she was going?'

'I do not think so, my lord. I do not know if she received a letter, but I think she did not leave word of where she would be.'

Nicolas swore beneath his breath, then, 'Thank you, girl—do you happen to know if my wife had any visitors yesterday?'

'I'm not sure, sir. Shall I ask Mrs Barrot?'

'No, I will do that myself, thank you. You may go.'

Nicolas waited until she had gone, then went to the closet and opened it. Most of Lottie's things were still there. Her jewel case was lying on the bed. He picked it up, opened it and saw that everything he or his relatives had given her was still there. The only things she had taken were her aunt's pearls, the diamond star her father had given her and various trinkets she had owned before she married him.

'No!' he cried in anguish. 'Lottie, damn it. Why didn't you tell me the truth?'

Nicolas felt the cold seep through him. He should have known Lottie would not sell those wretched diamonds. Why on earth had he lost his temper and accused her of being a thief? His anger had been a mixture of annoyance at the jeweller's manner in confiding in him that the marchioness had pawned her jewels and the meeting he had seen between Lottie and Hunter in the park.

What had he done? Nicolas was certain that she had left him—but where would she go?

Surely she would be at Rothsay? She was angry with him, but she wouldn't just leave him without saying goodbye—would she?

He had left her without a word. Why should she imagine he would care two pence where she was when he had accused her of a crime she had not committed?

She had lied to him, pretending that the necklace was having the clasp repaired. No doubt he had taken her by surprise. She must have been protecting her sister.

The jeweller did not know Lottie. If he saw Clarice he would assume that she was the marchioness. They were enough alike to be mistaken for one another if you did not know them. Nicolas would not be fooled for a moment, but he imagined that many people might.

The servants were not sure there had been a visitor on the morning he left the diamonds lying on the dressing table, but seen from a distance they also would take Clarice for her sister.

What a fool he was not to have known that at the start. It was the fault of his damnable temper—and the suspicious nature that had not quite believed in Lottie's goodness despite all his senses telling him that she was as sweet and good as she was beautiful—and he loved her.

He had been hiding from the truth for months now. Lottie was the woman he loved and he prayed that she loved him in return—a real, true abiding love that should have lasted for a lifetime.

Had he destroyed it by his careless words? Would Lottie forgive him once more? He knew he had hurt her too many times. Why should she care for him? He knew that he did not deserve she should—and yet he could not give her up.

Striding into his own bedchamber, he summoned his valet. He would go down to Rothsay. If she was not there, he would search for her until he found her.

* * *

'No, Lottie has not come here,' Aunt Beth said and frowned when Nicolas asked if his wife was upstairs. 'I thought she was enjoying herself in London with you?'

'She was—we quarrelled and she left without a word.'

'Whatever did you say to her, Rothsay? That is not like my Lottie. You must know that she is the most loving, caring of women and a true lady.'

'Yes, she is,' Nicolas admitted. 'It is all my fault. I said things—things that I had no right to say. It is hardly to be wondered at that she grew tired of me and left me.'

'Are you sure she has left you?'

'She took only a few clothes and jewels that came from you or her father. Everything I had given her was left behind. I have had it all sent down here, but if she is not here…'

Aunt Beth looked at him accusingly. 'You must have hurt her badly, sir. Lottie could not have done anything to deserve it. I know her. She is honest and loving, as different from—' Aunt Beth broke off and shook her head. 'Where can she be?'

'Would she have gone to her father's house?'

'If she has, it will avail her nothing, sir. Her father has closed the house and put it and the land up for sale. He says that he sees no point in trying to keep up appearances now and will manage better without the estate somewhere abroad.'

'What of Lottie's sister?'

'Clarice visited the house just before I returned here. She said she needed money, but I had only a few pounds to give her. I had given her money before and so had Lottie. She did say that she was going to ask Lottie for money—apparently, she believed it was owed her, because Lottie had everything and she had nothing.'

'Indeed?' Nicolas's mouth thinned. 'I suppose that means she intended to blackmail Lottie?'

'Lottie is fond of her sister, despite all, and would give her any money she had to spare, sir—but she would not give her anything that belonged to you.'

'I all but accused her of doing that very thing! What am I to do, Aunt Beth? Will she forgive me?'

'Most women would not, but Lottie has a tender heart and she may—but first you must find her.'

'Yes, I must,' he said. 'I shall go to her father's house immediately. If it has not yet been sold, she may have let herself in. After all, where else could she go?'

Where could she go now? Lottie looked at the boarded-up windows of the house where she had spent her childhood. The notices proclaimed that it had been sold, which meant it was no longer her father's property.

She could perhaps manage to get in and spend the night, but she would be alone without a fire or food. There was nothing for it but to find an inn and take a room for the night.

'I am sorry, Rose,' she told her maid. 'I had no idea that my father had sold the house. I am not sure where we can stay tonight. I do not have much money, only a few shillings. Perhaps we can find lodgings for that—or maybe the landlord would accept a piece of jewellery?'

'You will never sell your jewellery, my lady,' Rose said. 'There's no need, for I have three guineas in my reticule. I was paid before we left London and I can pay for our lodgings for one night.'

'In the morning…we shall go to Rothsay,' Lottie said and sighed. 'I have some things of my own there that I can sell. I shall repay you, Rose. Rothsay is your home and you must stay there, for I shall not be able to pay you a wage. It is very good of you to share with me like this.'

'You would do as much for me,' Rose said and smiled at her. 'We'd best tell coachman to take us to the nearest inn, mistress. It is getting late and we could all do with something to eat.'

'Yes. How sensible you are,' Lottie said and sighed. 'I should never have given my sister Clarice all the money I had—but I felt so guilty, because I had so much.'

And now, because of what Clarice had done, she had nothing. Without Nicolas the world was an empty place. The money and jewels had never meant that much to her, but they were a part of his world—and she had wanted to belong to him.

Rose nodded. 'Sisters are always trouble, miss. Mine used to get into scrapes all the time when we were little and because I was the eldest I got the blame.'

'Poor Rose. Clarice and I are twins. When we were small no one could tell us apart.'

'She would be the lady I saw coming from your room then, my lady. She was wearing a hat with veiling, but from a distance I thought it was you—but she didn't answer when I spoke to her, just ran down the stairs, as if she were in a hurry.'

'Yes, I dare say she was.'

Lottie's heart ached. Why had she not put those wretched diamonds away when she went into Nicolas's room that morning? It had not occurred to her that anyone would steal them—and only her sister would have dreamed of it. Rothsay's servants were all too honest.

She climbed back into the coach and gave the driver the order to find the nearest inn. She had been in acute distress when she left London, but now despite the pain in her heart, she could think more clearly.

What was she to do with her life? As Rothsay's wife she had had a purpose: the clearance of the Hollow and the setting up of a school for the tenants' children were just two of the plans she had made. Even had Nicolas visited only a few times a year, it would have been enough—or would it?

If Lottie were honest with herself, she knew that she wanted much more. She wanted Nicolas to love her as much as she loved him. He wanted her. His lovemaking had been passionate, even desperate at times, but he did not love her.

There was also Aunt Beth to consider. She knew her aunt could not live on her small income. Lottie would have to find work and support them both. Her pride had prevented her taking anything that Nicolas had given her, but perhaps she might accept a small part of the allowance he had made her for her aunt's sake.

No! She wanted nothing from him. He thought her a thief and a cheat. Somehow she would manage alone— but she must return to Rothsay and collect her things. Perhaps Aunt Beth could remain at the estate until Lottie had had time to find a small cottage for them and a position of some kind, though she hardly knew what she was fitted for. Unless she could be a teacher in a charity school? The wage would be very small, but there might be some accommodation with the job.

The worrying thoughts went round and round in her head. She must find a way of making her living somehow.

Nicolas stared at the empty house. The sold notice meant it was too late. If Lottie came here, she would know she could not stay. Where would she go then?

He wondered how much money she had left from her quarterly allowance. He doubted it could be much after her visit to the fashionable seamstresses in London. Besides, her aunt said she would have given what she had left to Clarice.

How had her sister managed to steal those wretched diamonds from under Lottie's nose? She must have turned her back or left the room for a moment, of course. It was his fault for leaving the necklace on the dressing chest instead of giving it to Lottie when he saw her. He wished that he could go back to that day—he would do anything if he could only unsay those awful words.

Lottie might go to Bath—but she had never visited her house there and could not know exactly where it was situated. Besides, if she had not taken her clothes and jewels, she would not think of living in the house he had given her.

Would she try to find work? Had she stayed at an inn? Or would she go to Rothsay? Many of her things were stored there. She would need them if she intended to live independently.

How foolish of her! She could not hope to survive on the wage that she would earn as…a teacher. Yes, he imagined she would try for something of the sort. However he had assuaged some of his guilt over his wife's hasty departure—he had told Aunt Beth that she was on no account to think of leaving his house.

'You will oblige me by living here, ma'am, and I shall make certain that you have an allowance—unless you are too proud or angry with me to accept it?'

'I have no intention of cutting off my nose to spite my face, Rothsay,' Aunt Beth told him. 'At my age I cannot afford to be too proud. Besides, I shall pray that Lottie will come to her senses. I feel that she really loves you and would be miserable apart from you. She would be greatly missed here, you know. Everyone loves her.'

'Yes, I am certain she was meant to be mistress of a house like this and why should she not continue as before? If she cannot forgive me, I will promise to keep my distance—but she is my wife and I shall not divorce her or permit her to divorce me.'

'That is foolish talk, sir.' Aunt Beth sighed. 'Have you learned nothing? Lottie may be coaxed, my lord, but she will not be bullied.'

'I did not mean…' Nicolas looked rueful. 'It is my damnable temper again.'

'You must learn to curb it, sir.'

'You are very right, ma'am. I must.'

Should he return to Rothsay and wait for Lottie—or should he make a tour of the district and discover if she had stayed at a local inn?

If she returned to Rothsay, Aunt Beth would do her

best to keep her there until he returned. She would be safe and comfortable, but if she were staying at an inn without much money she might be in trouble.

Chapter Fourteen

'Lottie, you foolish girl!' Aunt Beth rose from her chair and went forwards to embrace her. 'I have been worried out of my mind. Rothsay was here. He was convinced that you had left him.'

'Well, I have—or that was my intention,' Lottie said. 'Father has sold the house, but I suppose you knew that?'

'Yes. He gave me twenty-four hours to leave so I came here.' Aunt Beth looked at her anxiously. 'What else could I do, Lottie?'

'You did exactly right,' Lottie told her. 'I want you to stay here, dearest, just until I can find somewhere for us to live.'

'Could we not live at your house in Bath, if you will not stay here?'

'The house belongs to Rothsay. I want nothing of his, Aunt. He accused me of stealing his diamonds.'

'I don't know exactly what went on between you, my

dear, but I do know that he is sincerely sorry for what he said to you, Lottie. Do you not think you could forgive him?'

'You do not understand, dearest,' Lottie said and held back a sob. 'It is not just because of the diamonds. Oh, Aunt Beth, I love him so much. I thought I could accept this marriage of convenience, but it hurts too much.'

'Of course it does,' her aunt said. 'You have been in love with him almost from the start, I think?'

'Yes. I thought I could pretend to be the kind of wife he wants and needs. Rothsay does not want love from me. He merely desires a complaisant wife and an heir. I do not think I can be what he needs, Aunt.'

'Are you certain that he wants only that, Lottie?'

'What do you mean?'

'He has gone to your father's house to look for you. He seems genuinely distressed, my love. Could you not allow him to apologise to you? He has been good to us—to me. He has given me an allowance and told me this is my home. Even if we went elsewhere I should have a decent living. There are not so many men who would be as generous in the circumstances, Lottie.'

'No, Nicolas is the most generous of men—that is why it hurts all the more. How could he imagine that I would want to steal from him?'

'I dare say he is very sorry for having thought it, Lottie.' Her aunt gave her a shrewd look. 'Have you thought what will happen to the people here if you leave just like that? There may be no more improvements to the Hollow and certainly no school for the children.'

'Oh, do not remind me,' Lottie said. 'I feel so guilty. If I stayed for a few days just to make sure everything is in order… Perhaps it would be best to discuss the future with Rothsay. He may wish to divorce me. He must have an heir and he will need a wife.'

'Just so,' her aunt said and smiled. 'Besides, you must think carefully where you wish to go and what you will do. If you have a situation when you leave here, it will be more comfortable for you—and of course you will have to revert to your own name, Lottie.'

'Yes, I suppose I shall.' Lottie looked at her left hand. She would hate to take off her wedding ring, but it would probably be for the best. 'I shall wait for a few days at least. In the meantime I must find a way to sell a few of my possessions. I have some silver items that were my share of Mama's things…'

'You would never sell those, Lottie?' Her aunt looked shocked.

'I may have to. It is either that or the brooch Papa gave me for my wedding.'

'Better that than your mother's things. Besides, I have a little money left. What do you need?'

'I owe Rose three guineas. She paid for our lodgings—and I should like to give her a little more.'

'I will give you five guineas for her, Lottie. You can always repay me when you have money again.'

'Yes…' Lottie frowned. 'I had promised Lily Blake money for her dressmaking establishment. Perhaps I could ask Rothsay if he would consider giving her the money himself.'

'Did you not know?' Aunt Beth looked surprised. 'Lily came here while you were away. She wanted to tell you that she had the money and had decided to go to

Northampton and set up in business for herself. I thought you must have sent it to her?'

Lottie shook her head. 'No, I meant to do it when I returned. I wonder…do you think Nicolas could have sent her something?'

'I imagine he thought recompense was needed after what happened, though it was scarcely his fault, Lottie. Sam Blake was a fugitive from the law and any of the landowners around here would have told their keepers to shoot on sight. Rothsay did not instruct Larkin to do that, but the man acted within the law.'

'It is a bad law and should be changed. If I were a man, I should do something about it.'

'Well, perhaps your husband will one day, Lottie. If you guided his thoughts, he might do a great deal of good—as you could yourself if you stay here.'

'What are you up to, Aunt?'

'I am only asking you to reconsider,' her aunt said. 'I understand why you ran away—but men are sometimes wrong-headed, Lottie. They make mistakes. My husband was often misguided and even careless, but I forgave him—and I loved him. Your mother loved your father until the day she died, and she forgave him far worse.'

'Yes…' Lottie's throat caught with emotion. 'I know. Mama said we must always give others the benefit of the doubt—but Nicolas thinks *I* am a thief. How can I stay with a man who has such a low opinion of me? Papa always knew Mama was good, even though he let her down so many times.'

'Well, you must decide,' her aunt said. 'But at least let him have the chance to apologise.'

'I suppose I ought to speak to him. We must try to be civilised and make certain that the scandal is kept to a minimum.'

Lottie decided to walk to the lake. She had been back for three days now and Nicolas had not come home. Perhaps he had gone back to London. She was not certain what she ought to do for the best. Aunt Beth insisted she should wait for a while and speak to Nicolas and the servants were all so pleased to see her back home.

It was her home. She felt relaxed and comfortable here even though her heart ached. Having visited the Hollow and seen how much improvement had been made in the past weeks, she knew that it would be a crime if the work did not continue. The vicar had called on her, asking if she meant to set up her school and begging her to consider his curate for the post of teacher.

'Bernard is a good man and would do well in a local school, my lady. His stipend is very little and the poor lad cares for his sick mother. He cannot hope for preferment for some years, because he has no influential family to help him. If you could see your way to giving him a chance, he would repay you.'

'Well, I shall certainly interview Mr Bernard,' she said.

The young man did indeed sound exactly what she had hoped to find. His duties would be light and would not prevent him carrying out his work at the church, for the hours were compatible.

If only she could continue as she had been until the disastrous visit to London. Lottie wished that she had not taken it into her head to try to make Nicolas jealous.

The last night she had spent with him had shown her how very much she loved him, and left a constant ache about her heart. She was no longer satisfied to be a complaisant wife. She wanted to be loved and needed. Nothing less would do for her now. It would probably be better if she left before Nicolas returned. Aunt Beth was settled here and she need not worry about her. Lottie could establish herself somewhere and then her aunt…

Her thoughts were suspended as she saw a man walking towards her. For a moment she thought it was Nicolas and her heart raced. Then, as he came nearer, she saw that it was Bertie Fisher.

Lottie liked her friendly neighbour, but at the moment she would have preferred to be alone.

'Lady Rothsay,' he said and swept off his hat. 'I thought I might find you here. There was a great deal of talk when you did not attend the duchess's ball. People were speculating that you had left Rothsay. I decided to come down and investigate.'

'I am grateful for your concern, sir. It was just a little headache that kept me from that engagement. I am much better now.'

'You must know that I am your good friend, Lottie. If you are in some trouble, it would be my pleasure to help you.'

'You are very kind, sir.' Lottie smiled as she saw his earnest expression. 'I think I have been a little foolish, but there is nothing you can do to help.'

'Is Rothsay treating you properly? When he first announced the marriage, I thought it was merely because the family needed an heir, but I've changed my mind.'

'Have you—why?'

Lottie took the arm he offered and they turned back towards the house. She smiled up at him, because he was a good friend.

'Oh, because of the way he looks at you, and the way he acted on the night of the duchess's ball. He seemed like a man in torment.'

'Perhaps he was thinking of his lost love?'

'Lady Elizabeth Madison?' Bertie shook his head. 'I happen to know for a fact that she received a rebuff from him quite recently. I have it on the best authority—her own—that he turned down the offer of an affair. She was most put out and told me in a fit of temper. I do not think you need concern yourself about that lady. Any man who preferred that scold would have to be mad.'

'Oh, Bertie, you are a darling.' Lottie reached up to kiss his cheek. He grinned and kissed her back. It was not until they resumed walking that she realised Nicolas was coming towards them and had seen their embrace.

'Lottie—' Nicolas's expression was cold and angry '—I have been looking everywhere for you. What am I to infer from this—are you leaving me for Fisher?'

'Come off it, old chap,' Bertie said. 'No need to jump to conclusions. I'm a great admirer of your wife, but wouldn't dream of coming between you. What you saw—well, it wasn't what you think.'

'I was speaking to my wife.' Nicolas glared at her. 'If you will grant me a few minutes alone with Lottie, sir. I need to clear the air.'

'Not if you're going to bite her head off again.' Bertie squared his shoulders. 'I ain't one for quarrelling, but I ain't prepared to stand by and see you make Lady Rothsay's life a misery.'

'Going to challenge me to a duel? You can't be serious, Bertie. You know you don't stand a chance against me.'

'Have a damned good try.' Bertie looked stubborn. 'Lady's honour and all that…'

'Please do not be stupid, either of you!' Lottie lost her temper. 'You are both being ridiculous, I refuse to be a bone of contention between friends. It was a friendly kiss because I was miserable, Rothsay—and if you can't believe that, it is best I leave at the first opportunity.'

Lottie ran past them and into the house.

How dared they fight over her? Lottie was furious as she went up to her room. Why was Nicolas always so swift to think the worst of her? First he accused her of selling the diamonds, now he imagined she was conducting a clandestine affair with Bertie Fisher, of all people! He must still believe she was truly like Clarice.

She felt so ashamed. Aunt Beth thought she should continue to live under Nicolas's roof, but how could she? If Clarice was back in England for good it would only be a short time before people discovered that Lady Rothsay had a sister—and Clarice's reputation could ruin her. Between them, they would bring shame on Nicolas's proud name and his family.

She must leave as soon as she had spoken to Nicolas. It might be better if she went abroad. Nicolas must be regretting the day he offered marriage to Clarice and then ended up with her sister.

Sitting on the edge of the bed, she bent her head, covering her face with her hands. She could no longer hold back the tears. It had been foolish to come back here.

She should have found somewhere to live and sent for her personal things. When the door opened, she refused to look up.

'I am sorry, Lottie. Bertie is a good friend to us both and I am a fool for being jealous of any man who looks at you.'

'No, please, Nicolas,' Lottie said and looked at him. She wiped the back of her hand across her eyes. 'It is mere foolishness. I understand why you despise me—my sister is a thief. Her morals are not those of a decent young woman and you think me her equal. I am sorry. I should never have agreed to take her place.'

'Do you regret it for your sake or mine?'

Lottie's eyes closed for a moment, then she looked at him. 'For both our sakes, Nicolas. I find it does not please me to be the kind of wife you require—and I am certain you must wish you had never seen either Clarice or me.'

'Your sister is certainly a problem,' Nicolas admitted. 'I had hoped she might stay in France and not trouble us, but I dare say a way to control her excesses may be found.'

'What do you mean?' Lottie wiped her cheeks with a lace kerchief. Her eyes widened as he sat on the edge of the bed beside her. 'Clarice cares for no one. She must have known I would guess she had taken the diamonds.'

'She thought you would not give her up to the authorities. Do not fear, my love. I have no intention of handing your sister over to a magistrate. For one thing it would cause a scandal for us, and another—I owe her something for tearing up the contract, as I did. Though she herself did not sign it, she could have found a way to sue me for breach of contract had she chosen.'

'If she guessed that, I dare say she might,' Lottie said and gave him a watery smile. 'You were right, she is a thief. I am sorry you were forced to buy back the diamonds, Nicolas.'

'Be damned to the wretched things. They mean nothing to me. I would have left them in the bank, but I thought you might like to wear them.'

'I should have done if Clarice had not stolen them.'

'Why did you not tell me at once, as soon as you discovered the theft?'

'I knew only Clarice could have taken them. I went into your room to recover my pearls, which I left the previous evening—and when I returned she was there. She asked for money. I gave her what I had—and then after she had gone I discovered the necklace was missing. I wanted to tell you but I was ashamed of what she had done—and even if she is a thief she is my sister...'

'You thought I might have her arrested for theft?' Nicolas nodded. 'I had Blake arrested, didn't I? You could not know that I would have given him a lenient sentence and had him released early on promise of good behaviour. Believe me, Lottie. I had no wish to see the man hang or be given a long prison sentence.'

'I should have known—but you were so angry...'

'I have a wicked temper, my love. At first I resented being preached to by a woman—and then I began to know that woman and I understood that she spoke from the heart. I am very sorry Sam Blake was killed. If I could have prevented it, I would.'

Lottie nodded, looking up into his face. 'Did you send Lily Blake some money?'

'The twenty guineas you gave her and another hundred. I told her that she might apply to us for custom for her business when she was ready and we should recommend her. Was it enough for her to start up do you think?'

'A hundred and twenty guineas is a fortune to someone like Lily, Nicolas. She will have a fine establishment and should soon be famous and wealthy.'

'Will it make up for what she has lost?'

'I cannot speak for Lily—but if I lost a husband I loved and my children lost their father no money would be enough.'

'No, I feared not.' He sighed and looked regretful. 'What more can I do, Lottie?'

'Nothing,' Lottie smiled. 'You have done all that could be expected of you, Nicolas. However, you can continue the work at the Hollow and set up a school for the children.'

'Will you not stay and do those things? You are so much better at seeing what people need than I am, Lottie.'

'Do you mean that we should continue as we planned at the start?' Lottie could not look at him. Her heart was racing and she felt that she could hardly breathe.

'No, not as it was at the start, but as it could be between us now—if you can forgive me?' His hand reached out to lift her chin so that she looked at him. 'I care for you, Lottie, much more than I expected I should. I want you to be my wife, not because I need an heir but because I want to be with you. I want children with you, but I want so much more.'

'Are you sure, Nicolas? I do not think that I could bear it if you made love me to me and then rode off to London to the bed of your mistress the next night.'

'I have no mistress, Lottie. I gave her up once I'd agreed to your father's marriage deal and there has been no one else since, I promise you. Once I had tasted your sweetness I knew that no other woman would ever content me. You are the woman I need in my life— can you bear to give me another chance?'

He still had not said that he loved her, but Lottie knew that perhaps this was the closest Nicolas could come to telling her he cared. Elizabeth had hurt him so badly that there was a barrier inside him that would not let love in. He had lowered it partially, but it was still there.

'If you truly want me, I shall stay,' Lottie said after a moment. 'I must tell you now that I love you, Nicolas. I have loved you almost from the start. If you do not want my love, it would be fair to tell me now.'

'I thought I had forfeited all right to your love,' Nicolas said. He leaned forwards to kiss her on the lips. It was a long, lingering kiss, sweet and tender. 'You are my wife and I care for you as much as I am able to care for anyone, Lottie. I am not sure it is love as you know it, but I will not lie to you. There is something locked inside me that just will not come free, much as I might wish it. I want you, need you, care for you—is that enough?'

'Yes, I think so,' she said and touched his cheek. 'Perhaps in time you will feel able to love with all your heart, Nicolas.'

'Perhaps I love, but cannot express it.'

Lottie gazed into his eyes. 'Yes, perhaps that is so,' she said softly. 'Come to me tonight, Nicolas. For the moment I think we should go down—Aunt Beth will be worrying.'

Nicolas smiled. 'Wash your face, my love. You have a dirty mark just there.' He kissed the spot. 'I shall go down and tell her the good news.'

Lottie decided to change her gown before going to tea with her husband and her aunt. She went behind the screen and took it off, pulling on a fresh yellow silk gown. Hearing someone enter, she thought it was Rose and called out to her.

'Rose, will you brush my hair for me, please…?' She stopped and stared as she came out from behind the screen and saw the woman standing by her dressing table. 'Clarice! What are you doing here?'

'I came to see you, of course,' Clarice said. 'Are you not pleased to see me, Lottie?'

'Should I be—after what happened last time?' Lottie opened her jewel case, which was lying on the table, then held out her hand. 'Aunt Beth's pearls, if you please. I know you have them, Clarice. If you do not return them, I shall have you arrested. Aunt Beth would hate it if they were sold. Her husband gave them to her when she was married.'

Clarice reluctantly took the pearls from inside her glove. 'Give me some money, then. I don't mean two hundred pounds. I told you last time that I need at least ten thousand. Philippe is in such trouble. If he doesn't pay up they may kill him.'

'Has your lover been gambling again? He should learn

to play within his means, Clarice. I cannot give you such a sum, for I do not have it—and even if I had I should not give you Rothsay's money for a gambling debt.'

'You may be sorry if you don't. I need that money, Lottie, and I do not mind what I do to get it. Your precious Rothsay would not be happy if the truth came out, I think.'

'What are you talking about?'

'Why, I will tell all the world about the little deal that Father made with Rothsay. That the marquis bartered for a bride, and to make matters worse for both of you he was duped into marrying the woman he hadn't even bargained for. Imagine what everyone will think of you both then? Rothsay would not care for that to come out, I imagine.'

'You wouldn't, Clarice.' Lottie felt sick. She had just made things up with Nicolas and now Clarice was back making trouble. 'Rothsay will respond for sure. He could have you arrested for the sale of that necklace.'

'Really? I doubt it. I told the jeweller I was you. He believed me—and after all it is true, is it not?'

'No, actually it is not,' a voice said from the doorway. Both sisters turned to look and saw Nicolas standing there. He looked furious as he came into the room, and Lottie's heart sank. 'The original deal I made with your father was off before the wedding even took place. I married Charlotte Stanton, not Clarice—and I thank God for it every day of my life.'

Clarice scowled, her lovely face ugly with rage and bitterness. 'You think yourself so clever, Rothsay—but I have proof of the deal in the original contract and that is sufficient to cause a scandal. Do you want everyone to laugh behind their fans and say that Lottie was second choice?'

'They would not say that if they knew you, Miss Stanton.' Nicolas glared at her. 'However, you are correct in thinking I owe you something. Had Lottie not come in your place, it was my intention to offer you compensation for your loss.'

Clarice's eyes gleamed with avarice. 'I want twenty thousand pounds or my contract goes to *The Times* along with a lot of interesting gossip that would blacken your name, sir.'

'You may publish and go to the devil as far as I am concerned, but I shall not have Lottie harmed.' Nicolas was silent for a moment. 'I shall give you ten thousand— and I'll want the contract and a signed document that says this business is at an end.'

'If I gave you that, I could go to prison for blackmail.'

'How would that serve to protect Lottie and her good name? You, Miss Stanton, will go to Paris with ten thousand pounds in your pocket—and the promise of two thousand a year as long as you stay there. I shall offer this once only. Give me your word now or do your worst.'

'Damn you,' Clarice muttered. 'I need that money. I'll sign and I'll stay out of your way—for as long as I receive the two thousand a year.'

'It will be money well spent,' Nicolas said, his expression harsh. 'Go down to the parlour, Lottie. You aunt is waiting for you. I shall deal with this lady and then I shall join you.'

'Yes, Nicolas.' Lottie glanced at her sister. She felt

numb with shock. Surely Nicolas would never forgive this? 'Goodbye, Clarice. I hope we shall not meet again— until you have learned to respect others, at least.'

Chapter Fifteen

Lottie took tea with her aunt. She was apprehensive as she waited for Nicolas to join them, but he was a long time coming and when she asked the housekeeper where his lordship was, she was told he had an urgent message and had gone out. Too restless to stay in the house, she pulled on a warm pelisse and went out into the gardens.

It was chilly and she was about to return to the house when she heard the sound of gunfire quite close and then a man came charging at her. She hardly had time to see that it was the keeper Larkin when he pointed a shotgun at her, gesturing wildly in the direction of the park.

'It's your fault with your high morals, poking your nose in where it is not wanted and causing trouble from the moment you got 'ere,' he muttered. 'Well, he'll be sorry for what he's done—if I go down, I'll take you with me.'

Lottie shivered, a chill creeping down her spine as

she looked into the man's crazed eyes. She was alone and Larkin was clearly desperate.

'I have no idea what you mean, sir.'

'Don't you pretend with me, woman. I had a nice little thing going on until you turned up, laying down the law and getting folk on your side. Well, you'll pay for it and Dickon Blake will too, fer it's 'im wot told on me.'

'If you have been breaking the law, then you deserve to be punished,' Lottie said, standing her ground. If she turned and ran he would no doubt shoot her. 'You were swift enough to kill Sam Blake, and that, sir, was no accident. I would swear you might have shot him in the leg had you not wished to kill him.'

'Blake were in with us from the start, but he wanted out on account of his missus telling him she would leave 'im if he didn't give it up. Dickon and me both warned 'im, but he wouldn't listen so he had to be shut up—the way I'm going to shut you up now.'

'If you shoot me, you will certainly hang.' Lottie told him. 'My husband might be lenient with you if you come to your senses.'

'And very likely he won't fer it's 'im wot 'as 'ad me watched, spied on—and that rogue Blake 'as gone over to 'is side an' all...'

Lottie heard a rustling sound in the shrubbery. She did not dare to turn her head to look, but knew that someone was behind them. Larkin had become aware of it, too. In the moment that he turned his head, she rushed away to the right, fleeing deeper into the shrubbery. She heard Larkin shout, then another man's voice, and then the sounds of a struggle and finally a shot, followed swiftly by a second. Lottie gave a little cry of fear. Who had been shot—and would Larkin give chase?

'My lady,' a man's voice called as she hesitated, hardly knowing which way to go for the best. 'Larkin cannot hurt you. You are safe now.'

'Dickon—Dickon Blake, is that you?'

Lottie moved towards the spot where the sounds had come from and saw that Larkin was lying on the ground, bleeding profusely from a wound to his leg but still alive. He glared up at the man who stood over him, holding a shotgun at his head. Lottie saw that it was indeed Dickon Blake and that he also had a superficial wound to his arm.

'You are hurt, Mr Blake. What happened here?'

'He shot at me, but his gun misfired and I took him down,' Dickon replied. 'I'll not lie to you, Lady Rothsay. I've been a poacher and proud of it. In my opinion the woods should be open for a man to take a rabbit for his family—but I am not a murderer and I could not stand by and see him murder you the way he murdered my cousin.'

'I owe you my life, sir,' Lottie said. 'I think we should go back to the house and—' She was about to say that she would bind his wound and send someone to fetch the more seriously injured Larkin, who appeared to have passed out, but, before she could say more, several men came crashing through the shrubbery.

'Lottie!' Nicolas cried as he saw her. 'My God! I thought he might have killed you.' He glanced from her to the man on the ground, then at Dickon Blake. 'What happened here?'

'Larkin intended to murder me the way he murdered

Sam Blake. Sam wanted to make an end to the poaching. He was going to try to find work and look after his family, but Larkin couldn't allow that because he was the one masterminding the serious poaching in these parts—is that not so, Dickon?'

'Yes, my lady...' Dickon hesitated as if he would have said more, but Lottie frowned and he was silent.

'Mr Blake happened to be nearby and he heard what Larkin intended—and he shot him in the leg after he was shot at. Is that not how it was, Dickon?'

'I couldn't let him hurt you after what you've done for us at the Hollow, my lady. I thought you were like all the others at the start, but you ain't—and I couldn't let him do it, even if does mean I spend the rest of my days in prison.'

'I doubt you need worry about that,' Nicolas said. 'My agent told me you had been most helpful over the investigation into the poaching. I know you have had difficulty in finding work—perhaps you would care to take on Larkin's work? I shall expect you to deal honestly with me—and a man in need may be warned twice. After that he must be brought to me and I will see if he is a thief or just desperate.'

'Your gamekeeper?' Dickon stared as if he did not believe his ears. 'I've been one of them what stole from you, my lord—but if I take your money I'll serve you well. I never thought you would give me half a chance...'

'No doubt I should not have done so once,' Nicolas said and put his arm about Lottie's shoulders. 'My wife has taught me better manners, Mr Blake. You deserve no less than respect after what you just did, sir.' He beckoned to the keepers who were staring in astonishment. 'Take Larkin back to the kitchens and have him patched up. He will be arrested and tried for murder—and in his case I shall not be lenient. He will hang for the murder of Sam Blake and the attempted murder of my wife. You, Mr Blake, must also be attended. We shall talk later, for I am sure that a man like you will know what injustices have taken place in the past and should be righted—and I shall consult you concerning the affairs of the people at the Hollow. My wife has begun the task but it will be for me to make certain that things do not come to such a pass again.'

'Thank you, my lord.' Dickon bent to gather up Larkin's fallen weapon. 'I reckon it was a lucky day for us when you married her ladyship.'

Nicolas turned to gaze down at Lottie. There was an odd expression in his eyes as he replied, 'Yes, it was the luckiest day of my life—even though I did not know it then.'

'I think I should go back to the house,' Lottie said. 'It is most strange, but I feel a little...' She moaned and started to crumple at the knees.

Nicolas caught her in his arms. He turned and walked towards the house, carrying his precious burden and followed by his men and Dickon.

Aunt Beth had seen them from the window and came fluttering into the hall, her expression anxious. 'What has happened to her? We heard shooting—is she hurt?'

'No, it was a keeper who was shot—but she might have been had Dickon Blake not been there to help her. I have had an agent watching over things while I was away, but this afternoon everything came to a head.'

Lottie's eyelids moved. She opened her eyes and looked up at him. 'How foolish? Did I faint?'

'Bring her into the parlour,' Aunt Beth said. 'I dare say she will be better in a moment. These faints do not as a rule last long.'

'What are you talking about?' Nicolas asked, puzzled. 'I dare say it was the shock of being attacked by Larkin and then seeing two men wounded.'

'I very much doubt it,' Aunt Beth said as he set Lottie gently down on a daybed in the parlour. 'I do not know if Lottie is aware of it herself, but all the signs are there—though perhaps I should not say.'

'Now you have completely lost me.' Nicolas was exasperated. 'Is Lottie ill? Please have the goodness to tell me, for I have no idea what you mean.'

Lottie caught Nicolas's arm, as he would have moved away. 'I think what my aunt is hinting at is that she thinks I am with child, Nicolas. I have not mentioned anything, because I was not perfectly certain—though I have not seen my courses since…I left London.'

'You are with child?' Nicolas stared at her, then a smile showed in his eyes and his mouth curved into a huge grin. 'That is wonderful, Lottie. Do you suppose the night before you left…?'

'Yes, I would think so, though it is too soon to be sure, Nicolas. I could begin my courses tomorrow, though I am late and I think…I truly feel that I may be with child.'

'Here, Lottie dearest. Hold this to your nose,' Aunt Beth said and gave her a kerchief heavily soaked in lavender water. 'It may help you with the headache you may have after a nasty faint like that, my love.'

Lottie took the kerchief and inhaled the perfume

gratefully. She had been feeling a little queasy, but the strong lavender helped and she breathed more deeply.

'Should you not see what is happening elsewhere, Nicolas? You will need to send for the constable and have Larkin attended by a doctor. Even a man as despicable as he should be properly cared for, do you not think so?'

'Had I fired the gun he would probably be dead,' Nicolas admitted grimly. 'He is lucky that Blake got to him first. My keepers and agent will do all that is necessary, Lottie. I have no intention of leaving your side until I am assured that no other villains lie in wait for you. Forgive me for not protecting you properly.'

'It could not be expected that Larkin would try to kill me or that he would be in the rose gardens.' Lottie was sitting up now. She smiled and took his hand. 'Sit here beside me, Nicolas. Tell me just what has been going on here, please.'

'You were so certain that Sam Blake was innocent of any crime other than taking a rabbit or two. Therefore I had to wonder if Larkin was a dishonest servant as you'd suggested. When I went off to London I engaged agents to come down to Rothsay and discover what they could—and also to make sure that nothing happened to you. After what you'd said, I thought that it might possibly have been Larkin who took a pot shot at us that day. He probably wanted to give you a fright, but when you became involved with Lily Blake and took too much interest in things that could be dangerous for him, he decided to kill Sam.'

'Dickon told me that Sam wanted out of the large-scale poaching. Larkin would not let him give it up, because he thought he might betray the rest of them. I do not know who else was involved, but I think he was the ringleader.'

'He will be punished for the crime of murder. I shall give the others a warning—but I believe Dickon Blake will sort things out. A reformed poacher makes the best gamekeeper of all. My father once said that, but I fear I had forgotten much of what he told me. He went away from me when I was very young, you see.'

Lottie saw that Aunt Beth had left them alone. She patted the seat beside her and Nicolas sat down, reaching for her outstretched hand. 'Were you lonely as a child, Nicolas? Someone told me your mother died when you were very young?'

'She was very like you in some ways, Lottie, always wanting to help others. She had been nursing one of the young mothers at the Hollow and caught a fever. The doctor could do nothing and she died swiftly. Both my father and I were devastated. I think he could hardly bear to be here afterwards; he spent long periods away, and he scarcely seemed to know he had a son until just before he died. He apologised to me then, but it was too late. I had grown a protective barrier inside.'

'That isn't all of it, though, Nicolas?' Lottie's eyes were on his face. 'I know something of your affair with Elizabeth.'

'I did love Elizabeth in my way, but it was not enough for her. She once told me that the only time I came alive was when I played the pianoforte.'

'You do lose yourself in the music, which is why you play so well—but if she had loved you, she might have found a way to tear down the barriers you had built around your heart.'

'The way you have, Lottie?'

'Have I—truly?'

'Yes. I thought some of the hurt might still remain. I wasn't sure if I wanted to love completely, because it hurts to lose those you love—but I could have lost you today, Lottie.' He took her hand, lifting it to his lips to kiss the palm. 'I know that my life would be empty without you. You have made my heart your home, Lottie—and you rule both in my heart and my home. Without you I think I should be like my father and simply fade away.'

'What nonsense,' Lottie said and leaned forwards to kiss him lightly on the lips. 'For one thing I have no intention of going anywhere without you again, and for another—I want your promise that if in the future I should die and leave a child or children, you will love them and give them all the affection they deserve. Only a weak man gives up when he loses something, Nicolas, and I know you are not that. If my children live, then I shall live on in them—but it is most unlikely to happen. I dare say that you will be stuck with me for many years, perhaps the whole of your life.'

Her eyes twinkled with mischief and Nicolas laughed. 'You have my word, Lottie. You are right. I am not my father. I have my mother's spirit and she was brave like you. I promise that I shall always love our children—and now, my dearest, should you go up and rest?'

'Not yet, Nicolas. I shall change my gown for the evening, but it will be months before I shall need a nap in the afternoons. First thing in the morning, I intend to inspect the village hall and make sure that a part of it will do for my school.'

'And if it will not?'

'Then I shall expect you to build me a little school of my own, Nicolas,' she replied. 'I already have a very good master in mind and the sooner it is ready for the children the better...'

Lottie was brushing her hair before the mirror when the connecting door opened and her husband entered. She smiled and laid down her brush, standing up to receive him.

'Are you too tired, my love?'

'No, indeed I am not, Nicolas. Please do not imagine that I shall break if you touch me. I may be in a certain condition, but I am not delicate, and I do not think that making love will harm our child at this early stage. Perhaps later we may need to be more careful, but for the moment I am perfectly well and not in the least tired.'

He came to put his arms about her, gazing down at her face for several moments, before bending his head to kiss her. His lips were soft, tender, yet with an underlying passion that spoke of his hunger.

'How did I become so very fortunate?' he asked huskily. 'I was so careless in the way I chose my bride—and I found myself untold treasure in you.'

'Had you chosen more carefully I think we should never have met.' Lottie frowned. 'I am sorry about the things Clarice said and did. I hope she will stay in France and not trouble us again, Nicolas.'

'I have her receipt, and she knows that if she breaks the terms of our agreement she could find herself in prison. I believe she will stay away, but if she comes again, just tell me, Lottie. You must not feel sorry and give her money. Let me deal with her. Your sister is an adventuress. I regret to say it, for it must pain you, but you should face the truth.'

'I have,' Lottie said and sighed. 'I did not wish to believe you when you told me what she did in Paris, but I should have known. I shall not be foolish enough to give her money again. She must manage with her allowance or fend for herself.'

'We do not need to talk about her, my love.' Nicolas's hand stroked her hair, then her cheek. 'Come to bed, my darling. I want to show you how very much I love and worship you.'

Lottie gave him her hand, letting him lead her to the bed. Her heart was beating wildly as she lay down and drew him to her. Their kisses were sweeter than ever before, because for the first time both gave everything. All the barriers had been swept away, and Nicolas's eyes were free of shadows.

As Lottie surrendered to the tumultuous feeling of desire that overwhelmed her, she loved and knew that she was loved. Her nails raked his shoulders, her mewing cries of pleasure mixing with the rasp of his breath as he cried out and shuddered at the end. They lay together, flesh to flesh, lost in the wonder of the new happiness they had found, and then they slept.

* * * * *